Black Sun

Call of the Moon

Daniel Crux

INKWELL BOOKS

Writing-Publishing-Printing

Published by Inkwell Books
10632 North Scottsdale Road, Unit 695
Scottsdale, AZ 85254
Tel. 480-315-3781
E-mail info@inkwellbooksLLC.com
Website www.inkwellbooksLLC.com

INKWELL BOOKS
Writing-Publishing-Printing

<u>Acknowledgments</u>

My loving family, who continue to support my dreams even in the most trying of times.

Contents

Upon the twilight of the First Age of Terra, the Age of Progression, a series of great and cataclysmic wars would erupt between its human inhabitance and a mysterious race of invaders from the stars. The consequences of such devastating conflicts were far-reaching. The invaders were eventually defeated and repelled, but in the aftermath of these End Wars, governments would collapse, and humanity would face widespread starvation and extinction.

Thus would begin Terra's Second Age, the Age of Desolation, or, as it is more commonly known, the Thousand Year Darkness.

For seeming eternity, the human race would endure a dark age of utter chaos, a period of everlasting ruin and strife in which only the strongest and most capable survived. Through this desolation, a lone warrior would rise from the shadows. Seeking to reestablish order, this warrior would utilize a combination of hopeful words, what military power he held at his disposal and, most importantly, lessons learned from civilizations past to bring humanity's remnants under his banner.

Though this warrior's crusade would last many lifetimes, the human race, for the first time since its birth, would, at last, become united under a single cause and purpose. From this, order and culture would be revitalized across the ravaged earth, giving rise to a power that would rule over all, the Terran Empire.

With the Empire's birth and the warrior's coronation as the first Emperor, human civilization had officially been reborn, thus beginning the Third Age, the Age of Ascension.

But even with this Rebirth of Humanity, Terra remained broken and devastated, possessing few remaining resources to sustain its inhabitance. For humanity's continued survival, the Empire would turn its attention toward the final conquest, Space.

The foundations of this new age are marked solely by humanity's intent of settling its star system. Once space was reached, the Empire's first act was to establish space colonies in geosynchronous orbits around its homeworld. After vast expenditures of funds and manpower, the colonies would become the agricultural centers of this newborn nation, ending all lingering traces of the Darkness virtually overnight.

Even so, humanity continued to look to the stars, and soon lunar colonies were also developed for industry. Additional colonization and space exploration would continue unabated, with new settlements established on nearly all planetary bodies in the Sol System, from Mercury to the moons of Neptune.

Mining adventures, agricultural experiments, terraforming projects, and other endeavors were developed upon these colonies. Technologies that would also come to be used upon Terra itself, transforming the planet from a dark wasteland into a reborn blue and fertile world. New natural resources would also be discovered throughout, further nourishing humanity's growing empire as it began to transcend the borders of the Sol System.

Not long after the establishment of these colonies did Terran scientists finally make the discovery of faster than light travel in the form of the Arc Engine. With this breakthrough, humanity became further enamored with exploring the universe around them and expanding their reach throughout, establishing their beloved Empire's rule to the very borders of the galaxy. Seemingly, their only hindrance would be the various "alien" civilizations, which would inevitably seek to impede their progress, perhaps even attempt to subjugate them as those invaders had so long ago.

With that in mind, the Emperor would declare the formation of the Imperial Starfleet, the military arm that would defend humanity from its future enemies. It would not be long before the Imperial fleets and armies became as countless as the stars themselves.

Well into the Age of Ascension's third century, humanity would make first contact with an alien civilization in the further reaches of space. Unexpectedly, this civilization and many following it would turn out to be far more primitive than humanity had come to believe, varying from cave dwelling races akin to the ancient Neanderthals to some relatively advanced races that were equal to humanity's development in the midst of its First Age.

Even so, fearing the potential threat of these races, the Empire fell upon these worlds with great fervor, conquering in the name of humanity's progress while adapting whatever technology and advancement they found along the way. Not even the more advanced societies were capable of defending themselves against the mighty warships and combat ready men and women under the Emperor's service. Thus, humanity's dominion would spread vastly and rapidly throughout the Milky Way, challenged only by twelve others of similar power.

And yet even with the rebirth and growth of human civilization, the freedom offered by space also led to the establishment of much darker enterprises. As humanity expanded further into the darkness without end, its ability to maintain order throughout its colonies continued to wane. The equally continued usage of merchant lines to resupply settlements with whatever necessary resources made attractive targets to those who operated outside civilization's law.

Piracy had at last emerged.

Despite every effort to prevent its growth, piracy would soon become abundant throughout the galaxy. Men and women of all races and backgrounds would commit themselves to the dream of vast power and wealth, utilizing knowledge of the space around them to exploit shipping lines and plunder and pillage in reflection of the ancient Terran buccaneers. Amongst that number, the most successful in these endeavors would come to form the infamous Pirate Clans, establishing their dominions over the stars. All while retaining no mercy for those who may oppose them.

It is now the ninth century of humanity's Third Age. The galaxy progresses on as Terra, and the other twelve Galactic Powers struggle and conflict amongst themselves, each vying for complete domination. Throughout, piracy retains its sway, innumerable renegades sailing under the Jolly Roger's shadow.

This is a tale set upon one such band...

<u>Prologue: Semper In Obscurus</u>

She felt it again. Through the cold vastness of the abyss, she once more felt that unmistakable trace. The same feeling that she had first discovered not too long ago, an object of intrigue that had retained her attention, as limited as it was in her present state. Not unlike a single beam of light shining through a great and unforgiving darkness, or an emerging wakefulness slipping into a seemingly endless slumber. A presence that she had not felt for a long, long time, and even then never at this level of power. It was distant from her, at least for now.

She had been aware of it for some time, though it had only recently come within the scope of her perception. From out of the furthest reaches of all that is, it had emerged, initially as little more than the tiniest speck against an infinite background of nothingness. Over time, however, as it moved from one segment of the void to another, never staying immobile for any lengthy period, its true radiance gradually became apparent to her. For all that was within the infinite, that speck was the one thing that now captivated her after so long.

Indeed, it was quite a curious thing. A significant, unyielding presence, one that moved through the dark under its own will and direction, utilizing but the barest amount of its power toward the fulfillment of an apparent purpose. Rarely did it bring destruction into its wake, and only when such actions were necessary, namely to remove the most inhibiting of obstructions. Otherwise, it acted subtly, choosing to influence what lay around it as the closeness of a moon would influence the tides of a sea, bringing all under its spell to fulfill its wishes willingly. Very few were able to resist such influence, and those that were able did not retain their resistance for long. Such was the force of its will, even in the lightest of applications, that it seemed even the stars would succumb to its spell in due time. And those that were beyond its dominance seldom lay beyond its wrath.

But what she found most curious was not the power that this entity held, as apparent and radiant as it was, such that it shone well enough through the abyss for her to take her initial notice. Nor was it the purpose that had brought her from the distant reaches and into her perception in the first place, though that in itself did hold her intrigue. Rather, it was what it utilized to bring all around it under its will, what truly emanated through the eternal night, even more so than the light of its presence. It was its song.

Every so often, its beautiful melody would carry on through the void, reaching out to her. And for as long as she had been, she could not recall ever hearing something so wondrous, so enchanting that it seemed as though not even time and space could hinder it. So harmonious, so transcendent. A lullaby that carried through the void, reaching out to her in a distant voice. Causing her to stir ever so slightly, to shift from her dreams. In the barest of awakenings.

This should have been impossible; she knew all too well. For time since past and forgotten she had remained dormant and immobile, retained to the abyss around her as an infant to its cradle. She could do nothing, for she had become nothing. Nothing but perpetuity of dreams, the last remnants of her consciousness continually playing within the void. Dreams that led from one saga to another, one venture to the next, as if to make her forget where she was and had been for so long. All until the hour in which the final dream would end, and she would, at last, become genuinely one with the nothingness. To fade from all that was as the universe, and all else that had laid beyond her reach progressed onward. Likely to their oblivion.

Long had she resigned herself to her fate; for time innumerable, she had even lost awareness of it and all else. Now, however, through the power of this song, she had regained that awareness. As well as an all too certain desire, the very first thing she had lost upon entering her present state. The desire to move beyond the abyss. The desire to be free once more.

Such was the dominance of this desire that she felt constrained against the surrounding darkness. Though it presented itself as infinite, she recognized that it held boundaries. Boundaries that she knew she could not move beyond, or even struggle against, for she lacked the power to do so by herself. Boundaries that she could not even sense in her present state, thus maintaining the illusion that she was, indeed, surrounded by a complete and open abyss.

It would be a futile struggle, she knew, to attempt to free herself. At least, it would be if she had remained as alone and isolated as she had been. Now, however, she realized that, despite her present state, she was not truly alone. That there was indeed something, no, someone else out there. Someone who held inordinate power. Someone who possessed the gift of song.

Yes…that would be enough. If she could not free herself from the dark, then surely the one she felt, with all of its power, could come to her aid. All she need do was reach out, which, now that she was awakening, she could achieve. After all, while she could not move beyond the abyss, she could extend her power, albeit sparingly, through its boundaries. It helped that her power was not all too dissimilar from the one she felt.

There would be one hindrance. While she was aware of the one behind the song, it was not yet aware of her, and so would not be anticipating her contact. For that, she could not extend her power forward at just any moment; she would have to be careful and precise when she reached out, lest her reach not be heeded, or worse, hold a negative effect. She needed to present herself in the best possible way. A "right" and "opportune" time was, therefore, necessary, in which the singer would be receptive.

Fortunately, she was nothing if not patient. As long as she had remained in the dark, she could remain so a little bit longer, just as she could remain silent and docile that much more. The universe would endure through the interim, as it had from the beginning.

Thus for the present, she contented herself to that of a simple observer. To merely watch as the subject of her intrigue, her potential hope, continued. Taking another step toward its ultimate objective…

Black Sun
Call of the Moon

Chapter I: The Second Babel

Predecessor Ruins
Smyrna

This is really *getting old,* Alex managed to think as he dodged and parried another series of slashes. The alien, for lack of better description, only continued to attack with its axe, its massive stone blade rough and chipped but no less sharp, keeping the red-haired pirate on the defensive through the sheer quantity of its assaults. The crazed zealousness behind said attacks didn't help in the least, as the alien refused to relent, forcing Alex back through the ruined city. It was entirely driven toward removing the intruder from this apparently sacred land. The same crazed zealousness was unanimous with the rest of its kind; they were unremittingly attacking the Flint Pirates. Constant battle cries and screams only emphasized that drive, which Alex had promptly become annoyed with.

Fortunately, it wasn't long before the younger Flint gained an opening. Even through the abundant sounds that made up the current battlefield, he was more than able to pick up the telltale footfalls and clinking armor moving in from behind. And if that wasn't enough, the fevered, thundering roar that followed candidly alerted him to his second would-be attacker. Thus, taking advantage of the slight pause that his first opponent entered upon seeing his comrade's wild charge, Alex ducked and somersaulted to the right, narrowly evading the swing of the second warrior's axe, the latter in turn careening with his comrade. Rolling back to his feet, Alex wasted no time in slashing Forneus about, sending a crimson wave of energy that washed over the two warriors, obliterating them before they realized what was happening. Only the barest specks of falling ash remained.

Naturally, however, Alex did not have much time to recover, as the sharp ricochet of a ludicrously barbed arrow bouncing off a nearby ruin alerted him that there were still many more enemies to deal with. He turned to see another warrior taking aim at him with a bow, one that looked to be made from rotten wood, while a new group came charging in from the same direction, axes and clubs drawn and all crying out at the top of their lungs, or whatever breathing apparatuses they possessed. Charging forward, Alex simply dodged the next arrow before reentering the melee, slashing and scorching every enemy that he came across, utilizing a combination of Forneus' pyrokinetic powers alongside all too superior swordsmanship. As much as these aliens *thought* themselves to be warriors, they were nothing compared to what Alex and the rest of the Flint Pirates had fought before, especially during the second trip to Ephesus.

It was well over a year since that battle, which had marked the Flint Pirates' with their first significant victory. As the Circumgressus hadn't initially given them the coordinates to the second Predecessor energy device - or "Babel" - that would unseal Arcadia, the Flints had contented themselves well within the meantime, engaging in traditional brands of piracy alongside certain other ventures, both orthodox and not. Though they were nowhere near the great Morganna Flint's legendary fortune, much less any closer to resurrecting her long lost Gold Dragon Clan, the Flints and their followers had progressed well and gained much through that period, all but *officially* establishing them as the latest rising stars in the Milky Way Galaxy. After sixteen years in obscurity, the name Flint, at last, carried proper weight and infamy. As did the name of their vaunted starship.

Eventually, the Circumgressus did indeed identify the second Babel, this time located upon the distant world of Smyrna. Compared to the desolation Ephesus had embodied, its unlikely relationship with Smyrna might as well have been a study in contrasts. The latter was a world wholly abundant in life, from its grasslands and forests to its magnificent mountains, lakes, and rivers. Flora and fauna were both plentiful and always in significant diversity, such that it seemed as though Smyrna held no form of wasteland or erosion whatsoever. And to top it off, it also contained quite a few valuable minerals, up to and including deposits of hyperium, which was highly coveted, alongside various precious stones that would not look out of place upon numerous races' females.

Indeed, Smyrna was very much a gleaming emerald of great price. One that, by all facts and logic, should have been long annexed by one of the Thirteen, or at least one of the lesser nations. This notion, alongside the presence of the second Babel, with the inevitable surrounding ruins, and the overall feeling of otherworldliness that Smyrna held – one of its few similarities to Ephesus - had disturbed more than one of the Flint Pirates' number. Alex was starting to wonder if this would be a trend with any world that contained a Babel, or whatever other ancient knickknacks the Predecessors had left behind.

And then there was the final contrast it held to the first world. Whereas Ephesus had been wholly deserted of sentient life and civilization, it seemed Smyrna had been bountiful enough to support one. That in itself wasn't a bad thing but said civilization, as far as the datalogs read, was never recorded, much less classified with a Terran designation. It was apparently still in the developing stages of social and cultural evolution, specifically on the period that entailed warring tribes that fought and killed one another by day and worshipped eternally bloodthirsty war gods by night. And to make matters that much worse, said gods apparently dwelled within the ruins that contained the resident Babel, with a standing order to all tribes to slaughter and/or sacrifice any intruders that dared enter and "desecrate" their domain. Which, more or less, had led to the current situation that Alex and his compatriots were engaged in.

Charging into the middle of the advancing group, Alex executed a spin slash, sending a full one hundred eighty degree wave of flame throughout the formation. What wasn't completely obliterated was easily thrown aside, the resultant corpses thoroughly burnt. Unfortunately, this did little in disparaging additional warriors from attacking, as another group quickly moved in against him. Frustrated with their apparent lack of fear or self-preservation, Alex drove forward, parrying through the attacks of the first warrior to engage against him, then bifurcating its midsection with a fiery cut that its brass armor did nothing to withstand. Another, this one armed with a massive stone club that wouldn't have looked out of place on prehistoric Terra, quickly replaced its late comrade. Alex narrowly sidestepped to the right as it swung its weapon. By the time it raised it again, Alex had cleaved through its left side, effectively ending it as well, and then moved on, cutting down two more of the standard axeblade-wielding ones. Another, somewhat smaller wave of fire then followed, vaporizing at least three more as the younger Flint pressed on.

Ducking behind a nearby wall, if only to catch his breath, Alex turned to see another unit of warriors charging wildly toward a nearby raider contingent. The pirates easily cut down their attackers with a concentrated beam rifle barrage. A few stragglers managed to get through, however, but they were just as quickly dealt with as the raiders, switching to their Imperial daggers, Blue Dragon katanas, and other assorted melee weapons, engaged at close-range. The younger Flint couldn't help but laugh sardonically as the last combatant, once again bellowing a war cry as it attacked, was taken down by a dagger thrust that effortlessly pierced its chest.

Indeed, this was *nothing* like Ephesus.

Despite all their zealousness and drive to sacrifice the intruding Flint Pirates to their gods, the fact remained that the resident aliens were all too inferior and ultimately incapable of standing up to them. A curious humanoid breed, with dark green skin and bulky, well-muscled body structure that included two arms, two legs, a head that contained beady red eyes, a gaping maw of a mouth that held overly large fangs and equally large ears on either side, the aliens seemed all but outright built for power and tenacity. And that was before one got into the power behind their crude but still quite dangerous weaponry, ranging from the aforementioned axes, clubs, and bows to one or two more exotic arms, as well as the various furs, dislodged teeth and war paint they adorned themselves with, further elaborating their orientation toward war.

All that established, the aliens were indeed a viable threat to whatever else may have inhabited Smyrna. Compared to the Flint Pirates, however, who were literally thousands of years ahead of them in cognitive thought, skill, experience, and technology, they were little more than a nuisance. A particularly vicious nuisance, but still nothing beyond.

On the other hand, the aliens did have one factor going for them, which was consequently a factor the Flint Pirates tended to face: numbers. While it seemed like the Flints were always up against superior numbered enemies no matter where they went, they were now fighting an entire *civilization*. One that likely had a population well within the thousands, all of which were fanatically driven toward massacring the intruding pirates, both for themselves and their ever thirsting gods. Obviously, that made them entirely different from the average nuisance. It made them an actual, albeit unconventional, threat that the Flints couldn't take too lightly.

"Burn baby!" Alex called out as he punched the ground, generating a crimson shockwave that obliterated the remaining number of warriors that had surrounded him. There were, of course, more to come, charging through the ruins even as the cinders of their comrades were still raining down.

Reburying his frustration, Alex leaped into the air, executing another fire wave attack that burned through the initial four. Landing atop the remains of a structure, he spun around to parry the strikes of two more. Immediately, he opened up his left hand and launched a fireball into the chest of one, then spun again to slash the second at the throat, beheading it in a single movement. From behind the second, a third moved in with a massive spear in hand; Alex narrowly ducked to evade its thrust. Before it could perform a second, the younger Flint leaped back up and executed a rising slash, dividing the warrior into burning halves. Naturally, more were moving against him before said halves fell to the ground.

"Come on!" Alex hollered as he slashed Forneus about, cutting down two more without missing a beat. "Is that all you primitive screwheads got!?"

Though he doubted that they understood the insult, it was still more than enough to embolden a horde of the aliens to rush at him, deafening roars sounding throughout their charges. Thus Alex returned to the parrying and evading, slashing and incinerating, taking down one warrior after another in the elaborate pyrotechnic display that only Forneus could generate. All without having gained as much as a cut on his greatcoat.

And then, right as Alex cut down the last warrior in the squad, he felt the ground beneath him suddenly begin to rumble. That miniature earthquake was soon complemented by a thunderous stomping sound, and rolling dust cloud, from which a massive crimson eyed and iron horned/tusked charging war beast emerged.

"Whoa!" Alex yelled out as he leaped back, narrowly avoiding being impaled on its horn. *I didn't know the greenskins had a zoo!*

Landing some distance away, the younger Flint swung Forneus around in a style that Alex believed akin to an Ancient Terran matador with a red cape.

"Toro, toro!" the younger Flint called out as the war beast scraped its spiked hooves against the ground, its rider preparing to renew its charge.

This time Alex was a little cautious, such that he subconsciously gritted his teeth. Though he retained the advantage, the beast, for all of its bulk and thickened hide, demonstrated tremendous speed and agility. It would only take a few seconds for it to cross the distance and attempt to reconnect its horn or tusks with the pirate's body, if not snap at Alex with its rows of sharpened teeth. Again, much like an ancient matador, he needed to time his counterattack just right…

It all turned for naught; however, as a great, sweeping rush of black emerged from the beast's left side, overcoming it and its rider as an oceanic wave would. With final, anguished roars, the creature and its master were both devoured by the apparent darkness; their howls soon drowned out by the considerably softer, yet infinitely eerier 'shrieking' that the wave elicited as it swept between the ruins, drawing in additional victims as it went.

Staring into that darkness, Alex allowed an appreciative smirk to form upon his lips. "You're late, brother," he stated simply.

In response, a part of the darkness turned to move toward the younger Flint.

"Fashionably late. There's a difference," a voice replied as the darkness suddenly took shape, revealing a single, yet all too familiar figure. A figure that retained a piercing blue eye on his left side, while a black eyepatch covered his right.

"Besides, as a wise man once said…" an equally familiar grin unfolded as its bearer spoke… "'the main hero must *always* have a grand entrance.'"

Greatcoat flaring against the wind and Astaroth in hand, Jonathan Flint stepped forward to gaze at his brother, whose initial smirk folded into a full grin upon the elder Flint's approach. A grin that Jon matched, albeit with a cooler disposition.

That grin remained on Alex's face even as he leaped up and slashed Forneus about, launching another fire wave. As Jon neatly evaded to the side, the wave swept over an additional number of warriors, who, having possessed enough intelligence to wait until Astaroth's darkness dissipated, emerged and, roaring more battle cries, moved in against the two brothers. Simultaneously, Jon executed a wave attack of his own, sending a surge of darkness behind where Alex had been standing. It washed over another band of club armed aliens that had begun to advance, drawing them all into its void.

It was far from the end, however. For all that had fallen, those that remained were only further incensed to fight, rushing around the fire and the darkness to engage the sacrificial intruders up close. All the while, an additional number of war beasts, at least four this time, came surging in for the kill.

Thus, biting back whatever irritation they may have held, the sons of Morganna Flint rebrandished their Devilblades and let out battle cries of their own as they charged on.

——————— ———————

"Emperor's Bowels, can't these bastards take the damn hint!?" one of the raiders called out as he continued to fire his beam rifle, taking down more of the oncoming warriors with each shot. Unfortunately, for each one that he killed, it seemed there were two or three to take its place and continue the rush. "They'll be completely wiped out at this rate!"

"Not if they overrun us first!" another raider commented as he too kept firing, the crimson bolts easily piercing and striking down whatever he targeted, albeit with some considerable effort. As much as he would have liked to believe that these aliens, whatever they called themselves, would be quickly dispatched, the fact remained that there were more of them than there were pirates. And for all the refinements Professor Braun had made to their arsenal, the fact also remained that beam weapons eventually ran out of energy.

"They just keep coming!"

"Less chatter, more slaughter! The greenies have to break sometime!" another of their company, a dark-skinned woman with a permanent scowl across her face, roared as she let loose her rifle on full auto, spraying the incoming warriors with suppression fire. Though several went down, more than a few were able to wade through the fire and continue their charge, still roaring their battle calls as they went. Even the grenade that she lobbed after her initial burst did little to hinder the roaring horde; the aliens simply continued to charge even as bits and pieces of their comrades were still raining around them. Gritting her teeth, she could only slap another power pack into her rifle and continue firing.

They had been at it for a better part of an hour now, or so any of them would have assumed had they not been so busy fighting for their lives. Though their opposition was far from their usual adversaries, namely the Thirteen and their respective military forces, they were still proving more challenging to deal with than one would have initially believed. They just kept charging and charging, no matter how many of their kind were killed off. In fact, the abundance of death among their own seemed only to enthuse them with greater bloodlust. Leos and Taureans held greater restraint by comparison, as well as a sound knowledge of their mortality.

Fortunately, they wouldn't have to hold out for too much longer. Once the Babel was activated, the Captain's strategy would take immediate effect. After that, it was a sure bet that the aliens wouldn't be too keen on fighting them anymore, despite present circumstances. The Flints only need to maintain the effort until then, which was admittedly problematic but not impossible. After all, they had fought much, much worse…

A sudden, all too familiar clinking sound caused the assembled raiders to look up, taking immediate notice of a cylinder-shaped object that fell in their midst. One that had a telltale line of smoke rising from one end.

"Grenade!" one of them called out in warning. They all leaped away from the structure that had been serving as a barricade, splaying out to other areas of cover. A second later, the impromptu explosive device, which was little more than a chiseled, hollowed-out stone filled with munition powder, blew up.

In spite of its primitive construction, the weapon proved to be quite destructive, spraying stone shards in all directions at high velocity. Several of them struck the scowl faced raider in the back. And though her body armor shielding easily kept the shards from actually embedding themselves into her, the shock was enough to throw her onto the ground. She rolled onto her back, dazed and ears ringing.

She was not, however, so dazed that she didn't feel the footfalls near her, nor hear the faint bellowing and cries of warning that followed. Again instincts driving her, she rolled to the side as a great stone axe struck where she had lain. Surging to her feet, she drew her beam pistol and fired three shots, all landing in her would-be attacker's chest. The alien fell, but naturally, more of its brethren were quick to follow up.

Her scowl deepening at their rapid approach, the raider, who happened to be a former Imperial Marine, withdrew her pistol and replaced it with her dagger. Though she had long grown accustomed to the multi-racial buildup of her new "family," if not interstellar piracy altogether, she was still a Marine and a scion of Terra at heart and would be damned before some backworld alien trash got the better of her. Besides, it had been a while since she got to spill blood the old fashioned way.

There was a reason the dagger was the favored melee weapon of the forces of the Terran Empire. While swords and spears may have possessed greater reach, and axes and warhammers may have possessed greater power, only the dagger was ideal toward striking at an adversary's weak points, whether in an elaborate defense or within its very biology or mechanics. And if there was one thing Terrans – especially those who served or had served in His Imperial Majesty's Starfleet Marine Corps – knew, it was that all aliens had weak points. It was just a matter of identifying them, which Marines and those others adept at fighting up close were explicitly trained to do.

In this case, the greenskins had necks and were breathing the surrounding air. Thus, when the first one made its attack, charging forward to thrust its spear, the raider sidestepped it and then brought her dagger about, slashing into the left side of the alien's trunk-like throat, where the carotid artery would be in a Terran. Though she wasn't sure if she struck a similar organ, her slash was deep enough to elicit a line of surprisingly red blood, as well as to cause the alien to stumble forward, as if caught off-guard by the strike. Immediately seizing the opportunity, she then planted the dagger into the back of the warrior's head –inwardly wincing at how thick its skull felt – finishing him.

Withdrawing the weapon, she was just able to duck as the second warrior swept its axe. She leaped up and made a long gash into the front of its neck. Again the creature reacted in surprise, seemingly taken back that it had actually been struck. The startled hesitation allowed the raider to drop back down and perform a sweep kick that brought her opponent to the ground. Before it could move, she followed up with another, more solid kick to its head, which caused it to roll over. Rapidly, she plunged her dagger deep into its chest. Once more, that seemed to do the trick as the alien stopped moving from that point on.

Just as she stood up, however, she felt a force slam into her right side, knocking her several meters away. Her shield absorbed the blow, which would have undoubtedly crushed her innards in an actual impact, but the shock was more than enough to dishevel her for a moment.

Fortunately, she wasn't disheveled enough to stop from flipping back onto her feet, just as another one of the creatures smashed its club where she had landed. Bellowing with fury, the alien lurched at her, swinging its club while the raider maneuvered around it, inflicting a slash into the alien's upper left arm in the process. This caused the alien to howl with fury, once again leading credence to the theory that they were unused to getting struck, at least by the blade of an unholy invader such as herself. Enraged, it increased the savagery of its attacks, which she narrowly evaded or redirected, utilizing the momentum of the alien's swings to intercept the club and move it away from her, correspondingly inflicting multiple slashes into the creature, one a deep laceration into the being's chest. The responding roars nearly deafening her.

I've fought much *worse than you,* she thought, just as she lunged forward again and stuck her blade into the left side of the creature's chest. However, before she could withdraw the dagger, the creature dropped its club and grasped her arm, its grip locking onto it even as her shield resisted, and then jerked her forward. With a mighty howl, it reared back then head-butt her face. Again the shield deflected much of the physical blow, but the force was enough to knock her head about, clouding her vision and dulling her reflexes. The alien flung the raider into a nearby wall, knocking her onto her back once again, and reached for its fallen club.

The next thing she saw was the creature running toward her brandishing its club. She knew she wouldn't be able to get back onto her feet in time. Thus she did the only thing she thought of; she threw the dagger at the alien's head, where the blade penetrated deep into the creature's left eye socket. The alien let out another roar, more pained than infuriated, and dropped its club, its hand coming over its face in a futile attempt to stop the bloody torrent. She had obviously struck something vital.

"Thanks, Master Chief Hartman," she muttered, remembering her former

Marine instructor who had demanded pinpoint accuracy with a dagger and the requisite hundreds of hours of practice. The raider slowly rose to her feet and approached the seemingly blind and dying alien, ripping her knife from the greenskin's eye. Just as the newly rendered corpse fell face-first onto the ground, she felt a pair of oversized arms encircle her, yanking her up off the ground in an effort to crush her against their master's chest. Struggling to break its hold, she tried to slash her dagger about, kick something vital, or reach back to her pistol, but the creature would not be deterred, bellowing in rage as it squeezed against her shield, threatening to crush it. Glancing around, she realized her comrades that were close enough to support were engaged in hand-to-hand combat with several of the creatures. All the while, her shield came closer and closer to buckling from the pressure...

And then, with a sudden metallic impact, the alien warrior went limp. Instinctively breaking away from its hold, she dropped to the side just as it fell, face first as her third kill had done. When she turned around, she saw another blade sticking out from the back of its head. One she recognized as a kunai.

"Commander!" one of the other raiders howled in jubilation, followed by a bout of cheering as a single figure, dressed in a black and gold armored tactical suit, articulately straight-bladed sword in hand, leaped into the midst of the creatures and relentlessly attacked.

Easily evading the various axes and clubs of her would-be attackers, Fuma Kaguya slashed out once, beheading one of the aliens, and then proceeded to leap up and over as another came charging in with a spear. Landing just behind the alien, she deftly cut into its back, severing its spine. A following shuriken throw took down another, digging into its neck, before another spear-armed pair charged, only for the ninja to lunge forward, evading their blades, and then slash into the midsection of either as they passed. Both creatures fell to the grounds before realizing they had been struck, all the while Kaguya continued her assault.

Reacting almost instantaneously to the kunoichi's appearance, the aliens, as if realizing her to be the most substantial threat present, suddenly abandoned their attacks on the other raiders and, letting out additional war cries, charged en masse with their various weapons ready to strike. And yet, in spite of their numbers, Kaguya had no issue maneuvering around their attacks and striking in kind, cutting them down one after the other with her ninjato or throwing a well-placed shuriken or kunai into a particularly vulnerable area. Bodies fell to the ground in abundance. The earth seemed to quake continuously from the impacts.

The last to fall, and subsequently the largest of the group, was brought down as it swung its axe, only for Kaguya to leap up and over as the stone blade impacted the ground. With a confident flourish, she landed upon the alien's hunched back and stabbed her ninjato through its head, the tip extending out through the gaping, fanged mouth. With a final, almost sighing exhale of breath, the alien fell over. Kaguya withdrew her blade and neatly hopped off, landing back on the ground with promptness, just as the raiders ran over to meet her.

"Commander, that was awesome!" one of them blared out in clear approval.

Kaguya just nodded as she moved through the group. Before she could comment, however, an all too familiar rumbling sensation erupted across the field.

"Take cover!"

Moments later, two more of those war beasts came charging through the avenues, letting out twin bellows as their riders urged them on. Heeding their commander's orders, the group dispersed and opened fired as they hid, crimson bursts raining upon the animals from virtually every direction. And yet, despite the fact the supercharged beam shots easily pierced through the massive creatures' armor and hides, they continued to attack, seemingly through sheer willpower.

Kaguya ran toward one of the beasts and leaped onto its head, evading its attempt to impale her on its horn, and rapidly traversed its neck. The rider started to swing its axe upon her approach, but she was much quicker, skewering the alien on her sword and then throwing it off its mount.

Simultaneously, as she leaped off the creature's back, she launched three kunais out toward the second rider, one striking its head and the other two its torso. It too, fell off.

Landing back on the ground, Kaguya withdrew another kunai as she sought cover. Pausing, she considered for a moment; if the deaths of their riders and the abundance of beam fire weren't slowing either beast down, what good would her throwing blades do? Indeed, now without guidance, the creatures were running amuck through the ruins, bucking and weaving across the ground as they endured one beam shot after another, all the while attacking in kind where they went. One even managed to stomp and crush the debris that two of the raiders had utilized to take cover, driving the men to abandon their position.

Hoping that the beasts' brains were located in their heads, Kaguya sighed as she brandished her ninjato and readied to move in.

Before she initiated her assault, however, a barrage of beam fire streamed down from above, striking either beast in a virtual hailstorm of crimson. With a higher firing frequency and intensity than the raiders' weapons, the beam shots virtually shredded both creatures, their final bellows echoing through the ruins as the remnants of the carcasses splattered across the ground. Moments later, a black and gold gull-winged fighter swooped in and performed a flyby, then ascended back up to rejoin its battle above.

Appearing unaffected by the flyby, though concealing the minutest of smirks, it didn't take much for Kaguya to identify that particular pilot. Nor to tune into her comm. frequency, even amidst the renewed cheering.

"*Arigatou gozaimasu,* Corsair One," she said, eyes narrowing. "Though I was quite ready to finish them myself."

———————————— ————————————

Smiling in turn toward the only *slightly* begrudging thanks, Charlotte "Boss" Boyington was quick to reply.

"If you say so, Alfa One," she rejoined as she took her Corsair into a steeper climb.

As much as she would have liked to provide further air cover for the raiders, she, along with the rest of Corsair and Buccaneer Squadrons, had their problems to deal with. One of those problems soon made itself apparent as it unleashed a plasma shot at her. Banking to evade before twisting her fighter around, she fired a vulcan burst at her attacker. Several warshots later, a shrill scream erupted as her target, and its rider fell to the ground below in flames.

As it was on the surface, there were hundreds if not thousands of the aliens in the air, riding swarms of winged reptilians which, for lack of better description, Boss and several of her pilots had labeled as wyrms, flitting wildly across the sky, moving between attacking the Flint fighters and attempting strafing runs below. Usually, it would have been a massacre, a proverbial "turkey shoot" to borrow from Ancient Terran dialect, in which Boss and her contingent would have been entirely unhindered. However, while upfront, the wyrms appeared as every other winged reptile Boss had encountered throughout her life, they actually possessed one unique ability: they could ionize their breath and launch the resultant plasma out as an energy bolt. If that wasn't bad enough, the plasma bolt had an uncharacteristically high intensity. The Corsair's shields could stand up to a shot or two, but such attacks would take a fair-sized chunk out of them as Boss had discovered. It was one of the few times in her life that she had been caught off guard, much to her detriment.

Fortunately, that was the only real weapon the creatures and their rider possessed. They were otherwise no match for actual fighters, let alone the Corsair and pilots experienced through war and battles like Ephesus. As such, the Flint pilots, while retaining watch of the plasma fire, were making the most of it, decimating the aliens like the incarnate wrath of whatever gods they worshipped. All across the sky, wyrms were being torn apart by vulcan shots, their remnants virtually showering over the ruins below, usually accompanied by the death cries of their riders, while Corsairs continued their dance with little hindrance. A single fighter had yet to be lost, and more than one pilot was griping at the lack of a challenge.

That said, however, the aliens still outnumbered the Corsairs and Buccaneers many times over. And for whatever amount was shot down, more arrived to continue the fight, all but throwing themselves gleefully into combat. Thus the present dogfight, as opposed to a *massacre*.

Another set of plasma shots raced by the Corsair, forcing Boss to barrel roll to the right. Gazing behind, she saw a pair of wyrms on her tail, their riders letting out hooting bellows while raising an axe and a club, respectively, as the reptilians gave chase. Sneering, Boss banked to the left and entered a dive, knowing full well that both wyrms would follow. More plasma bolts trailed after her; she maneuvered into a zig-zag, evading each shot with practiced grace. Then, at the opportune separation distance, she snapped her fighter around without altering her velocity and fired a quick vulcan burst, obliterating one of the wyrms, before turning back. Seemingly incensed at the demise of its comrade, the remaining wyrm rider's beast fired additional plasma bolts at her, but, as before, the Blue Comet had little issue evading.

I still can't believe we're fighting these stone-throwers, Boss thought disparagingly as she continued her dive, the wyrm still following as she more or less expected. Just before she would have impacted the deck; however, she executed a Split-S, dipping her fight even further and performing a lateral turn, thus allowing her to fly straight back at her would-be opponent. As she expected, the sudden change in vector caused the wyrm's rider to momentarily halt his mount in midair, the reptilian spreading its wings lest it collide with the now ascending Corsair. That pause, albeit quite minor, was more than enough for Boss. Letting loose her vulcans, she shredded both mount and rider apart as she shot past, climbing to a higher altitude.

Closing in on an enemy formation, a term she used in the lightest context, Boss fired another crimson barrage, terminating several more of the beasts and their otherwise enthused riders. Boss shivered as she watched the carcasses fall to the ground; it seemed like the aliens did not fear death. She had a feeling it had nothing to do with their primitive culture but as if the aliens were biologically incapable of that kind of fear…

A sudden thundercrack exploded against her right shield, nearly causing

Boss to jump in her seat. Recognizing the sound, she knew, despite the bang, her fighter was not damaged. Looking over, she saw another wyrm moving toward her, its rider holding one of those stone grenades in its paw, ready to throw as it let out a fierce bellow. Gunning her thrusters, she quickly accelerated just as the creature threw its bomb, the explosion sounding off distantly behind her. Naturally, the wyrm pursued, moving as fast as it could to keep up with its black and gold "prey," its maw open with a plasma burst in the making.

It was then that Boss did something even she thought was rather cruel. Once she saw that the wyrm was directly behind her, she engaged, cut her engine power, and hit her flight breaks.

Within seconds, the wyrm and its rider literally crashed into her Corsair, smashing against her lateral shields with bone-breaking force. Obviously, the fighter was completely undamaged as before, but the reptilian was effectively knocked out or banged up enough that it couldn't fly, just as the force of the impact had caused the rider to lose its grip on the mount. As a result, both ended up falling, again with a defiant bellow from the rider as it dropped like a stone. This time Boss didn't bother to watch, instead bringing her drives back up and flying out again, seeking out additional targets.

Obviously, it didn't take long for her to find some, as no fewer than five wyrms came swooping toward her, plasma bolts firing rapidly. At least two exploded against her shield, but her fighter managed to weather the blows, and so she pressed the offensive, spraying more fire across the sky. This time she only managed to strike down one of the wyrms; the other four scattered around her shots in a surprisingly coordinated effort, moving around her bursts in a manner that only winged, fully organic beings could do. She managed to shoot down another reptilian before she flew through the pseudo formation, evading the follow-on plasma fire.

As she passed by the last wyrm of the group, its rider chucked its axe against the side of her Corsair. Needless to say, the axe bounced harmlessly off the fighter's shielding. Boss rolled her eyes as she shifted the craft over, firing a vulcan burst into the wyrm and the rider. Both were easily annihilated, leaving very little to fall to the planet's surface. After that, she looped around and dealt with the remaining two, narrowly evading their twin plasma shots before shooting them down as well. The last mount ended up being shot in the left-wing; it spiraled out of the air in a similar manner to an actual aircraft.

It was no more than a few seconds after her latest kill that Boss' sensors lit up in warning; another wave of enemies was incoming, numbering somewhere in the hundreds. Sighing with her growing aggravation, she looked toward the ruins below, specifically at the temple set at the very center.

How much longer? Boss thought concerning the temple, or more precisely, concerning the one within its depths. Not bothering to expect an answer, though she was sure that particular being could have replied if so inclined, she reoriented her fighter and engaged her sub-arc engines to full burn, aggressively charging at the newcomers.

Predecessor Temple
Smyrna

And so here she was once more. Her physical body standing within the core of the ancient mechanism, hand extended over the familiar orb as the energy pooled into the depths before her, while her metaphysical "self" had descended through that same energy into the darkness, and was now upon its epicenter. It had been as long and as arduous a process as it had before; a continued "fall" through a seemingly endless darkness, with the only apparent "light" being the surging energy around her. Even so, she had progressed through her descent all the same. She deduced, both from past experience and through her perceptions, that the emergence would not take much longer. That the light, steadily growing more apparent and powerful with each passing moment, would soon rise.

This suited her purpose, as it did those fighting above her. Though the battle currently being waged was nothing like what had been fought before, during the emergence of the first tower, it was still a battle all the same, and the longer it progressed, the more it would become detrimental for those who supported her. Fortunately, despite the number of alien combatants, she sensed no deaths amongst those who fought on her behalf, a myriad of injuries perhaps, but not one of the fighters had expired beyond her unique sight. However, their opposition remained enraged, fighting to retake the sacred ground that belonged to their twin, ever conflicting war gods. The ferocity with which the Flint Pirates engaged them didn't deter their battle lust; it only incensed the aliens that much further.

If the fight continued, she knew one of two conclusions would occur. Either her defenders would be overrun or, they would end up destroying the whole of the enemy army. The latter might have passed for necessary, as, short of *his* stratagem, it was unlikely the enemy would be dissuaded. All the same, however, such a course of action would retain consequences, not the least of which would be the trauma that her two primary supporters would suffer at once again having to destroy a whole civilization and culture. Thus for obvious reasons, neither conclusion was favorable to her, further necessitating the completion of her task at the earliest possibility. The fact it had likely been hours since she had initially began emphasized the critical nature of her timing.

Refocusing on the objective, as well as gathering herself for what was to come, she couldn't help but once again marvel at the ancient mechanism that she was attempting to activate. In her first experience, she could not see past the darkness around her, could not comprehend the sheer depth and power that the mechanism held within, nor the true force of the gathering energy that flowed into the depths about her. She still couldn't see beyond the dark, but that didn't mean she was ignorant of what it concealed. An infinite and astounding power, one that crossed the boundary between technology and "magic." No other articulated design could compare to it. A machine that held the specific ability of spanning the limits of space and time, to forcing open a gate that had long been closed. A gate that could only lead to providence, or so she believed. That thought catalyzed her surging sense of wonder.

How could any civilization or creed even conceive such a machine?

To create a device that altered the very fundamentals of existence, a power that even the most advanced civilizations of the present-day equated to the will of God, or gods, alone. Even she could not comprehend the sheer knowledge and understanding necessary to theorize the mere concept of it, let alone construct it and perfect it of whatever flaws it might have initially possessed. And she was perhaps the only being in the present era who knew how to utilize or at least activate it. Just as she was the only being who possessed even the most basic understanding toward its creators.

But that was all incidental. Focusing her power, she extended her reach into the mechanism's core. As a result, the energy began gathering even faster, becoming a torrent as it rained upon the epicenter. She retained her focus, guiding the "rain" into the mechanism as it continued to accelerate, such that it seemed the darkness itself would break under its collective force.

Soon enough, the barest flicker of light began to emerge…

Predecessor Ruins
Smyrna

"WAAAGH!" the alien called out as it charged, spear in hand, and ready to pierce.

"GROOOG!" Alex mockingly shouted back as he evaded the spear thrust, then surged forward to slash the alien across the chest with flame. It was not long before the enemy was utterly overcome by fire and reduced to ash, though by then, Alex had moved on, striking down additional adversaries as he went.

Fighting his way through the new slew of enemies, Alex, upon relocating an equally engaged Jonathan, turned back to back with his brother. Their blind spots covered, the Brothers Flint continued to fight, striking down and obliterating every adversary that came against them and their position. They seemed to be numbering infinity now; the air was filled with the sounds of bellowing war cries and feet stomping down on the ground as the charges went on.

"Well, this is another superb bedlam you've gotten me into brother!" Alex shouted as he battled no fewer than three of the aliens simultaneously. Swatting away the axes and club, evading a lateral swipe that would have knocked his head clean off, he proceeded to light one of the attackers' heads on fire. As the now howling being clawed at the flames, his two compatriots, seemingly oblivious to his agony, pressed their offensive. Alex had to hold Forneus up to deflect both of their weapons, momentarily holding them in place.

"What next? A frontal assault on Terra? Or maybe a wrestling match with a Cetian?"

"Has anyone mentioned you complain too much, Alex?" Jon replied as he slashed at his opponents, Astaroth's obsidian blade cutting through one of the stone-headed spears. He released a black wave, drawing the offending aliens into the nothingness, only for two more to move into their place, swinging their clubs at the elder Flint. Once more, Jon had little issue deflecting their attacks, then striking down either of the warriors, but even as they fell, more simply surged in to continue the battle. Inwardly he understood his brother's frustration, though he did well not to vocalize it.

"It's not like we haven't been through worse."

"I don't know. Even Drake's minions weren't *this* bloody obstinate!" Alex called back as he propelled another crimson wave at the marauding aliens, burning them into oblivion. The ashes swirled as an additional number rushed forward, calling out their eponymous battle cry as they brought their weapons against the younger Flint.

"At this rate, we'll end up repeating Sumatra!"

"No, we won't," Jon reassured as, mimicking his brother's move, he swept Astaroth about, unleashing another black wave that erupted over the oncoming aliens. Their howls echoed eerily as they were drawn into the void.

Another "greenie" charged the elder Flint with a thundering shriek, axe swinging. To the creature's surprise however, Jon didn't bother deflecting the strike with his Devilblade; instead, he raised his left hand and grasped the stone blade as it fell, holding it in place. With lightning speed, Jon impaled Astaroth through the being's torso, then ripped it out and executed an energy augmented palm thrust that knocked the alien back several meters into a nearby ruin, crushing it and a contingent of the being's cohorts upon impact.

In the brief calm, before the next gathering wave of enemies reached them, Jon stole a glance toward the temple. Though there was no way he could explain it to his brother, he knew all the same.

"The Judgment is nigh."

Comprehending his elder brother's message, Alex grimly nodded in acceptance. It was the only way they would be able to end this, at least *without* slaughtering another whole civilization in the process. They, as well as the rest of the Flint Pirates, just needed to persevere a little bit longer. As annoying and potentially hazardous as it was to do, for all of them.

Thus with renewed determination, the brothers separated and moved against the oncoming throng, utilizing the full might of their Devilblades. All the while, the enemy continued to swarm them, heedless of the pain, death, and destruction they faced.

Predecessor Temple
Smyrna

It was as before. From the endless darkness, the light sputtered into existence, steadily and rapidly growing, empowered as the various energies channeled into it. It was all or nothing now, she knew, and so focused the entirety of her power, forcing the energies to accelerate even more.

Soon, what had once been a mere glint against the black developed into the luminosity of a small star. Miniscule in comparison to those that shone across the galaxy, yet no less apparent in scope, such that, even against the backdrop of the infinite darkness, its radiance remained as visible as it was blinding. As more energy surged into it, the star multiplied in size and brilliance. It seemed as though the darkness actually withdrew from its light, that the night was at last giving way to the dawn.

Now, as the light surged, encompassing her, she could fathom its power. A power that, as its very name alluded to, bespoke of a civilization's passion to extend into the heavens, to unlock their gate. A passion that, according to specific mythologies, forced God, or the gods, to curse that civilization with confusion and indecision, giving birth to the variety of language. Thereby ensuring that their towers never reached completion, that the heavens would never be breached.

An ironic, yet no less triumphant smile formed on her lips as even more of the dark gave way to the light. Whether she and hers were destined to endure a curse of their own, or perhaps even outright damnation, by their actions, she would remain resolute as she had since the beginning. No matter what, she would see the towers complete, and the heavens bridged. She would see what lay beyond the gate. As would *he*.

And so the light became complete, the second key at last turned. From there, as it had once before, only silence reigned supreme…

Predecessor Ruins
Smyrna

Sweeping Astaroth across the front, Jon bifurcated another of the charging aliens with a well-placed cleave, cutting the torso off the lower body, before ducking underneath a club swipe of a second enemy, which he spun around and beheaded. He smashed his left hand into the ground, generating a line of black geysers and sending several more of the aliens into oblivion. Yet, the demonstration of superior force did nothing to dissuade the remainders. Against the omnipresent horde, Jon leaped into the air and fired another black wave, a larger one, which fell upon the aliens as an airborne predator, taking out significant quantities of the creatures before the elder Flint's feet touched ground again. He then renewed his charge, for without pause more followed.

Not far away, Alex remained just as vigilant, maneuvering through the latest grouping of aliens, cutting them down systematically before weaving a line of flames against those that he missed. Two enemy warriors managed to force their way through the fire. One swung its club at Alex only for the younger Flint to flip back and gain some distance. Not dissuaded, the second surged forward with its spear, but Alex ducked its thrust and then slashed upward, cutting the bladed end of the weapon off the pole. Not wasting a single moment, he sliced Forneus about, unleashing another wave of flame that immolated the warrior, its charred remains knocked back several meters before scattering across the ground. Heedless of its partner's demise, the first charged on, raising its club to strike from overhead. This time Alex leaped up and over before the swing was complete, the ground quaking from the impact as the younger Flint landed directly behind the alien. Abruptly, a fiery hand erupted from the being's chest, which it regarded with confusion before it was ripped away, allowing the newly rendered corpse to fall.

More of the aliens came charging in, but before Alex could deal with them, Astaroth's darkness erupted and surged over the group, overwhelming several of the numbers. Alex added his fire to the mix, immolating whatever few the darkness had left untouched while he came alongside his brother once again. More aliens charged at them, and more fell against a combination of fire and dark as the brothers waded their way through the mob.

"You would think these things had some sense of self-preservation!" Alex called out as he immolated another number of aliens, whose compatriots continued to charge regardless. "Think we're making a dent!?"

"In numbers, certainly," Jon commented as he ducked the club blow of one of the larger ones, then slashed it across the stomach. He just managed to move aside as the body fell, the ground shaking upon its impact. "In terms of morale, however…"

"Obviously!" Alex shouted as he also evaded the axe swing of another of the larger ones, this one big enough to dwarf even Kaiser, whose presence Alex was beginning to miss. Regardless, he was quick enough to launch upward with Forneus' blade, thus cleaving the creature into fiery halves. By the time he landed again, he was forced to deflect another axe blow, albeit this time from one of the smaller aliens, which he simply kicked away.

"Maybe wiping this particular civilization out isn't such a bad idea!"

Jon was about to comment when he felt the ground begin to shake again. Frowning, he looked over to see more of those war beasts charging in, their riders howling battle cries in abundance. Sighing, he raised Astaroth and prepared his next attack, only to pause when an all too familiar sensation began to wash over him. His smirk was that of triumph.

"And the kings of the earth, and the great men... " Jon began, all the while continuing to fight. *"...and the rich men, and the chief captains, and the mighty men... "*

Through the melee, Alex heard his brother's words but was unsure of what to make of his declaration.

"...and every bondman, and every free man... " Jon went on as he split another alien into halves. *"...hid themselves in the dens and in the rocks of the mountains... "*

He then unleashed another black wave, taking out a whole slew of enemies.

"And said to the mountains and the rocks, Fall on us, and hide us from the face of him that sitteth on the throne... "

The elder Flint's eye narrowed at the next oncoming charge. *"...and from the wrath of the Lamb. "*

Before Alex could inquire as to the quote, he too was gripped by the sensation. As were the aliens around him, their war cries and charges gradually giving way to confusion.

"For the great day of his wrath is come, " Jon continued, outright *feeling* the power now emanating from the temple, rising and rising further. *"And who shall be able to stand?"*

And then, all at once, an immense white light erupted from the temple ruins, momentarily overwhelming the surrounding space. All across the battlefield, the Flints and their enemies alike shielded themselves from the light of the Babel's activation, the enormous tower of energy beaming into the sky above, where it would continue on into the void. Another lock upon Porta Coeli had been undone.

However, Jon hadn't been so blinded as to prevent his shouting into his wristcom.

"All units take cover!" he ordered, just as he and Alex scrambled to the nearest safe area they could find.

Meanwhile, beyond the sky above, a black form began to move…

Flint Pirates umbra *Black Sun*
Smyrna System

Spectacular as always, Barbarossa thought as he watched the Babel emerge, almost overcoming space itself with its light. A light so pure and so powerful that it was perhaps the closest in existence to the true light of the heavens. The light of Aslan itself.

"Status."

"All targets locked in," the anonymous crewman that had momentarily taken over the tactical station replied, his report signified upon the bridge's viewscreen, which indeed showed all marked for the oncoming attack. "We're ready to fire."

Hearing that, Barbarossa allowed a small smirk. Even though he had long grown used to the captain's knack for strategy and tactics, there was something rather fulfilling about this one. The Leo found himself truly appreciating it and its irony. After all, what better utilization of a heathenistic faith than to use it against their practitioners?

Thus, Barbarossa sat back and looked over the Babel for a few moments longer, waiting for the word of his operations officer. Davis, knowing that appearance would be everything in this gambit, moved the *Black Sun* closer to the tower of light, as much as he dared without actually being swept into its current. Though there was no way he could put the ship into the exact position, he could make it appear, from the perspective of those on the surface, that the pirate vessel originated from the Babel itself. And like Barbarossa, and the rest of the bridge crew, there was something exhilarating about invoking the "Wrath of God" and scaring the waste fluids out of a warrior race such as Smyrna's.

This is going to rock, Davis thought gleefully as he brought the *Sun* as close as possible to the light, nearly licking his lips in anticipation.

Right beside him, Anna continued to study the sensors, specifically the gold dots that marked Flint Pirates from the green ones that marked the aliens. It was only when the last of the gold signals had moved to appropriate cover did she speak.

"All friendlies are out of the line."

Nodding, Barbarossa's smirk became a full fanged grin.

"Then, by all means," he waved at the weapons operator. "Let the Judgment commence!" he bellowed in righteous triumph.

With that, the crewman gleefully hit the appropriate button. The *Black Sun*'s missile launchers engaged systematically, firing their payloads into the open void. They immediately vectored downward toward Smyrna below.

Predecessor Ruins
Smyrna

The effect was near-instantaneous. From the sky above, the missiles fell, one after the other, upon their designated targets, both within and outside the ruins. As the explosions sounded across the field, the aliens, at least those that weren't obliterated, suddenly lost their previous drive and will to fight. All at once, their holy war against the invaders turned into a great retreat, the beings running away in previously unseen fear as more and more explosions erupted over them. Their collective thought apparently just what had they done to enrage their gods?

In a matter of minutes, the cries of pure, unrestrained fear grew more and more distant, until it was evident that no greenskins remained within the ruins. Once the last of the aliens were verified to have left the battle-ground, Jon transmitted the appropriate signal to the *Black Sun*, ending the missile bombardment. No sooner had the last explosion sounded did a great, collective shout of triumph erupt across the ruins, drowning out the lingering cries of the aliens, as the Flints came out of their shelters.

The Judgment, in distinct finality, had been cast.

Greatcoats wavering against the wind, the brothers moved into the open, dual grins of triumph across their lips as the roars and shouts continued in the background. Before them stretched a vast expanse of corpses, green-skinned and red-blooded, while much of the surrounding ruins had been desolated further. So much destruction, so much death. And yet, in the very image of their mother, the Flints had emerged victoriously once again.

As if to emphasize the moment, a group of Corsairs appeared overhead, their sub-arc engines screaming against the air as they performed the tradi-tional flyover. Once they passed, Alex turned to his brother, grin extending that much further as he dusted off his greatcoat.

"All in a day's work, brother."

Reflecting that grin's extension, Jon looked back toward the Babel, which continued to rise to the heavens.

"Yes," he concurred. "All in a day's work."

Chapter II: Back in the Void

Flint Pirates umbra *Black Sun*
Arcspace

It didn't take long for the celebrations to begin and escalate. In fact, as soon as the raiders returned to the *Sun,* they and the rest of the crew congregated in the lounge. The first drinks were consumed well before the pirate ship had broken orbit. And now that she was safely back within arcspace, the party wasn't looking to settle down any time soon, in case the wafting scent of alcohol, the loud background music, and the continuous banter didn't make it obvious. After all, pirates were well renowned for their love of parties, and those aboard the *Black Sun* were not about to break that tradition.

Thus, as music continually rang out from the nearby jukebox and over the surrounding air, the Flint Pirates went about their usual business following a successful endeavor: overt drinking, shouting conversation after conversation, challenging one another to various competitions – most of which either involved cards or die, if not more technological oriented implements - and wholly having a grand old time that only renegades like themselves could fully enjoy, let alone practice. Various forms of grog were passed around and readily consumed, each and every one of the present vidscreens was active and playing some form of media for an eager audience, assorted gaming tables were being fully utilized, and an abundance of laughter and banter mingled with the chords and verses of *The Boys Are Back in Town* as the latter rang over the surrounding audio system.

Overall, a typical scene for pirates when they were not pillaging and plundering somewhere in the galaxy, as the visos often emphasized. Many would remark that it was one of the few things the latter got right about their profession.

"To the Flint Pirates!" Anna called out as she raised her glass on high, inciting the rest of the table to follow her example.

"The Flint Pirates!" the others recited before clinking their glasses together and taking a swig. As usual, the core members of the Flint Pirates sat at their own table – which the rest of the crew had dubbed the "Captain's Table" as a result – and generally congregated amongst themselves. Despite the table's title, however, the Captain was notably absent from this particular celebration. As were three others, though, it was well noted among the crew that one of that number never attended such functions, while another one – subsequently the newest member of their company – was still adjusting to the Flints' lifestyle.

Regardless, the party continued.

"And now there are two," Alex remarked as he took another drink. "And with it, one more step toward the ultimate prize."

"Right, *one* more step," Davis pointed out from the side. "In well over a year since the first."

Alex shrugged. "Can't be helped, Davis. We can only reach the next Babel once the Circumgressus reveals it to us," he replied, adopting a smirk. "And it's not like it hasn't given us enough to do in the meantime."

Davis matched the first officer's smirk. "That I can heartily agree on," he said, taking a drink from his tankard. "To monitor the entire galaxy in real-time…" he exclaimed in a dreamy expression. "As well as every convoy, shipment, and exchange therein…"

With her usual annoyance toward the helmsman, Anna rolled her eyes at his display. "Somehow, I don't think the Predecessors had this in mind for its use."

Davis waved a hand demonstratively in the air. "I don't hear them objecting, wherever they are now," he shot back. "And I'm sure our dear science officer, wherever *she* is now, would have been the first to tell us so."

"Probably resting," Boss replied to the indirect inquiry. "I imagine those Babels take a lot of energy to engage."

"They do," Braun confirmed with a nod. "For all of the process' apparent simplicity, it still requires much in the way of psionic energy to energize the mechanism, and much more to get it to function," he took a slow sip from his tankard. "I can only fathom how draining it would be, especially for the average psion…"

"Which is something none of us will ever be able to figure out. Thankfully," Davis answered before shifting the conversation back on track. He, like everyone else at the Captain's Table, knew how drawn out their chief engineer could get. "As for the Predecessors and whatever intentions they have for their trinkets, I don't know about the rest of you, but I don't give a Taurean's ass."

The helmsman took another swig. "The fact is we have the Circumgressus, we know what it does, and most of all we can use it. Any other details, including whatever in the Fourth Circle it was 'meant for,' are incidental."

Alex considered that pronouncement for a moment. "Technically, only Lorelei and Jon can actually use it," he pointed out, recalling how his brother, as the *Black Sun*'s captain, was also given access to the device. Obviously, this was why the Flint Pirates were able to utilize it outside of their patron's purpose.

Despite that technicality, the younger Flint raised his tankard in acknowledgment. "Regardless, I don't believe you've ever spoken truer words, Davis."

"Here here," Boss added, raising her tankard, as did the others. "If the Predecessors didn't want their toys 'misused,' then they shouldn't have left them behind when they disappeared."

"'And that's assuming they didn't cheat a little themselves,' Kaiser claims." Gran, as usual, spoke up for the Herculean sitting beside her.

Now it was Anna's turn to shrug. "Don't get me wrong, I'm not complaining," she said. "I just don't want the thing blowing up because we didn't read the warranty properly."

Alex couldn't help but laugh. "Lorelei is the only one who can read it, and as pointed out, she's not complaining either," he added before taking another drink. *Of course, that in itself bothers me…*

"Well," Apache spoke up for the first time. Notably, after drawing an extra-long swig from his nauseous beverage. "Now that Smyrna's over and done with, and we've reaffirmed ourselves on our desecrating the Predecessors' leftovers…"

He then looked over toward Alex. "What's our next course, First Officer? After Nassau, I mean."

Suddenly feeling all eyes on him – including from those not seated at the table - Alex could only shake his head in response.

"I still have to speak to the Captain about it," he admitted as he refilled his tankard. "But, I think we'll be heading back to Ryugu next."

"Ryugu?" Anna repeated, raising an eyebrow. "Not that there's a problem with that, but why?"

All eyes shifted from Alex to Kaguya, who, as usual, was seated next to the younger Flint.

"I'm afraid I cannot answer," she offered simply. "However, I believe my lord simply wishes to discuss our progress."

"What? You mean he hasn't been kept up to date?" Apache shot back toward the kunoichi with pretend shock. "Or did you just slip up and forget your last evening call?"

Alex fixed the doctor a glare. "Apache…" he growled in a warning tone.

By now, it was an open secret that Kaguya reported to her father on all of the Flint Pirates' activities. However, very few of the crew held that against her.

Knowing better than to press the issue, Apache held up his talons in surrender. "Fine, fine," he answered, though inwardly retaining his disgruntlement. In truth, it wasn't that he had anything against the Fuma woman, but he did well to remember the days of conflict between the Gold Dragon and the Blue Dragon, as well as the blood feud between Lord Fuma and Lady Flint. And he knew Alex, despite his infatuation, also did well to remember. "But my point still stands. What does Lord Fuma need to hear from us that he doesn't already know?"

It was as good a point as any, despite the present tension. Kaguya took it all in stride as she answered. "As I said, I believe my lord wishes to discuss our progress with the Captain and the First Officer," she spoke in a measured tone. "And he wishes to do so in person."

"Besides, there have been some stirrings among the clans as of late," Alex added.

"Right," Boss nodded, as did several of the others. As scions of the gradually rebuilding Gold Dragon, it was Jon and Alex's responsibility to keep up with the other clans' activities and intrigues, especially if they came to involve them. And by extension, the rest of the *Sun*'s crew.

Davis let out a short 'heh' at the thought. "Lady Ching probably choked on a jiaozi," he deadpanned. "Or Lord Pargo sent out for new bedroom slippers…"

"Or Lady Levasseur has been even more bellicose as of late, and there might be a new Clan War on the horizon because of it," Alex pointedly shot back, causing Davis to glance upward.

Gran allowed a smile to form on her lips. "Regardless, it will be nice to revisit Ryugu," she spoke as pleasantly as ever, knowingly dispelling the tension. "We haven't made port there for quite some time."

"Not since Ephesus," Boss rejoined while withdrawing her familiar corn-cob pipe from her jacket, then proceeding to light it. "Considering how rowdy Nassau will undoubtedly be, it will be a quiet break before we head out again…"

"Assuming a certain someone stays clear of the geisha houses," Anna dryly declared before taking another drink.

Davis glared. "Dear god, can't you people let that go already!?" he nearly shouted, before looking glum. "They won't readmit me anyway…" he muttered under his breath.

"How terrible," Alex lamented sardonically. "Looks like you'll have to settle for one of your girlfriends then."

Davis sighed. "We've only been there twice, remember?" he pointed out. "Haven't had time to cultivate one yet."

He then looked charmingly toward Gran. "That being said, I could just enjoy the company of one of my lovely co-workers…"

Gran merely smiled. "An enticing offer to be sure, Mister Davis," she replied sweetly. "Unfortunately, I'll likely be indisposed upon arrival."

"Really?" Davis quired without turning down the charm. He reached for Gran's hand and, lifting it to his lips, placed a small kiss on her knuckles. "And what could be more enchanting than having a night on the town with a dashing, debonair rogue like me?"

"I don't know whether to laugh or regurgitate," Anna muttered under her breath. Alex felt a similar feeling of nausea.

Ignoring the general reaction around the table, Gran's smile took a sweeter tone. "As they say on Ryugu, *sore wa himitsu desu*," she answered, before leaning back a little, adroitly removing her hand from Davis' grip. "Besides, I don't think our Captain would appreciate me going out with roguish men."

That smile only became more extensive as she added. "To say nothing of our security officer."

Glaring down at the helmsman, Kaiser, having drunk the last of his prune juice, slowly crushed his tankard with one hand. A hard smile was etched across his lips.

"Point taken," Davis mumbled, not wishing to court the Herculean's displeasure. He quickly lifted his tankard for a swig. A long one at that.

"And all's right with the universe," Alex commented before taking another draught, the celebrations continuing around him.

In contrast to the party that he knew was in progress, Jon maintained silence and darkness in his quarters. Though, he was somewhat tempted to put one of his valued classics through the audio system. In fact, he had a particular song that would have suited the present environment, but that desire just could not compare to the peace and tranquility that silence and darkness afforded him. Instead, Jon reclined on his bed, his eye closed, and let his mind drift through its resident thoughts and feelings without a background theme.

Amidst the myriad of reflections, one, in particular, stood out: a specific memory from over a year ago. It had been a similar setting, albeit far less comfortable than his current one, lying upon a bed within starkly appointed quarters, his mind wandering in thought as background music played over his audio player, an attempt to drown out the loud rattle of the ship. They had just completed the mission to assassinate Anton Mercer, an assignment that would turn out to be their last as mercenaries, or "pirates for hire" as they had labeled themselves. The last before that fateful encounter on Aurora, where, with the pull of a pistol trigger, everything was set into motion.

In that old ship, Jon had rested on his bunk and pondered the last fifteen years of his and his brother's lives following his mother's Battle of Ephesus. A thought process that only brought despair and uncertainty. Now, within the confines of his lavishly adorned Captain's quarters, upon his far more comfortable bed, with the silence soothing his spirit, Jon again pondered a period in his, and by extension, his brother's life. Only this time, instead of it being fifteen years, it was but a single year, a year following *another* Battle of Ephesus. And, instead of despair and uncertainty, he felt as though the galaxy itself were at his fingertips.

Needless to say, it was a strange, almost surreal feeling. For a good portion of Jon's existence, he, and Alex beside him, had lived and struggled in destitution. Too many nights had he slept if at all, dreading the next day, wondering how he and his brother would be able to survive, much less prosper. Too many times had he feared the inevitable betrayal of his colleagues, or the continuous line of bounty hunters and his mother's old enemies moving unseen around them, all waiting for an opening or moment of weakness. And far too many times had he been forced to take on assignments from the lesser of clients, frequently for wages that were little better than a slave's, all so he and his brother could enjoy an all too fleeting peace until forced to search for work once again. A life, as Alex had once proclaimed, that their mother would never have wanted for them.

Admittedly, not too much had changed. There were still nights Jon did not sleep, though mostly due to reoccurring nightmares than anything else. And, he still feared the inevitable betrayal in his midst, as well as those seeking his blood and/or bounty. But now, he was no longer bound to the service of others, nor was he living each day strictly for survival's sake. Now he, and those who followed him could truly master their fate. He could genuinely captain his soul.

And so it had been for the last year. While it hadn't been entirely smooth sailing like some of the crew had wished, if not outright believed it would be, the Flint Pirates' ventures following Ephesus had proven to be both successful and profitable. By now, a fair percentage of their stores were filled with gold and other such treasures from a multitude of civilizations, up to and including all thirteen Galactic Powers. In fact, according to Anna's estimates, they had already gained three times the annual wealth of any standard band, and each member of their crew had more gold to his or her name than some planetary governors. Only the Clans, and certain other pirate groups, were more wealthy and prosperous, and yet none of them could meet the Flints' potential or success rate. Whereas such groups and organizations had been in operation since the time of the Pirate Queen, if not well before, the Flints had only been active for the past year.

Exhaling contently, Jon continued his ruminations. He and the rest of the Flint Pirates still had a long road ahead of them; he was under no illusions about that. Not just with Arcadia, but also with the reformation of the Gold Dragon and the settling of particular accounts, among other objectives. But for now, all that he and his band had accomplished over the last year would suffice.

He was so at ease he barely heard the door to his quarters shift open. But hear it he did, a frown spreading over his face. He recognized the interloper.

"I don't believe I gave you permission to enter."

The Captain could almost feel the responding grin as if it were sunlight.

"Sometimes one must take unilateral action," Lorelei quoted casually. "Besides, as the patron of this voyage, I believe I hold a permanent audience with this ship's captain."

Eye remaining closed, Jon said nothing as Lorelei, acting with presumed familiarities, strolled up and sat at the foot of the bed.

"I must say I was rather underwhelmed on this one. Compared to Ephesus, Smyrna lacked somewhat in exhilaration."

"I consider that a good thing. Ephesus gave enough 'exhilaration' on its own," Jon replied simply. "Besides, Smyrna was difficult enough without the Imps being involved."

"I suppose so," she agreed. "Though it begs the question as to why they've ignored us as of late."

It was only then Jon opened his eye. "Yes, it is rather disturbing."

Despite all the Flint Pirates had done over the past year, the Imperials had been somewhat inattentive. Sure, the Flints had several encounters with Imp forces since Ephesus, but the troops had almost always been acting in a defensive category, as convoy escorts or garrisons on worlds the pirates had chosen to raid. Beyond that, there wasn't so much as a word of Starfleet deploying a hunter-killer unit to capture or destroy the *Black Sun*, let alone a taskforce to bring the Flints and their cohorts, namely the White Siren, to justice.

"Any theories?"

"Nothing beyond the obvious I'm afraid," she answered. "The best I can ascertain is that they have other priorities. Or they simply intend to watch us work for the time being."

Or they're waiting for the right opportunity like Drake did, Jon thought, inwardly grimacing at the idea. Even now, he wondered if the legendary Admiral, the one who had cornered his mother at Ephesus sixteen years ago, was still out there, tracking the Flint Pirates whilst preparing to strike against them once more. In that regard, the thought that the Terran Empire as a whole had adopted his *modus operadi* toward the scions of Morganna Flint was unlikely, but not at all impossible.

"Well, whatever the case, we'll deal with them, and the other Powers, if and when the time comes," he said with a shrug. "For now…"

"Yes," Lorelei concurred. Though she was also disturbed at the unexplained disregard from the Imperials, she knew there was nothing they could do about the situation. For the present, they had more significant priorities.

"With Smyrna engaged, only five remain."

"And, assuming we proceed in order, the third one should be Pergamum," Jon replied, reaching out to the control console beside his bed. A moment later, a holographic star map illuminated the darkness. "Can't say I recall any planets with that particular name, Terran or otherwise."

"Neither can I. If it's like the first two, however, it will be a lost world."

Jon nodded. "A world forgotten or never discovered by any modern civilizations," he summarized. "Seems to be the running theme, doesn't it?"

"Unfortunately," Lorelei shook her head, her irritation toward the subject apparent. "The Circumgressus not revealing these worlds in the present time certainly doesn't help matters."

The Captain couldn't restrain his grin. It wasn't like Lorelei to allow her frustrations to show. But then, as he had noted throughout their partnership, there was much she did around him, and him alone, that she didn't do around others. Not that he had figured out how he felt about that.

"It will show up eventually. In the meantime, we'll simply return to traditional pirating, as we did following Ephesus."

"Among other assignments," Lorelei added.

"Oh?" It was only then Jon looked toward her, not knowing how he felt about that revelation. "You have more for us outside of Arcadia?"

Lorelei flashed her smile. "Let's just say Arcadia isn't my only objective, merely the primary. Or did you believe Arcadia was the only mystery the Predecessors, among various other ancient beings and civilizations, have left behind?"

Jon managed to keep from rolling his eye. "My crew and I are pirates, not archaeologists. And our arrangement was only for Arcadia..."

"Our arrangement, Captain, is that you and your crew aid my expedition first and foremost," she responded pointedly. "And while Arcadia remains the central focus of this expedition, it is by no means the only object of interest within."

Smile now gone, her gaze hardened. "As I told you on Aurora, this is not up for renegotiation."

Such was the force behind her unexpected outburst that Jon rose to sit and face the psion. Logically he should have been angered at her dictation, but he found himself somewhat perplexed. What was so frightening, or for another query, what was so important to her that she believed bringing him into line was the only viable strategy?

Regardless, he knew there was no room for argument; he had long agreed to her terms. And much more, it wasn't something he needed or *wanted* to argue about.

"Very well," he acquiesced, taking note of the surprise that briefly flashed over Lorelei's face. "As you informed Alex and me over a year ago, there is no backing out of this. So long as you allow us to continue our activities, I see no reason to even consider it."

He pretended not to notice her expression of relief, which she was quick to suppress.

"That being said, unless there's suitable payment or plunder involved, the rest of the crew won't be so agreeable."

"Don't worry," Lorelei appeased, just as quick to readopt her original demeanor. "You can be assured you and your crew will not be left wanting. In fact, you may even gain more than what you would from your little raids."

There was no ignoring the insult in that retort, Jon knew, but he remained impassive. Unfortunately, Lorelei seemed to detect his annoyance. Inwardly sighing, he deactivated the holographic star map and resumed his prone position on his bed, his eye once more closed.

"Is there anything else you wish to discuss?"

Even without her telepathy, Lorelei could sense his dismissal.

"No, I suppose not," she replied, before rising from her seat and stretching if only to demonstrate that she too was exhausted. It had been a trying day for her as well, after all. "At least, nothing that can't wait."

"Good to know," Jon countered, suddenly feeling the weight of the battle at Smyrna. "I suggest you get some rest; you might find Nassau rather chaotic when we arrive."

"Trust me, rest isn't something I wish to avoid," Lorelei murmured as she moved toward the exit. "Just be ready to pick up where we left off once we're both resuscitated."

"Over some form of beverage, I presume?"

"But, of course," Lorelei responded without turning around, matching his casual tone. "Neither of us would have it any other way. Until then, Captain," she said as the door slid open.

Alone once again in the silence, the memories quickly returned. Slowly, those thoughts slipped away as Jon's consciousness steadily waned for the final time that day. Only dreams remained from that point on.

With the scent of jasmine and orchids filling the air while the light of the surrounding candles illuminated his surroundings, Barbarossa continued to pray before the Star of Aslan. Compared to the more formal prayers he made on certain occasions, namely holidays commemorating Aslan and all who had served His will in times long past, the Leo now spoke to his god in near silence. Had any others been present, they likely would not have been able to hear him anyway. In truth, Barbarossa had always preferred this method of prayer. Somehow it felt Aslan would listen to such words more readily than the bellowing praises and declarations that made up the 'traditional' means of speaking to the Great and Magnificent. Besides, despite the celebrations that were now occurring in the lounge, today was no specific holiday, and so Barbarossa was free to pray as he wished.

As usual, in such times, he prayed for continued guidance from on high, as well as patience and temperance toward those with whom he served. Well over a year into his service to the Flints and their late mother's legacy, Barbarossa was still reluctant toward his present station. Admittedly he didn't detest it as much as he did in the beginning. In fact, he dared say he had come to rather enjoy the pirate's life, especially when it came at the cost of the Terran Empire and the other heathen races and nations beyond the Caliphate. However, he was still unsure of his place within a band of amoral infidels, many of which did not recognize a god of any kind, much less Aslan.

Throughout the year, Barbarossa had prayed and meditated on the subject to the Knowing. On the one hand, he knew he was exactly where Aslan wanted him to be. After all, if his being part of the Flint Pirates had been an affront to His plans, Aslan surely would have long liberated him before extending His wrath to the *Black Sun* and her crew. Alongside, He had continuously blessed Barbarossa with insight and fortune; the former to aid in his leadership when the Brothers were otherwise occupied and the latter taking the form of countless triumphs over his (and by extension his crew's) enemies as well as equally countless bounties that would both ensure his present comfort and gradually secure his return to his people. Indeed, he had endured much since his attempted hijacking of the *U-7501* seemingly long ago, but Barbarossa knew, above all else, that his god had not abandoned him, much less left him in desperation.

On the other hand, even knowing that Aslan was with him, Barbarossa could not for the life of him understand *why* he was where he was. He knew it was not to bring the light of Aslan to those around him; they would no more accept his faith than they would the faiths of their own races and creeds. Unlike far too many of his brethren, he was not insipient enough to believe that conversion by the force of a baneclaw brought true faith and adherence to Aslan. He also knew that, despite what the rest of the crew may have thought of him, he wasn't there to act as Aslan's executioner; again, had He wished for otherwise, He would have either presented Barbarossa the opportunity to fulfill His vengeance or He would have done it himself. And naturally, Barbarossa knew that he wasn't there on a whim. Whatever the reason, Aslan had intentionally placed him where he was to fulfill His plans. As he had always done since Barbarossa had been a cub.

So why? Why was he there, serving alongside criminals and miscreants? Beings that Aslan usually punished and made examples of to His adherents? Surely there was a worthwhile explanation, one that Barbarossa would understand had he known, so why hadn't it been revealed to him, in clear spite of all of his prayer and meditation? Whatever the reason, until Aslan gave him the answer he sought, Barbarossa could only pray for continued guidance, patience, and temperance. As well as to keep certain violent urges toward equally certain crew members - namely the unholy Red Devil that scourged and tormented him at every opportunity – in check.

And of course, there was the other subject that he prayed about, or more specifically, *against*. In spite of his better judgment, he retained that item, keeping it within a wooden box upon a nearby shelf, a place where none would suspect its presence, much less that it was in his possession. It had remained there since he had first received it from the Siren, and all throughout Barbarossa had refrained from so much as looking upon it. However, the strange sigil that it bore on its surface remained a fixture within Barbarossa's mind, alongside the power it represented.

Though it appeared dormant, its form inert, and its power sealed, Barbarossa knew better. Every now and then, he could feel its whisper, its temptation for him to take it out of its box, to awaken it and use it in whatever manner he saw fit. It was particularly active when he slept, oftentimes appearing in his dreams in some obscure form or another, claiming that it had "chosen" him, found him "worthy" of its "service," and that all he need do was take it and use it as he would his claws or fangs. Each and every time, Barbarossa would refuse, but merely doing so sapped the majority of his strength; it was as if the thing were appealing directly to his soul, bypassing his physical and mental defenses to reach his very core essence. He could only imagine such power in awakened form, which filled him with both terror and anticipation.

The only time it would not whisper to him was during prayer, through which Barbarossa was also reinfused with the spiritual strength and resolution to resist. However, this was only a temporary fix at best; as spiritual as he was, Barbarossa could not spend his entirety praying, and no matter how much time he spent speaking with Aslan, it would simply wait until he was done and open to its influence again. He feared that, short of Aslan's protection, he was only delaying the inevitable.

However, as much as he wished to rid himself of it, Barbarossa could not dismiss one simple fact: he would need it if and when he chose to act on his original objective. Indeed, as skilled as he was, Barbarossa knew that he was no direct match for the ship's captain and first officer, especially if they fought in tandem. The first time he fought the former, it had been under cover of darkness, and even then, the Captain had managed to defeat him through both skill and strategy. And, as much as he wished, he could not dismiss the brother. He did well to recognize the First Officer's brilliance, which was best shown with his handling of the *Black Sun* at Ephesus. And they were simply the primary opponents Barbarossa would have to face should he make another attempt on commandeering the *Black Sun*. Behind them was the Dragon Princess, their Stonewall guardian that he had previously fought alongside, as well as many soldiers and warriors that, for one reason or another, had forsaken their former nations and oaths for piracy.

And that wasn't dismissing the White Siren herself. A year later and he still didn't quite comprehend her methods or motives. She was determined in her quest and very territorial toward the Captain, yet it was she that had brought him the item, claiming that she wanted to see how he may use its unholy power. Even so, Barbarossa was not about to let down his guard around her, much less believe that, should he choose to take the ship and all else for himself, she would stand idly by. Especially with the Captain inevitably being involved, once again.

No, Barbarossa was no fool. As faithful and reliant as he was to Aslan, he would need that *thing*'s power once the time came. Thus he retained it, yet refused to give in to its temptations while praying to Aslan to strengthen him against its evil will. From there, he would continue to bide his time. And it would continue to remain in its box.

Suddenly, Barbarossa paused in the midst of his prayers; his enclave fell into total silence. A second later, his eyes opened, glancing slightly toward one end of the room.

Did I imagine it? His eyes continued to scan that section of his quarters. Though he wasn't quite sure, he thought he had felt something in that last second, something that, like a brush of wind, had moved nearby before seemingly vanishing. Too brief for him to get a fix on it, but he knew, whatever it was, he did not like the sensation it had caused. As if it were something that did not *belong*, much less hold a presence on his ship.

With utmost caution, his eyes glanced toward the box on the shelf. Had its contents, at last, managed to reach him as he prayed? His instincts told him this was not possible, and even if it were, it would have done more than simply brush by him; it would have once again attempted to draw him into its influence. As he stared at the box, he could somehow tell that what he just felt had not originated from it.

So, if it was not his apparent houseguest, nor was it the power of Aslan at work, then what had it been? Perhaps it had been the power of their Siren? A possibility, but a slim one. Barbarossa had encountered a few psions in his life, he had seen some of their skills in action, and throughout the various sensations they had elicited out of him, none felt so...*dark* as what he had momentarily experienced. He doubted the Siren was responsible, not that he had ever seen her at her most formidable strength, but somehow he doubted that her power was like that. Given her character, he would have guessed it as something of exceptional brilliance, vibrancy, and apparentness compared to the *something* he thought he had felt.

Unfortunately, that left very few explanations, none of which Barbarossa could rationalize. Therefore, if it was a figment of his imagination, it was of no consequence. If it had been real, it wasn't a life-threatening development. Again, not unlike the brush of wind.

Thus, the Leo closed his eyes and resumed his prayers, his murmuring once more echoing lightly through his domain ... but he couldn't dissuade the feeling that something was amiss...

The turbolift doors opened with a hiss, allowing Lorelei onto the selected deck. Resisting the urge to yawn and stretch, she exited and proceeded toward her quarters, where she could retire for the evening. With each step, the psion felt the weariness in her body, she needed sleep, she was barely able to hold herself upright.

She had not lied to the Captain, not that she ever lied in general, rest was not something she wanted to defer. Activating a Babel required the expenditure of tremendous amounts of her physical *and* psionic energy. The sensation was, to put it in terms a "normal" being could understand, not unlike raising a seagoing vessel from the deepest, darkest area of ocean with one's arms. It required vast reserves of energy and direction, as well as concentration. The smallest error could result in having to start

over or worse. The first time, at Ephesus, she had been rendered unconscious following the activation. This time she had managed to retain her
consciousness, but just barely. She had needed to forgo the party, much to
the disappointment of her fans and fellow Psirens, and spend the rest of
the evening alone and asleep. From what she understood, there would be
more opportunities to celebrate at Nassau anyway.

Still, she did have enough energy left to direct her special senses toward
the one in progress, if only to see if she was missing anything essential.
What she found was more or less standard for the Flint Pirates, if not
pirates in general. Short of fists and grog bottles flying about, it held
all the rambunctiousness and carousing one would expect. Chaos in
motion was the best way she could describe it, even though it wasn't as
destructive as one would have assumed. It helped that the principal crew
members, namely the Devilblade wielding first officer, the assassin raider
commander, and the giant security officer, were also present and ready to
restore order should the worst occur. Even the most daring or drunken - or
both - of their number knew better than to run afoul of their leaders.

Grinning at the image of it all, especially at the sight of Kaiser, for
apparently winning a bet on one of the sports vids, putting a hapless
Davis in an underarm stranglehold out of sheer thrill and triumph, Lorelei merely shook her head and continued onward. She knew she was
missing a good time, and a part of her felt morose over it, but it couldn't
be helped. She was exhausted. And once more, she would have more
opportunities at Nassau.

………H………

Lorelei halted, a cold feeling permeated her body, her eyes widened. For a
brief moment, as she had been observing the party, she felt something else
enter into her scope. Something that felt entirely out of place.

………He………

Abruptly she swung around, as though she had physically heard something
behind her. In fact, that was the best way she could describe the sensation;
rather than an image or a presence, it felt as though she had heard a voice.

A very, very distant voice, one that she could just barely discern. And, though she couldn't quite put her finger on it, it almost came across as a feminine voice.

………Hel………

Feeling increasingly uneasy, Lorelei summoned her remaining strength, preparing to draw upon her power if necessary. As much as she thought she actually "heard" that voice, she was more than capable of recognizing its underlying psionic nature. However, she also knew that there were no other psions on the *Black Sun*. Someone, or *something*, was telepathically reaching out to her through vast expanses of space. And despite whatever distance and interference may have laid between them, it was succeeding.

………Help………

The voice was still muffled and vague, but this time a clear word managed to solidify in her mind. Her uneasiness increased.

………Help………

………Me………

Who are you? Lorelei responded, trying to discern the source of the "voice." Whatever it was, it was not something she was familiar with or expecting. That alone instilled fear.

Show yourself!

The air in front of her shimmered, swirled, and coalesced into a slight form. A form that, while remaining indiscernible, could have been a young Terran child. Or…

………Help………Me………

And then, as fast as Lorelei blinked, it was gone; both the form and the voice. She was, for all intents and purpose, alone once again.

Remaining on alert, Lorelei looked about the deck, trying to find a telltale hint or trace of either the form she had just seen or the voice she had just "heard." Yet, even as her eyes scanned the physical realm while her mind scanned the realm beyond, she found … nothing. Nothing but the various presences of the crew spread across the ship, namely the ones who were continuing to party as if it were Terran Date 999.12.31.

Blinking again, reconfirming her surroundings, Lorelei decided that there was no point in making further attempts. For all she knew, it could have been a product of her marrow-deep exhaustion. With cautious steps, she resumed her walk to her quarters where much-needed sleep awaited.

Nothing else mattered.

<u>Chapter III: Nassau</u>

It was one of the most famous, or infamous, outlaw dens to ever come into existence, despite its appearance as an unassuming blue, mainly tropical world. Its name stemmed from an Ancient Terran colony situated in its homeworld's Caribbean Sea, which had been renowned for its brand of corruption and lawlessness – or "freedom" depending upon who was telling the story – once upon a time. And though it was technically an Imperial world, or at the very least it had been settled as one some time ago, it was not a place any law-abiding sentient, Terran or otherwise, would have wished to find his, her or itself, even in the direst of circumstances. Indeed, for all its moonlighting as a "republic", it was not a world for "proper" civilization, but for those who hailed from the direct opposite.

Its name was Nassau. And just like its ancient namesake, it was one of the most prominent "Pirate Republics" to ever exist in the modern galaxy.

Originally founded sometime in the early 700s, Nassau was something of a colony that never was. While it had remained loyal to the Throne, as well as enjoyed all the rights and privileges of a proper Imperial world for a time, the rapid expansion of its host nation and the colonization of more "valuable" planets resulted in Nassau being all but forgotten by Terra proper. The consequences of this were, of course, quite severe.

Without any real means of economic sustenance beyond some valiant but ultimately futile attempts at agriculture, Nassau quickly became a back-world colony, its citizens barely getting by with the most basic necessities while labor and business found their homes elsewhere. A constant lack of functioning government, always a byproduct of economic hardship, did not help matters in the least. The last Imperial governor that managed to keep the colony afloat under the Imperial banner, one Woodes Rogers, died long ago, and those that followed only exacerbated Nassau's failing state. Eventually, Terra stopped sending appointments - especially after the last one ended up "disappearing" in a tyrannoshark feeding ground - while the colonists openly refused to refill the position from their populace. Due to these outcomes and more, Nassau and its citizenry would be all but formally abandoned by the Empire and left unto themselves, with very little to live by, in an ever hostile galaxy.

Fortunately – or *un*fortunately, once more depending upon who was telling the story – it was neither long nor difficult for the beleaguered Nassuvians to find new means to not only survive but *prosper* outside Imperial oversight. As it turned out, there were quite a number of organizations that wished to operate more "freely" than others, and with Nassau being all but devoid of outside influence, it made quite an ideal hub for their activities. Indeed, there was no shortage of aspiring spacers and "entrepreneurs" in need of a base to operate from, especially one that *wasn't* completely isolated from the rest of the known galaxy. The fact Nassau was located in a reasonably accessible area of the Middle Rim made it even more ideal for such groups and entities.

Thus, after a bit of a rocky start – one that saw the last of the Imperial loyalists dead through various means – Nassau embraced its newfound destiny as a pirate haven and never looked back. A world in which, in the more romantic sense, all beings could enjoy proper freedom from the Powers and erstwhile civilizations, as well as seek out wealth, prosperity, and happiness for themselves. Alongside various forms of alcohol, contraband, and pleasurable company to match.

Naturally, it was an ideal destination for any renegade, and the Flint Pirates were no exception. In abrupt cessation, the *Black Sun* dropped out of arcspace and entered the system, from which it approached the titular world and made planetfall – Nassau lacked spacedock facilities – where it would proceed toward its new berth. Once again, in the form of its ancient name-sake, the harbor that the *Black Sun* had been directed to was, in fact, situated along a coastline, thus necessitating the starship to touchdown into the ocean and "sail" from that point on, not unlike an actual seafaring vessel. It certainly was a scene for any nearby residents to behold as the tremendous and powerful umbra, the Golden Roger proudly displayed on either side of her bridge tower, gently glided into its port of call and nestled into place. From there, the crew disembarked in their usual manner.

"Ah, nothing like the bouquet of fresh sea air," Alex commented as he and the rest of the *Black Sun*'s officers strode onto the deck. "Especially when it's mixed with the stench of rampant and unchecked hedonism."

"Taking on a poetic streak, Alex?" Davis quipped while running a hand back through his hair. As he had no lover waiting for him at their next destination, he had no choice but to make the most of his time in the present. Fortunately, love and companionship were never in short supply on Nassau. A chaste respite on Ryugu might actually be something he would *need*.

"Just speaking the obvious Davis," Alex retorted, before grinning at Jon.

The elder Flint simply rolled his eye in response before returning to business.

"Remember, three days. After that, we're back to the stars," Jon reminded the others. "Our launch time is set for 1900 hours then."

"We'll be here, Captain," Anna summarized for the others, who nodded their heads in confirmation. "Not like any of us want to call this place home."

"Fair enough," Jon replied. Even without his operations officer speaking for the rest of them, Jon doubted any of their numbers would have gone ashore in that particular place; as impressive as Nassau was to visit, no right-minded sentient would have ever wished to make a permanent home there. Even Davis seemed hesitant at the idea, though to his credit, the helmsman had experienced plenty of opportunities to desert in the past and had always returned.

Probably afraid Alex and I would hunt him down and drag him back, Jon thought somewhat cynically, though another part of him liked to think Davis actually *wanted* to remain a Flint Pirate. After all, he was certainly doing better with them than he would have with any other pirate ban. Just like the rest of the crew.

"Time is wasting, enjoy yourselves," Jon commanded to his anticipating and overeager group. "And hold no hesitation!"

"Aye!" the officers, and many of the surrounding crewmen, resounded at once. With apparent glee, they all went their separate ways, and Nassau would only become that much livelier as a result.

——————————————— ———————————————

After a few minutes on one of the local tram systems, the Flint brothers were back in the open, striding down the rather blandly titled Bacardi Street toward their intended destination. As they had expected, the street was mostly busy with both spacers and locals moving about to one place or the other, while the usual rowdiness played in the background. Though this particular area of town wasn't as chaotic as others, the sounds of tavern brawls and drunken misconduct were as abundant as the collective voices and footfalls. If not even more so.

As if to emphasize that precise fact, the brothers casually stepped aside as one of those fights, this one between a badly scarred Terran and a glaring Lacertan, moved into the street. Apparently too drunk to realize their respective adversary, both fighters ended up turning on the brothers, only to be dispatched with casual disregard as Jon blocked the Terran's attempted haymaker and countered with a far more direct punch to the face while Alex simply dodged the Lacertan's frenzied charge, smashing his elbow into its skull as it passed. With both would be assailants sprawled out along the street and firmly unconscious, the brothers moved on.

Eventually, they arrived at their destination: a three-story building with a mint green exterior, the brightly lit sign at the top reading "McHALE'S ISLAND." Spacers and locals alike could be seen sitting on the outer decks, enjoying drink, food, and conversation as waitresses served the former two, then slipped away before any of the more daring or drunken customers could reach out for a grab.

As Jon and Alex approached the entrance, a pair of Terran males, which the brothers recognized as staff members, pushed past with a third, far less built Terran male, in hand. Once they reached the end of the walk, the two apparent enforcers threw their equally apparent captive into the street, where he landed face first in a nearby puddle of questionable liquids. The two men returned to the tavern without looking back; the Flints shared a slight glance before following their example.

The building's interior was more or less as they had seen on the exterior. Seemingly every table and booth was filled with an occupant of some kind, talk abounded as more food and drink were passed along. At the far end of the tavern, a band with a skirted and bikini topped Lyran singer played, though neither brother recognized their current song. Either way, the pair moved to two conveniently open seats at the bar, where the tavern-keep – or at least the man who was working in place of the actual tavern-keep – greeted them.

"What can I do you two for?" an all too earnest sounding Terran male, who, despite his relative age, spoke in a near child-like tenor. If that alone wasn't an indication of the man's mental development, then his blank eyes and somewhat goofy expression certainly was.

Both brothers did well to keep the cringe off their faces. It was just like the man to forget who they were.

"Hello Parker," Alex spoke up, pretending nothing was amiss. "Glad to see you're still in good health."

A gaze of evident confusion quickly moved over Parker's face. "I'm sorry, do I know you from somewhere…?" he inquired.

"Let's just say we're frequent customers," Jon spoke up before Alex could make a sarcastic quip. He then glanced around the tavern to see if the one who *usually* manned the counter was present. "Is your boss in?"

Confusion remaining, Parker nodded nonetheless. "Skip's in the back," he explained. "Taking care of some office work."

"Sure he is," Alex deadpanned. "With or without his latest wife?"

"Hey now," Parker stuttered, suddenly defensive. "Just because Skip just got married again doesn't mean…"

"Right and I'm Nikola Tesla," Alex shot back, before looking toward Jon. "This is what, number seventeen?"

"I stopped counting a long time ago," Jon replied, turning back to Parker. "Assuming he's available, can we see him?"

Parker seemed to consider the two men. "I suppose so," he muttered. "But…"

"But?" Alex inquired, wondering where this was going to go.

"I need to know who you are and your reason for seeing him," the barkeep clarified dutifully as if he were still in Starfleet. "For security, you know?" he added with a wink. "Can't let the wrong people through and all."

"Of course," Jon complied as if it were completely understandable. He didn't have to look at Alex to know the direction of his thoughts. The younger Flint was always up for a practical joke.

"We're from the Judge Advocate General Corps, and we're here to discuss some…'issues' with Captain McHale regarding his service record."

Parker jerked to attention, his face lost all color, and his voice, when he was able to answer, stuttered and squeaked. "Y-y-you don't mean…?"

"Yes, I'm afraid so," Alex sagely added, with matching sympathetic tone. "JAG has been going over Captain McHale's file, particularly over his performance in the Third Leo War, and some uncertainties have risen," he then leaned forward conspiringly. "Uncertainties that may, at the very least, affect the Captain's pension…"

"…and at the very worst involve a board of inquiry," Jon finished.

"B-b-b-b-b-b-inquiry!?" Parker screeched in a barely contained outburst. "That's impossible! The Skip…"

"That is to be determined by the proper authorities," Alex replied staunchly and with projected authority. "But for now, we need to see Captain McHale at the earliest convenience."

"Ah, yes, yes, I understand," Parker nodded judiciously before throwing out an Imperial salute. "I'll get the Skip right away!"

Moving so fast that he nearly tripped over his feet upon exiting the bar area, Parker charged toward a nearby entryway, the door swung violently as he flew past.

"Bet you ten, he'll come out loud and packing," Alex offered.

"No bet," Jon scoffed as he glanced at his wristcom.

Alex grinned. "Bet you fifty, he comes out nak…"

"No bet," Jon repeated without ever looking up.

Almost immediately, a thunderous, bellowing voice hollered from the direction Parker had gone. One whose rancor was enough to abruptly halt all conversation and activity with its initial outburst.

"You sonsabitches!" The roar reverberated throughout the bar as the *true* tavernkeep charged out from the back area, an Imperial service pistol brandished in his hand. "You pondscumsuccors want to know what I did during the war!? I'll show you firstha…!"

Surrounded by the newfound silence and frozen postures of the clientele, the Brothers Flint stood with dual smirks of triumph as their target froze up in realization.

"Didn't see *this* coming, did you 'Captain'?" Alex quipped. "Or is it alright if we still call you Ernie?"

After a moment of stupefied shock, grand exuberance encompassed *former* Captain Ernst "Ernie" McHale's face as he placed his beam pistol back into its holster. Much to the brothers' shared appreciation and undoubtedly that of the rest of the establishment, the portly man was, in fact, clothed in a tropical-themed shirt, slacks, and sandals, the well-worn commissar cap atop his head the only implication of his former profession and service. Even so, both Jon and Alex noted the haphazard arrangement of the attire. Clearly, they had been thrown on in a hurry.

"I'll be damned," Ernie snorted as he looked the brothers over. "And here I thought you two were too busy with the family business to visit old friends."

"We were in the neighborhood," Jon shrugged nonchalantly. Despite his usual apprehension and distrust toward others, even he could not disguise his delight at seeing this particular 'old friend' again. After all, he and Alex had known him for a long time. "And we always make time to visit old friends."

"At least the ones that matter," Alex chimed.

His smile remaining prominent, Ernie nodded at the pair before giving a hand signal toward the band; music instantly filled the air. Disturbance alleviated, business "as usual" returned to McHale's Island, conversation resumed, and food and drink consumption recommenced. All as if the previous outburst had never occurred.

Order restored, Ernie wasted no time in embracing both Flints in respective bear hugs, complete with back-slapping and raucous laughter.

"You damned swabs! JAG officers… I should blast you both in the balls for that!"

Ernie stepped back and scrutinized the two sons of Morganna Flint. It had been years since he had last seen them. Though they stood tall, capable, confident, and exuded an aurora of danger, he couldn't help but remember the two young orphans who used to visit his tavern in between jobs.

"How've you boys been holding up? I mean beyond what the stories are claiming."

"Not too poorly," Jon replied with a wink. "We have had a busy schedule as of late."

"So I've heard," Ernie exclaimed. "Assuming the stories are true, I don't think there's a convoy from here to Proxima you and your merry band of eight-balls haven't touched."

"Or a world or station for that matter," Alex piped up with no shortage of pride. "It's amazing what you can do with a ship no one can see coming."

"Right, not to mention a crew that knows what they're doing," Ernie shook his head in momentary dismay. "I've seen too many of the opposite in my lifetime, both in and out of Starfleet."

"Hey, Skip!" Parker shouted, his service pistol at his hip. "I thought you were going to 'blast these thumb-sucking bastards back to Terra'!"

"Chuck," Ernie said patiently. "Do these two *look* like Starfleet types to you?"

Parker blinked as realization dawned. "You mean…" he sputtered, displeasure suddenly making its way into his eyes. "They tricked me!?"

"Nothing personal," Alex offered with a wink and a charming smile. "Just a bit of fun."

"That was *more* than a bit of fun!" Parker stated indignantly. "Impersonating officers of His Imperial Majesty's Starfleet is a major offense under Article 13…"

"Chuck, Chuck, they meant no harm," McHale spoke up again, grasping the younger man by the shoulder. "I mean come on, it's Jon and Alex Flint for crying out loud! Don't you recognize them?"

"Wha?" Parker let out, looking the brothers over again. "Jonathan? … Alexander?"

"Always a pleasure, Mister Parker," Alex replied smartly.

"Well, I'll be…!" Parker stammered in renewed shock, followed by some minor embarrassment at his error. "I'm sorry, it's just I haven't seen you two in a long while. I'm not that good with faces."

"No harm done," Jon answered reassuringly, then gestured at his clothes. "But in the future, this color scheme does not equate to Imperial grey."

Upon registering the black and gold and their symbolism, Parker nodded judiciously. "Right, of course," he replied, again with modest embarrassment. "I mean, really! You two aren't even wearing rank insignia…"

"Chuck," Ernie interrupted. "The bar needs tending; the patrons are starting to get rowdy."

Quickly, Parker glanced around the counter area, and sure enough, it looked like those present were plotting to ransack the liquor cabinets lest somebody refilled their drinks.

"Ah, sure thing, Skip!" Parker replied dutifully, then looking over at the Flints one more time. "Good to see you both again. I mean that."

"Likewise," Jon affirmed while Alex nodded.

Parker hurried behind the counter and started pouring refills while Ernie gestured for the brothers to follow him.

"This calls for a celebratory meal," McHale stated as they approached a particular set of doors. Specifically, the ones that led to his private dining area. "Christy!"

One of the men Jon and Alex had witnessed throwing out the 'trash' came over.

"Yeah, Skip?"

"Get these guys some Old Caribbean, on the house," Ernie ordered. "And get Fuji to fire up the *good* stuff."

"Got it," Christy answered, moving off toward the kitchen.

"Hey, Skip," another tavern employee called out.

"What is it, Willy?"

Willy pursed his lips as he pointed over his shoulder. "Jessica's yelling …"

"Who?"

"Number Nineteen."

"Oh, right, Jessica."

Off by two, Jon and Alex thought simultaneously.

"She's wondering when you're getting back 'on the job.'"

"Oh damn ...." McHale rejoined. "Tell her that we have VIPs and to get *presentable* and join us."

"Got it," Willy replied, then proceeded to yell over his shoulder, "Jess, Skip says to get your pants back on and get out here!"

"Apologies, just the usual marital bliss," Ernie sighed exasperatingly as he turned back to the brothers. The former Captain gestured again. "After you."

Jon and Alex entered the private dining room without another word.

The Harpy's Nest
Roguetown, Nassau

Resisting the urge to rub her temples, Lorelei could feel the beginnings of a migraine. And not one caused by the continual cheering for the various "specialty" dancers on the stage some distance away. Or the surrounding thoughts and *desires* centered on her and, to a far lesser extent, her companions.

"At the risk of repetition, was this excursion essential?"

"For the eighth time and counting, *yes*," Anna stated firmly. "It's about time we had a proper girl's night out."

"Is that what they're calling it these days?" Boss commented as she looked over their chosen venue. The Harpy's Nest, a name that she found ironic, was pretty much like every other drinking establishment on the planet, but with two differences. First, it was strictly females only – or at the very least genders that *leaned* toward female – and second, it had an all-male staff of various species that included dancers. The latter of which all wore minimal clothing.

"Because in this case, I find 'proper' is something of a misnomer."

Anna surveyed the tavern critically. "Alright, it's not exactly Antoine's, but considering everywhere else on this planet, this is probably the best we're going to get," she explained, glancing toward the stage. "And honestly, I can think of worst shows to have with dinner."

"*You* could," Lorelei muttered derisively. And knowingly. "But then you would consider the Emperor's Ball to be in poor taste."

That earned a glare from the operations officer. She knew *precisely* what the psion had meant by that crack.

"Forgive me, Miss Undine, but we can't have high society everywhere we go," she shot back. "Sometimes there are only commoners to mingle with. And subsequently steal from."

"Among other things apparently," Lorelei commented dryly as *another* staff member, this one a Terran of darker complexion, came to their table – to *her* specifically – and just managed to open his mouth before Lorelei could reply.

"No, I do not wish to have *that* particular 'service,' thank you."

The staffer stared.

"Nor that one," Lorelei retorted without turning to face him. "And I'm not so starved as to need the 'three for one special.'"

"We're okay here, thank you," Anna placated the glum-looking man as he turned away. "It wouldn't kill you to let them *speak* their offerings before shooting them down, you know," she hissed to Lorelei.

"Nor to appreciate the attention," Boss commented dryly. "Frankly, I'm rather jealous. You're the one they've repeatedly been offering backroom services to all night."

"Much to the displeasure of the other customers I might add," Gran piped up, detecting the tightening of facial muscles occurring at the other tables, and the number of eyes that had twisted toward Lorelei's direction.

Lorelei shrugged uncaringly. "The behavior is not new and gets annoying. It's one of the joyous 'perks' of being 'beautiful,' 'alluring,' 'exotic,' hailing from an otherwise 'unknown' race, and let's not discount possessing a well-endowed chest."

She took a drink from her tankard. "Needless to say, the populace's thoughts of intimacy and debauchery are something I've come to expect wherever I go. From the usual proletariat types to planetary governors, multi-billionaires, or beauty queens."

Anna arched an eyebrow. "You mean beauty *kings*," she corrected.

Lorelei's grin was sly. "Miss Weissfall of '06 had alternate tastes. Toward gender and *actions involved*."

A cold silence, save for the background dance music, ensued.

"You don't have to answer this if you don't want to," Gran spoke up shyly. "But I'm curious." She then willed herself to ask the question. "What's it like to pick up *those* thoughts?"

Despite Gran's discomfort – which Lorelei could understand perfectly – the psion was not at all bothered.

"How do you feel when a dog gazes longingly toward your leg?" she posited. "Or when an insect wishes to draw blood from your finger?" She then shrugged again. "It's all the same to me," she said, just as another suitor, this one a Monocerian, stepped up to try his hand.

And as with the others, Lorelei answered first, without looking back. "No, the dimensions of your 'real horn' is of no interest, your idea of 'bad' is repugnant, I really don't believe you can bend that way, nor am I your matriarch."

The psion then flashed that grin again. "Though I believe the ladies at table five would lap up what you're offering," she said, alluding to a group of hideous blobs, all of whom were looking at the Monocerian with evident hunger.

Lorelei smiled proudly as the admirer made a rapid retreat. "And that makes thirteen."

Anna glanced at the only one that hadn't spoken up since they entered the establishment. "You seem to be in good voice tonight, Kaguya," she stated dryly. "I don't suppose you'd care to enter in at any point."

For her part, Kaguya had purposely remained silent throughout the venture. For as long as she had been a member of the Flint Pirates, she still felt awkward in social situations like this one, where she wasn't required to strike a target or guard a valuable asset. It helped even less that – for once – she was in agreement with Lorelei regarding the chosen venue.

"Not particularly," she answered. "I'm simply enjoying the company."

She glared as one of the attendants that Lorelei rejected glanced at her with interest. "If not the surroundings," she specified as she dismissed the miscreant with a scowl.

"You people are way too finicky," Anna sighed in exasperation, taking another swig from her tankard. "We might as well not leave the ship next time."

"I don't know," Gran offered sweetly and reassuringly. "I'm having a good time."

"Really?" Boss inquired. She noted how Anna and Kaguya were curious as well.

"Certainly," the Lyran affirmed, this time without hesitance or discomfort. "I'm in the company of friends whom I respect and am comfortable around," she explained, turning her head around the table to simulate glancing. "I'm eating a decent night's meal," she continued, then "looking" down at her Nassuvian steak with grilled sea apples and chips, again for the others' benefit. "And listening to various melodious sounds."

She then smiled hintingly. "And I don't just mean the music."

The three glanced at the stage again and saw exactly what she meant. Regardless of their appearances and overall attractiveness, the dancers really were performing to the music quite well. One could only wonder the various sounds their bones and muscles made as they moved erotically with the beat.

After another short moment of silence, Anna gave a nod approval. "Well then," she exclaimed, a small grin touching her lips. "I'm glad to see that the night isn't a *total* loss."

"Don't be too sure," Lorelei retorted as she detected another 'paramour.' "The night is still young."

As the hopeful 'beau' opened its mouth, Lorelei spoke up first. "Not even an adaptor would work for that depravity. Besides, with your 'special' anatomy, you don't really need me."

Anna jerked and spat her drink out onto the floor. "Sorry," she apologized as she shoved her food away. "Didn't need that mental image."

And so went number fourteen and counting.

Old Billy Riley's
Roguetown, Nassau

"So there I was," Davis narrated to his undeniably captive audience. "Thrown against the floor, the big, red demon stalking toward me…"

"That must have been horrifying," the cute, large bosomed redhead squeaked, though no less captivated. "Being thrown to the ground by an actual devil…"

Davis smiled knowingly. "Well, truthfully, this wasn't an actual demon, but it was close enough. It even carried a flaming sword."

"Wow," his audience cooed. "Just like Gandalf facing down Durin's Bane…"

Davis' smile grew. "Now that you mention it, it did feel like that," *Whoever in the Eighth Circle "Gonorf" and "Dorian's Bone" are supposed to be.* "But, I was honestly too terrified to realize it at the time…"

"You…," the woman looked shocked. "You were scared?"

"But, of course," Davis replied smoothly. "I mean, I would have been a fool *not* to be. Only fools and liars pretend they're not afraid of anything." *And both end up dying rather quickly.*

He shook his head at the feigned thought, before returning to his story. "Anyway, I just managed to get back to my feet when the demon was on me again…" he continued, gesturing with his hands for the sake of his audience. The buxom redhead became more and more enamored with each word. Much to the evident disappointment of the being sitting at the bar counter.

"Kids these days," Juan commented with a shake of the head. "They believe any twaddle they hear."

"Hey, don't be like that," Ponce poked his comrade. "I mean, we used to tell even bigger lies back in our time."

"Yes sir, we did," Leon replied proudly as he looked up in the air in – near absent – thought. "Though if memory serves, you weren't nearly as smooth as this guy…"

"Aw hell, you say!?" Juan glowered. "I was smooth as Glacien ice!"

"Sure you were," Ponce flatly shot back. "Like that time on Massalia, where you tried to pick up that one Lyran gal…"

"Damn, that was hilarious," Leon laughed. "You claimed you were the reincarnation of Frick Sinotty or something."

"That's Frank *Sinotra,* you old bastard!" Juan retorted. "No one appreciates the ancient classics!"

On the opposite end of the counter, Apache kept a passive, increasingly alcohol-induced calm as he sipped whatever it was he was drinking in place of his usual brew, doing his best not to grimace or gag. When he tried describing to the tavernkeep his typical vintage, all he got was a disgusted look and a bottle of something called Cygnian ale, which had been claimed as 'popular' among avianoids. Apache had to almost hold his beak shut before he pointed out that Cygnians were more reptilian than bird, but he took the bottle anyway. A choice that he had quickly come to regret! He had been stuck with it ever since.

As the three old men on the other side of the bar continued to argue with each other about any given subject, Apache glanced back at Davis. He had to admit, for all of his flaws and baggage, the helmsman certainly knew how to pick up women. Besides the lady that was sitting with him, who looked as though Davis was her literal dream incarnate, the Aquilan saw an additional number of women attempting to eavesdrop with not so discreet interest. And much more, he was telling his story in such a way that not only did the aforementioned woman find it all believable, but it looked like she was becoming aroused. As if Howell Davis' voice alone were a natural stimulator. Indeed, as the Aquilan was witnessing, the Lady Killer well and truly lived up to his legend.

Much to the displeasure of the other 'gentlemen' in the establishment of course, from whom there was no shortage of dark scowls. Apache shrugged. It just meant more business for him – as well as another opportunity to torment the hatchling - in the morning. Assuming the helmsman lasted the night, of course.

But, compared to the Lady Killer's audience, the one at the far end of the tavern really surprised Apache. Standing at in front of one of the tavern vidscreens, which currently displayed the schematics of an arc engine, Professor Maximilian Braun held court. It appeared as if he was giving a university lecture, in front of the *two dozen* or so sentients that had gathered around in a half-circle seating arrangement, effectively turning that part of the tavern into a makeshift classroom. At first, Apache had tried to listen to what the Professor was going on about. But even with the effects of his so-called 'drink,' he barely made out a few words from the rest of the technobabble.

Whatever he was discussing, however, had a profound effect. Most of the audience looked as though they were being given commandments from their chosen deity, while others – namely the female attendants – looked ready to do unto the good Professor what Davis' audience was undoubtedly intending to do unto him at the end of his oration. The former would have confused most people, but Apache, being as old and worldly as he was, could understand. After all, if battle scars could be a point of attraction, as they indicate the bearer to be a warrior, then surely radiation burns and a body sixty-percent composed of machinery – though to the Professor's benefit *that* part of him still existed and functioned – would have had the same effect on an engineer. Alongside this, the gravitation toward intellect was always in force among the "Wrench Wench" community.

"…and for the third time, you didn't see Elvi!" Juan hollered. "He died early in the First Age for crying out loud!"

"But I did!" Leon defended. "I saw him on Libitum VI, driving a Cadillac Eldorado…"

"What in the Second Circle is a 'Cardiac'!?" Juan let out in apparent confusion. "And how do the damn Dorados figure in!?"

"Calm down Juan, before you blow your motor," Ponce admonished.

Apache grit his beak, straining to ignore the banter. Bad enough that he was stuck with a disgusting concoction that somehow passed for grog, but did he really have to put up with all this audio torture? If only Kaiser were next to him to silence the old bastards.

Unfortunately, the Herculean was a little preoccupied at the moment. At a table in the corner, that held a rather large pile of aurics on either side, Kaiser sat with his arm locked with that of an equally massive and monstrous Draco and had remained in that precise state for a good twenty minutes or so. The only indication that either being was still breathing was when their lock would shift slightly from one side or the other, only to reorient itself once the fighter reapplied his strength. That and whenever Kaiser, without so much as glancing away, reached over to drink his grog bottle, which, as a prior 'introduction' to his present opponent, he had unsealed using his eye socket as a bottle opener.

The whole display made Apache shiver underneath his feathers. What was it with Herculeans and their impulsive need to display their physical strength? He would have thought their Terran given name was enough of an 'honor' in that area.

"…Somehow I don't think that gal you spent the night with on Tamora III looked anything like this 'Ashakira,'" Ponce stated in disbelief.

"If you saw the images of her from Alexandria, you would think differently!"

"But she wasn't even Terran," Leon pointed out. "In fact, I'm not even sure if she was a real 'she'…"

"Hellfire… not all women have hair, you know!"

"And until that night, I didn't think 'women' sang bass," Ponce retorted sardonically as he took a drink.

"It was contralto you old sonofabitch! Though I admit, it was an incredibly low contralto…" Juan muttered under his breath.

Inwardly retching, Apache took a longer swig of his 'ale' as the three old Terrans, and those around the tavern chattered on. And once again he wondered, as much as he could through the alcohol-induced haze, what in the First Circle he had been thinking when he joined the shore leave.

Four Lions Inn
Roguetown, Nassau

It had taken him a while and much movement through the ever chaotic streets, but eventually, Barbarossa had reached his intended destination. For a few moments, he couldn't help but stare blandly at the edifice, a bright yellow building sporting a sign depicting four stylized Terran lions over its written designation. Considering its design and its somewhat unpolished state, it was all too likely that this inn was another leftover from the initial colonization and consequently hadn't been updated or revitalized since then. As a result, it was the perfect place to hold the awaited meeting, but Barbarossa wished the other party had chosen a more modern establishment for their 'reunion.'

He shook his head in minor disappointment. In reality, they could have held their meeting anywhere on the planet, and none of the inhabitants would have paid them mind. After all, it wasn't like such meetings and dealings were a rarity on this particular world, and if there was any real authority here, then it was obviously content to remain outside such affairs. So long as no significant disturbances were caused, something Barbarossa had failed to instigate, even though he was attired in his race's traditional battle armor and had moved through much of the city. If he had not alarmed the local population with his presence, and if his contact hadn't, then what did the rest of Nassau care if the two were to meet?

Ignoring the innkeeper – who was more interested in the blitz game playing on a nearby vidscreen anyway – the Leo proceeded to the tavern area of the inn. It was as loud and active as the rest of the city's establishments. Fortunately, it wasn't hard to find his contact; a telltale black curtain around one of the back booths was enough an indication, especially when it was the only 'closed' booth in the whole tavern. Smirking at the irony, Barbarossa proceeded to the cubicle, shifting it open, moved into the available seat, and closed the drape. Once more, none of the local sentients showed any signs of care or concern throughout.

"So," the being on the opposite end of the booth began after a long moment of silence. "This is Leo's greatest warrior. The one who refused his Caliph's direct command to return, all so that he may continue some misguided quest in extending Aslan's vengeance."

From the shadowed end of the booth, Barbarossa saw a pair of eyes flickered in bemusement.

"The one that the infidels of Terra have so creatively dubbed 'Barbarossa,' if only for the color of his mane."

Releasing an exhale through his nostrils, Barbarossa said nothing.

"Now I hear you are no longer fighting the jihad, but instead have degenerated into a miscreant pirate," the other sentient snarled in apparent distaste. "'Beast King' Barbarossa. That is the new epithet the Terrans, once more in a show of their usual creativity, have given you with your bounty, is it not?"

Again silence from Barbarossa. And still, the other sentient continued.

"To think, the mightiest of Leo would be so easily tamed, so reduced in pride and status he is now little more than a slave to a Terran captain," another snarl. "And all for what? Some misplaced hope to return home with honor? With tribute for His Holy Majesty that would stay his condemnation?"

Even through the darkness, Barbarossa could see the fanged smile.

"Or perhaps you have realized your proper place in Aslan's will," it said. "To be as far from His light, and the light of Leo, as the stars will allow."

The smile deepened, even more viciously.

"Or," it continued as if another thought had occurred. "You are merely *afraid* of returning to 'face the music' as the Terrans you have grown so comfortable among would claim."

Despite all the accusations, Barbarossa remained silent and unintimidated. Instead, he simply stared at the other side of the booth with clear inquisition. This seemed to dismay the opposite party.

"Well?" it sneered. "Don't you have anything to say for yourself?" it demanded, its own eyes glowering. "Or have your new Terran masters cut out your treasonous tongue to go with your new face?"

It was only then Barbarossa spoke.

"I happen to like this face," he stated with pride, a finger brushing against his 'X' shaped facial scar. "I think it rather becomes me."

He spoke further, lest another insult be made.

"And as for my silence, I had forgotten what you looked like after all this time," he allowed a fanged smile of his own to show. "I was simply refreshing my memory."

A long and quite amused laugh was his reward.

"Not only treasonous, but a flattering tongue as well," the other party declared as it, or rather *he*, leaned forward to display his full visage. "You have truly fallen from the light of Aslan, brother," the opposite Leo commented, in clear conflict to its proud smile.

"And you have become weaker within it Yusuf," Barbarossa said as he looked over his younger sibling, the second eldest of their generation, and very much appearing as such. Outside of his sibling's black mane, darker brown fur color, and relative youthfulness, it was quite apparent that they were part of the same litter. "Or is that the result of your last promotion?"

Smile remaining, Yusuf, in a mirror of his brother's prior action, brushed a finger against the rank insignia on his armor. Rank insignia that mirrored Barbarossa's markings, thus establishing their bearer as a Kapta.

"As you alluded to, it has been some time. And the role I played at Gallipoli certainly helped."

"Sure sure, charging madly into the face of enemy fire is always a guarantee for promotion," Barbarossa dryly commented. "Assuming one isn't killed in the process."

Yusuf smirked at the challenge. "As compared to you, 'Redbeard'?" he shot back. "As I recall, the glory you brought unto Aslan and our people was for attacking defenseless freighters from the bridge of a warship. Hardly something for the remembrancers to write songs over, much less inscribe onto the Pillar of Heroes."

Barbarossa was almost tempted to use a particular Terran gesture as his response. But Yusuf would have used it as an opening to proclaim him as a slave to Terran masters again.

"They were hardly defenseless," Barbarossa scoffed. "And I could care less about songs and inscribings."

Yusuf opened his mouth, but Barbarossa beat him to the draw.

"Unless we were to follow the Terrans' example and build a tremendous historical database like their Alexandria, such 'remembrances' would be forgotten in the next few centuries anyway," he asserted almost remorsefully. "No, all that mattered to me, and *still* matters, is giving Aslan His glory and our people their rightful victory. Nothing more, nothing less."

A short pause intervened before Yusuf spoke again. "And yet, for one who cares little about inscribings, your armor seems to have more of them than mine."

Barbarossa matched that grin. Indeed, while Yusuf's bronze armor had its share of inscriptions of valor, it was almost plain compared to Barbarossa's custom black armor. It also notably lacked its own Aslan's Star.

"That's one of the benefits of serving in the fleet," Barbarossa pointed out. "You can wear your awards without fear of being marked for enemy snipers."

"Better snipers than *battleships*," Yusuf retorted. "Just how many of those did the infidels deploy after you at Alterf?"

Barbarossa's next smile was of sad remembrance. "Too many," he avowed, remembering the battle in which Imperial forces had tracked down and finished off the *Canpenc* for good. The same campaign in which he was captured and then imprisoned shortly after. "But in the end, it could have been a lot worse."

"That it could have," Yusuf agreed with a nod, not wishing to even consider the idea. Even now, as far as Barbarossa had fallen from their people's grace, he still loved his elder brother. And he had no hesitancy in making that known, now that the opening ritual had been dealt with. "I am glad you survived, brother."

"As am I," Barbarossa returned the nod. "Just as I am glad that you were able to meet me here."

"Indeed," Yusuf replied, smiling the same sad smile Barbarossa had shown earlier. "Though I wish it were under better circumstances."

Barbarossa nodded again, this time in understanding. "I know. But for better or worse, we are here, and now."

The elder Leo then drew back the curtain slightly in order to signal one of the local tavernmaids.

"And, I imagine we have much to discuss."

Yusuf nodded yet again. This time, however, he was hesitant. And, much to Barbarossa's unsettledness, he was allowing it to show.

"Yes, we do," Yusuf answered, his voice also betraying reluctance. And displeasure. "And I fear you will not be pleased with most of it."

Chapter IV: Distant Echoes

He would have preferred to have been on the bridge, watching the stars race past as his current form of transportation flew through arcspace. However, as his "hosts" had plainly stated, they trusted him as much as they did most of his "kind" – perhaps even less, given his own unique set of traits – and would not permit him anywhere near vital areas of their vessel. He took this in stride, as he did with most things, and abided by their wishes, remaining in the domain they had graciously provided him and awaiting their eventual arrival. The latter wouldn't be that much longer anyway, something he didn't need a computer readout to tell him.

In the meantime, he continued to lounge upon the piece of furniture that would have otherwise been considered a bed, reading the book he was holding in his hand. An *actual* book! His hosts had insisted, outside that which he required, he not retain any technological devices while aboard their vessel. A reasonable condition, he thought, as he would have demanded the same of them had their arrangement been in reverse. And it helped that he was one of those types who preferred physical forms of reading and writing, as opposed to vidscreen or holoprojection based.

In any case, he went on reading his book, a particular Terran classic
that had been in his possession since his youth. A story that had been
conceived by one of the most visionary writers of Terra's First Age. A
writer whose wondrous genius could not have been genuinely appreciated
during his time, but was most certainly being appreciated here and now.
Its name was *The Dream-Quest of Unknown Kadath*, and it was likely the
best story ever produced by Terran hands.

Admittedly it had its flaws. It held nothing in the way of dialogue. Instead,
it was a simple first-person perspective from the protagonist throughout.
Its prose was quite purple, such that the descriptions and overall flow
could become relatively bland despite the story's extravagant and otherworldly subject matter. In fact, the writing altogether was rather amateur-
ish, as if it were the author's first real attempt at a novella instead of a
short story.

That all said, however, it was precisely in one prominent area that the novella's strength truly shined: its vibrant imagery. The described world centered
on the titular unknown, was as majestic as it was wondrous, a realm in
which the ethereal beauty and grandeur of Heaven lay side-by-side with the
alluring darkness and mystique of Hell. A place in which one did not travel
to, but rather one *dreamed* to enter, from which he or she traversed assorted
land and sea, filled with creatures of great design, cities, castles, and temples
of otherworldly opulence and sprawling mountains, forests, and caverns
that held much in the way of treasure and danger. A land in which one could
experience infinite adventure, with each passage more enthralling and exhilarating than the last. A place of dreams… and nightmares.

Inwardly he sighed as he read through the passages, feeling a certain
melancholy. If only the real universe were as vibrant and intriguing as the
dreamverse within those pages.

Placing the book down for a moment, he looked up, quietly imagining the
envisioned world. It seemed so close to him, to his mind's eye. Such that
by reaching out his hand, as he did at that exact moment, he could feel the
dense air of the Enchanted Wood or the sea breeze of Oriab. By taking

advantage of the near silence in his physical domain, he could hear the rocking and creaking of the mighty galleons that frequented the Southern Sea, or the playful banter of the cats that inhabited Ulthar. And if he let his eyes drift farther into the dreamscape, he could see the busying streets of Celephais, leading all the way up to the magnificent halls of King Kuranes.

But alas, none of it was, nor would ever be. As close as such a world was to him, it was still so far away, and utterly impossible to reach. By their very nature, dreams were as fleeting as they were temporary. One could envision distant worlds and ventures all one wanted, but one way or another, he or she would always be forced to return to an ever mundane "reality."

And eventually, as it had been for the story's protagonist, one could very well forget the dream…

A sudden beep on his wristcom snapped him back to the present. Frowning, he tapped it.

"What is it?" he demanded in clear annoyance.

The voice on the other end was obviously amused.

"My apologies. Was I interrupting something…*biological*?" it inquired in its usual rasping tone.

He frowned, knowing exactly what the voice was implying.

"Hardly," he answered in equally clear dismissal. "Now, if you would kindly explain the purpose of this call."

The voice quickly changed to seriousness, though not without its own hiss of annoyance.

"We are en route to the planet Nassau," it explained. "The *Black Sun* is confirmed to have berthed there."

He considered that. "I see," he answered. "Will your warriors be up to the challenge?"

A harsh laugh was the response. "I would not consider pirate scum a 'challenge.' Not even a haven of them."

The boast made him smirk. "I'm sure Robert Maynard and Raphael Drake both thought that as well," he pointed out. "You would be wise not to repeat their mistakes."

"And you would do well not to compare me to Terran filth," came the responding snap, which receded after it realized it had been intentionally baited. "Rest assured, my warriors will be ready."

"I should hope," he exclaimed. "Especially when two of her defenders are Devilblade Wielders."

A brief pause intervened.

"You will be contacted again once we have obtained her," it stated, before signing off as abruptly as it rang.

Sighing once more, he quietly picked up his book and continued where he left off. It was the only thing he could do now, to escape the mundaneness of his current setting. Of the realm from which not even dreams could help him escape.

However, as he reminded himself once more, all that would begin to change once he had *her*…

McHale's Island
Roguetown, Nassau

"No kidding," Ernie let out in grinning amusement. "…to an Imperial Governor?"

"Sure as the Big Bang," Alex replied evilly. "And the best part was he wouldn't shut up the whole time. He kept going on about how he was going to hunt us all down, see us all hang, etcetera, etcetera."

He took another bite of his entrée - something that Ernie had explained as "Lobster Thermidor" - before continuing.

"I mean seriously, the idiot is bolted to a bulkhead in a crucifix pattern, left with nothing but his skivvies and watching as his prized yacht is stripped around him, and he still thought he could intimidate us into compliance," Alex laughed. "It would have been pathetic if it wasn't so damn entertaining."

"I bet," Ernie chuckled as he drank his choice grog, Binks' Old No. 9 Brew. "So what did you end up doing with His Excellency? And don't say you shoved him out an airlock, that's way too simple for you two…"

"Is it anything that shouldn't be heard by ladies present?" inquired Mrs. McHale No. 19, otherwise known as Jessica.

Jon smiled courteously. "I assure you we did nothing of the sort," he answered as he took a sip of his Old Caribbean. "Quite the contrary, in fact. Once we obtained what we sought, we sent His Excellency back on his way."

"Still bolted to the wall, still stripped to his skivvies, but no longer yammering," Alex explained, his smile devilish. "We made sure to gag him before we left."

Ernie howled, loving every bit of it. "I bet the newsfeeds on Terra loved that!"

Jon nodded. "To say nothing of the cortex. From what we heard later, it was quite the scandal."

"'Governor Caught With His Pants Down – And *Not* In The Way You Think!'" Alex recited. "Or my personal favorite, 'The Governor's New Clothes – How The 'King Of Lombardia' Was Laid To Bare'."

Ernie laughed harder, nearly sloshing his drink. "See what I mean, Jen… *sica*?" the skipper just managing to avoid a disastrous slip of the tongue. "I told you these two were a riot!"

"I can see that, yes," Jessica stated before taking a sip of her drink, some sort of local cocktail that neither Jon nor Alex recognized. It was obvious she was still peeved about her private time with Ernie getting interrupted by the present company, though she was behaving amicably enough.

She'll get over it, Jon and Alex thought simultaneously. There was a good reason she was Ernie's nineteenth marriage attempt and counting.

"So," Alex spoke up again after a brief, somewhat uncomfortable pause. "Anything new happening in the galaxy?"

"Not much," Ernie shrugged. "Terra's been lying low as of late, but you obviously knew that. The Ophiuchians have been making overtures toward colonizing the Mumbai System, the Pegasians and the Pavons are going through some kind of trade war, the Dreyfus Company just got hit with *another* scandal…"

Ernie's eyes suddenly lit up in remembrance. "Oh yeah, and the Aquarians and the Pisceans are having a territorial dispute."

"Another one?" Alex quipped. "They've had more of those than you've had wives."

"Well, they are ancient enemies," Jon purposely interrupted before the less than dignified response was forthcoming. He did not fail to notice something more to that tidbit of news. "So, what makes this one different from those previous?"

"It's what they're fighting over that has everyone mystified," Ernie replied, clearly baffled by the conflict. "The Sognare Sea."

"Huh?" Alex gaped in confusion. "Why in the First Circle would anyone want that part of space?"

"That's what everyone is scratching their heads over," Ernie answered with an agreeing nod. "Up to now, both sides steered clear of that region…"

"As have everyone else," Jon stated, frowning. "What's changed?"

Ernie shook his head. "No one knows. Even the rumor mill is drawing a blank in that area. But whatever's happened, the Hegemony and the Confederacy have both laid claim, and neither one is willing to step back."

Both Jon and Alex knew what that meant, much to their inner disturbance.

"Has war broken out yet?" Alex asked.

Ernie shook his head again. "Not officially. But there have been skirmishes between the Aegia and the Ghaauh."

"And the other Powers?" Jon inquired.

"No direct response," Ernie specified as he took another drink. "Though obviously, they're standing by in case it spills over."

"As will the Clans," Jon surmised as he sipped his grog, considering. War anywhere in the galaxy was never a good thing, even for pirates. Not only did it mean more active military assets, and therefore more hazards for the Flints to avoid, but it simultaneously reduced operational space. And naturally, there was always the potential of the war expanding, gradually taking in faction by faction, until the whole of the Milky Way was out killing each other. Such was the way of the present universe.

On the other hand, Jon admitted, if they were willing to face the danger, a war between two Galactic Powers would provide more opportunities for them as well. After all, logistics remained an essential part of warfare, and there was only one proven method for moving vital supplies and equipment from one battlefront to another. And it wasn't like the Aquarian Hegemony, or the Piscean Confederacy didn't have it out for pirates, especially those operating in the name of the Golden Queen.

Alex, as usual, was entirely in sync with his brother's thoughts. "Any ideas when the shooting will officially start?" he asked.

Ernie shrugged. "Could happen any day now. Just needs the right spark in the right powder keg..."

As if on cue, a sudden explosion rattled throughout the building, causing lights to flicker and dishes to vibrate.

"Damn it to hell!" Ernie swore, his forehead wrinkling in pain. The Flints and Jessica looked on in confusion as the skipper's wristcom went off.

"That better not have been what I thought it was Gruber."

"I'm sorry, Skip, but it was," Gruber exclaimed.

Ernie rubbed his temples. "Is there anything left to salvage?"

"Tinker's looking at it now, but he doesn't have high hopes. For the time being, we're out of the brewing business."

"Great, just great," Ernie groaned, taking a moment to think. "Fine, we'll just focus more on the distilled stuff. Take McHale's Ale off the menu and offer specials on McHale's Gin and McHale's Rum to compensate. Add in McHale's Whiskey if necessary."

"What about McHale's Vodka?" Gruber inquired.

"Are you kidding?" Ernie made a gagging expression. "No way in the Third Circle are we subjecting the customers to *that* again!"

"You got it Skip," Gruber replied, signing off.

Tapping the wristcom, McHale looked back at the brothers, exasperation evident.

"The joys of private entrepreneurship," he declared in only *slightly* exaggerated frustration. He reached for his drink and took another, much longer swig. Jon and Alex shared a furtive glance, while Jessica watched her husband with distinct discomfort.

And then the tankard was placed back down with a hardened thud. "Now," Ernie said as if nothing had happened. "What were we talking about?"

Market Street
Roguetown, Nassau

Twilight began to fade into night, yet the streets and markets remained as abundantly rampant as ever. Moving amongst the crowds through Roguetown's most extensive market area, the five women blended effortlessly into the local inhabitance, with only the black and gold of their clothes distinguishing them from the background. The other sentients paid them no more concern than the rest, making no indication that they recognized their affiliation. The five remained alert all the same.

At the very least, we're out of that universe forsaken tavern, Lorelei thought as she moved along with the group. Truth be told, she had been to seedier places, but never for recreational purposes as Anna had wanted. It had always been aligned with her motives, namely to dodge authorities or to conduct business, but never because she wanted to "enjoy the sights."

Still, she had to credit the operations officer for the effort, if not the selection. Anna was doing her best for their collective enjoyment.

That being said, their present location was admittedly more to her liking. There was just something about an open market or, more precisely, the thoughts and feelings that tended to accumulate in such places, that enticed her. So many open minds focused on an equal number of various tasks, each generated from different purposes by beings of vastly different backgrounds. It helped even more that Nassau was more a hub in which sentients traveled to and from as opposed to a traditional colony or settlement. Those whose thoughts she sensed literally came from almost every corner of the galaxy at large. Only a more enlightened, as well as more stable, psion like her could appreciate such surroundings.

"Five hundred aurics for *this*!?"

The voice of Anna Reed suddenly sounded from not too far away. The young pirate was holding up a very tacky looking necklace, staring disbelieving toward a Pavon stallkeeper, while the other three women were perusing additional stalls nearby.

"I made one of these when I was seven!"

"Yes, but did you make it out of genuine Pavon gemstones?" the stallkeeper countered, as smoothly and as convincingly as one would expect from his salesbeing type. As their Terran given names alluded to, Pavons were essentially upright walking avianoids adorned with vibrantly multicolored feathers, exuding airs of extravagance and flamboyancy. The latter was especially emphasized with the copious amounts of jewelry this Pavon displayed on his being, which, even without reading his thoughts, one could tell were the *only* actual jewels in his stall.

"Pavon *rainbow gems* at that?"

Anna smiled. A smile that many aboard the *Black Sun* had learned to fear.

"And I suppose these came fresh from your fair homeworld?"

"Absolutely!" the stallkeep replied even more smoothly, then gesturing toward a particular stone on the necklace. "Take this stone, for example. Mined straight from the mountains of Petrus…"

Shaking her head at the discourse, Lorelei decided to follow the group's example and wandered to a nearby stall. As luck would have it, it was a local tea seller's stall. And much more, her products were the genuine article.

"Pegasian," the psion ordered, producing three aurics as payment.

Accepting the aurics graciously, the seller, an elderly Terran woman who had seen a multitude of ventures throughout her life before retiring to her present humble profession, immediately began the brewing process. With nothing more to do but wait, Lorelei turned back to the crowd, once more scanning through the thoughts and feelings that continued to tumble around her like the waves of an ocean, as she had once described seemingly long ago.

Suddenly, Lorelei's ears picked up a sound she hadn't been expecting: that of childish giggling. Looking over, she saw a small group of children running through the crowd, seemingly at play. Uncharacteristically she was startled. Though Nassau obviously held an indigenous population, she didn't think it was the kind of world one settled on to raise a family. Watching their antics, she also took note that the children were going around ostensibly without adult supervision, and while a few in the crowds took note of their presence, they didn't appear overly concerned by them.

It was only when she gleamed over the thoughts of one child that she found her answer. The children were orphans, by the death of their parent or abandonment, and taken in by one of the local religious institutions, which despite the world's social degeneration, were still considered sacred by the inhabitance. As such, the children were particularly knowledgeable of their surroundings, being aware of which adults were acceptable to be in proximity of and which ones to avoid entirely, as well as which alleyways and hiding places to run to should the latter come after them. Thus they remained unafraid as they ran through Market Street, uncaring of the grown-up affairs taking place around them as they went. One even took advantage of the local proprietors, lifting a coin bag from a stallkeeper as he ran by, the fully adult Lacertan not noticing it was gone until too late.

As she watched the children, Lorelei's senses picked up another presence moving behind them. At first, she thought it was one of their playmates trying to keep up, but as she turned her attention, she realized that this presence was different. And much more, not at all part of the aforementioned group.

Searching, Lorelei focused both her telepathy and her physical eyes, trying to identify the presence's source through the crowd. She knew it was out there, like a star whose luminosity was brighter than its counterparts. It shone through the surrounding hustle and bustle, such that it was almost impossible to ignore. Yet she couldn't pinpoint its exact location, much less identify the being of origin from the various faces and forms.

And then, something moved out from the crowd. Once again, seemingly trailing after the children, this one, appearing to be a young girl, moved through the street with an uncharacteristic grace, walking calmly between the adults as the other children continued to run. And whereas the adults were quite aware of the first group's presence yet appeared disinterested, those around her seemed the opposite. They didn't notice her being there, yet strangely, moved out of the way as she walked by. As if naturally inclined not to inhibit her.

However, it was only when she moved directly in front of Lorelei that the psion appreciated just *how* different this one was, much to her alarm. Before she realized it, the girl came to a stop in the middle of the street, the crowd once again moving around her without being *aware*. And then, slowly and ethereally, she turned to look at the psion.

Lorelei found herself gazing into a pair of all too familiar amethyst eyes. Eyes set upon an equally familiar pure white face…

"Your tea," the tea seller suddenly interrupted from within the stall, holding out a steaming glass.

Snapped back into the present, Lorelei blinked, straining to focus, finding that she was again facing the seller. Reflexively she turned around, glancing to where she had been looking previously, or at least where she *thought* she had been looking previously. Only the open streets, and the thoughts and emotions of those moving through it, lay before her eyes and mind.

"Ma'am?" the seller inquired, wondering if there was something amiss.

Turning back, Lorelei reached out and took the steaming cup, momentarily fixated on the blue liquid within. She nodded her thanks and, sipping the warm beverage, moved into the street.

Four Lions Inn
Roguetown, Nassau

"I…I see," Barbarossa nearly stammered before swallowing a drink of his raki, visibly shocked at all he had just heard. "I didn't realize things had turned out so badly after the war."

"Of course not. You had no way of knowing," Yusuf answered simply, taking his drink to ward off his disgust. "Suffice to say that the Third Terran Jihad cost us more than the infidels could ever have hoped."

That was the same conclusion Barbarossa had come to after hearing his brother's report, much to his horror. Ever since his initial Refusal, he had assumed Leo, having remained as untouched from the war as Terra had been, would simply continue in his absence. An assumption he now realized was only partially correct, and not by much.

Leo was still where he left it, yes, but now it was faltering, and faltering significantly. Whether through an indirect effect of the war, or a curse brought onto them by Dajjal, stagnation, and degradation within nearly all levels of society had since taken hold of his beloved homeworld. And with them inevitably came outgrowths of chaos and unrest, in which brother turned against brother and subjects turned against their Caliph, causing further degeneration of their civilization.

Fortunately, much of it appeared repairable, such that, unless a true disaster occurred in the interim, it would be some time yet before any revolution or civil war erupted. However, unless Yusuf was exaggerating – and Barbarossa knew his brother too well to believe that – it was only a matter of time. And with it, the potential destruction of their empire and their civilization.

Indeed, never in his darkest dreams would Barbarossa have ever believed his Caliphate would fall so far.

"How did all this happen?"

Yusuf shook his head. "The reasons are as legion as the stars. However, the central factor is the unanimous and unforeseen recall of the Cihat in the midst of the war."

He took another drink. "Besides the effects it held on our economy, it also called much into question with our Caliph and the rest of the leadership. Namely as to *why…*"

Barbarossa looked up, startled. "You mean that still remains unanswered?"

"Unfortunately. Only those in the upper circle know the actual reason behind the war's end, and they have deemed it necessary to maintain silence."

A shiver ran down Barbarossa's spine. What reason could be so terrible that even two decades or so since the war's end, none were willing to speak of it? However, that was the least of his concerns for the time being.

"What about Father?" Barbarossa pressed on. "Is he still on the Consei?"

"For now. With everything else, there has been much infighting within the Consei as of late…"

"Let me guess," Barbarossa answered blandly. "Several of the Conseiors have gone unto Aslan's side as a result."

Yusuf matched that blandness with his expression. "Not officially, of course. Fortunately, our father remains very much a part of this realm, and that seems unlikely to change any time soon."

He then eyed his elder brother slyly. "He says you have a lot of explaining to do upon your return."

"Heh," Barbarossa exclaimed, noting the underlying message. "Well, at least there's that," he said, smiling at the knowledge that their father was well. "And the rest of our family?"

Yusuf nodded once more, his grin returning. "They remain steadfast. Including Fatim and your bastard children, on the off chance you were wondering."

This time it was Barbarossa's turn to grin. "I never doubted her. Even if our species didn't mate for life, she would *never* forsake us."

Yusuf took another drink. "Yes, well, she remains as displeased with you as the rest. She wishes that, once you've come to terms with your 'Dajjal inflicted stupidity,' you return to her crawling, bloodied, and begging for her forgiveness."

Barbarossa's grin widened. Again he knew the underlying message.

"I take solace in my knowledge that I, in fact, retain a home to return to," he declared, downing the rest of his drink in one swig. "No matter how decrepit and poorly managed it has become in the interim."

Yusuf mirrored the action. "Funny that you say that now," he pronounced, placing his tankard back on the table audibly. "Because it may yet become *unmanaged* entirely."

Barbarossa raised an eyebrow, again feeling dread well within him. "What do you mean?" he asked inquisitively.

This time, Yusuf's expression was flat, as if he had been saving the worst news for last. "His Majesty is dying."

Now Barbarossa was genuinely alarmed. "Of what? And for how long?"

The other Leo shrugged. "No one knows the answer to those questions either. But suffice to say he has been approaching Aslan's side for years now, likely since whatever happened during the jihad."

Yusuf sighed, looking down at the table. "Only through sheer will, and the knowledge of what will happen once he does pass on, has he remained for this long."

Barbarossa nodded grimly. Through his father being a member of the Consei, he had met Caliph Salman several times over his life, as far back as when he had been a cub. All throughout, Barbarossa beheld a great and wise elder, an aged Leo that yet retained the strength and power of his warrior years, alongside accumulated experience and wisdom through his lifetime of venture and rulership. The ideal leader of their people as deigned by Aslan Himself.

Even more so than the Caliphate's fall from grace, Barbarossa struggled to imagine its Caliph being in such a weakened state. It was almost an affront against nature, let alone the will of Aslan.

This led to another inevitable question.

"What do you mean by that last part? 'What will happen when he does pass on'?" Barbarossa quired. "Surely, Prince Ismal will take the throne and sort this mess out…"

Yusuf closed his eyes and shook his head. "The prince disappeared nearly a decade ago. His whereabouts, as well as his continued existence, have yet to be established."

Another chill, this one much colder, ran through Barbarossa. "Then…?" he nearly forced himself to ask. "Who…?"

"I'm afraid Prince Mamluk is set to take the throne."

"What!?" Barbarossa nearly roared, hesitance immediately replaced with shock and fury. "That insane degenerate our next Caliph!?"

"I know, brother. I don't like it any more than you," Yusuf answered in a far more subdued tone. "Neither does Father nor many others." He then shrugged once more. "But what can we do about it? With the Crown Prince gone, His Highness is next in line…"

"For an execution," Barbarossa growled in outright hatred, now wishing he had not downed his entire drink. "His war crimes alone…"

"You mean his 'valorous acts of heroism,'" Yusuf mock corrected. "Up to and including his 'great victory' at Eboras."

Barbarossa snarled in distaste. Even after all this time, the Massacre of Eboras remained as much an affront to him as it had when it took place. "Only that bastard whelp would claim the slaughter of ten million defenseless innocents as a 'victory.'"

"Yes, especially when it only served to infuriate our enemies into fighting that much harder," Yusuf agreed, showing his revulsion. "'Hail Terra! For Eboras!' and so forth."

"This cannot stand Yusuf," Barbarossa hissed. "We cannot allow the Caliphate and all that is holy to fall into the hands of that monster!"

"I know, brother. But for the moment, we have no options. At least, none that would allow us to act openly…"

Barbarossa stilled, knowing what his brother was implying. There may yet be hope.

"How many others?"

Yusuf shrugged. "I couldn't tell you even if I did know. But suffice to say, Father, myself, and the rest of our family are among them."

Barbarossa took that in with visible relief. "Very well."

The younger Leo searched his brother's face, earnestly. "There are many hoping that the mighty Barbarossa would join our cause as well."

"You know why I cannot yet return, Yusuf," Barbarossa smiled, shaking his head, regretfully. "That being said, you also know where my loyalties lie. In fact, this may be for the better. In my experience, there is much advantage to be gained when operating on the outside."

Yusuf wasn't sure what his elder brother meant, but he knew better than to question him. "As you say, brother. Though you do realize neither your mate nor our father will be pleased by this."

"Heh. I would be disappointed if they weren't." Barbarossa raised his empty tankard. "The time of reckoning will yet come, brother. We need only wait just a little longer…"

"By the will of Aslan, brother," Yusuf replied, raising his own tankard.

Then, in a rather Terran-esque gesture, both tapped their tankards together and placed them back on the table, thus sealing their unspoken pact.

Market Street
Roguetown, Nassau

"That's, um, quite a collection you have there," Boss commented to Anna as the five walked onward.

"Thank you," Anna replied as if it were a compliment, glancing proudly over the various kinds of jewelry that now adorned her body. Save for her original golden cross, it would all go into a lockbox, specifically the one that held a good portion of her 'collection' once she got back to the *Sun*, but for now, she wore it with pride. "The salesman thought the same as well."

She then grinned slyly to herself. *After all, it was initially* his *collection,* she thought, recalling the Pavon she had dealt with before. The same retailer was now stripped of everything but his clothes and the costume jewelry he had tried pedaling to her. *Though I could have done without the remarks to my character and biology.*

"So," Gran spoke up brightly, having heard everything that went on between Anna and her would-be aggressor. "Where to now?"

"Hmmm…" Anna pondered, then spotted another tavern in the distance. "I suppose additional grog would be in order. A celebration of sorts."

"Of course you would say that," Boss laughed. Even before she had joined the Flint Pirates, Anna Reed's alcohol tolerance was almost legendary. "God forbid you go an hour without having some form of grog."

"And you?" Anna retorted. "I thought fighter pilots were notorious for their alcohol intake."

Boss smirked. "I didn't say I disagreed with your suggested course of action."

Anna nodded, then looking toward the others. "Any opposed?"

Gran shrugged. "The night is still young, as the saying goes."

Kaguya simply closed her eyes in acceptance. "I can think of no other alternatives."

Nodding at both of them, Anna looked over to the last member of their group. "And you?" she inquired toward the hooded figure, whose face remained shrouded. "Got any problems with another drink?"

Lorelei would have answered had she actually heard the question. However, just as the exchange was taking place, she felt an all too familiar feeling come over her. One that nearly made her body freeze in place.

.........Help.........

"Lorelei?" Anna questioned when the psion didn't immediately reply.

As if responding, Lorelei took several steps forward, apparently moving away from the group. Confusion coursed between them as the psion took several more steps, slowly and deliberately, seemingly in a trance.

Such may as well had been the case for Lorelei, as her fellow shipmates no longer registered in her consciousness. Instead, her focus remained forward. Where a particular child stood, gazing directly at her with eyes like her own.

For, as impossible as it seemed, they *were*.

.........Help.........Me.........

Then, before she could reply in any form, Lorelei felt something gradually reach out to her. Something that even she couldn't identify, but that was utterly overpowering. Something that, before she realized what was happening, began to encompass and engulf her form...

"Lorelei!?" Anna called out as she saw the psion suddenly jerk back, her hands reaching up and grasping her head, a silent scream echoing from her lips.

That was precisely when it all began.

With the suddenness of a hurricane, the first explosions began to rock Market Street as both physical objects, up to and including entire buildings, and thin air simultaneously detonated, sending fragments and shockwaves in all directions. Random articles and people rose into the air only to be flung or maneuvered in some way, either impacting the ground, the sides of structures, or other individuals. Various substances and forms shifted in composition, transforming into solid, liquid or vapor, fragmenting and assimilating rapidly and randomly. And in between, magenta energy danced and arced about like lightning, striking and lashing out in absolute furor.

Realizing what was happening, Anna, biting down her horror and disbelief, grabbed onto the thrashing psion, yelling her name and trying to snap her back. However, as if she were in the center of a vortex, she realized she couldn't hear her voice. That was right before she was telekinetically thrown back, with Gran and Boss just managing to catch her.

In the midst of this chaos, Kaguya began to move. Despite being dressed in a kimono instead of her standard tacsuit, she progressed just as efficiently, maneuvering toward the psion while fluidly and precisely evading the telekinetic forces. It was not long before she came upon Lorelei, who continued to struggle, seemingly unaware of the assassin's approach.

A kunai neatly fell into Kaguya's hand.

The other women quickly ascertained the Dragon Princess' actions. Without hesitation, Anna and Boss reached for their firearms; unfortunately, both knew that they weren't going to make it in time.

However, just as Kaguya was about to deliver the killing stroke, she was able to see the psion's face, to witness the sheer anguish that encompassed Lorelei's now twisted, tear-streaked visage along with the still silent screams of pain. It was only then, at the last possible second, she reversed the kunai, so it would strike handle first. And so it did, landing a blow against the psion's head, the force behind it enough to knock her wholly unconscious.

The chaos dissipated abruptly, with sound returning and objects and people falling onto the ground. Knowing it would not be long before somebody realized what had just happened, Boss, after passing Kaguya a scathing glance, picked Lorelei up and began moving away from the debris field. Behind her, Kaguya retained her kunai while Anna and Gran, beam pistols drawn, flanked their crewmen, ensuring that no one would follow them.

Anna's earlier inclination, notwithstanding, there was only one possible destination for the group. And though it was a tavern, their time there would not be for social engagement.

Chapter V: Signs of the Storm

McHale's Island
Roguetown, Nassau

Taking another sip of his Old Caribbean, Jon continued to lean against the balcony's ledge, gazing out over Roguetown at large. It was well past midnight now, the local sun having long since set below the horizon, thereby allowing the night to encroach and the city-wide artificial lighting to engage. Through this, Jon, in spite of the relatively "short" three-story height of his perch, beheld a rather spectacular view. Roguetown appeared as nothing less than a vast field of multi-colored lights extending all the way to the coastline. The accompanying "sounds of the city" were still there, the darkness having only emboldened activity throughout the area, but now distant and spread throughout the municipality. Ironically, this created a passive atmosphere for those well outside of it, Jonathan Flint included. Combined with the tranquility of his immediate location, the loudness, and banter being primarily contained to the tavern's first floor, Jon was at ease. Not even the distant sounds of weapons fire, which were reasonably abundant, dissuaded him from his contentment.

Knowing that the other Flint Pirates were spread out amongst those lights, Jon faintly wondered how they were doing. No doubt they were adding to Roguetown's chaotic elements, perhaps even contributing to the afore-mentioned weapons fire, yet all the same, Jon didn't feel overly worried. Though they were all from varying backgrounds, he knew they could generally handle themselves; even the least skilled of their group had since gained experience with their recent raids, if not Smyrna. And though there were a number of them that bordered on the unpredictable – namely a certain Lady Killer – he did not doubt their return to the ship in three days. With or without his having to take them out of the local stockade.

Jon couldn't help but laugh. He would bet good money on seeing several members of his crew, up to and including his helmsman, on the opposite side of a force field. Despite its violent, lawless nature, Nassau did, in fact, have a local security force. Usually, it was content to abide by the lawless-ness, but every so often, it would intervene in the more extreme cases, or at least in events that could not be concealed from public attention. And considering that a fair number of the Flint Pirates were prone to such extreme cases, Jon had a feeling he would indeed be dealing with them before the *Black Sun*'s departure.

But for the moment, that was of little concern. Undisturbed, he took another sip of his bottle and continued to look out over the lights; a distinct set of footfalls sounded from behind.

"How are things going in the basement?"

"You mean the 'brewery' slash 'distillery'? Not too bad, the earlier kaboom notwithstanding," Alex admitted as he joined his brother on the balcony, an Old Caribbean bottle of his own in his hand. "So far, Ernie's gang has it under control. Or so they kept repeating to me."

Jon mildly shook his head. "Let it be, Alex," he stated as he took another sip, a slightly longer one. "You don't need to fix every engineering prob-lem that presents itself."

"What's there to fix?" Alex retorted. "All that was missing was the mush-room cloud and someone quoting the *Bhagavad Gita*."

Coming beside his brother, Alex took in the view before him. "Anyway, I'm done for the night," he exclaimed, cracking his neck. "Once I finish off this bottle, I'm officially retiring for the foreseeable future, come hell or hangover."

"As will I," Jon replied, stretching in exhaustion. "God only knows what we'll be dealing with in the morning."

"More like the afternoon, but otherwise agreed," Alex corrected. "I'm not even sure the city will still be standing when we wake up."

"To say nothing of the universe proper," Jon countered before taking another drink.

Despite the alcohol, it didn't take much for Alex to understand his brother's reference. "All standard fare, brother," he reassured. "There's always a war occurring somewhere in the galaxy."

"I know, and this one won't be the first between two Powers," Jon acknowledged, shaking his head again. "But all the same, Alex, I can't help but feel something's different about this battle."

He looked away from the city in thought. "Usually wars are started over the acquisition of territory or resources, or more often than not ancient blood feuds," he said. "Yet while those can easily factor into this one, there still seems to be something amiss…"

"Yeah," Alex frowned as the possibilities began to weigh in on him. "I admit this doesn't sit well with me either. What could possibly be in that region of space for two Powers to fight over?"

"I can't imagine," Jon answered forebodingly. "The obvious answer would be some new discovery, one that would augment the power and influence of any who claim it." A scowl crossed his face. "But for that to work, someone would first have had to discover it and report it back."

"Right," Alex nodded. "And yet as far as we know, no ship or probe has ever returned from the Sea." The younger Flint shrugged. "Either way, I'm drawing a blank just like everyone else, Jon," he said, only mildly concerned. "And even then, it doesn't really have anything to do with us, does it?"

"No," Jon affirmed, turning back to the city. "It doesn't."

Shrugging again, Alex took another swig of his bottle, downing the remaining contents. Once he finished his drink, he glanced at his brother intending to say goodnight and retire to the quarters Ernie had provided them. It was then that the *second* 'kaboom' sounded, causing Alex to snap around.

"Now what!?" he glowered, half-expecting another accident somewhere around the tavern. Scanning his surroundings, he was surprised to see that the explosion, and those that followed in rapid succession, were taking place in another part of Roguetown, away from McHale's Island.

For the next few seconds, the Flints watched as chaos, seemingly focused around strange flashing violet-colored energy bolts, erupted in that area. Buildings were being obliterated, bodies and equipment flung high into the air as vivid amethyst lightning struck in all directions.

"What in the Fifth Circle…?" Alex gaped in shock as he turned toward his brother.

Witnessing the destruction, Jon's expression was one of pure horror, of a kind that was totally uncharacteristic of his usually inscrutable demeanor. Alex felt his blood freeze. He had seen Jon visibly horrified before, but this time it was different. This time, the younger Flint realized, it wasn't so much the destruction at hand that so overwhelmed Jon's taciturn nature, but rather his clear recognition of it. Or, more precisely, its source.

Realization dawning, Alex turned back to survey the devastation.

It can't be…!

Jon swung around and moved away from the balcony, all the while bringing up his wristcom.

"Foxtrot One to Alfa Romeo, come in," he spoke dispassionately at first, only to raise his voice when an answer did not come straight away.

"Foxtrot One to Alfa Romeo, come in!"

"Alf…Alfa Romeo here," Anna finally replied, her voice strained with shock. "Did you…?"

"Yes, we saw," Jon interrupted calmly, trying to defuse the situation. Too much volume would only attract unwanted attention. "What happened?"

"I…" Anna started to speak but then stammered. "I don't know, Foxtrot."

A brief pause intervened before Jon gave his next command. "Sitrep."

This time Anna was quicker to answer. "Lima is presently out, courtesy of Kilo."

Jon wasn't sure, but he suspected that Anna paused to flash a glare at Kaguya before continuing.

"We're on our way to you, proceeding discreetly and without visible pursuit. Recommend you have Alfa on standby."

"Acknowledged," Jon responded as he motioned to Alex. "Go downstairs and tell Ernie he's about to have more company."

Nodding, Alex moved quickly toward the stairs as Jon switched comm. channels.

"Foxtrot One to Alfa."

Old Billy Riley's
Roguetown, Nassau

"Owwwwww!" Apache groaned as he slowly rose off the ground where he had been thrown by the last explosion.

Behind him, a new set of ruins now stood where Old Billy Riley's Tavern had originally been, the entire building was demolished. Glancing back as he hazily dusted himself off, the Aquilan tried not to imagine how many patrons were buried under the resultant rubble. Had he not moved outside with select others to see where all the sudden bangs and booms were coming from, he could have been one of them.

What in the Seventh Circle...? Apache thought as he looked over his surroundings, doing his best not to gape.

Whatever it was, it had been vicious and widespread. Other ravaged or completely obliterated buildings could easily be seen, while assorted damage, ranging from scorch marks and smashed objects to craters and drifting ash, were equally abundant. And of course, amongst the destruction, bodies – or segments that were once part of a whole – abounded, among other associated things.

If anything, however, what disturbed Apache the most was the fact that, as he continued to survey the area, he surmised the event – once more whatever it had been - hadn't been deliberate. Instead, as rampant as it had wrought destruction over the city, it had also been seemingly incomplete, perhaps even entirely random in its approach. For all that was damaged or destroyed, an equal number of buildings and objects were left untouched, just as many of the surrounding populace still lived and breathed, albeit in abject shock and horror over what had just occurred. Not something Apache would have expected from a willful act of violence.

Unless...

"Foxtrot One to Alfa," Jon's voice called out from Apache's wristcom, which by some miracle was still functioning.

Hearing the suppressed strain in the elder Flint brother's voice, Apache suddenly had a sinking feeling he knew what had just happened. Discretely he raised his wristcom to his beak.

"Alfa here," he said, before coughing out some abstract dust. "Mostly."

The Aquilan could just hear the sigh of relief on the other end. "We have an emergency," Jon stated. "How long will it take for you to reach the Island?"

Apache considered. "I could be there in moments by flight," he offered, flapping his wings to make sure that they still worked properly. "But that might attract unwanted attention."

"Agreed," Jon answered simply.

The doctor thought over the route. "I'd say five to ten by foot. Fifteen if we proceed cautiously," he exclaimed, stepping back to the tavern ruins as rescuers began arriving on the scene. "Will that do?"

"Yes," Jon confirmed. "We'll be waiting," he said before signing off.

Once the channel was clear, Apache lowered his wristcom and looked over to a slowing moving smattering of rubble. "You heard all that rock pile?"

Kaiser, with a bit of effort, rose from the wreckage of the tavern, shaking off the abstract bits and pieces that remained on him. As he dusted himself off, he turned to look across where his earlier opponent had been. Apparently, the anonymous Draco had not been as fortunate as he, as Kaiser could only see the arm he had been using to wrestle extending out from the debris. Not only was it not moving, but it was also severely scorched and damaged; apparently, the reptilian had been struck directly by whatever had hit the tavern.

Shaking his head and standing by solemnly, Kaiser took a moment to quietly honor his now fallen opponent. The moment passed quickly, however, and Kaiser, after glancing around rather suspiciously, reached out to scoop up his winnings, which by some miracle or another had managed to remain composed and contained on the table.

"Classy," Apache quipped, rolling his eyes at the display.

Once the Herculean picked up the last coin, the two Flint Pirates inconspicuously exited the area just as the rescuers turned their attention toward Old Billy Riley's ruin.

McHale's Island
Roguetown, Nassau

After exerting significant effort and garnering attention from some rather unsavory characters, the group of women finally managed to reach McHale's Island with their unconscious companion. Escorted by the tavern employees sent to aid them, they made their way through the central bar, again enduring unwanted attention, and entered the designated backroom. Cautiously, Lorelei was laid out across a makeshift bed, her greatcoat then removed and reapplied as a blanket. Presently, Jon arrived with Ernie and a somewhat apprehensive Jessica.

"My god…!" Ernie exclaimed, seeing the psion for the first time. Jon and Alex had talked about her over dinner, but he never expected the mysterious alien woman to be this alluring. Much less in her present state. "She was the one who…?"

"It wasn't her fault," Jon declared as he assessed Lorelei's condition. The quickness of the response, along with the pirate captain's tone, was more than enough an indication for the tavern owner to drop the subject.

"Is it okay for her to be here…?" Jessica stammered with horror, gazing upon Lorelei's form as if she were about to reawaken and lay the tavern to waste as well. "I mean, she's trouble… what happens when…!"

"It wasn't her fault," Jon interrupted, this time turning his head and casting a withering glare at the obtuse women, one that reinforced the belying warning of the reply. All color drained from Jessica's face, and she immediately shut up. Stepping closer to her husband, she clung to Ernie's arm in a silent plea for him to protect her from Jon's growing wrath.

Ernie didn't bother to look at Jon; instead, he glanced with silent inquisition at the women who accompanied the psion. Reading their responding glances and body language, he deduced they concurred with their captain. Whatever had happened at Market Street, none of them believed that their charge was responsible. They seem united in their supposition that something beyond her own will had caused the incident. Of course, none of them had answers as to what that 'something' was. A moment later, Alex entered the room.

"Casualties?"

The younger Flint shook his head. "All crew present and accounted for," Alex replied, not bothering to hide his relief. "Through some twist of fate or another, none of them ended up caught in…" He trailed off as he saw the inactive Lorelei, an expression of sympathy crossing his face.

Jon nodded. Though he wasn't too sure how anyone else had fared, at least none of his crew had been harmed. That was his main concern, well before the rest of Nassau.

"What…"

As if on cue, Apache burst into the room with Kaiser trailing behind him in equal measure. It was only then that Jon and Alex remembered they hadn't identified their "family doctor" to Ernie, who, in turn, couldn't have informed his subordinates to be on the lookout for the Aquilan healer. However, since the doctor was accompanied by a perturbed looking Herculean, one who appeared to have just crawled out of a collapsed building, it was clear as to why none of the tavern staff had attempted to hinder them.

At first, the other Flint Pirates expected Apache to make an off-put exclamation, given that he was clearly as bad for wear as Kaiser. Instead, Apache simply bypassed all of them and came over to his newfound patient. Without a sound, he began his analysis.

"Shouldn't he have some kind of scanner?" Jessica whispered to her husband. "Or is he just taking a…"

"Doesn't need one," Ernie responded quickly before anyone else overheard his nineteenth spouse. "Aquilans have the sharpest optical sense of any race; their healers can identify ailments by sight alone. Rest assured, he's doing his job."

He studied the unconscious psion. *That being said, I wouldn't blame him if he is checking her out,* he thought, making a mental note to harp at Jon and Alex for holding out on him. Indeed, for whatever instabilities she might possess, this 'Lorelei' was smoking hot as far as unknown alien species went. If his present marriage turned out like the eighteen previous ones, Ernie definitely wouldn't mind her being number 20.

Of course, he mused restraining the urge to sigh, that was not in the realm of possibilities. His long line of marriages notwithstanding, he was no longer the picturesque image of a young Terran spacer. His body had long given way to the *slightly* overweight veteran he was now. Plus, seeing how fast Jon had come to her defense, Ernie had a suspicion that the aspiring pirate lord would take issue.

After a few moments, Apache looked up, visibly concerned. "Well, this is unsettling," he stated, turning to Jon. "Physically, she's in perfect health. Not so much as an allergic reaction to this planet's fauna. But…"

"But?" Alex repeated, suddenly wondering if he actually wanted to know.

Apache exhaled. "She has apparently gone through some kind of psionic episode. Her vitals, especially those tied to her brain and nervous system, have all risen alarmingly. In a way that usually relates to mental duress."

He then cast a knowing eye at his patient. "And given how composed we all know her to be…it must have been a considerable episode."

"A psionic assault," Jon affirmed, bringing to mind what everyone – save Jessica of course – was thinking. "One powerful enough to overwhelm her."

"Thereby causing her to lose control," Alex concurred. "How is that even possible for someone like her?"

Jon glanced at Kaguya. "Were there any other psions within the vicinity?" he asked, recognizing that she, of all of them, would know.

Kaguya shook her head. "None so powerful," she answered, continuing to speak just as Jon began to look away. "When I struck her down, she was crying and in considerable pain. Far more than I have ever seen her reveal."

Nodding, Jon felt closer to the truth. Despite the image she wished to present, he knew Lorelei was a powerful psion. One so powerful that - her ability to engage the Babels notwithstanding - she had chosen to conceal her actual strength and had gone well out of her way to ensure such concealment, even from him. Something that very few, especially within the company of pirates and criminals, would have done when endowed with such 'gifts.' Lorelei's uncontrolled rampage further elaborated just how powerful she was. As if the extent of the destruction hadn't done so already.

Kaguya's confirmation that there were other psions present gave Jon additional clues. Whatever had transpired, it was focused on Lorelei and Lorelei alone. If not, the remaining psions in the same vicinity would also have experienced the aggression, and Kaguya would have had to strike them down as well to end the chaos.

Overall, the conclusion was quite clear, but far from Jon's liking. Unless Lorelei had suffered a full psionic meltdown – which seemed improbable, as Apache had alluded to when referencing her usual composure – then whatever had destabilized her had come from an exterior source, thus characterizing the episode as a telepathic assault. More troubling, however, such an assault must have been tremendously powerful to overwhelm Lorelei's mental defenses, such that she displayed visible pain and anguish. Yet if Kaguya, being as attuned to the nature of psions as she was, had not detected the aggressor in the immediate vicinity, or had even traced the apparent target as she had done at Ephesus and elsewhere, then the assault must have been triggered from a great distance. One possibly beyond Nassau itself, much as Jon didn't want to think about it. Though they were rare, there were psions capable of such.

And of course, there was the *why*, which bothered him even more. Why would anyone make such an attempt on her? Granted, Lorelei had her share of enemies, as did everyone in the Flint Pirates, but Jon imagined there were far more pragmatic ways to elicit vengeance than a full-on psionic attack. And that was assuming it was even an attack at all. For all anyone knew, whatever had occurred could have had a completely different purpose or no purpose altogether, with the intensity of the action alone causing her to lose control.

All said Jon knew there was one clear truth. Whatever had happened, and wherever it had come from, Lorelei had suffered. Far more than anyone else caught in the wake.

What did this to you? Jon wondered as he moved to the table. Looking over the unconscious psion, he softly wiped a droplet of sweat from her cheek with the back of his finger.

Upon that contact, Jon suddenly felt something flash before his consciousness. It was the briefest of images; he was just barely able to make it out. What he did "see," however, invoked abundant, uncharacteristic apprehension. An apprehension that soon gave way to terror.

A great, featureless void. A sentient will trapped or imprisoned, desperately reaching out for salvation. Stars flickering, appearing in one area of space before fading away, only to reappear in another. Streams of color and fantasy, as unreal as they were beautiful, as beautiful as they were horrifying. Shapes and forms of unknown origin and nature, dwelling within a realm of dream.

All centered upon a lone, obsidian moon...

"Jon?" Alex's voice penetrated the elder Flint's trance.

Eye blinking, Jon took a breath and adopted the most serious of expressions.

"Inform the crew," he commanded as he turned to walk out. "We leave in one hour."

Boss jerked, Apache grunted, yet Kaguya grimaced. Only Anna quired, "Captain?"

"Just do it!" Jon barked as he exited the room, his voice, while forceful, betraying a disturbance that he would never have done willfully.

Exchanging glances of alarm, the Flint Pirates adhered to the order regardless. The next moment, Alex was on his wristcom, relaying those orders.

Midnight Lagoon Inn
Roguetown, Nassau

"What do you mean we're leaving!?" was the first line out of Davis' mouth the moment he closed the bathroom door. Notably, he was bereft of all manner of clothing, save for his wristcom, of course.

"You heard it right the first time, Davis," Alex's voice squawked through the communication device, already sounding agitated. "Get your junk together and get back to the *Sun*. We touch off in an hour."

Davis was beside himself. "Three days, Alex!" he hollered miserably. "We were supposed to have three days…!"

"Well, that's changed!" Alex shouted back, causing Davis to recoil. "We're leaving, no discussions!"

"Alright, alright," Davis let out, knowing better than to argue. He glanced at the nearby chronometer. "It'll take me a bit, but I should make the deadline."

He then considered for a moment. "Would this have anything to do with all the booms and bangs earlier?" The helmsman could almost feel the wave of aggravation from his First Officer.

"Just get back within the hour. Flint out."

"Shit," Davis muttered, now comprehending the direness of the situation. Though he had been preoccupied throughout the disturbance, enjoying the collective afterglow with the newest member of his interstellar fan club, Davis had at least heard the noise. It was only now, however, that he realized they weren't totally random acts common to Roguetown. And much more, the source was likely closer to home.

Sighing, he willed himself to move, reaching for the bathroom door while his mind scrambled to come up with an excuse for his early departure. He managed to make the most of his time in port, as he always did. The one waiting on the other side of the door, though she would be disappointed with their parting, was by no means unsatisfied with the evening. Davis knew she would be watching for his eventual return. He only hoped it would be sooner than later.

It was with that solemn thought Davis, at last coming up with a convincing excuse, one that *didn't* involve random explosions and causes of alarm, started turning the knob. And it was just as he began opening the door when another noise, one that was far louder than even the prior 'bangs' and 'booms,' erupted throughout the city. This noise filled Davis with even greater dread…for this noise was the bellow of the planetary defense siren.

Chapter VI: The Deep Ones

Nassau System

It was a rather innocuous little world, to borrow a Terran designation, he thought as the light of arcspace ceased, and realspace reemerged, their target's present port of call now fixed upon the bridge monitor. At their current separation distance, Nassau appeared like anything but a hive of scum and miscreants. Had it not been for its existing residents, his nation would have certainly seen it as ideal for annexation and colonization. Shame that the Terrans had beaten them to that. And it wasn't like water was a rarity within the galaxy.

For the present, however, such considerations were irrelevant. They weren't there to set up a colony on that innocuous little world, or even conquer it for that matter. They were there to take something from it, something that would be far more valuable to their nation than anything else that planet, no matter how inviting, might have held. And so they would claim it, for the glory of their realm.

"Detecting multiple signals moving to intercept," one of the bridge crew announced as he looked over his display. A tacwindow appeared on the bridge monitor displaying the ships, and images of the bands they represented, in question.

He frowned almost disappointedly as his eyes surveyed the screen. He would have hesitated to call most of those "ships," let alone combatants; some of them looked to be little more than collections of scrap gathered together around an arc or sub-arc engine of some sort. Not that he expected an Imperial battlefleet, of course, and it would make their objective easier to fulfill in the long run. But all the same, he couldn't help but feel dissatisfaction.

"The target?"

"Retained to the surface," another operator declared. "Coordinates twenty-five point zero three mark seventy-seven point three nine."

That didn't surprise him. There was no reason the *Black Sun* should have been in orbit to meet them, not after having just arrived at her berth. Again it made things that much simpler. If the *Black Sun* had been in orbit, she would have been far more challenging to isolate.

With that assurance, his hands – his *webbed* hands – gripped the arms of his chair in anticipation. "Proceed."

Upon that command, the taskforce accelerated toward the planet, paying little heed to the meager opposition that was rushing to intercept them.

McHale's Island Tavern
Roguetown, Nassau

"Talk to me, Willy," Ernie barked over his wristcom as he and the tavern staff began organizing their various weapons, preparing for the inevitable fight. Beside them, the Flint Pirates were also readying their respective weapons, anticipating that the trip back to the *Black Sun* would be more 'eventful' than they would have wanted.

From another area of the tavern, one lined with numerous monitors and other surveillance equipment, Willy analyzed the readout.

"Four ships, Skip. Full ID is still processing, but judging from their formation and arc ratings, I'm guessing three cruisers and a battleship."

Ernie wasn't the only one who jerked back, stunned. Nor was he the only one that gained a sinking feeling in their gut.

A raiding force, Jon mentally surmised, noting that there were no dedicated transport ships within the enemy group. And even if there were one or two present, it would have taken much more than that to pacify and occupy Nassau. Despite that, the invaders, whoever they were, had more than enough firepower for a hit-and-run assault.

"Alright, getting identification now…" Willy reported over the comm. to his all too captive audience. A brief, uncomfortable pause intervened.

"Shit!"

"Willy?" Ernie prodded, already knowing from that single word he wasn't going to like the answer.

"They're Pisceans, Skip," Willy conveyed, the reluctance in his voice as piercing as a cold wind.

Everyone in the tavern reacted to the identity of their uninvited guests. Jon and Alex exchanged a pointed glance. Pisceans attacking Nassau on its own was bad enough; after all, the Piscean Confederacy was one of the thirteen most formidable dominions in the galaxy and was every bit as advanced militarily as its competition. However, recalling the dinner conversation not too long ago, the brothers couldn't help but wonder if there was more to this raid than the obvious. Ernie seemed of a like mind.

"Do we have any idea what Dag they're part of?"

Being a confederacy, Piscean society was a collection of individual states that contributed to the whole rather than a completely unified entity. These states, or Dags, naturally varied from each other in specific characteristics, up to and including social makeup and military practices. Identifying the Dag of origin would grant a clearer image of the present opposition.

"That's a neg, Skip. Nothing matches up in the registry," Willy exclaimed as he looked over the arc drive signatures and hull markings of the four warships, which indeed didn't match anything recorded in the database.

Another alert soon flashed.

"Defense forces have engaged."

That'll buy us one, maybe two more minutes, Ernie sniffed somewhat derisively, his opinion of Nassau's defense fleet, the latter word he used lightly, apparent in his responding expression. It was one of those times he wished he still had the *Renegade*. Not that a single cruiser, even one of the vaunted *Ravager*-class, could hope to match three enemy cruisers and a battleship on her own.

"Inform me the minute they start deploying assault ships."

"Got it, Skip," Willy replied before signing off.

"When it rains, it pours," Alex dryly quipped as he slipped his Trafalgar back into its holster, fully active and armed at the appropriate setting. "On the other hand, it's been a while since we had a good ol' fashioned fish fry."

"To a point," Jon reminded as he adjusted his own Trafalgar. Unlike the other participants, it was doubtful he and his brother would use their guns in this fight, but it never hurt to have backup weapons. "Our primary concern remains to get back to the *Sun*."

Alex nodded, glancing over to the still unconscious Lorelei, now held in Kaiser's arms, ready to evacuate. "And I was seriously looking forward to a break from the action."

"Weren't we all," Anna agreed, before looking at Jon. "Any particular plan for this Captain?"

Jon shook his head. "Nothing beyond moving at best speed," he said, his lips folding into a solemn grin. "And killing as many aggressors along the way as possible."

"Fish in a barrel," Alex retorted, an anticipating grin spreading across his face. The responding groans were varied but loud. "What? Somebody had to say it."

Ignoring his brother, Jon looked toward Ernie. "Will you be able to hold out?"

"Against these fishheads? Please," Ernie retorted. "This isn't the first time my swabs and I fought Pisceans."

"I do not doubt that," Jon acknowledged. "But, you're still up against a considerable assault force."

"You just worry about getting back to your ship. We'll handle things on this end." Ernie smirked in agreement with Alex. "And believe me, fried fish with citrus butter, and wild rice is gonna be tonight's entrée!"

"I vouch for that!" Fuji added coming out of the kitchen, as he slammed a power cell into his extensively customized Arisaka beam rifle.

"All right, we'll take our leave," Jon pronounced, glancing at his crew to verify they were ready. "Save some fish for us. When we're in the neighborhood again."

"Great to see you, boys. Feel free to drop in anytime," Ernie replied as he slipped on his weathered Starfleet cap and pulled out his equally weathered Dragoon NP7 beam pistol. He flashed a sly grin at the brothers. "Just …no more stunts. As Chuck said, impersonating officers of His Imperial Majesty's Starfleet is a severe offense."

Ignoring the confused glances from the others, Jon and Alex both matched their friend's grin.

"We make no promises," Alex replied sardonically.

A few seconds of silence passed, as both the Flint Pirates and the McHale's Island staff willed themselves up for the unexpected fight. And then, with a single nod from the pirate captain, it was dispelled.

"Let's go," he commanded.

As one, the pirates moved out into the Roguetown streets. Things were about to become even more frantic than when they had first arrived.

Defense batteries flared across the cityscape, sending beams and projectiles into the darkened sky above. Unfortunately, the return fire was just
as quick and far more precise. The Piscean assault shuttles launched their
beam and missile weapons back at the defensive towers and platforms,
most ancient leftovers from Nassau's colonial days. A far more significant
number of detonations erupted across Roguetown. The escorting Piscean
fighters had similar success. Whatever craft managed to get off the ground
in time to attempt further defense of the planet was swiftly destroyed by
the shuttles' weapons, allowing them to continue virtually unheeded. From
there, it wasn't long before the shuttles touched down on the streets or
hovered above, allowing their occupants to enter the field where the real
fighting would take place.

Clad in stylized, variously marked turquoise armor and wielding assorted
hand-weaponry, the Piscean warriors either cabled or ran down the shuttle
ramps, firing green-tinted beam shots from their curiously designed rifles.
Any beings that remained unshielded and within the open fell instantly. Some
managed to return fire before being struck, their shots deflected by the shielding of the Piscean armor. However, the Pisceans were far from unchallenged;
a significant number of defenders had taken cover. Shielded and/or armed with
diverse weaponry, they were determined to repel the invaders.

Energy shots engulfed the unwanted raiders from all directions. Several were
struck down, their shielding and armor only defending them from so many hits
before the scaled flesh underneath was destroyed. Even so, the Pisceans were
not a race known for being easily thwarted. They pressed their assault through
the neighborhoods of Roguetown, individual units spreading out across the
streets to proceed with their objectives. All while the planet's beleaguered
defenders, several of which hailed from various military forces throughout the
galaxy, fought back, determined that neither Roguetown nor Nassau at large
would fall without significant cost to the invaders.

Under the strafing run of a supporting bomber, one such assault unit
progressed through a particular area of the city, capitalizing on their air

support and advancing upon nearby defensive positions with vicious effect. As spread out and undercover as the defenders were, only a select few of them had any viable combat tactical experience; hence they were incapable of mounting a strategic attack against proper soldiers. Thus, the Pisceans moved through the avenues in concerted form, striking down much of their opposition as they drove forward, taking only slight losses. Even the defenders' employment of a portable missile launcher did little to hinder them. Though they lost three of their own to the initial missile strike, it took but a single responding grenade to neutralize the launcher and its crew.

And then, seemingly out of nowhere, a sudden spray of crimson and bronze-tinted fire burned through the aggressors' rear line, the red beams readily bypassing shields and armor and cutting down no less than four of the fish-men. Swinging around, the Pisceans watched in collective terror as two Leos, both attired in their own race's battle armor, charged into their group.

Deafening roars reverberating, baneclaws extended, Barbarossa and Yusuf cut into their opponents with savage guile, slashing at whatever enemy was within reach and firing upon those not. The Pisceans scrambled to reform their unit and retaliate against these new, unforeseen foes.

Allowing his armor's shielding to deflect the oncoming green beams, Barbarossa dove at the closest Piscean, raking his claws against the fish being's torso. Though Piscean shielding and armor were both durable to an extent, it was no great difficulty for the Leo's baneclaws to break through the first and rend into the second, striking the organism underneath. Hissing with pain, the Piscean attempted to raise its rifle. Barbarossa was undeterred, following up with two more slashes to the head and torso, respectively, then kicking the now dying piscinoid away. Another Piscean fired its beam pistol at the Leo, but this time Barbarossa, if only out of reflex, evaded and returned fire with a single shot, striking his attacker in the head. Once more, the shielding and armor did nothing to protect the invader against Barbarossa's enhanced weapon, for which the Leo again inwardly thanked Professor Braun for his innovations, resulting in the enemy warrior falling to the ground.

Not far from him, Yusuf cut his way through another pair of fishmen, killing one directly while "only" being able to sever the other's rifle. The surviving Piscean reached down to its waistbelt and withdrew a curious-looking cylinder. With a quick jerk of its wrist, the cylinder extended into a traditional Piscean pike. Deflecting Yusuf's slash with its pole, the Piscean spun its melee weapon overhead and thrust it at the attacking Leo, only for Yusuf to evade. Rapidly executing two more thrusts in an attempt to impale the Leo, the invader screeched in frustration as Yusuf eluded each. Swiftly, Yusuf sidestepped the next stab and plunged his left claw deep into his enemy's torso. Though the beam gun parts of his bane-claws lacked the apparent enhancements of his brother's set, the claws, augmented by his armor's shielding, were more than able to break through his prey's defenses. With a high pitched shriek, the piscinoid dropped his pike. Yusuf deftly withdrew his left claw as he slashed the Piscean across the face with his right. Another fishman eliminated.

Sensing movement, the Leo pivoted on his left leg, narrowly ducking another pike thrust from behind. Completing his turn, he kicked the new attacker directly in the upper body, paralyzing its breathing and knocking it to the ground. Letting out another fierce bellow as he leaped on the momentarily stunned Piscean, the enraged Leo buried both claws deep into its head. The fishman no longer moved.

Also engaged in a pike attack, Barbarossa shifted to his right to deflect a slash aimed at his throat. Reacting fast, the Piscean retracted his pike into a shorter length and attempted to stab the Leo in the chest. Unsuccessful, it quickly spun the weapon to defend against the rapid follow-up claw attacks. However, the Piscean was so focused on the Leo's claws that it didn't anticipate the spin kick. Barbarossa smashed his heel against the side of the fish being's helmet, sending the attacker flying backward. It landed in a heap some distance away, allowing Barbarossa to finish it off with a pair of beam shots.

Two more fish creatures swiftly pressed forward with their pikes extended, while a third remained slightly behind them, trying to get a bead with its rifle. Ignoring the shooter for a moment, the warrior concentrated on the advancing pair, evading the pike thrust of one and deflecting the second. Barbarossa feigned to leap, then spun around, catching his prey off guard and slashing it across its back. A quick kick to the knees, claws extended, and the crippled, incapacitated piscinoid fell. Another kick sent the creature into a nearby building where local armed inhabitants happily ended its life.

Its incensed compatriot charged, swinging its pike at the massive Leo. Barbarossa dodged out of the blade's line, then crouched and tackled the Piscean, embedding his claws into its chest as they collided with a light pole. The injury wasn't enough to kill his adversary, however, and the piscinoid continued to stab at the Leo. Its strikes were incapable of piercing Barbarossa's armor, but one came close to connecting with the Leo's head. Aggravated, at the next thrust of the pike, Barbarossa deflected the blade tip with the back of his baneclaw, forcing the weapon aside, before proceeding to shred apart his newest victim, letting out another roar as he went. Seconds later, while tossing the new corpse to the street, an energy beam flew over his right shoulder, Surprised, Barbarossa dumped the body and jumped out of the way. The rifle bearer had at last lined up a shot.

Another polearm fighter resumed the attack, thrusting, stabbing anything to impale the red-mane demon. Again Barbarossa was forced to ignore the shooter in the face of the immediate threat, dodging or deflecting each pike attack as it came. A moment later, he grasped the pike and yanked it forward, slamming its unprepared wielder into his chest armor. It didn't take much effort to bury his right baneclaw into the fishman's lower torso, rip it away just as quickly and follow up with a trio of beam shots. The Piscean was dead before its body even began its final descent to the ground.

Spinning to face the rifle equipped warrior, Barbarossa saw he need not bother. While he finished off his previous victim, Yusuf had moved behind his adversary and impaled his baneclaws into the piscinoid's back and penetrated its chest, lifted the Piscean into the air, and flung it across the avenue. It landed against the side of a building, caving in the wall upon impact. It did not get up again.

Both Leos scrutinized their immediate surroundings, making sure that there were no more enemies in the vicinity. As there were none, they both visibly stood down, but only momentarily.

"There will be much more where they came from," Yusuf warned as he strode over to his elder sibling. "The bottom feeders are poor warriors individually, but there are always a lot of them."

"Indeed," Barbarossa acknowledged studying the dead Pisceans' armor, attempting to identify their dag's insignia. Unfortunately, nothing was recognizable to him. "I'm sorry, Yusuf, but I'm afraid this is where we part ways."

Yusuf nodded in agreement. As much as he would have loved to fight the Pisceans alongside his brother, both had their commitments to uphold. Alongside, Yusuf couldn't risk bringing Leo into a war with the Confederacy, or even a segment of it.

"My ship is on standby, brother. I can get off this Aslan forsaken rock at any time."

"And mine is already well within the process," Barbarossa conferred. He reached out and grasping his younger brother's shoulder. Though he knew deep in his heart it would not be the last time he would see Yusuf, he had a feeling their next meeting would be a long time yet. "Unto Aslan's glory, Yusuf."

Nodding again, Yusuf grasped his brother's hand. "Unto His glory, brother," he affirmed, then smirked. "And the fortune of His followers."

Smiling, Barbarossa retracted his hand and turned, moving in the direction where The *Black Sun* waited.

Yusuf watched as his brother's red mane grew distant. Though he remained tempted to call to him, to implore him to return to Leo with him, he again knew why Barbarossa would refuse, or more precisely, why he couldn't accept. Sadly, he was resigned to watching him go, all the while silently praying that Aslan continue to watch over his prodigal sibling. He also prayed for Aslan to watch over him, his family, and their Caliphate in their most desperate hour.

Prayers finished, Yusuf withdrew to his ship.

Ducking underneath the beam fire, Jon charged at the nearest Piscean soldier, slashing its chest with a darkness empowered knife-edge, striking it down, before turning away and forming a black wall to absorb the fire from another unit. He leaped into the air and landed amid the group. Performing a spin flash, the black emanating from Astaroth cut down whatever its blade didn't physically touch, thereby wiping out the entirety of that Piscean company. Without pause, the group continued moving through the streets toward the waiting *Sun*, the still unconscious Lorelei held safely within Kaiser's arms.

It wasn't long before they encountered another faction of soldiers firing their rifles as they approached. Kaiser and Apache took cover once more; Anna, Boss, and Gran returned fire, their enhanced weaponry taking down a fair number of the Pisceans immediately. Jon again charged forward with Astaroth brandished. Responding to the threat, the enemy soldiers scattered for cover, but that posed no great difficulty to the Flints, especially their captain.

Weaving through the fire and using Astaroth's energy to absorb whatever could not be evaded, Jon rushed what he assumed to be the squad leader, slamming the obsidian blade against its freshly drawn pike. The Piscean attempted to knock the sword aside and impale the pirate, but Jon was quicker, dodging to his left to both evade the stab as well as cut the soldier on its right side. The Piscean stumbled forward a few steps but didn't go down, thus prompting Jon to launch an energy wave to engulf and finish it. Several more beam shots struck his initial position prompting the elder Flint to leap away. A moment later, he landed directly behind another invading soldier, one swing of Astaroth, and the fishman was promptly beheaded. Spinning, he unleashed another black wave at a third Piscean, which had been attempting to sneak behind him for a back shot. The aroma of burnt fish wafted through the air.

The emergence of a nearby blaze indicated Alex's return; Jon had initially sent him and Kaguya to serve as the vanguard for their little group. Driving an enormous fireball toward another unit of Pisceans, the younger Flint swept through his enemies without hindrance, all the while the alien soldiers struggled to defend themselves, let alone inflict any kind of harm upon their attackers. The visible relish upon the Red Devil's face as he incinerated another squad of the piscinoids with a single sweep of Forneus only further established the lack of obstruction.

"I'm havin' fish tonight!" Alex shouted in an exaggerated colonial accent as he burned through a pair of enemy soldiers, cremating them before they could fire a shot at the younger Flint. Reaching out his left hand, he unleashed a scattershot of flame at another three Pisceans that were attempting to overrun his position, pikes in hand. Two of them were reduced to ash, while the third managed to spin its polearm through the flame, diminish it, and then move to impale. However, it was nothing for Alex to parry the strike and then bifurcate his adversary at the torso, both flaming halves falling to the ground.

As the second Flint went about his attack, another Piscean several meters behind him pulled a grenade from a hip pouch and moved to throw. It never completed the motion, as little more than a second later, a kunai impaled the soldier's hand and struck the grenade, causing it to detonate prematurely. Kaguya moved in with ninjato in hand, slicing her way through another line of soldiers as she went. Only one managed to get a rifle shot off before being struck, to which the kunoichi effortlessly swatted it from the air.

"I prefer *futomaki*," she commented dryly as she jumped back, narrowly evading another burst of beam fire. She swiftly retaliated with a multiple shuriken throw, the spinning blades piercing the Pisceans' shielding and armor upon impact.

Damn, Alex thought, momentarily transfixed with Kaguya as she fought, cutting down the Pisceans into proverbial Ryugu rolls. He wasn't so distracted, however, that he failed to notice another pike wielder move in from behind. Twisting around, the younger Flint deflected the attack then brought his sword around to slash the blade end of the pike off the pole,

Forneus' superheated edge quickly cutting through the Piscean weapon. From there, it was an even simpler effort to cut the soldier down before it could reach for its pistol.

Not to be outdone by the pair, Jon charged through another formation, slicing as he went before his opponents could bring their weapons to bear. Pausing, he formed another black energy wave, this one sweeping across whatever Pisceans remained standing from his initial attack. A thrown pike whistled past. A soldier was hiding in nearby rubble. Leaping, Jon landed directly behind the piscinoid and ran it through. The elder Flint then promptly withdrew his blade, allowing the newly rendered corpse to fall.

Suddenly, Jon's ears picked up a distinct noise. "Incoming!" he warned as he bolted for cover.

Sure enough, another bomber came streaking down from the sky, shooting a spray of beam and rocket fire over the immediate vicinity. Buildings and avenues went up in a matter of moments, while the death cries of multiple beings rang through the air.

Unfortunately for the Piscean pilot, however, the Flints had managed to gain cover just in time – Jon and Alex having raised shields to absorb/deflect any fire – and so were only lightly touched by the attack. Retaliating, the brothers launched respective waves of flame and darkness toward the bomber, which had foolishly twisted around for another pass. The craft was instantly overwhelmed, its destruction alternating between an explosion and an implosion. Whatever parts remained rained down to the streets below.

Pausing for a small moment to witness the bomber's destruction, Alex turned to the others. "Come on!" he signaled as he and Jon started moving again. The pirates were quick to keep up.

─────────────────────

What a day! What a day! Davis inwardly ranted as he let loose his Antilles 94 into anything that looked even remotely amphibious. It had been bad enough when his shore leave had been so abruptly cut short, especially after all the trouble he went through to make the night worthwhile. But now he was fighting his way through a planetary invasion just to get back to his ship. And as if that wasn't bad enough, he seemed to be the only Flint Pirate in this area of Rougetown. There were other allied combatants, sure, but most of them were hardly putting up a fight against the Pisceans, let alone killing them. Only Davis seemed to be making any progress, his supercharged Antilles breaking through the fishnoid's shields and armor with relative ease, but he was still only one man. And there seemed to be an infinite number of Pisceans.

Shooting another one of the enemy soldiers in the chest, Davis continued to run down the street, moving ever closer to the *Black Sun*. Despite what his fellow crewmates may have thought of him, the helmsman was familiar with combat. He was a reasonably good shot, as the line of dead Pisceans behind him could attest to, and he was apt at finding any cover and firing points that were available, as demonstrated when he scored a headshot on one of the charging pike wielders. After that, he threw himself behind a nearby pile of debris just as its rifle-armed brethren renewed their fire.

Taking a moment to catch his breath and evade the shooting, he adjusted his pistol's setting slightly then peered up over the stack of stones and rubble to return the favor to his aggressors. No, he wasn't inexperienced with combat in the least; he had seen his fair share both within Imperial service and his life of piracy. The problem was, unlike certain crewmates of his, Davis was not a one-person killing machine by any stretch of the imagination. He could definitely hold his own in a firefight – which he was doing now – but he wasn't a Marine or a raider, and he certainly wasn't a Devilblade Wielder. He could take down a fair number of the fishmen, but at this rate, one of them would eventually get him. He was not so convinced of his immortality to believe otherwise.

Damn it! Davis glowered as he struck down two more Pisceans, forcing the others to dash for cover. That was enough for him to move again, and so he abandoned the debris pile and continued running, firing at seemingly every angle as he went.

There is no end to these sardines, the helmsman fumed. *Kill one, and there's always another or two to pick up the slack! It's a goddamn trout farm!*

It helped even less that they had close-air support, as Davis' ears picked up the telltale sounds of a bomber diving down behind him, strafing beam fire along a set of buildings. He dared not look back; he simply thanked whatever power might be in the universe that it hadn't focused on him and continued moving.

A few minutes later – which might as well had been hours from his perspective – he rounded another corner and nearly ran right into another Piscean troop. Fortunately, he was quick enough to duck back behind the building as green beam fire erupted all around. Without taking much time to aim, he returned fire to keep the attackers on the defensive. One of those wildly aimed shots managed to clip an intended target in the shoulder, the resultant screech of pain alerting the others that their shields and armor were useless against the dark-haired pirate. As a result, the other the piscinoids paused their advance, spread out, and took cover. Capitalizing on the break in the fighting, and using the retaining walls of the building's garden for concealment, Davis crawled away, willing himself to keep moving toward the *Sun*.

A small distance away, the Lady Killer stood up to continue his run for the ship. No sooner had he exited his hiding spot than he heard another telltale noise: a piercing battle cry from behind him. Twisting around and bringing his pistol about, Davis nearly managed to squeeze the trigger when the charging Piscean smacked his Antilles out of his hand with its pike. Cursing, Davis dodged the initial thrust and then attempted to grasp the polearm and yank it away, but his hands were unable to grip the pike through the Piscean's shielding, which naturally covered its weapon as well. As such, Davis could only dodge several more times before his adversary finally got smart and swept the pike through his feet, knocking the Terran to the ground. It was all Davis could do to raise his hands – one last feeble attempt to grab the pike before it struck – as the Piscean poised its weapon for the kill…

It never made it! A beam, a familiar crimson beam, burned through the

Piscean's back and out its chest. Acting on instinct, Davis rolled out of the way as the corpse fell, its armor clanging against the ground like a collection of metal buckets.

"Get your sorry ass up Lady Killer!" a harsh Terran voice barked as more beam fire erupted, followed by additional Piscean death cries. "Before you become fish chum!"

Ears burning, Davis recognized the voice which, alongside that particular gun, could only belong to one being in the universe. He scrambled to his feet and reclaimed his Antilles. Embarrassed, yet relieved, he aimed at another Piscean only for his target to be shot square through the left eye. The helmsman turned toward the source of the fire, which was advancing swiftly through the area, gunning down any and every Piscean he saw.

"For the record, I was doing quite well before you showed up!"

"Sure you were," the tall, muscular built Terran male sneered, his fading brown hair falling over the collar of his black shirt. He continued to reduce the ranks of the Piscean assault teams with his Grenada J-34 beam pistol, while effortlessly moving about in the manner of an action viso hero. "You were amazing against Nemo back there!"

"Screw you!" Davis snarled as he fired more shots from his Antilles.

As good as Davis was, however, he was *nothing* compared to the man he was fighting alongside. The man who had yet to miss a single kill. Not that he would ever have admitted it to the bastard, who as far as the helmsman was concerned personified the smug arrogance of his combatant type. Whether marine, soldier, or raider, they were all the same to him.

"And screw that stupid shirt!"

No sense of taste, Bartholomew Cheney, sub-commander of the Flint Pirate raiders, thought as he struck down another fish type with a headshot. Indeed the black and gold emblemed shirt he was wearing, which read, "I'M JUST ONE BIG FREAKING RAY OF SUNSHINE AREN'T I?" with a stylized, smiley-faced sun alongside, was one of his favorites, as well as something of a novelty in this day and age. It made him further adamant not to get shot, even more so than the obvious.

Additional beam fire erupted just as Davis opened his mouth to comment further. So much in fact that Cheney ended up grabbing him and throwing him behind another set of rubble before joining him.

"Don't bother, son," the sub-commander ordered before promptly shooting the attacker off the top of a nearby building without ever looking up. The fresh corpse fell to the ground with a hardened crash, again reminding Davis of an action viso. "Just shut up and be a Fish Killer for five more minutes!"

With that, the senior raider abandoned his cover and went back to shooting anything that moved an inch against him. Glowering, Davis took another breath before following the raider's example.

What a day!

Finally, Jon thought as he and those with him made it back to the port where the *Sun* was moored. It was evident the Pisceans had been unable to board her, though not for lack of trying. A large number of the fishmen had spread out across the dock, attempting to advance on the umbra. Several more were coming up out of the water around her, just managing to reach her hull. Fortunately, she was not unguarded. A contingent of raiders had taken position about the dock as well as the hull, defending their ship and oncoming crew members against the horde. And as indicated by the large number of dead Pisceans encompassing the area, the invaders had yet to accomplish this particular objective.

There wasn't much time to assess the situation, however, as the aggressors had noticed the new pirate group's arrival. Several green-tinted beam shots launched at them. Glowering simultaneously, the Flint brothers both raised energy shields to absorb/deflect while the others returned fire, taking out several of the attackers. Immediately, Alex and Kaguya charged in, adding their blades to the fight, while Jon took momentary cover behind a collection of crates.

"Foxtrot One to Papa Bravo," Jon called out over his wristcom, raising his voice to be heard over the constant beam fire. "Status report."

"I'm already aboard, Captain," Braun replied, evidently at his post. "All systems are engaged and awaiting imminent departure."

Though a part of him wondered why, and how, the Professor had gotten back to the ship so fast, Jon knew better than to question the situation. There were higher priorities at hand.

"Crew?"

"Seventy-three percent have returned by this time," Braun reported just as quickly. "More are coming in as we speak."

As if to emphasize that last point, an all too familiar roar erupted across the dock. Barbarossa had arrived. He rushed a group of fishmen that the raiders hadn't managed to kill, baneclaws properly brandished. The Pisceans were caught off guard and unable to mount a defense as the infamous Beast King savaged them, not unlike an actual Terran lion hunting fish in a river. Only one of their number managed to strike a glancing blow, its pike grazing Barbarossa's shoulder armor right before the Leo shredded it with the rest of its brethren.

Taking a moment to acknowledge the Leo, Jon then shifted back to Braun. "We'll hold out until all crew are accounted for," he informed the Professor. "But standby for emergency launch regardless."

"Understood."

Cutting communication, Jon was forced to leap away. A Piscean grenade landed near his initial position and obliterated everything in the area.

"Get going!" Alex called out to Kaiser and Apache after immolating another soldier and enlarging the opening he created for them in the enemy's line.

Unfortunately, the younger Flint didn't have time to see if they moved out or not. Alex ducked the pike attack of a fishman, which let out the Piscean equivalent of a battle cry as it lunged. He raised Forneus to strike but switched to forming an energy shield to deflect the attack of a second Piscean advancing from the left, and a third moving to impale him in the back.

And me without teriyaki sauce, Alex thought bemusedly as he jumped back, skipping on top of the third's head in the process. With a backward kick to its skull, the pirate vaulted away, his weight and movement knocking the Piscean off balance. It stumbled and inadvertently impaled its comrade on the left, collided with the corpse, and bumped into the other pikeman. Still airborne, Alex laughed and unleashed a fire wave that took out all three at once, before promptly landing a short distance away, where another horde naturally came at him. Alex resumed deflecting and evading beam fire and pike attacks. *Or a decent Moscato that compliments fish for that matter...*

That was as far as he could think, more screeching soldiers charged from the left. He raised an energy shield to repel their pike thrusts, then attempted to turn and counterattack. Another Piscean charged in from the opposite side, and no less than three additional Pisceans were waiting for him from behind. Alex glowered at all of this, especially as further opponents kept coming after him. Compared to Imperial Marines and their ilk, Pisceans – not unlike an actual school of fish – were not much individually, but could be quite effective in groups. For every Piscean Alex cut or incinerated, more moved in where their comrade had been. The symmetry around their attacks – again not unlike an actual school of fish - didn't help in the least. Even with Forneus, Alex found himself becoming more and more defensive.

As the youngest son of Morganna Flint, he had no intention of getting killed by something usually found on a wall plaque. And though he was surrounded, such that he had to generate a full three hundred and sixty-degree shield, it wasn't hard to gain breathing room. Focusing his Devilblade's power, he let out a roar, unleashing a superheated, outward expanding fireball. The Pisceans closest to his position were vaporized, those farther out incinerated, their ash blowing around the dock. Those on the peripheral edges of the *school* were fatally burned. And yet the onslaught kept coming....

Screw the teriyaki, Alex thought as he went back to cutting and burning every Piscean he could move against, focusing on the attack to keep them from defending or stacking up against him again. *Chips and tartar sauce will do just nicely!*

Some distance away, Kaguya was in a similar predicament, a horde of the Pisceans were focusing their attention on her. She wasn't sure if they recognized her as the daughter of Fuma Kotaro or assumed because she fought with a "mere" ninjato and assorted throwing blades, that she would be easier prey. They were moving to surround and overrun her position. Inwardly, she smiled; this was nothing she couldn't handle, this *mai odoru*.

With an overhead swing, she cleaved a Piscean in two as it charged, parried the strike of another, then turning, keeping the other piscinoids in her peripheral vision, she sidestepped out of the way of a pike counterattack and, with one hand, severed her opponent's foremost leg. She then knocked the polearm aside and spun her sword around, allowing her to impale the Piscean through the torso.

"Pirate scum!" the Piscean hissed as it dropped its pike and grasped onto the blade, forcing it deeper into itself while flashing its fang-like teeth.

"Sashimi," Kaguya responded derisively before ripping away her sword, the body falling to the ground.

That wasn't the end, of course. Responding to the charge of additional combatants, the kunoichi twisted around and launched three kunai, which struck three of the approaching soldiers in vital areas. She spun and ran forward to bring her sword against the rest. As she wasn't wearing her tacsuit - a fact she was beginning to find highly annoying - she had to concentrate on evasion, weaving around and deflecting/redirecting each pike thrust and beam shot. Her enemies' superior numbers continued to leave her with little maneuvering room, but the Dragon Princess had survived much worse, even amongst their kind.

Slashing another across the chest, Kaguya banked to her left to evade the pike thrust of its comrade. She reversed her ninjato and impaled the fishman through the back. Unfortunately, she realized upon withdrawing her blade that she hadn't hit any vital innard; as a result, the Piscean twisted around to stab her with its pike, forcing the ninja to jump away. Countering, she launched a shuriken from midair, but, as she ducked to avoid a thrown pike from another adversary, her aim wasn't as sure. The spinning blade only managed to embed itself into the fishnoid's shoulder. It turned, screeched that high-pitch battle cry, she assumed it was a battle cry, and rushed at her.

Definitely like mai odoru, *'with a clear mind, the right technique at the right time delivered at the right speed to the right target at the right distance,'* the Dragon Princess ruminated, remembering an old tactical formula of being "in the zone."

Landing, she crouched and charged against the alien's right, bifurcating it at the waist with a diagonal cut she knew would be critical. Not taking any chances, she finished it off with another shuriken throw, to the back of the alien's neck, where it pierced deep into its spine.

And the horde continued to surge toward her, though now a little more cautious and respectful. Kaguya, turning to face the oncoming Pisceans, was surprised to see a flurry of crimson bolts strike them from her left, each a precision hit to critical areas. The chief raider of the Flint Pirates watched as her number two moved onto the scene, his pistol trained and awaiting additional targets. She also noticed Davis trailing some distance behind him, shooting at the Pisceans with determination, if somewhat panicked, but nowhere near as much precision.

"Commander," Cheney nodded respectfully to his superior as he moved past.

"Master Chief," Kaguya replied. Joining him, both warriors brought their weapons about and charged back into the fight.

Breathing heavily as he flung himself behind another debris pile, Davis peered at the nearest *Black Sun* entryway. He knew he had to get over there and inside; their quick getaway depended on him being at the helm, far more so than his aiding in the present fight. And of course, there was also the fact he wanted to stay alive and breathing, which he would have a much better chance of doing inside the *Sun*'s hyperium hull than out here in the open, caught between the sardines from hell and potential friendly fire. He had no illusions about the latter with certain crew members, namely those he owed money or otherwise had past relations with their significant others.

Unfortunately, he couldn't move from his current location. He was overcome with fear, and his leg muscles were quite strained, having run through a relatively large portion of the city in order to reach the ship. He would be lucky to stand back up, let alone make a run under fire toward that entryway.

"Three days…!" Davis muttered as he held his Antilles close, nearly jumping when an explosion occurred near his position. Despite his terror and quivering legs, he was starting to feel anger coarse through his veins, not that he knew where to direct it, of course. The injustices he had to endure were intolerable. "Three days without running or shooting! Was that too bloody much to ask for!?"

"Story of our lives, Davis," a familiar voice retorted, causing the helmsman to jerk. Somehow in the middle of his little tirade, Alex had landed right next to him and was now observing his subordinate's present state with open bemusement.

"Alex!" Davis gasped, just as another beam shot struck the debris pile, sending rock shards and metal fragments in all directions. "Thank god!"

"I should hope," Alex rejoined as he peered over their cover, Forneus in hand. "I don't suppose you were with a Dagon's daughter at some point…"

"Wha-!? Hell, no!" Davis growled, visibly disgusted at the very idea. "Just because it's female doesn't mean I'll bed it!"

"A considerable portion of the galaxy would say otherwise," Alex scoffed. In truth, he doubted Davis' lust was so intense that he would even take to fish people. Just as he also doubted that Davis was the reason for all this. "Not to mention certain crewmembers…"

"Look," Davis stated, returning to the matter at hand. Though he was reluctant, he knew he had a better chance with Alex than with anyone else outside his captain. "If we're going to get out of here, you need me at the helm. For that, I have to make a run for the ship. I need you to cover me.

Got it?"

Alex looked toward the ship and back at Davis. "What's it to you?" he asked.

The helmsman could barely believe it. "Goddammit Alex! We're in the middle of a firefight for crying…!"

Yet another beam struck nearby, Davis nearly soiled his pants.

"I see it as a good bargaining opportunity," Alex replied, completely unperturbed, even as he moved out from cover to launch a wall of flame at a group of nearby Pisceans. "Especially since I can get you there instantly."

Suddenly, Davis was interested. "Really?" Did the younger Flint unlock some new ability with Forneus that he hadn't seen yet?

"Sure, but it'll cost you," Alex declared, just as another shot struck the ground behind the pirates. Surveying the fight, Alex saw additional Piscean soldiers moving onto the dock and advancing toward their position. "Unfortunately, I can't name the price right now, but rest assured you will owe me."

"Fine!" Davis hollered, seeing the reinforcements coming in as well. "Just get me the hell out of here!"

"With pleasure," Alex grinned wholeheartedly, right before reaching and grasping Davis by the throat and lifting him. Despite the obvious temptation, he didn't apply pressure. And though he struggled, Davis was unable to break the younger Flint's grip, while his eyes failed to move away from the Red Devil's grinning face. It was only then that the Lady Killer realized what was about to happen.

Looking toward the intended destination, Alex, after encompassing a field of flame around Davis, *flung* his captive down the dock. The helmsman flew like a burning comet through the air, naturally screaming all the way. And then, as indicated by a massive clang, Davis sailed through the entryway, slammed into the nearby bulkhead, and fell to the deck floor.

"Score!" Alex chimed victoriously before rebrandishing Forneus, leaping over the debris and returning to the fight. Uttering a rather large and loud line of cuss words, Davis scrambled to his feet and ran toward the bridge.

———————————— ————————————

Swish, Jon thought in bemusement, having paused briefly to watch Davis' impromptu flight. Had he not been in the middle of a battle, he would have commented more, but he remained as committed to defending his ship as those around him.

Parrying a slash from his adversary's pike, Jon turned his wrist outwards and swept the weapon aside, forcing it out of the fishman's hand, only for another enemy soldier to move against him from the left. Instantly, he generated an energy field, absorbing the fishnoid's pike, which the soldier was keen enough to release before being sucked into the void alongside its weapon. Now unarmed, it was defenseless against Jon's quick spin and extension of Astaroth. Green blood flowed from the slash around its throat. Turning, Jon unleashed another black wave to eliminate the rifle bearers, yet, as he had come to expect, several more of their kind advanced to replace their comrades, forcing him to put up another shield to absorb their fire.

I was correct, Jon concurred as he watched the newcomers move in, only to scatter once he used Astaroth to redirect their fire. Though their shields deflected the ricocheting beam shots, the force of the hits was enough to catch them off-guard and make them seek cover away from the vaunted Black Angel. *We are their objective.*

He had suspected it since the fight had begun, but it was only now that Jon was able to confirm that hypothesis. Indeed, there could be no other explanation for the Pisceans' assault on Nassau, not when they were focusing so many troops upon the *Black Sun* and her crew. Granted, Jon doubted Nassau had anything else of equal value to the *Sun*, and as he and Alex had discussed with Ernie before, the Flint Pirates had been making quite the name for themselves as of late. Surely the capture or destruction of either would grant the Piscean Confederacy, if not the specific Dag that was perpetrating the attack, inordinate prestige amongst the other nations of the galaxy.

At least, that was what Jon hoped. Compared to *another* explanation, which he dreaded far more…

"Papa Bravo to Foxtrot One!" Jon's wristcom suddenly beeped. "All crew are now accounted for! We may depart at any time!"

Hearing that, Jon enveloped himself in darkness and charged through his Piscean attackers, those unable to dodge in time were absorbed wholesale. Once he reached a clearing, he allowed the darkness to dissipate.

"Acknowledged," the elder Flint stated before tapping the appropriate command on his wristcom, signaling all other Flint defenders to return to the ship. He extended his hand and black holes formed in front of the remaining Pisceans, halting their approach and absorbing all attacks. The pirate captain maintained the black voids until all other Flint combatants were onboard. Then, with a flick of his hand, the voids sped forward in a great wave, encompassing any Piscean soldier that remained at the dock. Turning, Jon ran for the open entryway.

Piscean *Gnaiih*-class battleship *Grah'n* Nassau System

Yet another barrage of neon green beam fire discharged, followed by another of Nassau's would-be defenders being struck. Explosions rippled across her hull an instant later. He found himself frowning at the display, an expression that remained even as the enemy vessel – which might have passed as a cruiser if it wasn't cobbled together with scrap and refuse – gave into her wounds and detonated. His frown only deepened when another ship, a frigate he guessed, attempted to replace its comrade, launching a spray of torpedoes as it passed. It took but a moment for the torpedoes to be intercepted and blotted out, and another to destroy the frigate.

"They are truly a valiant breed, these pirates," the *Grah'n*'s captain commented from the side, actually appearing impressed with the opposition. Even now, after so much loss and destruction, these *pirate scum* remained willing to fight the taskforce. All in clear spite of their significantly reduced numbers. "Far more so than certain others amongst our kind…"

He smiled and nodded. Yes, the pirates were dying in droves, but the fact remained they were putting up a fight, doing all they could to hinder the invaders from occupying their world. Valiance, as the *Grah'n*'s captain stated, valiance that would have greatly benefitted the Confederacy if it was embraced by all factions. A harrowing thought to be sure, seeing such bravery and dedication in ordinary miscreants, as opposed to the warriors and leadership of certain Dags, which would have undoubtedly fled at first sight of the enemy. Not that he, or any other member of the taskforce, held any kind of kinship with the "outsider" blocs of the Confederacy. They were all the same in terms of race and civilization, but that was as far as it went.

Hopefully, that will soon change, he thought, as he watched another mishmashed pirate ship obliterated by one of his cruisers' missiles. And it would once everything fell into place.

"Picking up arc readings from the surface," the tactical officer called out to the captain. "The *Black Sun* is ascending."

Within a second, the main monitor illuminated and zoomed in, showing a distinct black and gold profile launching itself from the surface into space. His dismay flared at the sight of the umbra. He had sincerely hoped they would be able to capture her on the surface, but it seemed his troops were insufficient for the task. Inwardly he cringed; he would endure much from their "guest" later for this failure.

"Ignore the remainders," he commanded, just as another of said "remainders" was obliterated by missile fire from another one of his cruisers. "All ships, intercept the *Black Sun* at once!"

Flint Pirates umbra *Black Sun*
Nassau System

When it rains, it pours… Jon thought, repeating his brother's earlier statement, as he watched the silhouettes of the Piscean warships enter into view. They were already starting to move away from their initial opposition, or what had at least attempted to be their initial opposition, as indicated by the newly created debris field, and set an intercept course toward the *Sun*. He exhaled through his nostrils. *We are definitely their objective.*

"Piscean taskforce now moving on intercept course," Barbarossa reported as he looked over his display, gazing at the tactical profiles of the battleship – a *Gnaiih*-class – her three cruiser escorts – all *Hlighr*-class – and their various support craft with interest. Piscean ship designs were quite unlike those of Terra or Leo; their surfaces were smooth and organic in appearance as if they were specifically designed to emulate aquatic lifeforms, yet all the same quite predatory.

"Shall we engage?"

Ignoring the collective expectation of the rest of the bridge crew, Jon took a moment to consider. By all appearances, it would have been an easy battle. The *Sun* had fought against much worse in the past, and her crew was as well attuned to fighting in space as they were upon a planet surface. One battleship and three cruisers would be mincemeat in a fight with her, whether she engaged them under cloak or in the open.

On the other hand, as he watched the enemy ships continue to close in, Jon sensed something was off in their approach. The *Black Sun*'s capabilities were well established, at least as well established as the resurgent Flint name that she carried, so much so that whoever was commanding the taskforce would have been fully briefed on them. And yet, rather than take an elaborate stratagem as Drake had done at Ephesus, the Pisceans were moving for a traditional frontal attack. Something that should have been an obvious suicide, even if they did have additional ships waiting to join the taskforce.

If Jon's hypothesis was correct, they were not after the *Black Sun* or even the Flint Brothers. For the true target, the Pisceans would indeed have come prepared.

"No," Jon stated, deciding then and there not to risk it. "Cloak the ship and activate the Psi Disruptor."

Barbarossa raised an eyebrow. "Captain?" he inquired, already feeling something amiss. He wasn't the only one either, as several other eyes looked toward their captain in confusion.

"You heard me," Jon replied, then turned to the helm. "Mr. Davis, course is at your discretion. Get us away now."

Though confused by Jon's behavior, Davis immediately complied. "Aye, sir," he answered as he began plotting the appropriate course.

"Cloaking," Barbarossa reported. "Psi Disruptor online."

Jon nodded, continuing to watch the Piscean ships as they advanced. If his supposition was right, the Pisceans would be completely blind to them now, more so than if he had simply cloaked the ship. Unfortunately, there was no way for him to verify that, at least not at this time. He had a feeling that would change soon.

"Course plotted and locked in," Davis announced, taking one more breath. "Arc Drive standing by."

"Engage," Jon commanded, in the form of an Ancient Terran captain whose name escaped him.

With that, the *Black Sun* entered into arcspace, leaving Nassau, and those invading it, all behind her.

Chapter VII: Ignotum Per Ignotius

Perhaps she had overexerted herself; maybe she had acted prematurely altogether. In either case, she had not anticipated such a disastrous outcome. Not when she had simply intended communication with the one she sought and nothing more.

Regardless, the damage was done. In her haste to reach out, she had inadvertently overwhelmed the one she sought with her power. That had been far from her intent. She hadn't thought, as much as she could 'think' in her present state, that it was possible, as much of her strength was still largely restrained to the abyss around her. But then, in that initial thought, she had only considered its volume rather than its *nature*. An error on her part she realized now. Her attempted outreach would have been entirely foreign and incomprehensible to the one she had chosen. The results spoke for themselves.

Despite everything, however, her actions, as limited as they had been, were not quite a failure. Surely the songstress was aware of her now after hearing her voice calling out from the abyss. Perhaps not as aware as would have been preferred, but the songstress now knew of her existence.

That would suffice, especially after the inadvertent shock created with the contact. Anything more would be a tremendous risk, more than she was willing to make at this time.

Overall, while not as cordial as she had hoped, it was all proceeding by her will. Now that initial contact had been made and her existence firmly established, the songstress and her allies would be gradually drawn to her. Though her perception was once more quite limited, she was cognizant enough of events happening in the galaxy at large; aware that at least two impetuously powerful empires were now in conflict over her, or at least what they believed her to be, and threatening to evoke a great war to claim her. This, alongside the ramifications of her initial contact, would retain the attention of the songstress' allies. They would search to discover what was occurring within the "sea of dreams" that surrounded her, and how it affected their patron. They would come for her, and the songstress would travel with them.

That made her even more hopeful. An emotion, as with all others which were slowly returning to memory, that she had not held in a long, long time...

Flint Pirates umbra *Black Sun*
Arcspace

"Alright," Davis began, already feeling a migraine coming on. One that had *not* originated from the grog and companionship he had been enjoying earlier.

"Now that everything has finally settled down, with us being out of the line of fire, and the ship flying at seven or eight times the speed of light toward the nearest cluster I could dredge up... perhaps someone can now answer the standing question..."

And then, not unlike lava from a volcano, or a flash of light from a self-destructing starship, the next line of words exploded from the helmsman's mouth in a virtual bang.

"What in the Seventh Circle just happened!?" he yelled, nearly slamming his fists on the table in frustration. "First, our patron saint goes off the deep end, and then, out of nowhere, we have another Galactic Power gunning for us! And it hasn't even been a full a day yet!"

"Technically speaking," Gran casually, and helpfully, pointed out. "It's more likely to have been a single Dag, as opposed to the whole Confederacy," she turned to the rest of the table, projecting reassurance. "Otherwise, we would have been facing much larger numbers, right?"

"To say the least," Alex replied with a bored expression. Not even the sight of Davis blowing a transmission board did anything for him at this time.

"One Dag, Two Dag, Red Dag, Blue Dag, whatever!" Davis continued to ramble. "Point is, someone is coming after us again, and dammit all, it isn't some Lacertan scavenger band!"

He then cast a glare at Jon. "And don't even bother trying to convince us that Lorelei had nothing to do with it or that the Pisceans weren't after her specifically…"

"And how in the First Circle did you come to that conclusion?" Anna interrupted, her expression just as bland as Alex's. Despite her words and reluctance toward agreeing with the helmsman, she had a good feeling Davis was onto something.

Davis shrugged. "Well, obviously they weren't after the *Sun* or the Flint Pirates at large, and they certainly weren't looking to conquer Nassau. Otherwise, they would have sent an entire fleet instead of a simple raiding force. Yet, all the same, they were focused on us specifically. They. Wanted. Something. We. Had."

He glared at Jon again.

"All just after half the city was fried with psionic lightning," he exclaimed snidely. "A pure coincidence, I'm sure."

Though some were obviously annoyed by the helmsman's tone and phrasing, his point nonetheless stood.

"The Psi Disruptor is active," Braun added on with a thoughtful tilt. His right hand, in its usual manner, automatically moved up to contact, so that Braun could rest his head against its metallic palm. "Which would mean they have psions amongst their forces…"

"Or they would be tracking the telepathic signature of the one among us," Davis finished for him, still glaring at the captain.

The Psi Disruptor was one of the first new additions to the *Black Sun* after Ephesus. As its name suggested, it disrupted psionic energy, effectively concealing the ship and its occupants from any kind of telepathy, as well as providing limited defense against telekinetics. Drake's little trick of utilizing psions to track the thoughts and feelings of the *Sun*'s crew, and therefore the *Sun* herself, would not be repeated.

"And I sure as hell didn't see any of the fishheads shoot fire and lightning from their fingertips."

Again the point resonated with the group.

"So how about it, Captain?" Davis spat, almost challengingly. "Is anything I just said wrong? Or are you going to pretend this is not happening?"

"Davis…" Alex growled in warning, flame flickering on his fingertips.

Jon raised his hand, signaling Alex to stop. Though hesitant, Alex nonetheless complied with his brother's wishes.

"It is as you said," Jon confirmed. "The Pisceans were clearly after Lorelei, and it's all too likely to be connected to her prior episode."

"'All too likely?'" Anna inquired, curious, as were the others.

Jon pressed further. "How many of you are aware of what's occurring around the Sognare Sea?"

Almost instantly, heads snapped back at the mention of the Sea.

"Way I heard it," Cheney entered in. "Both the sardines and the merfolk have claimed it as their own, and are gearing up to kill each other over ownership."

"So what?" Boss pressed. "How does that connect with Lorelei and her wiping a quarter of Roguetown off the globe?"

"Basic logic," Jon elaborated. "Sognare is too unstable to warrant any kind of territorial expansion, much less formal colonization or resource gathering. With that in mind, it's not the Sea that the Aquarians and Pisceans want in itself…"

"…but rather something in it," Anna concluded, seeing where Jon was going. "And whatever it is, they believe Lorelei is a key component in acquiring it."

Kaguya nodded, coming to the same conclusion. "At least one Dag believes so," she said, reminding everyone of what Gran had pointed out before. "Which itself indicates that the others are ignorant of her value."

"Assuming anything is actually there, of course," Davis snapped, skepticism all over his face. "And it still doesn't explain what caused her to go *vespertilio stercore rabidus.*"

Jon nodded, conceding the point. "Quite true, we're missing too much information. All we have are three pieces of an undoubted whole: the Pisceans and Aquarians are in direct conflict over Sognare, at least one faction of the Confederacy is after Lorelei…"

He then nodded at Alex. "And, based on recent events and those two prior facts, Lorelei is connected to Sognare in some way."

"It's been reported that the Sea has an adverse effect on psions in particular," Alex added. "Something about them perceiving it as a 'dream' or 'nightmare' in reality…"

"I've read those reports as well," Braun concurred. "Though in such cases, the subjects were always in relative proximity to the Sea. Nassau, by comparison, is practically on the other side of the sector."

"But, Lorelei is more powerful than the average psion," Barbarossa pointed out, before looking toward Apache. "And since we're speaking of our patron, I don't suppose she's active enough to provide additional answers."

"Far from it," Apache shook his head. "She's still taking up space in my sickbay, and that doesn't look to change any time soon."

"Well," Anna said, shrugging. "Kaguya did hit her pretty hard," she exclaimed, before casting a darker glance at the kunoichi, who pretended to ignore it. None of those who witnessed the event were under any illusion of the assassin's original intent toward the psion.

Again Apache shook his head. "Her injury is more psionic shock than anything physical. Whatever came over her was quite powerful, but that's already been established."

"'Came over her'?" Gran posited, suddenly quite hesitant. "Or 'reached out to her'?"

A cold shiver went over the entirety of the room as all twelve occupants considered that hypothesis. As much as they all wished to dismiss it as an exaggeration, none were able to do so. With everything that had occurred, along with all that had been established as fact, it was not feasible to discount the possibility.

"Whatever the truth, we need more information," Jon declared, narrowing his eye at the others. "For that, we'll start with the obvious: identifying the enemy and their objectives."

He nodded to Anna. "How many Pisceans do we have in the crew?"

Anna immediately recognized his intent. "One," she said, then looking back at Kaguya and Cheney. "Among the raiders."

Cheney nodded in confirmation. "Jaws," he said. "Good fighter, though I wouldn't share quarters with him," he grimaced. "Pisceans have a whole different idea toward personal hygiene than most."

"I don't suppose he took offense to our killing his brethren earlier." Davis retorted, still angry at the loss of shore leave.

"Please, he was practically in the center of it," Cheney snorted, bemused. "Whatever Dag attacked us, he'll know."

144

He glanced back at the captain. "Just as I get a distinct feeling, he'll take great pleasure in killing more of them in the future. The kid has a definite grudge against someone."

"That's one," Jon said before considering further. "For the second, a conspiracy like this will be fragmented and widespread, which means very few will have enough for a projected whole."

He then looked at Alex, the vestiges of a smirk forming across his lips.

"Fortunately, Alex and I happen to be well acquainted with someone who could help."

The younger Flint's look of confusion quickly gave way to frustration noticing the bemusement within his brother's expression. Groaning, Alex closed his eyes.

"Ciel."

"Ciel," Jon confirmed with a smile, before turning back to Gran, who, barely concealing a smirk of her own, nodded at her unspoken orders.

Tragedy Inn & Bordello
Penzance

Casually exhaling a lungful of light grey smoke, Ciel held her cigarette wand in hand as she looked at her desk monitor, where the Flint Brothers' faces remained prominently displayed.

"I must say this is quite the predicament you're in, *mes chers*," she exclaimed while, again casually, tapping some excess ash into a nearby tray.

The madam did nothing in haste. Her's was a world of sensual pleasure and sinister secrets. Many came to her for the first and left after inadvertently revealing the last. Patience was always rewarding and indicative of the moment action was required.

"If everything I've been hearing is true, you have officially ended up in the middle of the largest blood feud since the Plantagenets and Valois."

"So we have learned, firsthand," Jon replied dryly, Alex and Kaguya standing just behind him.

The younger Flint was trying to remain visibly neutral, and failing quite miserably if the chiding gazes that were continually flashed at him were any indication. Kaguya glared at the face on the monitor screen, her desire to launch a kunai into the madam evident. Ignoring both of them, Jon continued.

"That being said, we're very much in the dark with everything else…"

"Which is where I come in," Ciel finished for him, inhaling slowly and exhaling another collection of smoke from her wand. She glanced at Alex. "As you are aware, I can supply more than mere information, *mon chéri*."

"Yes," Jon confirmed with a nod, pulling Ciel's attention back to him. He leaned forward with utmost seriousness. "For now, we need to learn as much as possible about this vendetta, up to and including how it began and the identity of the ultimate prize."

"Because, they're clearly not fighting over fishing rights," Alex quipped.

He had thought to lighten the tension of the exchange. He promptly regretted it as Ciel flashed an alluring grin toward him.

"So you can still speak, after all, *mon amour*," she purred and stretched suggestively. "I was afraid some other cat had gotten your tongue."

She then flashed her eyes over to Kaguya. Her expression, while retaining affability, became far less friendly.

"Or a little *yariman hime* for that matter."

Not the first time since the conversation began was Jon glad Ciel wasn't physically present, as he could imagine all the things Kaguya would have attempted had she been. Or, for that matter, what Ciel would have tried in reverse.

The two had met some months ago, when the *Sun* had last visited Penzance and Jon, needing certain information, had chosen to visit Ciel while in the colony. Though Ciel had always been respectful to him, in a way that Jon suspected an aspiring bride treated her future brother-in-law, he knew it was *only* when Alex was present that she was especially forthcoming on the information he, or they, sought.

Unfortunately, he had made the mistake of allowing Kaguya, who had heard of Ciel and her enthrallment with Alex, to join them. His thought was the extra security would be beneficial, and he trusted in Kaguya's stoic deportment. He had been wrong... oh, so wrong!

The result had been significant property damage to Ciel's establishment and injury to its employees, namely Ciel's bodyguards. Jon and Alex had to physically remove Kaguya from the building lest she deliver on highly specific threats to the madam, and vice versa. Since then, the two had maintained an intense contempt for each other.

In this present exchange, Ciel superficially concealed her disdain with her usual affableness. And she was doing it so well that she actually came across as pleasant, at least forwardly.

Kaguya didn't even bother. *"Va te faire foutre, boudin."*

Jon quickly intervened before Ciel could slash at her monitor and end the communique.

"We're pressed for time," Jon stated evenly. "So, if you could give us everything worth knowing..."

"Payment?" Ciel inquired, returning to business at the proverbial flip of a switch.

Jon smirked. "I'm sure we can work something out to your satisfaction... next time we're in Penzance."

Quickly taking the hint, with her eyes again flashing at Alex's as the barest traces of an anticipating grin formed on her lips, Ciel nodded in acceptance. She knew better than to question the Flints in that area. Their reputation toward repaying debts, whether in the form of collateral or vengeance, was well established. And as a bonus, it would undoubtedly give her another chance at putting the Fuma witch in her place.

"Very well," the Lynx replied, before eyeing the trio carefully. "I assume you're all aware of the mythology surrounding Sognare?"

"Let me guess," Alex deadpanned. "It's regarded as a sacred realm by certain races and civilizations…"

"Or the realm of the damned, depending," Ciel continued. "Regardless, it has been recorded by various cults and religions, past and present, as an ethereal existence. And though they each have their explanations behind such an existence, there is a single commonality."

Again she eyed her audience carefully.

"The belief is the 'sea' is merely an expanse," she explained. "An extension of another existence."

Alex attempted a question, but Jon was faster.

"And what is this core existence?" he asked, the intensity of his inquiry surprising Alex and Kaguya, to say nothing of Ciel.

After taking a moment to adapt to the elder Flint's change in demeanor, Ciel continued.

"That, too, changes between the mythologies," she elaborated. "But the most prominently believed, especially amongst the Pisceans and the Aquarians, is an all too specific form."

Her lips then drew into an ironic smile.

"The Black Moon."

A chill ran down the elder Flint's spine, one that quickly spread throughout his body as the image he beheld upon Nassau returned to his mind's eye. A lone obsidian moon, dwelling within the depths of a vast multicolored tumultuous sea…

Not noticing his brother's sudden discomfort, Alex raised an eyebrow.

"*The* Black Moon?" he declared, wondering about that phrasing's significance.

Ciel nodded.

"*The* Black Moon is a facet of many mythologies and religions. Often claimed as the domain of gods or devils…" she smiled ironically again. "Once more depending upon the point of view."

Inwardly forcing back his shock, Jon returned to the subject at hand.

"Basically, a domain of superior beings," he summarized, before considering. "Or, more simply, a domain of greater power."

Again Ciel nodded and continued.

"Which some claim can be bartered for or wielded by those who find the Moon. So you can understand why the Pisceans and the Aquarians are especially interested."

Now it was Kaguya's turn to look agitated.

"Those two races have been fighting each other for a long time. Longer than most. They have known of the existence of the Sognare Sea," she hissed, barely civil. "Why are they interested in Sognare now?"

Maintaining her business demeanor, despite her desire to spit in the Dragon Princess' face, Ciel shook her head.

"I'm afraid I have no solid information there…"

"But?" Alex questioned, noticing the phrasing. Namely, the usage of the word 'solid.'

Ciel smiled at Alex, her eyes sparkled. He had caught onto a subject that the other two had missed.

"There have been rumors," she spoke, far more conspiringly now. "Which, if true, both the Confederacy and the Hegemony have gone well out of their way to silence. Some years ago, an Aquarian monitoring station detected…*activity* emanating from the Sea. *Psionic* activity."

A renewed chill swept through Jon, one that expanded over Alex and Kaguya as well.

"Go on," Jon encouraged.

Ciel, showing the first signs of hesitance, continued regardless.

"It was a telepathic signal. One that was initially short-range, such that it barely registered. However, as time passed, the signal grew stronger and stronger until it was detected by multiple stations and posts. All while physical activity within the Sea became further erratic."

He feared he knew the answer, but Jon asked anyway.

"When exactly did this begin?"

Knowing full well why the elder Flint had asked that particular question, Ciel paused to take another pull on her cigarette. Exhaling, she waited a few seconds before answering, contemplating.

"Approximately thirteen years ago. On the precise date of Undine's debut performance."

Jon closed his eye while Alex and Kaguya both stared at each other, astonished. All at once, so much was clarified; now they understood the totality of the situation. What they would soon be facing, and what was transpiring within that section of space.

And yet they still felt so lost...

Chapter VIII: Changing Tides

Flint Pirates umbra *Black Sun*
Deep Space

It wasn't his favorite classic song of all time, but Jon couldn't help but feel that *The House of the Rising Sun* was appropriate for the occasion. The solemnness of the melody, as well as the lyrics, and the vocal rendering by the long-forgotten singer, were apropos for the present situation. If it weren't for the detrimental effects it would have on morale, Jon might have played it over the *Sun*'s intercom system, as he often did for his crew's benefit. Instead, he settled for it playing in the background of the observation deck, all while he looked out over the stars.

For the time being, the *Black Sun* was traveling at cruising speed through open space. Both the cloak and the Psi Disruptor remained active, just as Lorelei remained incapacitated. The crew continued performing their duties, though the abrupt departure from Nassau, as well as the fact they were being pursued by the Pisceans, had generated a melancholy that encompassed the ship. They had faced worse, but the early end to their shore leave and the factors within had not been taken well by most. Fortunately, discipline remained in force. That was never much of a problem with the Flint Pirates, which, if nothing else, had a Herculean as head of security. And, despite the multitude of battles, the ship continued to function as well as it had since her initial departure from Ryugu.

The voyage to the Blue Dragon homeworld had also been delayed. Though Lord Fuma had voiced his disappointment over his students and daughter not being able to make their scheduled meeting – apparently there was much to discuss – he nonetheless understood that the Flints had to take care of their own business before returning to Blue Dragon space. Notably, he had not offered aid, and Jon had not requested any. Both recognized that this was the Flints' issue to resolve, and Jon liked to think Lord Fuma trusted it would indeed be taken care of without having to involve his clan. Granted, Kaguya was still with them, but as long as she wore black and gold, she acted on behalf of the Flint Pirates alone. Overall, their tardiness in meeting with the Blue Dragon Lord was a non-issue, though it left a sourer taste in Jon's mouth than their emergency departure from Nassau had.

The Flints were left to deal with their present dilemma: the Black Moon and all entailed with it. Despite that knowledge, Jon frowned. Even Ephesus felt simpler in comparison. For all they had endured before and during that battle, it had been an active conflict between the Imperials and the Flints. Something that they were able to fight their way through, though not without some help.

The present conflict was much different. It was a gradually emerging war between two ruling empires – something that the Flints, by all rights, shouldn't have had anything to do with – over an element that, assuming it did exist, could very well shift the balance of power in the galaxy. A conflict that could not be dealt with so readily, nor so aggressively as that private war with Drake. A conflict in which one trod carefully and delicately, lest they cause all else to become embroiled within.

It helps even less that we have no direction at this point, Jon mused. Indeed that was a problem. Reviewing the information Ciel had provided, there remained the question of how the Flints would proceed. The most obvious route was to take the fight to the enemy, as had been done at Ephesus. However, Jon retained caution toward that approach. He still didn't know enough about said enemy, and the possibility remained that they were prepared to go against the *Black Sun* proper. Yet at the same time, they couldn't stay on the run; eventually, they would get cornered, regardless of the *Sun*'s speed and stealth. Such was the central disadvantage of being one ship against many.

For the moment, Jon, and by extension, the rest of the Flint Pirates, could do nothing but wait a little longer. Surely they would gain further answers once Lorelei reawakened. Until then…

A frown crossed his expression as, through the music, his ears picked up the door opening from behind. Followed by footfalls that did *not* belong to his brother.

"You aren't the one I was expecting."

"Yeah, sorry about that," Cheney replied with a shrug. "Last I saw him, he and Professor Braun were going down the deck cackling maniacally. Something about taking over the universe by breakfast."

Wouldn't that solve all of our problems, Jon thought as the sub-commander of the raiders came to stand by him. Even without looking directly, the captain could depict the former marine's latest shirt. The words "PAX SUPERIORE VI TELARUM" written around an ancient "peace sign" with two stylized rifles underneath. All in black and gold, of course.

"Quite the view," Cheney commented as he looked over the stars. "Think we could find my house from here?"

Ignoring the quip, Jon decided it wouldn't hurt to ask.

"I don't suppose the Dread Soldier Cheney has any answers to our current problems…"

"Dread *Pirate* Cheney," Cheney corrected. "That changed when they found out I joined your merry band. And as for answers, sorry, they pay captains to have those. Me, I'm here to shoot bad guys."

"Fair enough," Jon rejoined.

It was a little strange having another member of the crew who was as flippant as Alex, but the captain wasn't offended. If anything, the former marine had well-earned that right, alongside the permission to address the captain so casually.

A brief moment of silence ensued before Cheney spoke up again.

"I do have a few questions," he said, re-earning Jon's attention. "Do you think this is all connected to Arcadia in some way?"

Jon had considered that possibility but ultimately decided against it.

"Unlikely," he replied. "If it were, the psionic activity within Sognare would have begun with Ephesus, not Lorelei's song."

Cheney nodded, considering. *Ephesus...* he thought momentarily, before moving back to the present.

"And what about Lorelei?" he posited. "How do we know that she isn't further connected with this?"

He quickly continued, lest the captain would interpret that question the wrong way.

"Don't get me wrong; I like her and all. But as everyone seems to point out, we don't know anything about her background. Just that she's a self-proclaimed scholar seeking some thingamajig called Arcadia."

Cheney mused a little more on that fact. "For all we know, she could be a physical manifestation of the Black Moon, sent out into the galaxy to learn, explore, and otherwise have a good time, and what happened on Nassau was her originator's attempt to reel her back in..."

That earned a raised eyebrow from Jon.

"Did you think of that?"

Cheney sniffed. "Hell no, I'm not *that* screwed up," he exclaimed with a shrug. "Let's just say the subject has been discussed...multiple times...by many...over assorted forms of grog. That was the prevailing theory. "

"I see," Jon observed.

He had wondered what the crew would claim about Lorelei after the psionic attack. He also took note of how they kept it quiet around him.

"Well, despite that highly intriguing theory, and any others like it, her *real* background is irrelevant at this point."

Cheney did not overlook the staunch directness of the captain's tone as he continued.

"Perhaps she's directly connected to this Black Moon; perhaps she isn't," Jon surmised. "Whatever the truth, it doesn't change our present circumstances. And even if it did, she will remain regardless."

This time, the raider eyed the elder Flint carefully.

"Because the ship will go gooey kablooie without her? Or because you'll make sure she sticks around?"

A stern leftward glance told Cheney he had overstepped his bounds. The sub-commander, in an attempt to defuse his captain's ire, raised his hands and spoke quietly.

"I'm only asking what any other officer would in my place. To say nothing of the rest of the crew."

Jon, though angered, nodded in acknowledgment of the raider's intent to understand, not insult.

"Because, whatever she thinks or believes," the Captain answered in a more subdued tone. "She is one of us."

Now it was Cheney's turn to nod, having received his answer.

"Alright," he conceded. "Though you'll find more than one person on this boat would claim differently." Again he followed up before Jon could reply. "Not the majority mind you. But they're there all the same, in not so obvious places."

Knowing precisely what the raider was referring to, Jon retained his gaze toward the stars.

"They always are," he murmured in a near monotone. All while the music continued to play in the background.

————————————————————

After everything they went through just two days ago, Anna found it strange to be standing in the same room as another Piscean, especially when it – no, *he* – wasn't trying to kill her. Or Gran or Kaiser, for that matter, as they were standing toward the back of the room. As Gran had translated, the security officer had insisted on being present, just in case said Piscean did feel something toward the deaths of his fellows.

Nerves aside, upon actually meeting the Piscean crewman for the first time, Anna saw that he was nothing like the soldiers that attacked them on Nassau. Even discounting the fact he was presently wearing Terran designed clothes – naturally, black and gold-colored, with a slogan on the shirt front that read "EAT AT CHUM'S" along with a cartoon fish wearing an Ancient Terran sailor's hat – the fishman was as different to those previously encountered as a shark was to a minnow. A rather apt analogy in Anna's opinion, as Jaws – whose human given name was also entirely appropriate – honestly reminded her of a shark. A Terran tiger shark specifically, given his blue-grey colored exterior and the darker stripe markings that ran down his back. Other than the fact he was essentially an upright walking, muscle-bound fish, she would never have tagged him as being of the same race as those they killed on Nassau.

For his part, Jaws did not hide his disdain toward the aforementioned fishmen. He was presently looking over various images from the encounter on a holographic vidscreen.

"Yes, it is as I suspected," the Piscean spoke, in a growling tone that held obvious distaste. "These hagfish hail from the Rohu Dag."

He reached out with a webbed hand and brushed it against the holographic screen, specifically over the armor markings currently magnified.

"Their markings confirm that dag," he spat. "As does their collective stench."

Anna wisely bit back a quip on that last comment. It was just as Cheney had said before, no love lost.

"What can you tell us about this particular dag?" she inquired. "Besides what they wear and how they smell?"

Jaws seemed all too happy to oblige.

"Rohu is a minor dag," he explained. "With very little in the way of resources and military power." He glanced back at the imagery. "As a result, it's oft-overlooked by the others, much less considered a proper rival to them. I suspect they wouldn't have been worthy of our notice either, had they not attacked first at least."

Anna nodded, though she came to an all too different conclusion. In her experience, it was the smaller groups and organizations that required the most attention. More often than not, they were the most ambitious, the most power-hungry, the most willing to expand their territory and influence by any means. And, the most easily and often overlooked.

In this case, it wasn't too hard to see what their enemy's aim was. The Rohus – she assumed that was the proper reference – clearly believed that their seizing the Black Moon would, among other things, allow them to subjugate the rest of the Confederacy to their banner. And much more, they were keen enough to act during the present political turmoil, effectively moving in the background while the other dags hashed it out with the Aquarians.

That said, it still didn't explain how they managed to connect Lorelei to the Moon. Anna had a feeling there was much more involved with that affiliation.

"Who's their Dagon?"

"Inanga," Jaws replied. "I'm afraid I do not know too much about him, other than that he is considered an agitator..."

"An agitator?" Gran translated for Kaiser.

The Piscean nodded. "In spite of his position, he has repeatedly challenged the other Dagons, as well as the Dagoth himself."

To increase his visibility, as well as his reputation as a more prominent player, Anna thought, again, experience coming into play.

"Why hasn't he been removed?"

This time the Piscean shrugged. "I cannot answer that either," he said, somewhat reluctantly. "Though I would suspect he holds some measure of cunning."

Anna agreed. It made sense; cunning often went hand in hand with ambition and political acumen.

"Anything else we should know about?"

Jaws seemed to recall something. "There have been rumors. About an outsider having entered into Rohu's service." He then added before anyone could ask. "A *Terran* outsider."

Anna wasn't the only one who showed visible interest. Kaiser, ordinarily stoic, was now intent.

"Could you elaborate on that?" Gran requested for the security officer.

Reluctantly Jaws shook his head. "I'm afraid not, as I have not heard any specifics on this individual," he answered. "But I felt it significant somehow."

The operations officer considered that information. Her instincts told her this was significant, especially when Pisceans made no secrets about what they thought of other races as did most Terrans for that matter. An interspecies crew aboard a Piscean ship wasn't unheard of but was *highly* irregular.

"Very well," Anna concluded. "Thank you, Jaws. You have been most helpful in this matter."

With surprising cordiality, the Piscean accepted the thanks with a rather Terran-like gesture.

"My pleasure, ma'am." He again looked at the still projected imagery. "I trust we will be fighting these miscreants again in the future?"

"Seems that way," Anna shrugged.

"Good," Jaws replied, before flashing a fanged smile. "As you can surmise, I hold no love for these erstwhile 'brethren' of mine." Then, in another Terran-like gesture, he stretched out his arms. "Now, if there isn't anything else…"

Anna smiled and nodded her thanks; the Piscean accepted the gratitude and dismissal. Then, turning, he acknowledged Kaiser and Gran and left the cabin, the door shifting closed behind him.

Waiting only a few seconds after the fishman's departure, Anna looked over to the Lyran. Gran immediately understood.

"He was truthful throughout," she answered the unvoiced inquiry. "Not that I suspected him…"

"Neither did I," Anna agreed.

It was no secret how territorial and antagonistic the Pisceans were between the various dags. It was only in the face of outside opposition – namely the other twelve Galactic Powers – that they were indeed a united civilization.

"But it never hurts to be sure."

Anna glanced at the frozen images of the dead Rohus.

"At the very least, we have a better understanding of what we're up against," she exclaimed, before eliciting a slight chuckle at her own words. "This time around anyway…"

"Well," Boss spoke as she looked over the designated tactical data on the nearby vidscreen. "So far, we have one battleship and three cruisers, alongside their respective fighter and bomber compliments."

"Plus troop transports in case the fight shifts to a terrestrial setting," Barbarossa pointed out as he moved to his drink cabinet, pulling out a bottle of raki and two accompanying glasses.

At his insistence, they were holding the apparent tactical meeting within his quarters. Even after a year or so since his joining up with the Flints, he was still uncomfortable being among the rest of the *Black Sun*'s crew. Outside of his duties anyway.

"Obviously, this is nowhere near the bulk of their forces."

"Agreed," Boss nodded thanks as she took an offered glass.

Though she wasn't too fond of Leo raki, it was nonetheless considered a great honor for a Leo to share it with another. Especially when that other was neither a Leo nor a follower of Aslan.

"At the same time, however, I don't think they'll have as much as the Thirteenth Fleet. Otherwise, they would have sent more ships to Nassau."

Barbarossa signaled his agreement while taking his seat across from the Blue Comet. It still surprised him that he felt comfortable in her presence and valued her insight and input. He was continually having to modify his blanket hatred of all things Terran.

"Regardless, we're still facing an entire dag," he said as he poured raki into each glass. "And there's always the possibility others may get involved."

"Only if they learn about Lorelei," Boss stated as she viewed the white liquid. "Somehow, I don't see that being spread around the Confederacy anytime soon."

The Leo shrugged. "You never know."

Raising his glass, he tapped it against Boss'. Both took a drink. The Leo closed his eyes to heighten the appreciation of the body and aroma of the raki; Boss tried not to wince at the intense flavor.

"On the other hand," the fighter ace voiced a sudden thought, re-earning Barbarossa's attention. "There is also the possibility that they possess unconventional forces as well. They are, after all, hunting a psion," she pointed out.

"The Captain seems to suspect as much," Barbarossa concurred, recalling the retreat from Nassau in a more understanding light. "As do I."

"It can't be psionic troops of their own," Boss deliberated, taking another drink. The flavor was still intense, but it was growing on her. "As Davis pointed out before, they would have been among the assault forces."

The same conclusion had entered Barbarossa's mind.

"That doesn't necessarily mean they lack psions," he replied. "Only that none of them are frontline troops."

The ace shrugged. "They wouldn't have stood a chance against Kaguya," she declared, recalling that specific part of Ephesus. "Which leaves two possibilities: first, they possess some type of anti-psionic weapon or capability…" She looked at Barbarossa. "Or second, they do have a psion or two in their muster. Just not combat-trained, as you said."

Barbarossa nodded. "In the case of the latter, the psion in question would have to be quite powerful," he surmised as he sipped his drink. "If only to properly subdue Lorelei."

Despite herself, Boss smiled. "Left an impression on you as well, didn't she?"

"Humph," Barbarossa answered, understanding her reference. "I had long suspected the strength of her power. And that, for whatever reason, her refusing it."

"Yeah. If our patron were a weaker level psion, she probably wouldn't be able to activate the Babels."

"She comes across as one who holds immense power, yet is reluctant to utilize it," Barbarossa spoke sagely. "Like an Emperor who does not wish to overuse his authority…"

"Or a Caliph," Boss replied in turn, before shrugging again and taking another sip of the raki. "I suppose she has her reasons."

"As she does with everything else. Anyway, I don't think we will be repeating Ephesus," the Leo exclaimed. "But we will be up against a considerable force regardless."

The fighter ace had estimated as much. "One that, at the very least, will be equivalent to an Imperial battlegroup," Boss said, looking back at the vidscreen. "And it will contain some heavy firepower if that *Gnaiih* is any indication."

"That was probably the dag flagship," Barbarossa posited while taking another sip. "Though I wouldn't be surprised if they had one or two battlecruisers to supplement it."

"If not additional battleships proper," Boss followed, shaking her head slightly. "We have our work cut out for us on this one, Kapta."

"Indeed, Commander," Barbarossa agreed once more, raising his glass toward the opposite fleeter and flashing a fanged smile in the process. "Yet, I suspect neither of us would have it differently."

Matching that smile, Boss again clinked glasses with her fellow veteran.

———————————— ————————————

Door shifting open with a slight 'woosh,' Kaguya entered the area in relative silence, her kimono swaying gently with her movements. As she had expected, the sickbay was deserted outside of its sole occupant. No doubt, Apache was somewhere agitating others or simply being agitated himself. That suited her immediate purposes quite well; she didn't want anyone else present as she went about her task. Just as she hoped, the one she came to see hadn't awakened, though if need be, she could always repeat her previous action from Nassau.

Quietly she approached the designated bed. Its occupant indeed remained reclined, dormant, but still very much alive. For the briefest of moments, the Dragon Princess held uncertainty toward the latter. Besides the *Sun* potentially self-destructing if the worst were to occur, she didn't want to imagine how Jon, or anyone else on the ship, would accept such an unseemly death. Only the weak and those at the end of their lifespans passed on in their sleep. Not someone – as much as she didn't want to admit it – as powerful and as ambitious as this psion. For all of her faults and evils, Lorelei deserved better.

Kaguya scrutinized the immobile form in the bed. Despite her skill at gathering intelligence, she still knew virtually nothing about the psion. As always, the hatred toward the alien woman began to rise. The same hatred she had held since that fateful exchange with Jon over a year ago. And would likely retain well after she, at last, struck her down.

Not usually given to emotion, Kaguya wanted to end this woman once and for all. This was the woman that had led Jon – who, alongside Alex, meant more to her than anyone, outside her biological brother, would ever know – onto a path of inevitable destruction. A path that promised much at its end, but would deliver death before it could ever be reached. A path upon which she feared Jon, Alex, and all who followed them, would ultimately be lost. Perhaps were already lost, given all too recent events.

Indeed, she would never forgive Lorelei. For setting the Flints on that path, for taking her family away from her, there would be no clemency, no absolution. Only unending fury and vengefulness, from which a quick and precise killing stroke would eventually emerge.

And yet…and yet for all of that hatred, Kaguya also felt something else toward the one before her. A feeling that she couldn't quite identify, but knew to be present and well within her.

It was that feeling, and that feeling alone, that stayed her hand on Nassau, just as she had been ready to eliminate her target. A sentiment had surfaced when she saw the pain and anguish upon Lorelei's face as if her very soul was under torment. Not even the threat of Kayuga's potential death – she had been well aware of Boss and Anna reaching for their weapons at the time – had swayed her from her kill. Much less the purported destruction of the *Black Sun* or any other safeguard Lorelei had put into place to keep the crew from turning on her.

Was it pity? Sympathy toward her plight? The wastefulness of such a death? Kaguya did not know.

For all of her intelligence and power, Lorelei remained as vulnerable in her sleep as any other target, and Kaguya had never held reluctance to strike in that manner. It would be so simple to draw a kunai and impale a vital organ or slash her throat, or more bloodlessly snap her neck. Or to utilize one of the nearby medical instruments – despite Apache's best efforts, she knew his inventory – for a more "creative" execution. Or even whisk her away to the nearest airlock, in a more traditional pirate manner.

Yet Kaguya would do none of that; *could* do none of that, not even if it solved all of their immediate problems with Sognare and the Pisceans. All because of something internal holding her back now as it had before.

Inwardly sighing, she whispered to the still form.

"It is not your time to die. Nothing more, nothing less."

Resolved, Kaguya, after casting one last glare at the still dormant woman, turned around and exited the sickbay as quietly as she had arrived, proceeding down the corridor toward parts unknown. So apparently focused on her eventual destination, she never detected Apache as he stepped around a nearby corner. The Aquilan intently watched the Fuma woman until she disappeared down the passageway, then transferred his gaze to the entrance of his sickbay…

<u>Chapter IX: Quest of the Dreamer</u>

"Where…where am I?" she espoused, yet could neither hear the words nor feel herself speak them. In fact, it was fair to say that she sensed nothing at all, nothing within the vast, apparent emptiness that surrounded her, an emptiness that held neither light nor darkness. Comprehension was as abstract as it was impossible, yet appeared as infinite as the void of space itself. All the while she remained fixed within its apparent center, uncertain of her very existence within this realm.

Yes, she was aware, yet that was the extent of her present state. For, once again, she felt nor sensed nothing, not her own physical body, no foreign object or entity beyond her, not even the words that she had just uttered. She merely was and nothing more.

This was quite disconcerting, to say the least. Even within the dark depths of Ephesus and Smyrna, she at least had sensed something to be drawn to, to descend toward. For as seeming as the nothingness was within those prior abysses, they still contained the dormant Babels, sleeping but waiting for her to reach them. Waiting for her to awaken them.

That was not so here if it could even be called "here." It was all pure "nothingness." She wondered how anything could dwell in such a setting, let alone retain a sense of self and individuality. To simply "be" in such a void. All unfathomable. All otherwise impossible.

And then...there was something.

...At last...

Though she did not actually "hear" the words, she was able to sense them. As if they had been read out before her, against the surrounding nothingness.

...You can hear me...

"Who are you?" she mouthed, once more not hearing her own words nor physically feeling herself utter them. Despite those hindrances, however, she, at last, felt something more. Another presence within the void.

...I know not, for I have not been for so long...

She considered her next words carefully.

"Could you be..." she hesitantly posited. *"...Arcadia?"*

A brief pause intervened as the source of the words seemed to consider.

...That does seem familiar...

Another pause followed; she suddenly felt herself being observed in some manner. As though she were being scrutinized by an inquiring, physical eye.

...Indeed, you remind me of them...

"In what way?" she felt herself ask.

Though she obviously could not depict it, she sensed a small smile in response.

...Your song...

...It's just like theirs...

Confusion was all she perceived. Who was...?

...Unfortunately, our time is short...

She blinked – or at least believed she did – as she suddenly felt something else. Something, which began to erode through the nothingness. Gradually taking form in her comprehension.

…Allow me…

Light, or at least what she believed to be light, began to pierce through the void…

…*The honor*…

——————————— ———————————

Lorelei blinked again. Only this time, she realized she had *actually* blinked. Not only that, but she had somehow regained her physical form. She was standing, clothed in her standard ensemble, black and gold great-coat whipping slightly about from a seeming wind. She felt her hands, *saw* her hands when she looked down, clenching and opening them. Her ears picked up the sounds of her actions, of her booted feet moving against a solid floor, of her breathing and her heartbeat.

And yet, while her five basic senses reclaimed their function, she still felt a vast nothingness from her sixth, most prominent sense. No matter how far she reached out mentally, no matter how much she sought for anything else, anything at all, she still only depicted a sheer openness, sheer empti-ness. As if there was no other life, no separate *existence*, around her.

An apparent contradiction, she decided, as there was much her aforemen-tioned senses beheld before her now.

In place of an abyss, a magnificent cityscape now surrounded her, a metropolis unlike any other imagined or conceived. Elaborate towers extended grandly about, as if deliberately reaching toward the great beyond, while streets and avenues crisscrossed in virtually every angle and direction. Elegant plazas and avenues resided evenly, each differenti-ated by arrangement and composition. Various edifices and designs, with unique intrigue and grandeur, were placed in specific areas to break any potential monotony — all shining gloriously against the pale starlight above. The variety of color, shape, and texture contained within the cityscape was indescribable.

To any other who beheld it, who stood within its hold, the city would have appeared nothing less than the work of gods given form. But not her. Lorelei slowly pivoted, perusing the metropolis in apparent alarm. Uncertainty emerging within her as she looked about as if trying to catch her bearings.

"Am I...?" she exclaimed, distant and bewildered as if she were lost. Or worse. "Is this...?"

"No," a new voice, an all too familiar voice, spoke from behind her. "This is merely a projection I have manifested."

Lorelei turned and faced a child. A child that, despite the obvious difference in apparent age, shared her form. The psion trembled with astonishment as she beheld a replica of her younger self.

"Now we can speak more openly," the child explained in Lorelei's voice – albeit a younger version – while watching the psion with amethyst eyes.

"You..." Lorelei exclaimed, gazing at the child in perplexity. "That form..."

The child nodded in understanding. "I hold no apparent form, comprehendible or otherwise," she clarified. "For the sake of stable communication, I have undertaken this state of being gleaned from your mind."

Again the psion blinked, perplexity turning to uncertainty. As strange as it was to look upon her younger self, Lorelei was more concerned about the entity that had assumed her identity.

"Who are you?"

A glint of sadness entered into the other's eyes. "I do not know, as I answered before," she stated sincerely. "For I have not been for so long."

An interesting choice of words, Lorelei mused, uncaring if the 'other' picked up her thoughts – such as they were – or not. She instinctively sensed immense power was behind that form. Something that, despite its lacking identity, was far more than what she usually dealt with or encountered.

Suddenly, a memory returned to her, as well as an observation.

"I sense no hostility from you," the psion declared, studying the 'child,' both physically and psionically. "Yet on Nassau…"

"Yes," the 'other' acknowledged. "The transgressions of that contact were not of my will. I merely reached out to you, without accounting for your response to such contact. I misjudged."

Lorelei folded her arms, looking dubious. "You could have sent a note."

Now it was her younger self's turn to blink. "I'm afraid I'm not capable of such…"

"Nevermind," Lorelei cut her off. Apparently, humor was beyond her – assuming it was a 'her' – as well.

Sighing, the psion chose to press on.

"Regardless of what happened, you have my attention now," Lorelei exclaimed, moving closer to her other-self. "And, as you also said before, our time is short."

Lorelei knelt before the child so that she could stare directly into her eyes.

"So, what do you want with me?"

Her other-self nodded as she returned the gaze. "I need you…" she explained. "…to free me."

"You're a prisoner?" Lorelei's responded, her eyebrow arched in amazement.

"Yes, though not in the way you would believe."

As if to consider her words carefully, the other-self paced slowly, moving in a small circle.

"My prison is not one of stone or energy fields, but rather one of nothing-ness. A pure abyss, in which I cannot see, hear, nor touch."

The duplicate then turned back, seemingly to emphasize.

"A prison in which I may only *dream*. And nothing beyond."

"I don't understand," Lorelei replied.

Again her other-self nodded. "It is not something so simple to fathom, but it is the truth. For time immeasurable, I have been trapped in the greatest of voids, with not but my dreams."

The child gazed up toward the projected sky. "Dreams as infinite, and as brilliant and captivating, as the stars beyond us," she said, before glancing back down, solemnness creeping into her expression. "Yet nothing so existent."

A thought nibbled at Lorelei's mind. She was unable to identify it before her other-self turned back once more, continuing with her explanation.

"And for time foreseeable, I would have remained as such. Likely until I became but a dream…"

"But…?" Lorelei inquired, sensing something … more.

"But then, I heard your song," the child clarified, passion infusing every word. "And everything changed."

Perplexity returned to Lorelei in a rush; she didn't even bother concealing it. Slowly she stood.

Sensing the psion's discomfort, the child elaborated. "I do not quite understand how, but through your song, I have once again become *aware*. Aware of what lies beyond my prison and my dreams. Aware of the vastness you call 'existence,' which I was undoubtedly a part of at one time."

She continued before Lorelei could say anything. "Aware enough to *yearn*," she stated, now displaying the first vestiges of emotion, gesturing with her hands. "To *desire* to become part of it once more."

The child then stepped in front of Lorelei, determination shining from her eyes. "This is why I have sought you out. So that I may yet be free."

"How do I know you weren't imprisoned purposely?"

The child blinked, apparently not having thought of that herself. "Perhaps I was," she posited in admittance. "Though if that is the truth, then I cannot remember as to why," she shrugged. "Just as I cannot remember who, or what, I was before my incarceration."

Lorelei exhaled, considering the declarations silently. As she had estimated before, the being before her, despite its choice of form, was immensely powerful. Powerful enough to have overwhelmed Lorelei's defenses, even inadvertently. With that in mind, it was doubtful the being was imprisoned randomly. The individual may have been destructive, such that another powerful being, or a collection of powerful beings, were forced to act accordingly. In that sense, it would not do well for Lorelei to reverse that sentence... even if she knew how. And yet, the more she studied this being, the more she rejected her concern. She sensed there was so much more to the one before her than a mere prisoner, or even an instrument of destruction.

Lorelei continued her internal debate for what seemed like hours as opposed to minutes – not that time truly mattered in that realm, she imagined – until finally closing her eyes in resolve. Whoever, whatever, stood before her, she knew she could not turn away. Though she did not understand *why* she still *knew* regardless. The better part of her felt she would be remiss not to set it free. Thus she resigned herself to the inevitable.

"What would you have me do?" Lorelei inquired, looking back at her other-self.

It was only then that her younger self smiled in seeming genuineness. "To begin with, seek me out. I lay within the center of a great sea."

Yet again, Lorelei raised an eyebrow. "I don't even know where to start..."

Much to her surprise, the child laughed. "Do not worry, for there is one who holds the means to find me." Again the younger self was all too willing to clarify. "An explorer, one who has entered the sea before you."

"Who was unable to reach you apparently," Lorelei pointed out, somewhat sardonically.

Another nod of acknowledgment. "Yet came closer than those before. Or those since."

Briefly pausing for that to sink in, Lorelei continued. "And where may I find this explorer?"

The child seemed to hesitate and consider that question as if she was attempting to come up with an understandable explanation.

"Within the heart of the sacred moon. That is where he fell upon leaving the sea."

Lorelei sigh in frustration. "I suppose exact coordinates would have been too much to ask for."

She held up her hand as her mirror image looked frustrated.

"I will see what I can do," Lorelei declared. "Though I cannot guarantee resolution."

"That is not a concern," the being replied, resuming her original unreadable expression. "For as I said before…" Then, in a manner that unsettled Lorelei to her very core, the child's eyes seemed to flash knowingly. "Your song is just like *theirs*."

Eyes widening, Lorelei started to inquire further; however, a great light engulfed her, the city around her, and the child before her all faded away into…

Flint Pirates umbra *Black Sun*
Deep Space

The first sound that Lorelei perceived upon her somewhat prolonged awakening – her eyes gradually blinking into focus – was the sound of music. Terran music, she realized, identifying the accompanying piano and harmonica. The voice of a Terran woman joined the song. She spoke the somewhat downtrodden lyrics in what might have been a colonial accent but sounded much older than that, while the piano and the harmonica were joined by drums and a bass guitar. It all came together in a harmonious, if saddened, melody.

"*Rainy Days and Mondays*," Jon clarified from beside her bed, having noticed her awakening. His audio player was the source of the song. "In case you were wondering."

Lorelei recognized the *Black Sun*'s sickbay. It wasn't long before everything else returned to her memory, up to and including the events that quite obviously resulted in her infirmed state.

"How long was I out?" she inquired, groaning as she started to get up.

"Three days," Jon replied casually as if it were no great matter. Though appearing nonchalant, his eye never left her as she gradually reoriented herself. "Quite a lot has happened since."

It wasn't hard for Lorelei to telepathically gleam the reasons, as well as all that had occurred since Nassau.

"So... wow... I now understand," she exclaimed with a frown. It felt like the universe was completely different from what it was before Nassau. "For what it's worth, I was as unaware as you were."

Jon nodded. "I believe you. Though I can't speak for some of the crew..."

"Nothing I'm not used to," Lorelei countered, gradually pulling herself into an upright position on the bed, slowly stretching her limbs. Three days lying immobile wasn't enough to put her out of shape, but she still felt stiff and strained as she reoriented herself. Just as she felt the first vestiges of a massive headache.

Jon continued to watch her throughout, his gaze steady and unmoving. "Was it like Kurzis?" he inquired, after a brief moment.

The mere mention of that name was enough to cause Lorelei to shiver. It had been over a year, yet the memories of the tainted jungle planet, and the derelict starship within, remained grossly vivid. Even now, the psion – to say nothing of the rest of the crew – was hesitant to talk about it.

After a small moment of repose, she shook her head. "No," she answered. "What I felt on Kurzis was corrosive and undoubtedly malevolent."

She frowned as she considered the next line of words. "This...This 'Black Moon,' or whatever dwells in its place, however..." she hesitated, but only for a few seconds. "It cannot be so easily described or categorized. It's powerful, and overwhelmingly so. And yet, entirely foreign at the same time, its intentions beyond even my estimation."

The psion looked toward the captain. "All that I understand is that it is imprisoned, and seeks my aid in its liberation."

Jon mused over this revelation. While Lorelei had been incapacitated in sickbay, he and the others had researched much on the Black Moon's subject matter, and while it had been oft claimed as the dwelling place of gods or devils, it was never declared a prison. But then, not all iterations of Hell depicted Satan being trapped in the center of Cocytus.

Whatever the case, it seemed Lorelei had much to tell, and the information had been received directly from the source itself, apparently. Thus, after another relatively long moment, Jon nodded at her again.

"Get cleaned up," he commanded as he stood up. "We're holding a senior staff meeting in an hour."

With that, Jon exited the sickbay, allowing Lorelei to collect herself in silence.

"So let me get this straight," Davis proclaimed dubiously, leaning back with his arms folded over his chest. "Your little episode on Nassau, our being hunted by an entire sardine school, *and* the whole of the galaxy facing a potential war between two Powers, is all tied together in a psionically empowered SOS? One for a jailbreak no less?"

He let that linger around the table for a moment before shaking his head in sheer disbelief. "Frankly, I don't know whether to laugh my finely chiseled ass off or cry diamond tears at our newfound misfortune. Only this ship would be so unlucky…"

"No one's shot the albatross yet, Davis," Alex dryly pointed out. "Not that you're one to talk about ill-fortune. Or should I remind you of some little 'expeditions' of yours, like Zayed II?"

Davis visibly shivered at that reference. "I'd rather you didn't," he snarled.

"Regardless, the point still stands," Barbarossa followed up, gazing at the psion with dubiousness. "Even by my standards, this seems beyond belief."

"I know it's quite difficult, but I assure you it remains the truth," Lorelei staunchly answered. "Whatever is at the center of this, whether it really is some god or demon, it seeks liberation and believes I am the only one that can grant it."

"Yeah, funny how that works," Boss proclaimed as she lit her pipe, taking a momentary puff. "Anyway, how do we go about this? Because I get the feeling running and hiding is not an option."

"It wasn't at Ephesus. Why should this be any different?" Anna coolly rejoined. "Granted, we seem to be facing somewhat less than we did there."

"So long as everyone else stays out of it, and that will only last a short while. Eventually, the rest of the Piscean Confederacy will get involved, and the other Powers with them," Cheney pointed out, visibly disliking his estimates. "Doesn't matter who shoots it, that bird's goin' down."

"In flames," Alex flatly agreed, before adding on. "And yes, I understand the irony of that statement."

Jon concurred with that sentiment. It was only a matter of time before galactic heat death, and their running and ducking into the nearest aster-oid belt would surely accelerate that process. Thus, there was only one solution to the problem, one that he and Lorelei with him undoubtedly, had already resigned to following. As would the others, but he wanted them to realize it themselves.

Fortunately, he didn't have to wait long as emphasized by the perturbed side glance his brother gave him before stating. "All in all, we really have but a single option in this," Alex proclaimed to the rest of the table. "*Fly Me to the Moon…*"

"Seriously!?" Davis thundered toward the younger Flint, nearly slamming his fists on the glass table. "You actually want to go through with it!?"

"*Want* has nothing to do with it. We *have* to," Alex countered, before turn-ing to his elder sibling. "You want to explain it, or shall I?"

Jon shrugged. "You're doing a good job so far."

Nodding at the compliment, Alex turned back to the helmsman. "As you so eloquently pointed out, Davis – at least up to your referencing your ass, which was the *last* visual any of us needed – everything is centered on the Black Moon or whatever's on it or in it. This upcoming Aquarian-Piscean War, the resultant galactic turmoil, and our apparent part in all of it is based squarely on who can reach the Moon first and claim it for themselves."

Davis opened his mouth to reply, but Alex was faster.

"And yet, whatever this thing is, it's sentient enough to realize it's trapped in some hellhole, and so needs someone to pull it out," the First Officer let that sink in before continuing. "We do that before the Pisceans or Aquarians reach it, we may be able to prevent the war and galaxy-wide power shift. And as a bonus, it would undoubtedly stop harassing Lorelei as well."

"Assuming it doesn't turn out to be some galactic devourer entity," Boss posited around her pipe. "How do we know it wasn't locked away for good reason?"

"We don't," Jon admitted in place of his brother. "It could very well be Death, the Destroyer of Worlds, in true form."

He inwardly mulled over that very possibility but managed to push it aside before anyone besides Alex and Lorelei noticed.

"However, that remains an uncertainty, whereas our present circumstances are quite valid," Jon stated to the others with authority. "And our course set as a result."

Though obviously – and understandably – apprehensive, a collection of nods moved around the table in response. Like it or not, a war that would inevitably embroil the galaxy was a much more appalling issue than a possibility of eldritch malevolence. An issue that would not be resolved by ignoring their part in it, no matter how reluctant they were.

"Well then," Barbarossa spoke up after another moment of quiet, glancing at Lorelei once more. "I don't suppose your correspondent informed you of *how* to reach it?'"

"Or what you have to do to free it," Anna added. "Somehow, I get the feeling it will involve more than papier-mache and a raft."

Lorelei shook her head. "Unfortunately, I was not provided any specifics," she elaborated, much to the group's dismay. "Only that I was to seek out an 'explorer.' One that allegedly made it closer than the others."

"Great," Davis growled in frustration. "That narrows it down, doesn't it?"

"Actually…" Gran volunteered, her tone one of consideration. "It just might. We know there have been expeditions into Sognare, right?" she stated helpfully. "Perhaps one explorer managed to return…"

"Not too likely," Boss rejoined. "Those expeditions tend to disappear completely."

Alex shrugged. "Doesn't mean there wouldn't be at least one survivor, and it gives us a place to start looking," he said as he engaged his holoprojector, generating a screen in front of him.

"Searching for stardust in the cosmos…" the helmsman grumbled, totally disgruntled at the possibility of being caught up in another war. As if Ephesus hadn't been bad enough.

"Everything leaves a trail, Davis," Alex admonished. After a few moments of inserting commands, he found what he was looking for. "Got a hit," he confirmed. "An Aquarian expedition five years ago disappeared like the rest."

He ensured everyone was listening before adding. "However, there was indeed a survivor," he affirmed, projecting the designated image around the table. "Captain Jennis, the leader of the expedition. He was found in an escape pod, adrift just outside the Sea."

"He could have ditched before entry," Davis pointed out petulantly. "Like any other sane sentient would have done…"

"Funny you say that," Alex rejoined. "The report also claims that he was found 'maddened upon recovery,' and was committed to an asylum, or equivalent thereof, on Aquarius after return."

"Oh, great," Davis deadpanned. "Just what we need, a guide that's somewhere beyond the rim."

"Not to mention beyond our reach," Anna exclaimed as she looked over the data. "It also claims that he disappeared from his cell two years into his commitment."

"We could not have gotten to him on Aquarius anyway," Gran translated for Kaiser. The Security Officer held his own dubious expression.

"So what does that leave us?" Boss questioned, still retaining her pipe. "Beyond braving the Sea by ourselves."

"Which would make us 'beyond the rim,'" Apache quipped, his arms folded over his chest.

"Fortunately, I brought this up with our host," Lorelei stated as everyone turned their attention to her again. "Our explorer, for better or worse, has 'fallen within the heart of the sacred moon' to quote the source."

Despite the ambiguousness of the claim, it got the group thinking.

"How many moons does Aquarius possess?" Boss inquired.

"Four," Anna answered. "But we don't know if this particular moon is around Aquarius..."

"Doesn't matter," Cheney responded. "Wherever this Jennis guy ended up, he couldn't have gone far."

"And there's also the 'sacred' part," Gran added. "We just need to find a natural satellite that the Aquarians see as divine."

"Yeah, but 'heart of the sacred moon'?" Davis retorted again. "Wouldn't that mean he would be in its core?"

Gran shrugged. "Maybe he dug himself there?" she suggested, smiling. "Isn't that a traditional method of escape and concealment?"

"As insane as this gill-man is, I doubt he's physically capable of such,"

Cheney retorted dryly, having picked up on the Lyran's sarcasm. "Just as I doubt he held access to a drilling platform…"

"Maybe he had a scooping utensil?" Apache mildly added.

"Or maybe it's not actually a moon," Alex interrupted, his eyes fixed on the holographic datawindow in front of him. "But rather an organization."

With that, the image of Captain Jennis was replaced with a different one: a cortex page displaying a curious header, written in Aquarian. Despite the language, however, those present had no issue reading the script.

"The Vaos Selino?" Kaguya recited curiously.

"Order of the Sacred Moon," Boss translated, sniffing derisively. "I'm guessing they're not a sanctioned religion."

"Probably not," Anna responded, amused at what she was reading. "But then, the Black Moon does have a fair amount of cult worship around it, so this isn't surprising."

"At least they're not into sacrificing virgins," Davis muttered. "Though how do we know this isn't a grand coincidence?"

"I was just getting to that," Alex replied as he added another datawindow display. One that wasn't on the previous site.

Reading it, Davis deadpanned. "Annual 'pilgrimages' into the Sea. Should have seen that coming."

"As well as the usual stream of terrorism, within the Hegemony and without," Cheney indicated, also looking over the display. "If I'm reading this right, it wouldn't have taken much for this group to infiltrate that asylum."

"And spirit Jennis off into the night," Boss agreed. "Or their 'heart' as the case may be."

"Which in itself confirms his value," Barbarossa nodded to the other two veterans. "They certainly believe him to be their deliverer or at least one who holds the means to reaching their promised land."

"And the previous pilgrimages?" Gran inquired, having 'read' the displayed

179

data through a series of clicks that were generated at her section at the table.

"Officially they 'rendered themselves unto the Moon,'" Davis read, sarcastically. "And were 'permitted unto paradise.'"

"Canaries in a mineshaft," Anna sniffed toward that tidbit, recalling a comparable Terran adage. "Obviously, they're hoping Jennis will ensure the next pilgrimage goes better."

"Yet they've had him for three years," Braun spoke up for the first time, his right arm automatically scratching his head as he leaned toward it. "Surely, if they're as vicious as claimed, they would have reamed the information out of him by now."

"Clearly they haven't," Jon asserted, directing the meeting back onto the subject. "Where is their main temple located?"

Alex took another moment to gather that information. "For obvious reasons, the Vaos Selino doesn't have an official church," he clarified as he scanned the data. " But their 'center of worship' is suspected to be on Timas IV, within the city of Ianessa."

"Right on the Seashore," Davis declared, recalling the location of that particular world. He shrugged, looking toward Jon. "That explains our heading, but what about the rest? How do we proceed?"

Jon looked at Lorelei; she nodded at his unspoken inquiry.

Chapter X: World by the Sea

Piscean *Gnaiih*-class battleship *Grah'n*
Deep Space

Continuing his stride down the corridors of his flagship, Dagon Inanga did his best not to cringe as he grew closer and closer to his destination. There were a great many things in the galaxy that caused him agitation – incompetence amongst his subordinates, *greater* incompetence amongst his fellow Dagons, the continuous reminders and inclinations that his Dag did not hold the power and prominence that it should have, the scar that ran across his deadened left eye. However, none of those inflicted agitation upon him as much as that which was at the end of his trek despite its relatively limited presence within his existence. He was headed to see a being that caused ire like nothing he had ever experienced.

For as long as their arrangement had been in place, Inanga repeatedly questioned what kind of beverage he had been consuming during its consideration, let alone its negotiation. Surely he had not been in the best state of mind when he had first listened to that *creature*'s words and much more believed that they could serve to his and Rohu's benefit. There could be no other explanation, especially when more prominent – and therefore vastly more inept – Dagons had refused the being's services. If only he could return to that fateful day and forewarn himself from touching that particular bottle.

Unfortunately, it was what it was. As much as Inanga detested the one on the other side of the door he had just reached, he knew that, until they gained what they sought, the creature was here to stay. There was no getting rid of him otherwise, given his abilities, which undoubtedly surpassed every weapon and armament that Pisces held in its vast arsenal. Up to and including Pisceans of similar power, much to Inanga's disbelief. He still shuddered at the memory of that "demonstration" from not too long ago...

As if to emphasize the latter fact, the door shifted open before Inanga could announce his presence into the intercom. Glowering at the deliberateness of it, Inanga took a moment to reinforce his resolve before entering what was undoubtedly the darkest part of the *Grah'n*...where the bane of all that was, dwelled.

"I've been expecting you," a disarming Terran voice commented, its owner casually reclining against a nearby bed, an all too familiar tome in its grasp. To this day, Inanga had never seen him without it; he was beginning to think it was part of his hand. "I trust you have *not* succeeded in tracking down the *Black Sun*?"

Inanga's glower only deepened at the jab. More so toward the casualness behind it rather than the words. "'We have been having difficulties, yes," he forced himself to admit. "But it shouldn't be long now..."

A bemused chuckle interrupted him. "In other words," the Terran spoke as he placed his tome down and brought himself into a sitting position. "They've completely evaded you, and you're hoping I can help narrow down their likely berth."

Inanga's lips receded to display his barbed teeth. "I warned you before," he growled. "That insolent flippancy would not be tolerated..."

Another chuckle, another interruption. "And I believe I warned you as well, Inanga," the Terran countered, the Piscean becoming angrier over the eased usage of his name. "That as long as you retained my services, you would allow me my little amusements."

It took much of Inanga's restraint – and the knowledge of what would happen if he tried – to keep from reaching for his holstered weapons. His hand especially twitched toward his pike, while the desire to carve out the Terran's heart remained a fixed compulsion …as it had been since the beginning.

Ignoring the Dagon's ire, the Terran casually rose from his bed and moved toward the desk provided with the rest of his quarters. Various objects – some conventionally scientific while others of far more arcane design and purpose – were meticulously positioned across the surface.

"Fortunately for you, I had anticipated this outcome," the creature stated, moving some of the items aside, revealing a built-in control panel. He tapped a switch causing a holographic starmap to appear at the center of the room, in turn drawing Inanga's singular attention.

"I estimate the Flint Pirates have long established our objectives, as well as the present state of the galaxy along with them," the Terran expounded. "This, alongside identifying their patron's connection, will undoubtedly drive them to seek the Black Moon."

Inanga gazed at the starmap in consideration. "Would it not be more likely for them to simply run and hide in the safest point until all is concluded?" the Dagon questioned. "They are pirates, after all."

Another chuckle sounded, this one toward Inanga's apparent lack of understanding. "As your soldiers can attest, at least the few that survived Nassau," the Terran prodded once more, much to Inanga's reemerging ire. "These are not ordinary pirates."

He shook his head. "No, if they didn't run and hide from Drake, then they will not do so from us. Just as they will not allow the potential eruption of a galactic war."

Inanga sneered. "There will be no war. Once we gain the Black Moon, none will resist its power, let alone stand against it."

"Quite," the Terran concluded. Though he had his own doubts, he saw no reason to argue the Dagon's point, especially when it would distract from the immediate goal. "Under that hypothesis, the Flints will seek a means of access into the Sea…"

He then tapped another switch. "Which is where *this* enters in."

A second later, one of the dots in the map shifted in color, while another holographic projection appeared before the Dagon, one that showed a specific data set.

As he read its contents, Inanga's single functioning eye widened in astonishment.

"How did you come by this?"

The Terran smirked, knowing that he had accomplished what the entirety of the Confederacy's intelligence organs had failed to do. And that was before assessing their quarry's destination.

"Research and some educated speculation. I am a scientist, after all," he explained proudly. "Whether or not he indeed holds what many have sought, that is the *Black Sun*'s destination all the same."

Inanga nodded, accepting the logic. Granted, it was all tied to his "guest's" belief that their quarry was indeed seeking the Moon, and not retreating into the void as he would expect of their kind. But then he recalled Nassau, as well as the infinite tales of the deeds of the Flint pirates at Ephesus. He found himself agreeing with this creature. The Flints were no ordinary pirates. No more than the Golden Queen had been.

"It will take us several days to travel there," Inanga stated as he turned to head back to the bridge. "I suggest you make yourself comfortable again."

"Yes, about that…" his "guest" spoke up, causing the Dagon to halt his pace. "When we do arrive, I insist on participating."

Cautiously the Dagon turned, seemingly choking down his initial response.

"May I inquire as to why?"

The Terran shrugged. "Given all that occurred on Nassau, I fear your soldiers will be of no match for the Flints or their raiders. Let alone *her*."

Inanga opened his mouth to argue, but his "guest" beat him to the response.

"I will not tolerate another mistake."

The Dagon didn't miss the underlying energy of that statement. Nor the feeling of power – for lack of better word – sweeping over his conscious mind. Like a current surging toward a shoreline, indicating the real strength of its source, which lay within the deep.

Again withholding his initial response – which would have been a gulping action as opposed to a quip – the Dagon knew better than to contest.

"Very well," Inanga exclaimed, before turning again. "If nothing else, it will get you off my ship for a good while."

Despite the subtle barb, the Terran nodded in apparent satisfaction.

"Indeed," he answered, an anticipating smile extending across his lips. "This is something we will both appreciate…"

Flint Pirates umbra *Black Sun*
Timas System

It was not the most prepossessing of worlds, yet, as Jon gazed into his command scope at the image of Timas IV, he couldn't help but sense a mysterious grandeur about it. Quite unlike most planets that he and his crew were used to, the fourth planet of the Timas System was covered entirely in water, granting the biosphere a solid blue surface against the light of the resident sun. An enormous sapphire in space, even more so than the likes of Ryugu or Nassau, or Terra for that matter. All lay beneath its encompassing sea.

Such planets were relatively common amongst the Aquarians and Pisceans, who often terraformed – or aquaformed Jon supposed was more accurate

– worlds to their liking the way most colonial civilizations were predisposed to do. And it certainly wasn't the first "waterworld" he, and likely the majority of his crew had seen. Yet, despite that apparent regularity, there was still something about Timas IV that stood out, as if what lay underneath its waves was far more than even his preconceptions would allow.

Whatever the truth, the data on his command scope showed an otherwise unremarkable Aquarian world, with a single major city – the aforementioned Ianessa – and various smaller settlements. That alone told Jon much about Timas. Namely, the Aquarians had believed it held promise at one time, such that they put time and effort into creating a true city rather than a standard colony, only to have changed their minds, all but abandoning the world after the city's completion.

Shaking his head at a nagging feeling, Jon retracted the scope.

"Status."

"Nothing on sensors," Barbarossa reported. "Short of another umbra, there appear to be no other ships present."

"Not much on communications either," Gran provided. "I'm picking up some sparse chatter from the planet, but nothing system-wide."

"That figures," Davis quipped from the helm, once again vocalizing what the rest of the crew were thinking. If the Vaos Selino was indeed down there, it had chosen the perfect world to establish its faith. One could only wonder what that faith truly entailed to require such isolation.

The helmsman glanced at Jon. "I don't recommend drinking any fruit-flavored beverages while down there, Captain."

"Duly noted," Jon answered. That particular reference had been one of the grimmer historical records gleaned from Alexandria's archives, and Jon had little doubt the Vaos Selino's anchorites retained similar practices in a given scenario.

"Take us down."

Inhaling, Davis inputted the commands into the helm. A moment later, the ship accelerated again, moving toward the planet steadily. As her cloak remained active, it was doubtful anyone would notice the umbra entering the planet's atmosphere, but the bridge crew held their collective breath all the same as the darkness of space gave way to ambient blue and white. After all that had occurred over the last few days, the Flints were prepared for anything.

Despite that apprehension, the *Black Sun* achieved reentry easy enough and continued her descent into the ocean, which cascaded around her invisible form. Jon always felt a certain irony whenever he watched a starship dive into a planetary sea, and the *Sun* was no exception. As he observed the submergence over the viewscreen, with water gradually overlapping sky, that irony felt even more emphasized.

He found himself wondering through the descent. Was the *Black Sun* – if not the umbra altogether – truly that far removed from the Ancient Terran submarines of the First Age? Especially those that roamed the Atlantic during the Second World War?

From the overwhelming blue and initial surge of bubbles, darkness gradually enveloped the bridge's main monitor as they descended into the depths, only without stars in its background. Not that it mattered, as the sensor readout at the corner of the viewscreen provided enough data on the *Black Sun*'s direction and continued submergence. It wasn't long before the bottom was viewed, at which pointed the umbra ceased in its descent and continued steadily toward its destination. Outside the various oceanic life that swam and waded around her hull, nothing seemed particularly interested in the four hundred meter long vessel. Assuming they were able to detect her.

Of particular note, however, was the lack of any other seafaring vessels, or Aquarians for that matter, within the immediate vicinity. In fact, no matter how far or how deep the *Black Sun* channeled, sensors only detected the presence of non-sentient lifeforms. And though none of those present spoke of it, Jon could tell that they were all deeply disturbed by this discovery.

Then, after what felt like hours of undersea travel, the *Black Sun* reached its destination: a deep valley that held something none of the present crew-members had anticipated. Beyond the outlying mountains lay not a small settlement, but a seeming metropolis. Mighty towers, not unlike those one would depict in a terrestrial city, extending from the ocean floor, glistening through artificial illumination. Majestic statues of various Aquarian figures placed about in equal form, alongside vivid undersea gardens. All the while, fair numbers of sea creatures traversed between the edifices, all toward respective destinations of their own. Needless to say, the effect upon the onlookers was almost immediate.

"That," Anna breathed in barely subdued shock. "Is no minor colony."

Alex shook his head. "Why haven't we heard about this place? Surely, this was intended to be a major hub."

"Intended, but not implemented," Jon concurred, considering. What he saw now all but verified what he assessed before. The Aquarians initially had big plans here, and then…they didn't. However, that was not their immediate concern.

"Where is he?" Jon asked, without so much as turning his head. It didn't matter, as everyone in the bridge knew who he was addressing.

Lorelei, her eyes fixed upon the city before her, rose from her station and moved over to stand next to the captain's chair. If she held any emotion toward the metropolis, she kept it well hidden; her expression betrayed nothing. Nothing but complete focus, both physically and psionically.

After another moment, she reached out and pointed with her right hand. "There," she said, indicating a specific tower. "He's in there."

Quickly, the viewscreen magnified upon the designated tower. Though architecturally indistinguishable from those around it, there was some difference. Specifically, the tower narrowed as it extended from its base, eventually culminating into a point at its summit.

A spire, Jon thought, keeping his expressions neutral. He did not want his crew to be shaken any more than they already were.

"Assault team to the hangar deck," he commanded as he rose from his chair.

—————————————— ——————————————

It was a grim company that gathered within that section of the hangar, standing in a group while the nearby technicians continued their tasks. Along with everything else, the *Black Sun*'s crew was now well aware of what occurred as of late, and much more, what the Flint Pirates would be doing about it. Not that any of them had expected less; their unscheduled departure from Nassau had all but emphasized the direness of their situation. So when news broke about the Sognare Sea, a potential galactic war, and their band embarking to prevent/subside all of it, it generally came across as confirmation of the worst outcome rather than an unwelcome surprise.

Even so, one could tell that none of the crew were looking forward to the upcoming voyage into the Sea. The gathered raiders, all dressed in their respective tactical armor and retaining their choice weapons, appeared as though they were about to embark on a suicide mission. Not that any could blame them, given the obvious.

"Your part of the mission should be clear enough," Jon spoke over a holographic representation of the spire. "Array yourselves throughout the tower and standby for the contingency. As we locate the Vaos Selino's den and move into it, the probability of detection will increase, thus necessitating an armed response."

The captain gazed over the raiders. "We do not have exact numbers of the cult's ranks, but we can safely assume that the entirety of Ianessa is under their control and that they will have acolytes spread throughout."

Outside a few furtive glances, no response was forthcoming.

Jon continued. "Our primary objective is the contact and possible retrieval of our target. In either scenario, the cultists *will* be aware of our presence after that point," he gazed with utmost seriousness toward the infiltrators. "Our only chance of escape is for you to cause enough confusion on the outside to allow for a direct evac."

Once he saw that information sink in, he turned to Cheney. "Master

Chief?"

Cheney nodded, taking his cue. "This will be the first time fighting Aquarians for some of you," he explained as Jon tapped the display, which shifted over a digitized image of the designated alien. "You have nothing to worry about, Aquarians bleed and die just like all other biologicals."

The former Master Sergeant continued. "Having said that, they are an amphibious race as you may have surmised. When they're in the water, they gain a finned tail for power swimming."

The image displayed as such, the two legs of the model merging to form a mermaid-like apparatus.

"When they're out of the water, that tail shifts into two legs that they can walk or run with," the model then shifted back. "Since the city's underwater, this pretty much grants them free rein on the outside, which means they can appear and attack from virtually anywhere, so long as they can access the interior."

The screen shifted again, this time displaying the stylized, armored form of an Aquarian soldier.

"As far as weapons and combat skills go, your typical mergrunt is armed with traditional beam and projectile weaponry, as well as a trident as their choice close combat weapon."

The trident formed at the side of the warrior, retracting and extending to display its telescoping capability.

"The cultists will no doubt be similarly armed, but unless they're former members of the Aegia, they will be no different from your average civilian with a gun or blade."

Cheney let that sink in for a minute. "That being said, they will retain superior numbers, so don't get overconfident out there. Do whatever it takes to maintain the initiative; cross every 't', dot every 'i', and kick every ass."

He nodded to Alex, who took over the briefing.

"Your equipment has been modified specifically for this assignment," Alex stated. "On the chance you end up submerged, your oxygen masks, weapons, and hydro-thrusters have been calibrated for the local seawater. Even so, given the enemy's advantages in that environment, I strongly recommend you seek dry land at the first opportunity."

It was then Kaguya stepped in. "Once the primary objective is completed, we will retreat to the uppermost accessible level for evac. Failing that, you can go to the alternate points detailed in your wristcoms. Due to our mission area's layout, there is no shortage of access points. Memorize each and every one of them."

After a collection of nods, Jon assumed the briefing.

"One final detail. Given its size and isolation, Ianessa may hold other evils beside the Vaos Selino." Jon paused, letting the team absorb that statement. "Be prepared for anything."

Another set of furtive glances, but again no verbal response. Finding that acceptable, Jon nodded toward the company. "Let's go."

Ianessa, Timas IV

For all the apprehension, the underwater flight into the city progressed smoothly. In spite of the shifting current, the Condor proceeded through the field of towers with little inhibition. Again the local sea life seemed disinclined to challenge its approach, seemingly aware that it was bigger and stronger. That being said, Jon did note a curious detail. Upon glancing out the viewport during the flight, he watched as what he assumed to be a fish swam by the shuttle. Though he wasn't quite sure, as he was unfamiliar with the species, Jon thought the fish moved somewhat erratically. Just as he thought he saw a peculiar look in its eyes – it possessed three on each side – which seemed equally unfocused.

Regardless, the Condor eventually approached one of the docking stations, where it swung alongside and connected. Typically the Flints would never have used such a forward means of entry, but Jon felt it was prudent this time. Besides the fact they were up against an unaware opposition, the chosen station was one of the city's outermost. It would take longer to reach the spire that way, but circumstances dictated stealth and concealment were more essential than directness.

Standard deployment followed with Cheney and the raiders going first, followed by Kaguya, Alex, Jon, and Lorelei, respectively. Once the team was safely in the tower, the Condor detached from the docking station and moved away. Jon had explicitly ordered the pilot to remain within the city space, both to facilitate a rapid evac and for a swift response if necessary. This was another irregular practice. Both basic strategy and common sense emphasized that the evac ship remain outside the combat zone until time of withdrawal. However, as the enemy seemed to lack any type of a defense – and once more, was ignorant of the assault team's entry – it was better to forgo the orthodox approach.

Jon felt reassured wth the unconventional tactics upon seeing Ianessa's interior for the first time. The glimpse was neither welcoming nor hopeful. Before the assault team, a sparsely illuminated corridor lay open, littered with debris and rubble and framed with cracked, broken walls. An apparent ruin, for lack of better description, with no indication toward its cause or origin.

"Welcome to Ianessa," Alex dryly commented as he stepped forward, gazing over the surroundings with the same unhopeful expression as the others. "Home to those with sweaty brows."

He shrugged toward the resultant dubious glances. "What? No one here plays visgames?" he inquired in equal dubiousness.

Shaking his head at his brother's reference, Jon checked his wristcom. As had been read by the *Black Sun*'s sensors, the city was far from deserted; there were a fair amount of lifeforms within, though spread about invariably. And despite all facts and logic, the elder Flint had a sinking feeling that they were not all cultists.

"Move out," he commanded, prompting the group to deploy, regardless of their growing inhibition.

——————————— ———————————

Due to the city's layout, it took quite some time for the assault team to make any significant progress. Whereas similar establishments would have had streets and avenues to advance through, Ianessa only had buildings interconnected by access tubes. And obviously, none of the present company was going to risk utilizing one of the local transit systems, even if they were in working order. For that and additional reasons, it was an elongated, tedious trek from the edge of the city toward the spire.

Devastation was the only commonality throughout the structures. Though none of the damage was such that water had broken through, the shattered debris, broken constructs, various marks, and fluid splatters, some of the latter might have been Aquarian blood, were as abundant as they were disturbing. It was quite clear that some form of unrest had taken place long before the *Black Sun*'s arrival, there would have been telltale signs of an outside invasion, but none of the Flints could ascertain what it was exactly. Not that there weren't theories passed around.

"Some kind of class revolution?" Alex offered as he looked around, still on alert for any potential obstructers. "Those things happen, you know."

"Sure, but isn't the damage a little much for that?" one of the raiders commented. "And wouldn't we have run into someone by now if that were the case?"

"I don't know, but whatever it is, it's making me piss my pants," one of the gruffer raiders commented, gazing over a set of tears, or what may have been claw marks, in a sidewall. "This is unnatural."

Ignoring the banter, Jon glanced at Lorelei again, as he had done systematically since their arrival. For what it was worth, the psion didn't seem any more disturbed than the rest of them. This indicated much to Jon, especially as he recalled Kurzis; whatever had taken place on Timas was apparently not the same event. Otherwise, there would have been the presence of Taint – the malevolent psionic residue that had emerged over and corrupted the aforementioned jungle world – and Lorelei would have been far more disheveled as a result.

The psion's composure didn't make whatever had transpired around them less disturbing, though. It was clear that something dark and sinister had occurred upon this world. Perhaps neither as dark nor as sinister as whatever had attacked the *Daedalus*, but still an unnerving matter. The fact they had yet to encounter another sentient, although they were now well within Ianessa and lifeforms continued to be detected throughout the cityscape, only emphasized that discord.

Could this be connected to Sognare as well? Jon wondered, considering. He surmised the only thing that separated Timas IV from other worlds of its type was its proximity to the Sea. However, even with that datum, the elder Flint couldn't come up with an explanation of the current circumstances.

And then they turned another corner and entered a relatively extensive space, some type of open gathering area. A majestic window filled one wall, granting a spectacular view of the surrounding cityscape. However, that was not the sight that caught one of the raiders' attention.

"Captain..."

Jon quickly turned at the raider's alert and gazed toward the spot identified by his outstretched arm. The scene he beheld generated further dread.

At long last, they had found an Aquarian. A long-deceased Aquarian impaled to the nearby wall in a crucifix pattern. Stripped of all but torn, ragged clothing, its torso laid open from disembowelment and its head rendered eyeless. All while additional lacerations of various shapes and indications splayed across its form, including what appeared to be bite marks.

"Okay..." Alex let out, his voice measured. "This is usually the part where one gets the proverbial hell out."

Kaguya took a moment to analyze the body. "Wounds were inflicted when he was still alive," she explained. "Tortured to death."

"Put up a fight, though," Cheney gestured at the spread arms, whose clawed fingers indeed showed blood around them. "Whoever did this to him had a helluva a time about it."

Again Jon gazed toward Lorelei. "Anything more?"

The psion stepped forward, evaluating the remnant. "This was a civilian," she stated, gazing over the ruined form. "Possibly a laborer, given his physical structure."

She then willed herself to look up at the eyeless face. "Much more, his final expression is not just of pain and anguish," she said. "Rage?"

The sudden sound of clamoring rapidly shifted the team's attention, all bringing their respective weapons about. Upon turning, however, they saw that a simple piece of debris had fallen from the ceiling, causing a relatively loud impact upon its drop.

"Let's continue," Jon ordered as he withdrew his Trafalgar, taking one last glance toward the hanging corpse before turning and moving away. The rest were quick to follow, all on high alert as they went.

Even so, despite their caution and vigilance, none appeared to recognize a subtle change in their surroundings. The further they penetrated the city, the more that which was around them began to stir, gradually drawing closer to the assault team as it progressed...

Black Sun
Call of the Moon

Chapter XI: City of Rapture

Flint Pirates umbra *Black Sun*
Timas IV

Humming the notes to something he had once gleamed from Alexandria – *Electricity, Electricity,* he believed it was called – Braun continued to adjust the internals of his right arm at the Lounge bar counter. As usual, it was a tedious task that took up a fair amount of his time and energy, but it was still something that needed to be done regularly. Given how vital his artificial limb was to his operation, he could not let it fall into disrepair. Or worse, become *irritable* over whatever uncalibrated parts Braun had not addressed.

Given all that was happening, it was somewhat surprising to see the rest of the Lounge was decently occupied – if subdued in noise level – with many of the booths filled and a game in progress at the billiards table. That is, until one realized, as Braun did in his ever jovial manner, that there wasn't much to do here at the bottom of the resident sea, especially when all the action was undoubtedly happening off of the ship. Not that those around Braun were complaining, of course, with grog being consumed as much as any other social occasion, and the usual jokes, gossip, and conversation being passed around with equal earnestness. Again, only the noise level was substantially lower than the norm, such that there wasn't even background music playing. As if the crew were collectively afraid they would awaken something in the depths with their ambient noise level.

Once the final adjustment clicked into place, the arm's outer plate slid closed, thereby completing the adjustments. Smiling at his work, Braun brought his limb up to examine it, flexing its black and gold fingers gracefully, only for the limb to suddenly launch itself outward at various angles. It reached toward the tankard of a nearby patron, flailed at the ceiling lights, and grabbed for Lloyd's arm. Braun was forced to haphazardly restrain it every time, beating it back into submission in the usual fashion.

"The usual glitches, Professor?" Anna observed as she came over and took a seat beside the cyborg, signaling Lloyd for a drink.

At that, the arm reached out once more – this time toward Anna's posterior while she was in the process of sitting down – but Braun restrained it before it could make contact.

"Yes, the usual glitches," Braun replied in seeming admonishment, pounding his right arm back down to his side. "Nothing out of the ordinary, I assure you."

"I bet," Anna glanced at the man widely hailed as Terra's most significant scientific mind as he forced his false limb into submission. Even now, she did not know what to make of him, and she had a feeling the rest of the crew, up to and including the Flint Brothers, had a similar problem.

Doing well to notice the operations officer's bland expression, Braun espoused a frown as he, at last, subdued his arm.

"May I inquire toward your presence here, Miss Reed?" he asked without a hint of displeasure. "I would think you would be on the bridge at this time…"

"Not much to do right now except wait, so Barbarossa's giving everyone leisure time," she shrugged as Lloyd passed her a tankard, which she accepted with a nod. "At least until Gran picks up the inevitable distress signal."

Taking a drink, she looked at the engineer. "And what about you? Shouldn't you be dealing with the fact we're several thousand meters underwater?"

Braun shrugged, as much as he could with his cybernetics. "She'll hold out well enough," he exclaimed as Lloyd passed him a refilled jug, which his right arm was quick to grab. "I wouldn't be much of an engineer if I didn't waterproof my work."

"I suppose not," Anna agreed, glancing upward. She almost anticipated the dripping. "Any bets on how well it's going?"

The scientist seemed to consider the query. "About as well as can be expected in the present circumstances. No doubt, they're still making their way toward wherever this explorer is being kept."

Now it was Anna's turn to frown. "Would be nice if they do so without running into trouble this time around. Though we both know that's not going to happen."

"Indeed," Braun concurred with his usual bemusement. "Given all that's happened in the last few days, I'm surprised Miss Granuaile hasn't picked up that distress signal yet."

"Give it time," Anna shrugged, suddenly feeling the makings of headache she didn't think was from the depth pressure. "This particular day is still young, after all..."

Ianessa, Timas IV

The deeper the assault team journeyed into the city, the more extensive the devastation from *whatever* had taken place. Though they still had yet to run into any structurally compromised areas, damage and telltale signs of violence remained abundant as they progressed, seemingly growing more and more chaotic.

Additional bodies were also discovered as they pressed on. Though only a select few were as "elaborately presented" as the one they had initially found, certain cases were borderline unhallowed. Much of their number had decomposed beyond recognition, and all bore similar signs of vicious struggle and aggression. Shattered and broken limbs, seemingly infinite cuts, lacerations and disembowelments, various forms of dismemberment, and potential signs of cannibalism. All were accompanied by the same postmortem expressions of rage and virulence that the first corpse had held as if the Aquarians had remained in apparent bloodlust even as their bodies failed.

It was quite evident to the assault team what had taken place. Rather than an outside attack of some kind, the destruction that had been wrought upon Ianessa had been at the proverbial hands of its inhabitance. Whatever had happened, it had inflicted nothing less than pure madness upon the citizenry, causing them to turn upon each other like rabid animals, all sense and morality seemingly removed. Once again, Kurzis came to mind, as those that had been with that past assault team recalled the Taint corrupted flora and fauna that had been encountered prior to the *Daedalus'* discovery. And yet, somehow, they could surmise that this evil was different, the lack of Taint notwithstanding.

Among other things, Jon mused, *these corpses don't appear to be physically mutated.*

Though the bodies were warped beyond their original forms in one way or another, said warping appeared due to physical trauma, not any type of metaphysical blight. As eroded as the wildlife on Kurzis had been, they had somehow retained their baser survival instinct, whereas these Aquarians had clearly been thrown into thorough crazed aggression, attacking any that were around them. And much more, a few corpses showed signs that the individual had turned on themselves, mutilating their body in extensive, insatiable fervor. Not even those possessed by rogue Devilblades acted in that manner.

That all said, there was one similarity between Kurzis and Timas that Jon, and those around him, did well to recognize. They were being watched. By several obviously aggressive, yet seemingly cautious, stalkers.

"How many?" Jon whispered to Lorelei, who remained beside him as they kept moving.

"Eight presently around us," Lorelei stated, frowning at what she read. "With more approaching."

"Are they the cultists?" Alex murmured, holding his Trafalgar, anticipating an attack at any second.

Lorelei shook her head. "No, their minds…" she started, but trailed off as unsettling darkness crossed her expression. "…I believe they're the original citizenry."

Jon opened his mouth to press further, but Lorelei already knew what he would ask.

"However, I am detecting more abundant sentience toward the city center," she explained, before glancing furtively toward the captain. "All positioned around a mind, not unlike those around us."

It was only then the pieces fell into place with Jon, his eye widening in realization, and an all too certain dread from within.

Then picking up on sudden movement, Jon raised his own Trafalgar and fired off a snapshot, the resultant crimson beam launched into his target. With a shrill cry, the hideously scarred, one-armed Aquarian fell back and did not move.

Acting just as quickly, Alex brought his pistol up and fired into another aggressor as it charged the squad. The rest of the assault team was quick to follow as six more assailants ran screeching toward their position. Six beam shots impacted the feral, for lack of a better word, Aquarians that, upon the death of the first, abandoned their hiding places for an immediate strike. In a matter of moments, several more fresh corpses were rendered into the area, the last dispatched by one of Kaguya's shurikens. Deathly silence once again reigned following the previous anguished screams.

Alex, his pistol still at the ready, moved over to check the being he and Jon had shot. As expected, it was a horrifically mangled, twisted creature with many wounds, some self-inflicted. The rest of the team never lowered their weapons or stopped scanning their surroundings.

"Just what in the Seventh Circle happened to…?"

"The worst possible outcome," Jon spoke. "This planet is mere lightyears apart from the Sea…" A cold swell came over him as he continued. "What do you think happened upon the Black Moon's initial awakening?"

It took a moment, but eventually, the rest of the group made the connection. The emerging psionic activity from the Sea had done far more damage than any of them had realized. It had plunged the inhabitants of Ianessa straight into hell.

"*Kisama…*" Kaguya breathed in uncharacteristic shock. She tried to fathom what that kind of uncontrolled psionic power would do to any mind, sentient or otherwise, within its range. Even the outermost touch would have caused permanent damage.

"These poor bastards…" Cheney muttered, now gazing at the corpses with sympathy. They never had a chance against that kind of force. Nor would they have been able to foresee its occurrence.

Alex closed his eyes momentarily. "No wonder the moonies set up shop here," he let out, suddenly feeling disgusted at the notion. "This must be holy ground to them."

Even Lorelei couldn't help but feel a heavy heart as she looked over the surrounding bodies. Indeed they had suffered and suffered greatly. And worse, contemplating what she perceived of the Black Moon's apparent will, she had an inclination that, much like Nassau, this had all been unintentional. The citizens of Ianessa had been caught within the wake of its stirrings, and nothing more.

Even so, it made her, and several others, once again wonder. What exactly were they trying to set free? Was it something that had been purposely imprisoned? What…what would happen upon…?

Another feral cry sounded from behind, this one distant but drawing closer.

"Let's go," Jon commanded.

Nodding in near unison, the group began moving forward, new shadows trailing them as they pressed further.

Flint Pirates umbra *Black Sun*
Timas IV

"How do you think it's going?" Davis inquired as he continued to look out over the cityscape from the observation deck viewport. No matter how long he stared at it, Ianessa never seemed to become less ominous, less like an underwater haunted house. It was rather unnerving.

Casually smoking her pipe, Boss took in a lungful of smoke and exhaled before answering. "Well, it's still standing," she observed with minor interest. "And it doesn't look like any major action is taking place, though that can change at any second."

"Obviously," Davis commented sarcastically as he folded his arms. He had a feeling that *something* had already occurred. Not that he thought a group headed by two Devilblade Wielders and the greatest assassin in the universe would have much trouble from a bunch of religious fanatics. "Though I wonder why it's taking so long…"

Boss shrugged. "They do have a lot of ground to cover. And they're proba-bly running into minor hindrances along the way," she offered. "Other than that, however, I don't think it'll be much longer."

"Here's hoping," Davis replied, just as one of the local fish, or he assumed it was a fish swam by the viewport. He cringed upon sight of it; somehow, it didn't feel natural. "The longer we stay here, the increasingly disturbed my calm becomes."

Boss let out a 'heh' around her pipe. "You do realize we're heading into a far different, far worse Sea after this, right?"

"One worry at a time," Davis rejoined. Another fish swam by, and it appeared just as grotesque as the previous. "At the very least, we'll be in space again," he said, doing his best to ignore the turbulence in his stomach. "I hate being underwater."

Boss couldn't help but smirk. "Are we displaying signs of hydrophobia, Mr. Davis?"

"Please," Davis admonished. "Some of my more natural environments usually include water in some way: bathtubs, showers, hot tubs, various beaches and waterparks around the galaxy, all with proper female companionship, of course."

The ace resisted the urge to roll her eyes as the helmsman continued. "But several thousand leagues below?" he shook his head. "If I wanted that, I would have joined the Imperial Naval Patrol instead of Starfleet. Much less become a *space* pirate…emphasis on *space*."

Boss nodded at the thought. "It does lack a certain charm compared to space," she admitted. "But at the same time, I can see why some people would be enamored by it."

Davis sniffed. "I always thought Hemingway was overrated. Did love Verne, though, present circumstances notwithstanding."

He watched as another fish swam by. "'The sea is everything,'" he quoted. "'It covers seven-tenths of the terrestrial globe. Its breath is pure and life-giving.'"

The helmsman could almost feel the ace's intrigue as he went on. "'It is an immense desert where man is never lonely, for he feels life stirring from all sides.'"

He shrugged. "I could say similar stuff about brothels. But when put into that context, I can also see how giant blobs of water might inspire such fascination."

For obvious reasons, Boss couldn't help but blink. "Forgive me," she exclaimed. "But I never thought of you as well-read…"

Davis laughed. "Ancient history," he said, memories seemingly coming into play. "Nothing really interesting, though."

Flippancy aside, Boss retained her intrigue, but ultimately decided not to prod. "If you say so," she pronounced simply, exhaling another breath full of smoke.

Silence made its grand return as both continued to look out over the city beyond.

Ianessa, Timas IV

It took longer than any of them would have liked, not helped by the seemingly continuous run-ins with psionically maddened Aquarians, but eventually the assault group made it into the spired tower. Almost instantly, the team felt as though they had stepped into a different world from the rest of the city. While the spired tower was as much in ruin as the rest of the metropolis, it held several differences. Namely, there was an obvious lack of corpses lying around, though blood and fluid splatters remained as part of the devastation, fair numbers of lit candles filled the space with light, and the presence of crimson banners in specific areas. Banners that proudly displayed a blackened crescent moon, alongside equally blackened Aquarian writings.

"Pardon me good sirs, ma'ams," Alex recited as he looked over the assorted banners. "Do y'all have a moment to discuss our lord and savior the Black Moon?"

That earned him a hushed chuckle from the other raiders, as well as a semblance of a grin from Kaguya. Jon, however, was more focused on the shadows that were approaching from a nearby corridor. Upon his signal, the group immediately dispersed and took cover along the broken surroundings, training their weapons as the shadows grew across the ground. It wasn't long before murmuring – no, *chanting* – voices accompanied those shadows.

Sure enough, a line of obscured figures soon appeared. All garbed in crimson, the blackened crescent proudly displayed throughout. Quite unlike the Aquarians the assault group had been dealing with, these acolytes seemed to be passive, though the Flints did well to note the beam pistols and retracted tridents that some of the robed figures were carrying. Fortunately, they seemed otherwise preoccupied with their apparent ritual, and so passed by without ever noticing the squad.

Why do I get the sneaky suspicion they're not praying for love and peace? Cheney thought as the assault group began to move out of their hiding places. As luck would have it, the acolytes were heading further into the tower, and it was a sure bet they would go someplace relevant. The Flints knew better than to let that opportunity slide, and so followed, but retained their caution.

"Holy shit," one of the raiders exclaimed as the group peered out from the corridor into the immediate space. Though some of the others could have done without the crass retort, it remained an appropriate exclamation toward what lay before them.

Vastly bigger than any of the spaces they had moved through, it was quite obvious they had, at long last, found the temple. Additional banners hung from the ceiling and nearby walls, while several murals and weavings depicting varied images of the black crescent – oft with adoring worshippers below it – were spread around the immediate area. Acolytes moved about the space, either practicing their rituals, conversing, or otherwise going from one place to another, all quietly and reverently as one expected. And of course, there were armed guards spread about, appearing as intimidating and humorless as any secular counterpart would.

"Looks like we hit Jonestown," Alex murmured, keeping his eyes on the nearest acolytes. Though they appeared otherwise focused, almost to a disturbing degree, neither the younger Flint nor the rest of the group was about to take any chances. "So, shall we get started?"

Jon looked over and nodded at Cheney. With a return nod, the master chief signaled the other raiders, who immediately moved forward and began to spread out around the temple, all while remaining out of sight from the occupants. In a matter of minutes, they would all identify and take position in various fire zones, ready and waiting to attack at the given word, or more likely given sounds of conflict.

Satisfied, Jon and Alex both concentrated and formed shrouds, adorning themselves in faux crimson garb. However, Alex then remembered Lorelei.

"We might have a problem..." he told Jon, gesturing over to the psion and her black and gold attire.

Jon saw what he meant. "Alex and I will go ahead..."

"Please," Lorelei retorted, right as her form began to change. Much in the manner that the Flints had formed their Devilblade empowered shrouds, the psion's color and profile shifted and fluxed, culminating in her taking on crimson hooded garb of her own. With her non-Aquarian features as effectively veiled, she appeared no different from the Flints or the surrounding religious sect.

Quite obviously taken off guard, the brothers could only glance at each other and shrug. However, before they moved out again, Alex had yet *another* realization.

"Wait a minute, where's Kaguya?"

"I'm here," a voice spoke from behind him. Turning around, he saw that the kunoichi had also taken on the local dress.

"What the-?" Alex let out at the ninja.

"Clearance sale," she stated as if anticipating what Alex was about to ask.

Jon raised an eyebrow. Not so much because the assassin somehow managed to slip away, gain her new garb, and then return without any of them noticing, but somehow she managed to fit it over her ninjato as well. In fact, Jon couldn't find any sign of the sword along her back, which somehow felt... off.

Even so, he had higher priorities. And now that they were all ready, he saw no reason not to proceed. Passing the same nod he had given Cheney toward the other three, the apparent converts stepped out into the open and began to move, with Lorelei at the forefront to guide them. Moments onward, they all but disappeared into the sea of red, appearing no different from the oblique figures that surrounded them.

Slowly, reverently, they progressed ever deeper into the unholiest of domains.

Chapter XII: The Whisperer in Darkness

Flint Pirates umbra *Black Sun*
Timas IV

As with the rest of her species, and all other sentients that possessed sense and taste toward the acoustic, Gran held great appreciation toward music. Though she had no aspirations to enter the music field personally, she still had her favorites from various races and cultures. A list that was continually growing as she encountered more and more compositions, and was in turn, aided along by helpful crewmates that, knowing of her culture's love of melody, provided her with works that they thought she would appreciate.

As she was the only one present on the bridge at this time, being the obvious candidate to keep watch while the ship remained underwater, Gran saw no reason not to relax at her post and allow for some background music. Her current playlist consisted of songs given to her by the Captain, all of which naturally originated from Terra's First Age. Ancient Terran music was a great fascination for Gran. For such a primitive, divided culture, Ancient Terra produced some of the finest melodies, and with only the most basic of instruments. She was still amazed at what the human voice could accomplish on its own, to say nothing of wooden constructs with but strings and hollow points in key areas, or elongated brass tubes and eponymous "drumheads" stretched over spaced out shells. Even the stranger of Terran instruments, such as the outlandish "bagpipes," produced sounds that could captivate and mesmerize when used appropriately, of course.

Presently she was listening to a song entitled *Do It Again*. Like most Terran classics, the original creators and performers had long faded into time's passages, yet Gran could tell from the song alone that they had been among the great composers of their age. With but a relatively mere combination of strings, keys, and percussions, the composition took on a unique rhythm, one that was neither too mellow nor too blatant and flowed like water from beginning to end. Almost to an entrancing quality, such that Gran could practically feel herself become lost in the music.

If only the lyrics made sense... she thought with a minor sigh. In her opinion, that was the song's lone downfall. Though they weren't completely abstract, she had a feeling that they were written under heavy narcotic influence. The best she could surmise was that they centered on discord, albeit in the strangest of occurrences. Water thievery, and the impotence of resultant justice. A man forced to abandon his cheating lover for another, much worse woman. Excessive gambling and trickery. She supposed it all fit the song's title, given the repetitive nature of the verses' subjects; otherwise, any attempt to draw a deeper meaning only led to the first signs of a resultant headache.

Regardless, Gran could easily see why her captain was fascinated – perhaps even obsessed – with the works of Terra's Age of Progression. Indeed they held a quality to them that modern works, Terran or otherwise, seldom matched...

Despite her fascination, however, Gran wasn't so absorbed by the music that she didn't hear her console beep in warning. Frowning, she tapped a few keys, causing the beeping to cease while a new set of sounds entered her headset. Almost immediately, her hands snap up to her earpiece, an expression of equally sudden panic running across her face.

No!

Abruptly ending her music, Gran then tapped her comlink. "Second officer to the bridge!"

She didn't know if it was due to his usual promptness or the anxiety in her voice, but Barbarossa exited through the turbolift no more than a few moments later.

"What is it?" he demanded as he moved to the Lyran.

"I'm detecting multiple contacts incoming from arc," she reported, picking up the shift in the Leo's musculature response. "I can't identify their drive signatures from here, but…"

"It's safe to assume our Piscean friends are back," Barbarossa finished for her, frowning. Somehow he knew they'd show up. "ETA?"

"Approximately twenty minutes," Gran stated after a quick estimate.

"Battlestations."

Alarm klaxons, the dimming of overhead lights, and the flashing of red promptly followed. By the time Barbarossa had taken his seat in the command chair, the bridge was filled, designated personnel hurriedly retaking their posts. All the while, the viewscreen, and multiple display screens flashed to display the incoming contacts…

Ianessa, Timas IV

Compared to the hindrances they previously encountered, it had been relatively easy for Jon, Alex, Kaguya, and Lorelei to enter the temple. As was to be expected, none of the acolytes could be bothered to grant any of the four a second look as they moved through their ranks. Even the guards flanking the temple entrance didn't so much as glance up as they passed, with one eliciting a drawn-out yawn in the process. Not that any of them had expected much more than that; so long as they were attired in red with a black crescent etched somewhere, none of the cultists had any reason to suspect them.

See the uniform and not the face, Jon thought, remembering another Ancient Terran adage, one still applicable in the Third Age. It helped that the other cultists, who were chanting in much the same way as the initial group, were passively entering the space, thus making it much easier for the Flints to blend in. That behavior in itself was suspicious to the team. Was there something about to happen?

As for the temple, it was more or less what they all expected. Having been established in a former playhouse of sorts, the area was configured in an enlarged ground floor and several balconies enclosed around a fragmented stage. More red banners and candles were spread throughout the space. Compared to the faded grandeur that the Predecessor temples held, the Vaos Selino temple was merely decrepit looking, as well as appearing hastily cobbled together, being little more than weavings and candlelight placed around a broken, forgotten interior. The abundance of fallen debris, some of which were as large as boulders, only emphasized its decaying condition.

In spite of that, however, the cultists seemed content with the chamber, as those entering didn't appear put off by the dilapidated surroundings. It didn't take the team long to notice their apparent congregation was moving toward the front areas of the chamber, their chants growing steadily louder. Four more armed guards stood motionlessly in front of the stage, observing the group's approach. Even Jon felt disturbed as he and the others watched the proceedings from the background, having taken cover behind one of the larger wreckage fragments.

"I suppose youth service is out of the question," Alex quipped. Beside him, Kaguya drew a kunai into her hand, ready to strike at a moment's notice.

Rather than reply or take similar action, Jon glanced at Lorelei, who nodded back in her usual manner. As enigmatic as the response appeared, the message was clear enough to the elder Flint. They would see soon enough.

It was then a new figure appeared. Another cultist, this one dressed in black shimmering robes, walked on to the stage with an air of great self-importance. Moving to the center of the stage, conveniently just behind the wall of guards, the newcomer held out his hand, signaling those in the audience to silence.

"The Vaosin," Lorelei clarified as if the cult leader wasn't obvious enough. "Basically, the Order's 'Anointed One.'"

Both Jon and Alex sniffed derisively.

"'Do not lay hands on the anointed,'" the elder recited.

"My ass," the younger retorted.

"*Lunis ka* my children," the Vaosin began.

"*Lunis ka*," the gathered intoned in unison. Even with his features other-wise obscured, it was easy to tell that the cult leader was quite pleased with the response.

"On this day, we are gathered for a great and most holy task," the figure declared with typical drama. "For our Sacred Moon has once more granted illumination…"

Was that a pun? Alex thought.

"Once again, it calls to us. For us to render our souls unto its holy light," the 'anointed one' proclaimed to his audience. "For the galaxy around us remains in turmoil, ever poised to turn and devour itself as a great serpent, bringing destruction and damnation to the unfaithful."

The Vaosin raised his webbed hands for effect. "Only by the light of the Moon may we find salvation. Only upon its holy plain may we find para-dise," he avowed. "For the time of judgment will soon be upon us, and those found wanting will be cast aside, never to rise."

Light and paradise from a black, barren moon? Jon mused while remain-ing attentive.

"And so," the Vaosin continued. "May you rejoice, my children! For the Moon has chosen you!" he declared with even more drama. "To render yourselves unto its divine light! To ascend unto the waiting paradise!"

Shit, Alex thought, *more canaries for the mineshaft.*

"Upon a great ship, you shall journey across the Sea, guided by its sacred gleam," the dialogue went on. "And though you may face many trials, by your faith, my children, you shall brave them! And in the end, reach that which has been promised!"

Another raising of the hands by the leader resulting in mass murmured praises.

"You will join your brothers and sisters, those who have given themselves unto the Moon, and have received its gift of eternal peace! You will be freed from the chaos that devours our galaxy, freed from the pain and suffering of mortality!"

Then the lowering of said hands. "You shall be saved, my children," the Vaosin affirmed, feigning closeness to tears. "We shall all be saved."

"*Lunis sava,*" the gathered chanted in apparent solemnity.

Once more, despite his obscurity, one could just depict the satisfaction in the cult leader's features.

"Your chariot departs within the hour," he announced joyfully. "Take only that which you need."

He then placed his hands together into a makeshift circle over his chest, emulating a full moon, and bowed head.

"*Lunis fe.*"

"*Lunis fe.*" the acolytes replied, mimicking their leader's gesture.

With the end of their anointed one's affirmation, the gathering began to disperse. The Vaosin and his bodyguards watched their exodus with intent clearly looking for any form of dissent within the ranks, or at least any indication that one of the soon to be departed knew what truly awaited him or her.

"Well," Alex snorted, "that was enlightening." He watched the mass of robed figures move off then glanced over to his brother. "Any objections to taking out the good reverend along the way?"

Jon considered. "I suppose we would be doing the Aquarians a favor," he said, looking upon the departing acolytes. "To say nothing of them…"

"It also serves our purposes," Lorelei spoke up, earning the attention of the other three. "The entrance to the lower levels is presently locked, and the only key is in his possession."

Detecting no sign of treachery among his followers, the Vaosin turned and marched off the stage, with his bodyguards dispersing as well.

"We will need it in order to proceed," Lorelei finished.

Jon and Alex both looked over to Kaguya.

"You know what to do," the elder Flint indirectly commanded.

Nodding, Kaguya withdrew her kunai back into her robe sleeve and rose. With subtle motion, she moved away and disappeared completely into the surrounding space.

―――――――――――

Letting out a subdued exhale at the monotony, Cheney continued to stand his watch. He didn't know how long it had been since the main group had entered the temple, but it felt like an eternity had passed since then. An eternity of standing around in near boredom, while the locals went on about their business in front of him, seemingly unaware of the mortal danger they would face should they do anything out of the ordinary. He could imagine it was much the same for the others.

By this point, the raider contingent had more or less spread to their assigned positions throughout the tower, ready and waiting to initiate crowd control and/or the diversion for the grand escape, all the while staying on the look-out for additional developments. Waiting to execute a plan was a monotonous task, but it had to be done. There was no telling what could set the moonies off, much less make them aware of what was occurring in their beloved temple. It helped that they were freaky little shits as it were, either walking around in a strange daze while chanting, or praying – or both Cheney suspected – or conversing to one another in hushed tones. And that was before one got back to the subject of the armed guards, who Cheney also suspected had certain personal parts of their anatomy removed. Whatever the case, the sooner they got out of there, the better he would feel.

That being said, he was far from unprepared for the worst. Whereas the most heavily armed cultist in sight merely held a bigger gun than the others, Cheney, like the other raiders, was dressed in his custom tactical armor and equipped with everything he needed to do his job. Everything he needed to bring semi-divine retribution upon the heretics around him … and then some.

Compared to most pirates, Cheney had a different perspective on being "armed to the teeth." To him, it was not about how many weapons one possessed at any given time, but rather what one needed to kill with. In such a case, he only needed three specific instruments to eradicate anything and everything he came across: his Navassa H-89 beam rifle for his primary, his Grenada J-34 beam pistol for his backup and, as part and partial for any Imperial Marine, his V42 dagger for everything the first two were inadequate to handle. All fine-tuned and customized to his exact preferences, and all weapons he knew he could expertly kill or incapacitate with, depending upon which was necessary. The cultists wouldn't have a prayer – pun intended – if and when the shooting started.

That went for the younger ones as well; he was sorry to say. Amongst the sea of red fabric, Cheney could pick out a few shorter figures from the rest. Apparently, the Vaos Selino also incorporated a children's ministry. A frown crossed his face; he couldn't tell if the little ones were armed, much less willing to fight, but he wouldn't have put it past the adults to have indoctrinated them in violence.

Unfortunately, child soldiers were all too common throughout the modern galaxy. Whether through ethnic warrior traditions or grownups simply utilizing cannon fodder, there were many cultures and independent factions that armed their young and sent them into battle, oft times well ahead of the adults ushering them. Cheney had fought more than a few in his time, some of which had even been surprisingly good combatants, but it had never gotten easier for him. Would he have to fight more here when the shooting started?

It never changed seemingly. Even now, he thought he caught a glimpse of metal within one of the children's robes, a sinking feeling welling in his stomach as a result. Dread Pirate or Dread Soldier, it was all the same…

He grit his teeth, forcing those thoughts away. Such a line of thinking had never been beneficial, and most certainly wouldn't help him in the present setting. Besides, he had long accepted that the galaxy was a wretched place and that his lot in it was to kill. If anything had changed at all, it was that he now killed for his own fortunes rather than those of Terra or an Emperor he had never met. That, strangely, made it much more worthwhile.

And then, Cheney's eyes caught movement. One of the robed figures – one of the *smaller* robed figures – suddenly turned his head in the pirate's direction. A cold swell came over the raider as a result; what was the little bastard thinking?

Slowly the diminutive figure began to move away from the adults and other children, quietly wandering toward Cheney's hiding spot. Swallowing, Cheney silently reached down and withdrew his dagger. He hoped and prayed to God – the one true God – that he wouldn't have to use it on a child. Also, for obvious reasons, the action could not start yet. As much time had passed, the main group had clearly not reached their objective, and there was no telling what would happen if the Flints' presence was discovered now. And that was before his side came into play. For all he knew, every one of the cultists could have been armed, not just the guards.

Go away brat, Cheney thought as the younger Aquarian continued making its way toward him. *There's nothin' you want to see here.*

Yet the child continued to approach, despite the former soldier's inward warnings. It was obvious now that the kid thought he had seen something and, in typical fashion for his age, was too curious to adhere to his undeveloped survival instincts. Thus, taking in a resigned breath, Cheney quietly waited for the little one to get close…

Suddenly, one of the adult cultists called out from the background. Upon hearing her, the child turned its head, pausing in its movements to listen more. Then, once confirming the call, it turned away completely and ran back, its earlier curiosity forgotten in the face of its concerned parent.

Letting out another, much longer exhale, Cheney sheathed his dagger. That had been far too close for his comfort, but at least the worst had been averted. Praise the Lord and Hallelujah!

That being said, the mission was far from over, and there were plenty more where that kid came from. Thus, only relaxing so much, the Dread Pirate Cheney remained at his watch. All the while, those before him equally remained unaware of his presence.

——————————————— ———————————————

It was only a few minutes after the main group had obtained the designated key that they proceeded through the *formerly* secret door and further into the apparent temple depths. None inquired toward what Kaguya had done to obtain those keys; rather, it was safe to say that the Vaosin was well and truly somewhere in the Malebolge now. And knowing how the assassin worked, it was also safe to assume that the false prophet had passed on "creatively."

In either case, they were now moving through a series of darkened corridors, whose collective purpose and arrangement had been lost when Ianessa fell. Whatever they were originally meant for, now they came across as nothing less than a great dungeon or chamber, appearing just as decrepit as the rest of the city. If anyone had to guess – except Lorelei, of course – they were now likely utilized as the Vaos Selino's secret prison, meant for those who questioned the *former* Vaosin too expressively or otherwise denied the Vaos Selino's divinity. Or they simply detained any that had gained the cult's direct interest but refused cooperation.

The more things change… Jon thought, recalling similar institutions from Ancient Terra, as well as during the Thousand Year Darkness. Not that he was surprised; he had learned long ago that religious intolerance was another universal constant, no matter the race or specific faith. And the cult already moonlighted – for lack of better expression – as a terrorist cell.

Of course, what truly disturbed him – as well as Alex and Kaguya, if their responding expressions were any indication – was the silence of it all. If there were sentients locked away behind those doors as suspected, shouldn't they have heard their approach and reacted accordingly? Shouldn't they have been calling out to them, pleading for liberation, or crying out for deliverance? Yet outside the sounds of their footfalls, there was nothing else: just an eerie, perhaps even deathly silence, not unlike that of a crypt or mausoleum.

And though he was partly tempted, Jon was not about to inquire to Lorelei about it. Even with the hood of her shroud based robes drawn, he could tell she was unsettled by their present surroundings. Only the universe knew what she was feeling from within those "cells."

Eventually, after a fair amount of walking, the group finally reached the specific cell.

"Here," Lorelei stated, holding her luminator up toward a blank metal door.

Though the door was indiscernible from the others they had passed to this point, the three warriors couldn't help but feel a certain ominousness surrounding it. After all, none of them knew what to expect on the other side; they already knew that the good Captain Jennis had been exposed to the Sea not too long ago, and had been in captivity since. Two years of which had been spent under the Vaos Selino's tender mercies.

Even so, as they had previously established, there was no turning away from this. Thus, Jon nodded the inevitable command to Kaguya.

Reproducing the key from her robes, Kaguya moved up to the door and inserted it into the appropriate slot. With an ill-omened hiss, the door slowly slid open, showing even deeper darkness within.

"Hassa...hasfa loka..." came a low, murmuring voice from within the gloom.

"Captain Jennis?" Jon called out, doing his best to ignore the accompanying stench. It was clear the captive had not left his cell in the last two years – and likely had lacked access to a workable plumbing system – the result being an almost overwhelming fetor. The luminators confirmed much of the latter.

"Good lord!" Alex nearly stammered, his light shining between various low quality food remnants and unmistakable bodily waste. Such was its effect that he reached to burn it all away with Forneus, but was stopped by a hand motion from Lorelei.

"Lossa...valikana..." the voice continued to tremble from a corner of the cell. The group directed the luminators accordingly.

There, what might have been an Aquarian, was crouched down against the wall, huddled within a brown, heavily stained and torn blanket, continually muttering in sheer incoherence. The limbs that extended from the blanket were withered, almost completely devoid of muscle tone, while long, matted hair hung from the head that was presently shielding itself from the light. And amidst the mixture of rotten food and undisposed refuse, there was another smell: one not unlike a dead fish that had been exposed to open air for far too long.

Silently and almost serenely, Lorelei moved away from the group – ignoring their questioning gazes – and knelt beside the disheveled being. And then, just as slowly, she reached her hand out, attempting to touch his shoulder. The act was immediately met by near-violent defensiveness.

"Asfa...! Eldrio le caba...!" the entity now yelled out in greater volume. Reacting fast, Jon and Alex went for their Trafalgars while a shuriken slipped into Kaguya's hand. All three were quickly halted by another one of Lorelei's hand motions.

Allowing a moment for the prisoner to settle down, Lorelei once more reached out, this time making contact with its shoulder. And this time, the prisoner did not react violently. Rather, its physical tremoring stilled considerably, while its muttering, ever slowly, drifted away into a calming silence.

Then, in seemingly whole minutes, the three at the cell's entryway watched as the creature's head, again ever slowly, turned away from the corner and drew to look toward the one now making contact. Indeed the face on it was Captain Jennis', as the trio remembered from his image profile, but like the rest of his body, it also was withered and diminished, with hair of an abnormal shade of green, even for an Aquarian, extending in virtually every angle. All the while, two whitened eyes, obviously long blinded by the perpetual darkness, attempted to focus on the psion.

"Lotis...ema cada...?" Jennis managed to breathe, bringing his hand up to Lorelei's, grasping it lightly.

For her part, Lorelei nodded. "Yes," she said as if answering the gibberish question.

At that, a look of joyful peace entered Jennis' face, his mouth extending into a smile of rotten teeth. *"Epla...!"* he let out, almost breathlessly. *"Esta re callum...!"*

Though neither Jon, Alex nor Kaguya understood the wordage, they at least understood the emotions behind them. Whatever gibberish Jennis was spouting, it was not Aquarian nor any other recognizable language. However, the former explorer appeared pleased with Lorelei's answer.

Suddenly, Jennis reached his other hand out – much faster than initially – and placed it against Lorelei's, holding it with more strength than previously displayed.

"Etoi..." he whispered to the psion. *"Lepla va gal ata!"*

Softly, Lorelei grasped the hands of the explorer, holding with clear intent. In that instant, Jennis' blinded eyes, at last, focused, gazing directly into Lorelei's amethyst set, almost as if they had regained their sight.

Minutes slipped by, with the pair maintaining contact – both physical and meta – with one another. Throughout, the three at the doorway watched as a curious pair of lights began to emerge from either: purple for Lorelei and a mysterious orange from Jennis. At first, the dual lights only enveloped their bodies, swirling and shifting about as lightning amongst two storm clouds. Yet as time went by, those lights grew more and more in span and vibrancy, such that the whole cell soon became enveloped in them, obliterating the surrounding waste in the process.

In time, the three at the entrance were forced to shield their eyes as the pair of contradicting, yet harmonious lights emerged from the cell, seemingly to engulf the whole of the prison. If not the entirety of Ianessa…

And then, all at once, the lights vanished, darkness settling back in. As the three unshielded their eyes, they watched as Lorelei, in respectful reverence, lowered Jennis' body to the floor. She brought her hand over his face, closing his eyes with a single sweep.

Solemnity settled in as the warriors watched. For all that he had suffered, Captain Jennis was at last free. Both from his present tormentors, and from whatever demons had taken hold of him long before.

After a moment passed, Lorelei spoke once again. "I have the information," she said as she rose, looking back at the group. "I have what we need."

It was Alex that inquired first. "What we need…?"

Lorelei nodded, at long last smiling. "The course…" she explained. "…that will take us through the Sea."

Flint Pirates umbra *Black Sun*
Timas IV

"Piscean fleet emerging from arcspace," the tactical operator reported as he looked over his monitor. Sure enough, the screen displayed a multitude of Piscean ships suddenly appearing near Timas IV, reappearing in realspace one after the other. The fact there was more than four this time wasn't lost on the bridge crew, who stared either at their monitors or the viewscreen.

For his part, Barbarossa frowned as he watched the influx of the Pisceans through the command scope. As he had discussed with Commander Boyington earlier, he had expected the four ships that appeared at Nassau to have been but a meager part of the Rohu Dag's larger fleet. Yet now that he saw it in actuality, he was beginning to realize they had their work cut out for them. Even so, he was far from intimidated, much less willing to let the Pisceans have their way.

"Standby on missiles and torpedoes," Barbarossa commanded as he had the scope retract. "We'll wait for them to achieve orbit, and then…"

The tactical station promptly beeped in warning. "Missiles launching from the Piscean ships!" the tactical operator called out as multiple new signals emerged on the viewscreen.

Barbarossa went on high alert. A missile attack directly after reemergence? That didn't make any sense. Even if they had somehow detected the cloaked *Black Sun* at the bottom of the sea, there was no way the Pisceans could have locked onto her so quickly. And much more, why were they attacking with a missile spread rather than torpedoes? Surely those would have done far more damage, especially against a single target.

Unless, of course, the *Black Sun wasn't* the actual target.

Barbarossa's eyes suddenly widened with realization. "Intercept!" he roared, hoping and praying to Aslan he was wrong.

Missiles erupted from the *Black Sun*'s midship launchers, flying out and then ascending through the depths. By the time they emerged from the sea, the Piscean missiles had entered the atmosphere and were descending rapidly. A flurry of explosions sounded as the two groups merged, with the *Black Sun*'s swarm deflected the oncoming barrage as much as possible.

Unfortunately, the *Black Sun* was simply unable to produce enough missiles to deflect the whole spread. As such, several Piscean missiles plunged into the water and continued onward through the depths until they reached their intended target.

Grinding his teeth, Barbarossa could only watch with the rest of the bridge as the missiles fell upon the city. Explosions flashed within the watery depths as buildings shattered and fell, while the resultant pressure waves caused further damage. And that was only the initial assault.

Barbarossa understood precisely why the Pisceans had attacked the city immediately. The enemy knew the *Black Sun* – and Lorelei with her – was already on Timas IV, and that to approach the planet meant opening themselves to attack. As such, their only choice was to force the *Sun* out of hiding by effectively holding Ianessa, and the Flint Pirates that had embarked there, hostage, bombarding the city piecemeal until the umbra came out into the open. Even if it risked what the Pisceans had been seeking, they had obviously decided that the *Sun* was the larger threat.

And much to Barbarossa's ire, he knew there was no choice on their end either. Not while their forces remained in the city, entirely vulnerable to the Pisceans' assault.

"Second barrage incoming!" the tactical operator reported in alarm, just as another set of signals were detected and displayed.

Barbarossa let out a final growl before giving the order. "Decloak the ship and move to intercept!" he commanded, the bridge crew scrambling to comply. "Standby for direct combat!"

Upon those commands, the *Black Sun* rematerialized and rapidly ascended through the ocean depths, much as her earlier missiles had done. In a matter of minutes, she breached the surface and proceeded ever upward into the sky, her obsidian hull shining brightly against the water spray,

All to meet an oncoming enemy once again.

Chapter XIII: Approaching Dread

Ianessa, Timas IV

The group had just begun making their way back to the main temple when the quaking erupted. The intense force of the cascading pressure waves pitched the tower about compelling the four to brace themselves against the walls. For a time, it seemed as though the tower would topple over from the shock, but fortunately, the Aquarian construct resettled into its original equilibrium, allowing the four to stand without support once again.

"The Pisceans," Kaguya exclaimed, her eyes looking toward the still darkened ceiling.

Jon and Alex didn't have to look to Lorelei to come to the same conclusion. "Double time," the elder Flint brother ordered, prompting the group into a run down the corridor. Stealth no longer mattered at that point. Though they had gained what they came for, enemy incursion – by a much greater threat than Vaos Selino adherents could ever hope to be – was imminent.

"Foxtrot One to Charlie Two, sitrep," Jon called out over his wristcom as the group continued to move.

"Foxtrot One, a Piscean fleet just appeared out of arcspace, thus the earlier missile barrage," the Condor pilot spoke evenly, obviously trying to mask his discomfort. "Bravo Sierra is already moving to intercept."

All four easily saw the logic in that. The Pisceans had deliberately attacked the city to force the *Black Sun* out, and Barbarossa had taken the only choice they had.

"Acknowledged," Jon answered, momentarily considering. Barbarossa would take the *Sun* well into the fight, that was for certain, but it would only hold back and dishevel the Pisceans at best. There was no way she would keep the assault forces from entering Ianessa. "Standby for pickup. We're en route now."

"As you command Foxtrot One," the pilot replied before signing off.

Within seconds of the comlink's termination, Jon and the others picked up the sounds of voices and hurried footfalls coming down the corridor. Those sounds quickly took form as a number of red-robed figures emerged, opening fire with their energy weapons.

Figures, Jon and Alex both thought simultaneously as they dispersed their shrouds and charged forward, Devilblades in hand, while Kaguya threw her cloak to the side before drawing her ninjato. Apparently, somebody had found what was left of the Vaosin, and that the dungeon key was no longer in its possession.

The beam fire was everywhere, but the bolts were easily absorbed/ deflected by the dual energies of Astaroth and Forneus, thereby allowing the three warriors to advance into close quarters with the worshipers turned combatants. At the pirates' approach, the cultists switched to their tridents, which they managed to extend right as the three were upon them, but once more, it barely mattered. Without bothering further with energy attacks, the Flint brothers slashed into the first two cultists that entered their reach. At the same time, Kaguya easily rushed under a trident thrust and struck her would-be attacker's lower torso. The three newly rendered corpses fell to the ground simply enough, with only more to follow.

226

It was over in less than a minute, and with little difficulty. Only one of the cultists managed to last longer than the others, having produced a pocket gun at the last moment before Alex reached him. However, the younger Flint easily evaded the surprise attack and proceeded, slaying his target well before he or she could fire another shot. After that, the corridor fell back into its earlier silence.

"There will be more," Alex stated, earning nods of agreement from Jon and Kaguya. That much was obvious; the cultists were now alerted to their presence and would do anything in their powers to hinder them. At least until the Pisceans finally reached the city.

"Let's go," Jon ordered, getting the group to move again. It would be a long run, but they were sure to make it. The only question was would their ship be in a position to receive them.

Flint Pirates umbra *Black Sun*
Timas IV

Another swarm of missiles surged at the *Black Sun*, only to be intercepted by the ship's phalanx emplacements. Through the myriad explosions, more rampant beam fire followed as the Piscean warships closed in, the green energy shots easily deflected by the umbra's shields as her beam cannons twisted around, returning the attacks with their crimson barrage. At least one *Throd*-class destroyer was obliterated, but the rest managed to evade, continuing their onslaught as they maneuvered. And that was before their support ships moved in, adding their volume of fire against the lone pirate ship.

Looking over the numerous enemy contacts as displayed on the main monitor, Barbarossa felt himself glower with dismay. As had been expected, the Rohu Pisceans had brought many more ships with them this time around; if not their dag's entire fleet, then the greater portion of it. Presently they were fighting in a higher orbit, with the enemy warships spread out yet still concentrated on the *Sun* while their fighters dueled with

Boss' Corsairs. No bombers or dedicated strike craft had been deployed, and Barbarossa could understand why. Their objective wasn't to destroy the *Black Sun* so much as hold her down.

"Torpedo status!?"

"All loaded and ready to fire!" the tactical operator reported, just as the ship quaked again from more enemy cannon fire. "Enemy cruiser closing from starboard!"

Barbarossa turned just in time to see a monstrous *Hlighr*-class cruiser coming at them, her main cannons already firing. Beams slamming into the starboard shields, the *Sun* again shook with violence, forcing Barbarossa to grip the arms of the command chair.

"Evade and return fire!"

Hearing that, Davis brought the ship into a climb and pitched her over, unmasking her underside stern cannon to the *Hlighr*. The cruiser began to turn to its starboard side to evade, but it was much slower than the *Sun*, and her larger size only enhanced her target profile. Two crimson beams launched from the stern cannon, striking along the Piscean ship's portside in quick succession, causing such damage that the stricken warship began to roll toward her starboard. Clearly, she had lost helm control. A third cannon shot would have doubtlessly finished her, but by that point, a trio of *Vulgtm*-class frigates sped into firing range, covering for their larger comrade with beam fire of their own.

Barbarossa scowled as the *Black Sun* launched another missile barrage in response, forcing the three smaller ships into evasion. Once again, the *Black Sun*'s primary weakness was evident; she was only one ship. And while she could easily have annihilated the Piscean fleet on her own – at least in a conventional battle – the fact remained she was far less ideal as a lone defender, and the Pisceans were taking clear advantage of it by keeping the bulk of their ships scattered. As a result of the latter tactic, the *Sun* was bogged down; the Flints were forced to divert time and energy into hunting down and destroying individual ships, one after the other, thereby extending the fight considerably. Not an ideal scenario in a defensive battle, as Barbarossa knew well from experience.

If only we had other ships in our service... Barbarossa thought with irritation as the *Sun*'s bow cannons fired, taking out another Piscean ship, another cruiser, a *Hrii*-class if his eyes weren't mistaken. That was an additional problem; the Pisceans were throwing a lot of ships at them, but they were all "lesser" types, ranging from frigates to cruisers.

A bold strategy to be sure, using smaller, more maneuverable – as well as more numerable – ships to hinder a superior but very much singular adversary, the Leo contemplated. *However, the Rohus possess at least one battleship in their fleet, and perhaps more of the same,* Barbarossa recollected. *Where are they?*

"Torpedoes incoming!" Anna called out in warning, just as the sensor screens displayed the newly launched projectiles.

"Redirect phalanx!" Barbarossa ordered.

Despite her most glaring disadvantage, the *Black Sun* remained the most powerful ship in the galaxy, which more than evened everything out. This was best displayed as her phalanx emplacements redirected their fire to the oncoming torpedoes; standard weapons of their design could never hope to pierce through torpedo grade shielding, yet in a spectacular display, the projectiles were instantly sniped from the immediate space.

No sooner than the collective glare of the explosions diminish did Barbarossa roar. "Fire our torpedoes! Full spread!"

Upon that command, the six projectiles launched from their tubes and sped out into space, each one directed to a specific target point. Though the Piscean fleet was fairly spread out, more than a few enemy ships had grouped to concentrate their firepower, making them ideal targets for the *Sun's* higher yield weapons. Naturally, those ships detected their approach and so directed phalanx fire at each one. But, quite unlike the *Black Sun*'s armaments, the Piscean guns were easily deflected by the torpedoes' shields. It helped that said weapons had been enhanced in all areas by Professor Braun's efforts.

Moments later, six larger scale detonations erupted, the fire consuming whatever Piscean warships and craft were in their immediate proximity. Those that weren't destroyed were easily rendered into flaming shards, their burning, deadened remnants now flinging aimlessly about the battlefield. Eventually, they would all be drawn in by Timas IV's gravity well, the resulting atmospheric entry completing the torpedoes' work. In the meantime, however, there were plenty more Piscean ships to fight, with those that had not been harmed, or those just damaged by the barrage regrouping and returning the *Sun*'s fire with their beam weapons.

In response, the *Black Sun*'s main cannons unleashed their wrath, obliterating or severely damaging one Piscean after another with each attack. Alongside, those Corsairs that weren't committed to the dogfight added their fire, strafing the enemy warships with their wing-mounted beam cannons, exacting additional destruction throughout.

Still, Barbarossa knew, it wasn't enough. They were inflicting heavy damage on the bottom feeders, but it didn't matter as much. The opponents in front of him were not the ones he should be hunting.

"New signals coming in from arcspace!" Anna announced, entering commands into her station. A second later, a new display appeared on the viewscreen, showing the new contacts. "They're too small to be warships!"

Barbarossa nodded. "The assault force," he exclaimed.

Another sensible strategy on the enemy's part; rather than have the immediate ships deploy assault troops in the middle of a firefight, a portion of the Piscean fleet remained outside the system, where they could launch arc booster equipped transport craft at the appropriate moment. And with the *Black Sun* drawn into fighting the enemies around her, it was all the more likely that one or two transports would slip through and reach the city.

It also explains where their capital ships were deployed, Barbarossa thought with some derision.

He had initially hoped to at least eliminate the enemy flagship, as well as keep their shock troops from reaching Ianessa, but neither objective would be accomplished now. Even so, he could at least make things easier for the captain and those with him.

"Standby for missile barrage! Target and fire after reemergence!"

Though he complied with the orders, the tactical operator didn't look hopeful. "I don't think I can get them all, sir!"

"Just get as many as you can," Barbarossa replied, then looked toward the helm. "Mr. Davis, come right, mark four five! Bring us toward their point of entry!"

"Aye, sir!" Davis responded as he brought the *Sun* into a right turn. Their new course would bring them closer to the estimated emergence point for the assault shuttles, thereby giving the missiles less distance to reach.

Unfortunately, the Pisceans saw that the *Black Sun* was moving to intercept and so began to move in as well, again concentrating their fire as much as they could. As before, the umbra's shields deflected the oncoming beams while her cannons returned their fire, destroying or critically damaging more Piscean ships as a result. Even so, the earlier specified weakness remained in play, and more than a few enemy warships moved into position to cover.

Sure enough, Barbarossa and the bridge crew watched as the assault shuttles emerged into normal space, already speeding toward the planet. With any Piscean ship or fighter in range moving to protect them.

That would not stop the Flint Pirates.

"Missiles, fire!" the Leo commanded in another roar.

With that, missiles erupted from the *Black Sun*'s sides, twisting and speeding toward the targeted shuttles. All at once, the Pisceans moved to intercept, firing their missiles and redirecting their phalanx at the incoming shots, scoring several hits and resulting explosions. Even so, more than a few missiles made it through, reaching and obliterating a fair number of the shuttles before they could enter Timas IV's atmosphere.

It was then Barbarossa saw something peculiar. At first, it appeared as though a missile was going to hit its targeted shuttle, having bypassed the warships' phalanx fire and the fighters sent to intercept it. However, right before it could strike, the second officer thought he saw a flicker of energy around the shuttle, only momentarily visible, but quite like an energy shield. And then, the missile, despite also having been enhanced in power and performance by Professor Braun, was deflected, its detonation never reaching the Piscean craft. Thus, the shuttle continued unharmed, eventually reaching Timas IV's outer atmosphere.

What was that? Barbarossa questioned. Unfortunately, he couldn't focus on it, as another pair of cruisers came charging in, their main guns firing at the *Black Sun*'s bow. The Leo warrior shifted his attention back to the fight, commanding the *Sun*'s weapons to return fire.

No longer under threat, the Piscean transport craft easily descended through Timas IV's airspace, then continued to dive into her ocean, proceeding on toward the awaiting, and utterly defenseless, city.

Ianessa, Timas IV

Pandemonium ensued as the denizens of Ianessa realized all was not well. Though the earlier missile attack had been mercifully brief, it had been enough to cause great panic and confusion, and indicate that the moonies were no longer the only presence within Timas. In typical civilian fashion, they had attempted to flee, though to where specifically it was doubtful even they had considered, all but trampling over each other as they moved en masse toward the various exit ways. Only the harsh words, tridents, and occasional beam bursts from the outlying guards kept them back, though it was quite clear they would only do so for a short time.

Cheney, however, wasn't concentrating on the developing riot. Like the other raiders, he had realized what was happening the moment the city quaked, and that an enemy incursion was imminent. He could only mutter a near-silent curse as he readied his beam rifle, waiting for the first breach to be made in his immediate area, which he knew would be soon.

Sure enough, several parts of the surrounding walls exploded open, with multiple Piscean troopers surging through the breaches, beam weapons already firing. Numerous cultists – namely the unarmed masses – were immediately cut down, propelling the survivors to scramble madly toward any safe haven. Regrettably for them, the intruders were very adept at shooting retreating targets, and only the most fortunate were able to avoid the constant beam fire. Those that were armed, namely the aforementioned guards, attempted to fight back, but they were no match for actual soldiers. They, too, were brought down easily, despite their attempts at resistance.

It was only when Cheney, at the opportune moment, shifted around his cover and fired a three-shot burst into one of the fishmen, did the raiders make their presence known. With a flurry of crimson fire, several of the Pisceans were laid out with the dead cultists, while those that remained shifted their attention accordingly. Moving to gain cover of their own, the Pisceans returned the fire earnestly. Though several more of their number fell as they went, it was enough to keep the pirates effectively pinned. Cheney was forced to duck behind his shelter as a multitude of emerald beams smashed into it.

I'm getting too old for this shit, Cheney thought dryly as he waited for an opening. It was ancient, if cliché Terran expression that had been uttered by many a veteran in his present position, and Cheney saw no reason to discontinue the tradition. At the very least, the opposition wasn't much, if the abundance of Piscean death cries were any indication.

Stepping out, Cheney unleashed another barrage. He scored hits on several Pisceans, their power armor once more rendered useless against Professor Braun's enhancements, before ducking back to avoid the return fire. This time, however, Cheney didn't remain behind his cover, he crouched down and sprinted to another part of the area, firing as he ran. Two more enemy combatants became corpses with torso shots. Two or three Piscean shots managed to hit him during the transition, but his armor's shielding deflected them easily enough.

Once behind another structure, he reached down to his waist compartments and withdrew a specific grenade. "Bang!" he called out overhead, signaling the other raiders toward his intentions before throwing the device into an area where several Pisceans had taken cover. A second later, the device landed and burst, generating a specifically directed shockwave that, guided by the grenade's sensors, surged through the spaces, eliminating the threat and ruining much of the architecture in the process. Those that survived the initial blast were rendered completely dazed, and therefore easily cut down by the responding fire from the other raiders.

"Terran scum!" Cheney heard a hiss from behind. Instinctively, he deftly dodged the impending pike thrust, swung his rifle around, and fired another two shots into his would-be attacker. It fell, but there were two more with him, their pikes extended and ready to strike.

Knowing better than to go for his dagger, the sub-commander turned his rifle around and used the buttstock to block and parry both attacks. Quickly, he dropped down and fired another shot into one of the pair. Had the enemy been human, the beam would have pierced his or her gut, but Cheney rolled, jumped to his feet, and fired a shot into the thing's head to be sure. The body was in the process of crumbling when its comrade swept its pike and connected with Cheney's shoulder. His shielding prevented the piercing, but the impact flung the rifle out of his hands. The fishman hissed, believing it had the former marine, it quickly raised its pike to impale the pirate.

Unfortunately for it, however, Cheney was much faster on the draw. Swiftly extracting his pistol, he fired a multi-burst shot into the fish's guts, causing it to recoil with each blow. By the time Cheney stopped firing, the Piscean was effectively forced against a wall, the body slumping back and falling to the ground. A great smear of blood followed the corpse down.

Cheney immediately reholstered his pistol and dove for his rifle, which had naturally landed in an open area. Rolling across the ground after he grabbed it to avoid the responding beam fire, he quickly ducked behind another formation. Utilizing the structure for cover, he continued to fire upon the oncoming horde, taking down several more enemies in the process.

This just keeps getting better and better, Alex thought as he unleashed another wave of flame at the cultists, incinerating or severely burning the figures. As with most religious fanatic types, it appeared the moonies were blindly dedicated to their "holy" cause. It seemed like the entirety of the cult had been sent to hunt down the intruders, and they were all attacking with a fervor usually reserved for actual soldiers. Not that they were making much headway in avenging their *former* Vaosin, though they were doing well at detaining the four from their impending departure.

The cultists were also becoming increasingly well-armed with each new wave. This latest group had set up a megagun at the end of the corridor, which was continuously firing as the would-be shocktroopers pressed their attack. Naturally, the heavy beam fire, while otherwise effective against conventional troops, was easily evaded or deflected by the brothers' Devil-blades. But the frequency of the attacks hindered their progress. Alex had just cut down another trident armed cultist when he was forced to raise another wall of flame to deflect attacks.

"The moonbrains have quite the arsenal, don't they!?"

"At least we know where all the tithes went," Jon rejoined dryly as he moved through another grouping, unleashing a flurry of black waves that savaged the enemy fighters as he passed. He reached his left hand out to generate another black hole, absorbing the enemy's beam fire and redirecting the blasts among the cultists. Unfortunately, even he was forced to throw up a bigger void to absorb the repeating megagun fire. He swept Astaroth about and launched another black wave at it, but the overpowered beam spray reduced its effect. He glared as he was forced to defend again.

Not far from his position, Kaguya moved into a dead run, cutting her way across three more cultists as she went. At the end of the hall, she jumped to the side, avoiding two moonies firing at her location. Two kunais launched from midair took out the attackers. She returned to her dash, this time making a sprint toward the megagun nest. The gunnery crew responded accordingly, turning the weapon and aiming at the approaching assassin. Kaguya maneuvered around the fire efficiently enough, all the while readying her ninjato as she drew closer.

Unfortunately, just as she reached the gun nest, one of the beams shot ricocheted and struck a glancing blow across her right thigh. She stumbled from the force of the blow and the shock. Unlike the raiders that followed her, Kaguya's armor was not designed for durability but stealth and maneuverability. It lacked shielding, was more flexible than deflective, and therefore offered little protection against heavier firepower. Hissing back the resultant pain, the ninja just narrowly moved to the side of the corridor, evading the follow-up shots.

"Kaguya!" Alex yelled as he flicked his left arm out, eliciting a fire shield over her as she crouched against the sidewall. He started to move in against the megagun, but additional cultists charged him. Choosing to parry their tridents while he maintained Kaguya's shield, the younger Flint held both prongs for a brief moment, then threw them back and unleashed another fire wave, incinerating the pair before they could counterattack. He turned and sprinted toward Kaguya's position, but the megagun crew had anticipated this and aimed their weapon upon him. Cursing, Alex generated a second fire shield for himself. It provided a defense but also slowed his progress. He glanced over to Jon, only to see his brother also being forced back by the rapidly increasing numbers and sheer determination of their opponents. The situation was deteriorating fast. If they weren't careful, it could escalate into another full out massacre, as it had been on Sumatra.

Taking advantage of the new aim of the megagun, Kaguya attempted to skirt around her barrier and renew her attack. The megagun flankers saw her movement and turned quickly, firing their beam rifles to hold her back.

Frustrated with fighting off the cultists and the megagun impeding their exit, Jon executed a full three hundred and sixty-degree power slash then slammed his left fist into the ground. The resultant wave of darkness erupted across the space, easily overcoming the attackers. The darkness didn't cause actual harm but rather obstructed visual senses in their entirety.

That was more than enough for the three warriors to act. Without any way to track the infidels, the surrounding cultists were completely vulnerable and quickly eliminated. Within minutes, the corridor was filled with abundant death cries as the Flints went on the offensive, wholly unhindered.

What was surprising, however, was that the megagun and its flankers continued firing, despite visibility being nonexistent. Even the constant beam fire failed to illuminate the sheer blackness, such that the repetitive sounds of discharge were the only indication that their weapon was fired at all. Firmly believing in the divine protection and guidance of the Moon, the gunnery crew figured that whatever they struck, their beloved Moon would sort it out. With divine fortune, they would kill the heretics, darkness be damned.

Thus, the gunner was surprised when he heard the flanker to his right elicit a cry of pain, followed by the unmistakable sound of a body falling over. This was immediately followed by the more horrific scream of the flanker to his left, as well as a sudden wave of heat washing over the gun nest. Had the man spontaneously combusted? To make matters worse, the one behind him, monitoring the megagun's external power system, repeated shrieked in apparent agony before going silent. The megagun soon followed in that silence, its beam fire coming to an abrupt and entirely unintentional end.

It was only then that the darkness receded, and much to the gunner's horror, standing directly in front of the inoperable megagun, the three heretics looked upon him like black and gold clad demons, their swords held at the ready. The gunner pulled back the megagun trigger helplessly, hoping and praying – literally – that the weapon would fire.

After a short moment, the gunner remembered he had a sidearm. The gun never cleared the holster before, much like his comrade, he too went up in flame, burning out like a dying candle. Nothing remained of him, or the megagun.

Once more unopposed, the four moved forward. As they progressed, however, Lorelei felt uncharacteristic acrimony encompass her as a new presence entered her awareness…

———————————— ————————————

With the sound of an underwater explosion, the shuttle breached the tower wall. The hatch promptly opened to allow its passengers inward. Following their protocols, the Pisceans spread out with weapons at the ready, looking for any sign of the enemy. Though they were technically outside the main combat area, at least for the moment, it wouldn't do well for any of their numbers to be caught by skirmishers. Bitter experiences from Nassau kept them from putting anything past the Flints and their entourage.

All except for one. Unlike his escort, he was well aware that the Flints had not placed any of their raiders within the present surroundings. As such, he casually exited the shuttle, his dress shoes making far softer impacts against the floor than the Pisceans' greaves, only to stop after taking but a few steps into the tower. Slowly inhaling, he looked upward, allowing both his conventional and *special* senses to take in his new surroundings.

In all honesty, he was rather disappointed with what he found. After all he had heard and researched about Ianessa, he had expected it to be more… *enrapturing*. Instead, he only felt the barest traces of residual energy, while the presences outside the tower were little more than sub-sentient. Only the latter indicated that this place had been touched by the Black Moon at all; otherwise, it was virtually no different than any other Aquarian city, beyond its proximity to the Sea.

Even so, he wasn't there to take in the sights. And Inanga had made it clear that they had a schedule to keep; the good Dagon was in no way fooled about how his beloved fleet would fare in a prolonged fight with the *Black Sun*. Nor, after Nassau, how his troops would last against the Flint raiders.

Shaking his head, again wishing he had gained better help for his agenda, he nonetheless nodded to the Piscean squad leader, signaling him to continue. Though visibly put off at being commanded by a Terran, the squad leader nevertheless complied, directing his soldiers to move forward. With brisk motions, the Pisceans filtered out, moving deeper into the tower and closer to the action. He, of course, followed along, while keeping his focus on a specific presence therein…

Black Sun
Call of the Moon

Chapter XIV: The Outsider

Timas IV

Boss grimaced as several beam shots slammed into her Corsair's shields. They weren't strong enough to pierce them, of course, but it was always an unnerving feeling whenever she took a hit or several in this case. Regardless, it did little to slow her down. She twisted her fighter around and fired her vulcans at the oncoming Piscean craft, managing to shoot down two of them almost simultaneously in one pass. The remaining Pirhas counterattacked just as quickly, forcing her to barrel roll out of their line of fire. She accelerated, turned again, and scored another one of their number then sped away, her Corsair easily outrunning her would be opposition.

Persistent little fish, Boss thought as she unleashed her vulcans on another group of fighters, only managing to shoot down one before the rest scattered. Whatever their capabilities amounted to, the smallcraft were as fish-like in form as everything else in the Piscean arsenal. Combined with the sheer determination of their pilots, and what actual skill they may have, the opposition functioned more like a large school of rabid piranha rather than conventional fighter squadrons. Their sheer numbers only emphasized that image.

Of course, sheer numbers only amounted to so much against superior flyers, and the Flint pilots were quite obviously the latter. Outside of damaging one or two, the Pisceans had yet to take out even one Corsair, while their ships were being eliminated by the dozens. That being said, however, the enemy fighters were not going down as fast as Boss would have liked. The *Black Sun* was also having a hard time reducing the ranks of the large task force. If the Pisceans intended to drag out this fight, they were doing a hell of a job.

"Break now, Two!" Boss called out to her wingman before jerking her control stick. The two Corsairs split formation as another Piscean group moved in, charging headlong and firing. Minutely shaking her head at such novice tactics, the Terran ace nonetheless brought her fighter about as the Pisceans flew past, firing her vulcans into their bunched formation. Several more fell as a result, and by the time the Pisceans managed to turnabout, Boss and her wingman were well passed them. Not that they would have been able to pursue anyway as another pair of Corsairs attacked the fighters.

It wasn't long before she was shot at again as two more Piscean fighters charged from the left. This time Boss banked her Corsair out of their beam fire and spun into a barrel roll to evade as they flew by. She started to twist around to shoot either target in the ass, but much to her surprise, one managed to squeeze off a missile before she could complete the maneuver. Cursing, she engaged her countermeasures and went into a dive, the missile trailing after her.

Fortunately, the missile ended up losing its target and overshooting, disappearing somewhere beyond her scope. Unfortunately, her threat indicator sounded as she was locked on again.

"Corsair One, below you!" Corsair Two called out in warning, emphasizing the danger.

Despite the outcry, Boss already identified the threat. Upon executing her dive, she inadvertently entered the sights of an enemy *Nyth*-class destroyer, which wasted no time in training its guns upon her. Moments later, Boss had a whole storm of beams and missiles flying at her which she was forced to maneuver through on her current vector. Any attempt to pull out would leave her open to a direct hit.

Experience and instinct simultaneously engaging, Boss waded through the projectiles, systematically moving her Corsair into whatever opening presented itself. It was tricky, but by no means impossible for her, even though it seemed the *Nyth* had fired its entire arsenal. Recognizing an opportunity, she maneuvered her fighter on course for the perfect attack run, which the Pisceans would only realize too late.

Smirking as she came over the *Nyth*'s topside, Boss triggered her fighter's wing-mounted beam cannons, firing repeated bursts as she flew over. As expected, the destroyer's shields and armor were utterly incapable of deflecting the fire, resulting in several explosions ripping across the enemy ship's hull. By the time Boss finished her run, the *Nyth* was still intact, but beginning to drift as secondary explosions began to erupt across her.

All in a barrel, Boss thought rather smugly as she moved away from the dying destroyer, Corsair Two joining her wing. It was only one ship out of many, especially if the Pisceans had several more in reserve as she suspected, but it was a satisfying kill all the same. There was just nothing like properly fried fish, after all.

Still, it didn't look like the fight would be ending anytime soon. Once more, the Pisceans were doing well keeping the Flints locked in place, and therefore unable to support their comrades down below. They were undoubtedly fighting Pisceans themselves at this point, and perhaps something more if Boss' eyes and sensors hadn't lied to her before. When that one shuttle…

A combination of beam fire and noise from her threat indicator snapped her back. More enemy fighters were now tracking her from directly behind, firing their guns in rapid succession. Boss banked again with Corsair Two following, evading the fire and turning about to face their latest foes.

Ianessa, Timas IV

Slapping another power cell into his rifle, Cheney continued fighting, waiting until there was a break in the enemy fire, only then rising from his cover and counterattacking. More Pisceans fell, joining their buddies on the ground, but a fair number of them were still living and breathing, thus ensuring Cheney and the other raiders withdrew into their respective covers. It was getting rather agitating; the fight had to have been going on for over a half-hour now, and the fishies showed no signs of slowing down.

If only we had a Delphinian among us, Cheney thought blandly as he again waited for a break in the energy discharges. He was starting to wonder if the Pisceans were ever going to run out of troops. *At the very least, they're easy to kill individually,* he mused. Two more death cries from the other side validated the observation, all the while the raiders had yet to lose anyone.

Still, the former Imperial Marine knew it couldn't go on like this indefinitely. Eventually, one side had to give in this contest, and Cheney had no intentions of his being 'the one.' Thus, he waited for another break before dashing to an alternate set of cover – one that would allow him to effectively flank the Pisceans – firing his rifle as he went. He didn't get any kills during the transition, but that didn't matter; once he reached his new roost, he was more than able to fire into the ranks of the enemy, taking down three more of them before being forced to duck. A fourth and fifth soon followed when the fishes attempted to move against him, cut down by support fire from the other raiders.

That was when he heard it, even amongst the constant gunfire. The sound of multiple footfalls entering the battleground and taking up with the opposition, all the while the volume of fire increased exponentially. Cheney frowned; it was the third round of enemy reinforcements since the start.

Just what we need now, he thought sardonically as he gripped his rifle, preparing to fire again. Additional numbers or not, they were still fish. Thus they would die just as well as the ones he had taken down already. *More chum for tonight's...*

He never completed that sentence as his ears picked up another sound, the sound of cries – *non-Piscean* cries – not far from his position. Hearing those, he immediately rose, rifle trained for support. However, upon his eyes meeting the horror before him, he involuntarily gasped.

One after the other, raiders were lifted from their hiding places and into the air, just barely managing to cry out in the process. Even those that attempted to fire in support were eventually dragged upward by the same unseen force. Those few who managed to get off a shot – as well as hit the mark – could only watch helplessly as their fire was easily deflected. Once in the air, their fates varied; some were strangled, while others were forcibly hurled into nearby hard services, and even more, were gruesomely contorted midair.

It wasn't long before Cheney was also pulled upward as if by an invisible rope that was wrapped around his throat. Struggling to breathe, he dropped his rifle as he instinctively reached for his throat with both hands, desperately attempting to break the chokehold. Yet, no matter how much he fought, the bands around his throat tightened.

Quickly, he identified the source of the attack, a single figure walking through the center of the battlefield with mocking casualness. The Dread Pirate's vision was blurring rapidly; the raider was unable to comprehend the sentient fully, but he could just depict his silhouette, it was a Terran male. That was more than enough for Cheney; his right hand abandoned his throat and reached for his pistol. If he was going to die, then he sure as hell was going to take this bastard with him.

Unfortunately, he had just managed to draw the pistol when he was suddenly flung across the hall, slamming back first against the sidewall. Even with his shielded armor, the sheer force of the impact reverberated through his body. He also knew, through his hazing consciousness, that he would have easily been pancaked if not for it. And it was a safe bet there was now a fairly detailed body outline etched into the wall, much like something he saw in one of those vistoons that regularly played in the *Sun's* lounge.

And yet, his original drive remained as he moved to bring up his pistol. With his vision becoming increasingly blurry, Cheney was nearly able to fire off a shot before the gun was ripped out of his hand. After that, he was pulled away from the wall and slammed into it no less than three more times.

With the last impact, Cheney felt blood escape from his mouth as he was, at last, dropped to the ground. Feeling very much like an abused ragdoll, it was nothing short of a miracle that he was still conscious, enough that he could force his hand over to his dagger for one last attempt.

"You may all wait here," the figure commanded to his apparent Piscean allies, who had abandoned their cover and were now moving to secure the surrounding space. "I promise I won't be long…"

Through force of will that he never knew he possessed, Cheney drew his dagger and, with all of his remaining strength, flung it toward the voice's origin before falling unconscious.

As such, he never witnessed the dagger halting in midair, mere centimeters away from its target's head. In response, the Pisceans raised their rifles at the freshly incapacitated raider's form, but the target gestured for them to stand down. Once more grudgingly, the remaining Piscean troops followed the command, proceeding with their original objective.

The figure reached out his hand and had the dagger descend into it, blade first. Holding it for a moment, he observed the object with apparent curiousness, seemingly intrigued by the weapon.

"Indeed," he spoke to no one in particular, brushing a finger along the glinting blade. "These are not ordinary pirates."

With that, he lifted the dagger from his hand and flung it back across the room, where it embedded into the wall, squarely beside its owner's head. Ignoring the anxious glances from his escorts, the Terran then gave one final bow of acknowledgment to the downed raider before turning, proceeding without hindrance toward the temple entrance.

"Finally," Alex commented, effectively vocalizing for the rest of the group.

After all they had gone through to get there, the temple center was a surprisingly welcoming sight for the pirates. The fact it was also presently deserted only made it more so; with any luck, the entirety of the cult's fighters had been wiped out on their trek back.

For his part, however, Jon felt that something was off as they entered the center. Not that he expected the cultists to be lying in ambush, the area was far too large for them to entrap the four intruders, but he would have thought there would be more cultists waiting for them upon their reemergence. If not the cultists, then certainly the invading Pisceans. Jon wasn't fool enough to believe they hadn't entered the city by now.

Even so, for the moment, it seemed they were free from enemy aggression. Thus, as the group proceeded through the temple, Jon brought up his wristcom.

"Foxtrot One to Charlie Two," he called out, trying to reach the Condor again. Faint static was the singular response, much to Jon's inner dread. "Repeat, Foxtrot One to Charlie Two, come in…"

"Kaguya?" the elder Flint heard his brother speak in clear disturbance, stopping short his third attempt to contact their transport.

It was easy to see what had taken Alex back. Standing in the middle of the temple, Kaguya's widened eyes were fixed upon the central entrance, while tangible fear and anxiety radiated from the kunoichi's form. And if that wasn't enough of an indication that they were in trouble, Jon, and Alex, could almost feel vestiges of energy emanating from that entryway, a kind of feeling one experienced with an approaching storm, or the distant surging of a flood.

Simultaneously, all three warriors redrew their respective blades, now watching the distant doorway with clear intent. Jon didn't bother raising his wristcom to check on the raiders outside; whatever was about to meet them had obviously dealt with all prior opposition. The pirate captain could only hope that the raiders had somehow survived the attack; otherwise, he would deal with the casualties later, after he survived the oncoming battle.

Beside him, Alex's more scientifically oriented mind raced to define what it was they were about to face. Whatever was entering the temple center was clearly psionic. A powerful psion at that, for even the barest traces of his, her or its power was enough to set Kaguya on edge, and the Flint brothers as well. He briefly wondered if he had felt this power before. Was this was the same power that had tainted Kurzis? Brief consideration was sufficient for him to realize it wasn't; as overwhelming as this power was, it was nowhere near as repugnant and horrific as what they had found on the *Daedalus*.

That didn't make it any less of a threat, one that would have to be summarily dealt with before the Flints could leave the city and return to their ship. That knowledge remained among the three as the doors at last opened, allowing a single figure to enter, slowly and near silently into the temple.

"Ah yes, I was expecting to run into you first," the figure spoke as his eyes fell upon the three pirates, casually ignoring their obvious intent to kill. "Though I would prefer to forgo any further conflict, if possible."

For all of its overwhelming power, the figure that stood before the three Flint Pirates was surprisingly disenchanting to behold. Yet, all the same, the being's physical presence was horrifying in its own right, such that the Flints each felt themselves grow more defensive as they looked upon him.

A tall, thin male of clear Terran physiology, the newcomer nonetheless appeared more entity than human. An imposing caricature of a sentient being that, for all its obvious existence, should not have *been*. This, however, wasn't brought on by any form of ugliness; quite the contrary, the apparent man was rather handsome, retaining a well-proportioned face, pale white skin, long blonde hair that went even further down his back than Jon's, and yellow-tinted eyes that gazed out over his surroundings. All complemented by a prim white dress suit with an overcoat.

And yet, instead of emphasizing attractiveness, this apparent beauty only made him that much more repulsive, more abhorrent. His face was *too* well proportioned, as though it had been artificially molded rather than birthed. His pale white skin was of a cold, sickly nature, as if sunlight, or light of any kind, had never touched it throughout existence. His blonde hair, meanwhile, as opposed to Jon's golden sheen, was dull, pale, and decrepit in tone, making the being that much more cadaverous. Only the yellow eyes seemed to retain any form of life, yet these were the most terrifying of all. The three found it difficult to return his gaze. It was as though pure chaos, pure evil, gleamed outward from those eyes ... and it was all cast upon the Flints.

Even Jon, who retained his taciturn expression, felt his instincts telling him to run, to somehow find a way to escape, find some way of avoiding combat with this ... *creature*. He forced such feelings back, knowing that the fight was inevitable, before addressing the newcomer directly.

"I suppose you're the collaborator we've heard about."

The being nodded. "That would be me, yes," he confirmed.

Jon inquired further. "Do you possess a name?"

"Certainly," he answered, taking a bow. "I am Doctor Laurentius Kraft, a humble scientist, and researcher."

Alex raised an eyebrow. Somehow, he had heard that name before...

"And as I said, I wish no further conflict," Kraft continued.

Despite that claim, Jon could tell that there was something underneath the apparent doctor's words. Something malevolent.

"Let me guess," the elder Flint exclaimed, grip tightening around Astaroth's hilt. "You want us to turn Lorelei over to you."

Kraft smiled. "If you would be so kind," he replied, almost jovially. "In return, my hosts and I will allow you to leave this place without further hostility."

"Sure," Alex shot back. "All so you can lay claim to a power that you cannot possibly comprehend, let alone control."

The doctor chuckled. "Only for lesser beings such as yourselves," he rejoined knowingly, before focusing his power. "I, on the other hand, possess a fair shot at it."

His already present smile was emphasized as he directed his power over the three. *As you may so easily behold.*

At that, the Flints encountered the full brunt of the doctor's power, and the results were clear. For brief moments, the three felt as though they stood at the center of the storm, or the raging flood they had only just picked up before. Each felt as though a surging, monumental force had settled upon them, threatening to crush them completely.

And then, all at once, it was lifted away by its source, seemingly allowing the three to breathe again.

Kraft took on a sterner, less patient expression. "To complete my quest, I must reach the Black Moon," he stated. "And for that, I need her."

He then reached out his hand. "So please," Kraft went on. "If you would kindly…"

Dual black and red energy waves were the Flints' immediate answer. Responding instantly, Kraft projected an energy shield to dispel both waves and then leaped back, evading three kunai as they embedded themselves on the temple floor. He was still airborne when the Flint brothers were upon him again, bringing down their blades with simultaneous motion. And yet, despite their valiance, neither Astaroth nor Forneus so much as grazed Kraft. He evaded their strikes with surprising fluidity. Kaguya appeared behind him; her ninjato raised to strike. Kraft dodged this blow as well. He then moved overhead.

Mundane fools, Kraft telepathically broadcasted as he crossed his arms together. Upon doing so, a surge of yellow energy, the exact unearthly color of his eyes, encompassed him, momentarily blinding his opponents.

That blinding light was followed by beams forming and launching, raining across the temple, and forcing the three raiders to evade and deflect the resulting destruction. Kaguya counterattacked with a shuriken, but Kraft easily foresaw the attack and deflected it with another shield, to which he followed by firing a series of energy discs at the female ninja. Rather than simply evade, Kaguya charged forward, using her ninjato to deflect every one of the discs as they arced toward her, from there leaping at the psion, poised to strike. Unfortunately for her, Kraft remained faster, initially dodging her strike before generating another energy shield at point-blank range, knocking her away.

As she recovered, Alex and Jon both surged forward in her place. At their approach, Kraft fired dual-energy bursts to halt them, but the brothers remained steadfast, deflecting the blasts with their Devilblades before launching another set of energy waves. Rather than raise another shield, Kraft mimicked the Flints' technique and fired off an energy wave of his own, canceling out the previous two. He then fired off more of those energy discs, but Jon and Alex evaded those as well as Kaguya did and closed the distance, each slashing at Kraft with their blades, only for the psion to avoid each of their strokes. However, Jon noticed his opponent had some diffi-culty maneuvering around his attacks – reacting rather sluggishly to them – compared to how efficiently he dodged Alex and Kaguya's.

Kaguya soon rejoined the fray by moving toward Kraft's side, hoping to take the psion off guard while he fought the brothers. However, Kraft again dodged, floating away from the three while materializing and firing additional beams. Complementing the latter, more energy orbs emerged overhead, generating neon yellow pillars that flowed down to the temple floor, forcing the three on the defensive. Jon countered by firing off a scattershot of black holes, which all converged on Kraft's form. This too was deflected as Kraft created another barrier, then fired off a swarm of laser-like beams at the elder Flint. Jon was forced to generate a shield of his own to absorb the shots.

Stepping to his brother's side, Alex hurled a vertical wave of fire at Kraft, forcing him to bank to evade. A line of kunai immediately followed the wave, but the enemy psion weaved around it as well. A dual-energy burst aimed at the combatant's heads was his retaliation. Alex erected a fire barrier while Kaguya rolled around hers, then drawing another shuriken and throwing it at Kraft's head. This time the psion merely ducked his head, allowing the shuriken to pass and embed in the wall behind him.

At that moment, Jon emerged from a black portal just above the embedded shuriken, his blade set to impale. However, Kraft disappeared before the elder Flint could strike and materialized behind Kaguya. The ninja reacted fast, spinning about with her sword set to decapitate. Before her blade could touch the psion's neck, however, Kraft telekinetically froze her in place and instantly lifted her into the air. As the Dragon Princess struggled to break free, he paused to observe her efforts for the briefest moment then flung her into the side of the temple, smashing her against a nearby wall.

"Kaguya!" Alex called out as he saw the assassin slide to the floor and not get up again. He launched a fiery tsunami at Kraft that filled the space. "You'll pay for that!"

You may try, plebian, Kraft telepathically replied as he flitted back, dodging the fire and the follow-up slashes from both Flints. Again Jon noticed the doctor's slightly slower reaction to his attack, but he wasn't able to consider it as Kraft hurled another swarm of energy bolts at the pair. Rather than defend, the brothers charged through, weaving around the beams as they again closed in on their opponent, executing reprisal attacks as they sprinted toward the creature. Kraft again dodged and deflected each strike, his arms remaining crossed as he floated through the air.

Focusing on speed in that instant, Alex leaped at the psion, hoping to overpower him before he could telepathically foresee the attack. However, despite his effort, Kraft reacted just as quickly, telekinetically hurling Alex against a support pillar and lobbing several follow-on concentrated bursts as the younger Flint struck the column. Alex was forced to create a barricade of flame to protect himself from the impact, energy shots, and falling debris of the now destroyed pillar.

Simultaneously, Jon spun another black wave above the psion, forcing Kraft to shift some of his energy to deflect being absorbed. This action was enough for Alex to drop his guard and move again. Multiple fire twisters sprang up around the psion, engulfing him in a tornado of flame. When Kraft, encased in a yellow energy field, moved through the inferno, the younger Flint followed up with a midair power slash, only for that attack to be averted as well.

Maintaining that barrier – enhancing it in fact – Kraft suddenly spun and launched the energy field as a supersonic comet directly at Alex. The field's tremendous speed multiplied the force of the impact exponentially. It smashed the pirate backward into a large ornate statue. For a short moment, Alex was able to maintain consciousness, just enough to attempt another move. Smiling, Kraft merely rapidly expanded the energy field simulating an explosion, burying the younger Flint in a large pile of twisted metal and polished black rock. Flame vaporized the debris but once dissipated the younger Flint collapsed, and did not reengage.

Only one impediment now remained, much to Kraft's satisfaction.

That same impediment surged after Kraft, who narrowly dodged this initial energy enhanced slash. Glowering at the psion, Jon pivoted then lunged, executing a combo attack before launching another power wave at near point-blank range. This time Kraft dissipated into whiffs of smoke before reforming overhead and generating another swarm of energy blasts that darted around the space in multiple vectors, forcing Jon back on the defensive. Weaving around each blast as they burst through the temple, Jon counterattacked by opening multiple black holes which not only raced at Kraft from numerous directions but drew in the psion's shots as well. Kraft snaked around each hole, but the momentary distraction they created was enough of an opening for Jon to draw close again.

Just before Jon's blade could connect with his opponent's body, Kraft vanished, dual globes of energy now filled the space previously occupied by the psion. They raced against the elder Flint from either side. Only a timely leap up and over the orbs kept them from connecting with Jon. But Kraft wasn't about to let him gain another opening. The psion surged after the pirate, forming six more energy shots – larger ones this time – and firing them at the Devilblade Wielder. Jon generated a black hole and disappeared, remerging against the sidewall of the temple, only to repeat the action to avoid another newly formed blast. It slammed into the sidewall where he had just been standing. Jon was forced to move around the temple several more times, dodging every attack Kraft launched at him.

Suddenly, the temple seemed to fill with shadows, black forms that moved, firing energy waves at the psion, then shifting up, over, around, disappearing into the floor, walls, ceiling and open air only to reemerge again and again, and with each reappearing draw closer to the psion. Kraft could not discern which form was the elder Flint. He turned around the space analyzing each shadow, dodging each attack, searching for the pirate captain. Distracted, he didn't notice the small black hole open directly behind him. Quickly reaching out through the energy portal, Jon swung Astaroth at his enemy's head. Only then did his blade connect with his adversary's flesh, managing to inflict a deep cut upon the doctor's right cheek. One deep enough to gush blood as Jon slipped back into the portal. The shadows disappeared.

Seemingly taken off guard by the contact, Kraft wiped his cheek and glanced at the red splotches on his fingers. Undeterred, he suddenly spun and caught the descending blade of Astaroth in a yellow energy vice. Forming another three energy bolts, he launched them at the pirate captain. Jon managed to evade two, but the third one was too fast. Thus it struck him in the chest and exploded, throwing him back several meters. Only by stabbing the now freed Astaroth into the ground did he manage to keep from flying back further. But the damage was done, Jon felt as though his whole chest was crushed, bleeding and burned.

Hovering up to the pirate, who was utilizing his blade to stand, Kraft reached up with his right hand and brushed some more blood away from his cheek. Observing the larger smear, he then looked Jon dead on.

"You're rather... different," the psion exclaimed observantly. "Aren't you?"

Glaring, Jon flicked his left hand and fired off a black energy volley in response. Raising his barrier to deflect, Kraft snarled and retaliated instantly, launching a full barrage at the weakened pirate. And though Jon drew the darkness around himself to absorb the oncoming fire, he knew it wouldn't be enough to prevent injury.

And yet, none of the yellow beams so much as grazed him. Instead, as

Jon opened his eye, he saw that a transparent violet barricade had now formed around him, deflecting the onslaught as easily as Kraft had done with their attacks. A myriad of explosions erupted before him, but no more damage was done.

It was then Kraft's smile returned. "At last," he said as he touched the ground again, unfolding his arms. "Our lady of the hour."

Stepping out from the shadows, Lorelei gazed intently at the opposing psion, all the while, ignoring Jon's gaze – at least outwardly – as she moved past.

Undaunted, Kraft nodded at her. *I must say I've been looking forward to this,* he spoke to her with his telepathy. *To stand before the legendary White Siren...*

Savor that feeling, Lorelei coldly replied. *For I assure you, it will not last.*

Despite the threat, Kraft remained pleasant. *There is no need for such apprehension,* he attempted to soothe, *as I told these three, I did not come here for conflict.*

And yet... Lorelei replied, looking over to Alex and Kaguya's still forms. *It seems you have created one anyway.*

Kraft smile disturbingly emboldened at this. *So I have. Regardless, I'm afraid I must have you come with me back to the* Grah'n. *And from there, lead my associates and I through the Sea.*

Lorelei's gaze narrowed. *Obviously,* she retorted, *I refuse.*

A violet aura emerged over her, just as the ground began to tremor, and surrounding rubble and debris began to float into the air.

Instead, in reprisal for all the harm you caused, willingly or not, she continued, just as energy began to gather around her hands, *I will take your life.*

Again Lorelei felt Jon's gaze against her back, but she forced herself to ignore it. That was something she could deal with after this fight.

Shaking his head mildly, as if disappointed, Kraft could only sigh. It seemed there was still work to be done, and conflict to be had.

A true pity, he stated as he refolded his arms once more lifting off the ground.

Ascending into the air, greatcoat flickering around her as violet and yellow energy crackled and surged through the temple grounds, Lorelei prepared herself. For better or worse, she was now committed to battle, and there was no way she would back down at such a juncture. Not even as her audience continued to watch, uncharacteristic astonishment and uncertainty emanating from that single blue eye.

Thus, after a final brief pause, the psions flew at one another, a thunderous crash and eruption of energy bellowed upon contact.

Chapter XV: Thunder and Fury

Flint Pirates umbra *Black Sun*
Timas IV

"Picking up additional contacts coming in from arcspace," Anna reported amidst the quaking. She then looked up. "One of them is the *Gnaiih*-class previously encountered at Nassau."

Barbarossa flashed a fanged smirk. *The enemy flagship,* he considered with clear satisfaction. *So the Pisceans are at last moving their central force into action.*

That, of course, meant several things. The first and most obvious was they had made a serious dent within the present forces. A fact reinforced by the abundance of debris throughout Timas IV's orbit, though enough Piscean warships remained to keep the *Black Sun* busy in the meantime. The second, however, was they would be facing far more serious firepower now with the addition of battleships and battlecruisers to the enemy's present fleet. Not to mention the additional number of fighters and support craft they would be bringing with them into battle, though that was more

Commander Boyington's problem to deal with than Barbarossa's.

The third and most important was the opportunity now presented. If they could destroy the bulk of the Rohu Dag's forces, then it would nullify the present threat to both the Flint Pirates and the galaxy at large, at least for a time. Again, it would only be a brief period before the rest of the Confederacy learned of Lorelei's connection to the Black Moon, but for the time being, only the Rohus were aware of it. Thus, if the Flints could eliminate them as an offensive force, not only would that take down one of the larger threats against them, but it would also buy them enough time to sort out this entire affair, especially as the other Dags continued to squabble with the Aquarians. Once that was accomplished – however that was to be accomplished – the fixation of the Black Moon would cease, galactic war would be averted, and the Flints could put this whole chapter behind them. Aslan would remain on high, and all would be well with the universe.

Of course, that would only work if two objectives were achieved. First, they actually had to destroy enough of the Rohus' ships to force a withdrawal, as well as render them incapable of further pursuit. And second, they had to figure out how in Jahannam they were going to deal with the Black Moon. Again obviously, Barbarossa and those present could only achieve the first objective.

"Hard to port!" Barbarossa bellowed as he lowered the command scope, studying the oncoming enemy contacts. They would be entering Timas IV's space within the next few moments. "Take out that cruiser off our bow!"

With that command, the *Black Sun* shifted in vector, her bow cannons already angling toward the designated enemy. The cruiser instantly took notice and focused her fire, while her nearest allies supplemented the attack. However, none of them were able to pierce the *Sun*'s shielding. The umbra's cannons quickly completed their shift and fired, their shots easily breaking through the cruiser's shields and piercing the hull. Fire instantly erupted as the Piscean ship's structure was ripped open – not detonating completely but fracturing enough – rendering her inactive.

No sooner did the flaming cruiser begin to drift into Timas IV's gravity well did the reinforcements appear. The newcomers open fired, sending a virtual storm of beam and projectile fire at their lone black and gold adversary.

"Evasive maneuvers!" Barbarossa commanded as he retracted the scope, the ship rocking around him.

Again the *Sun*'s shields were holding up, but as proven at Ephesus, they wouldn't last forever. It especially didn't help that there were torpedoes mixed into that barrage.

"Bring us around their formation! We'll strike the battlecruisers first!"

In truth, Barbarossa would have rather hit the enemy flagship up front, but he knew that particular ship would be well within the center of the formation and thus out of reach until its escorts were properly dealt with. As such, the *Sun*'s cannons again angled and fired upon the myriad battlecruisers within the formation. Quite unlike the cruisers, destroyers, and frigates the *Black Sun* had been dealing with to this point, the battlecruisers held up to the barrage, though not without a great portion of their shielding being chipped away. They returned fire in earnest, as did the rest of the fleet.

"Getting a little hard to move around, sir!" Davis called out as he guided the ship, doing all he could to dodge the incoming fire. Even so, for all of his skill, there was only so much he could do with so many guns and rockets blasting at them. Obviously, he couldn't evade them all.

Ignoring the exclamation, Barbarossa watched as the cannons at last breached one of the battlecruisers' shields and began blasting into the hull underneath. It soon erupted in flaming debris, as did some of the other ships that were struck. But, the Pisceans simply moved others into place and returned fire. As more beams and missiles struck the *Sun*'s shields, though thanks to Davis' maneuvering not many were successful, Barbarossa could already tell that this was going to take longer than he would have liked.

All the same, this was not an opportunity he, nor those around him, would miss. And not just because of the reasons Barbarossa had earlier considered; the Pisceans had attacked him, and those around him, and so would pay in full. No matter how many ships they sent after the *Sun* or troops they sent after their comrades on the surface, the enemy in front of them would be bled dry, and their desolation would be remembered beside the Thirteenth Fleet's harrowing at Ephesus.

Thus was the fate of all who took arms against the Flint Pirates. Especially when the Beast King commanded them.

"Maintain evasive!" the Leo ordered, just as enemy fighters began to emerge from the newcomers. The *Sun's* Corsairs immediately came around to intercept, and Barbarossa could tell that they would have their hands full. The final round had well and truly begun.

"Reload missile tubes and standby for barrage!"

Ianessa, Timas IV

With jolting light and escalating fury, the battle waged on. Maneuvering through the air as beams of violet and yellow flashed, only to be evaded or deflected, the psions continued their duel. The air quaked from their combined power, energy rippling between them as destruction incarnate. All while their lone audience remained standing upon the ground below, utterly captivated by the onslaught.

Flitting back in a zigzag pattern, Kraft fired a barrage of energy bolts; Lorelei extended her hand and form a violet barrier to guard and deflect. Without pause, she charged at her opponent, an equally violet energy blade extending from her right hand as she came over him, slashing downward. Kraft banked to the right to evade as Lorelei swung her left arm out and generated another psionic blade. The doctor moved quickly to flatten his body and dodged this blade as well. Undeterred, Lorelei spun in an elaborate dance that forced Kraft to retreat a fair distance to escape.

Returning to the offensive, Kraft hurled a large burst of yellow energy at the pirate, only for Lorelei to retract her blades and form another barrier, deflecting the strike yet again. She renewed her charge; blades outspread as she surged at her adversary.

This time, it was Kraft's turn to form a barricade, deflecting Lorelei's initial strike, before retreating again as she used her opposite blade to shatter the field. Kraft created and fired another beam spray, forcing Lorelei to veer to her left and counterfire with homing shots, which caused her opponent to dematerialize to elude injury.

Reforming next to a temple pillar, the doctor was surprised as Lorelei had anticipated his move and was waiting for him. She charged, her right blade reigniting as she slashed at Kraft's neck. Dematerializing yet again, the opposing psion dodged the blow. He reappeared behind the pirate, but Lorelei twisted around and swung at her adversary, left blade flaming. Kraft evaded, executing another complicated evasion as his foe kept up the momentum. The doctor then triggered dual point-blank energy shots at the psion, but Lorelei easily spun around and slashed at the doctor's exposed back. Only a timely formed barrier prevented the blade from making contact.

You fight with such grace, Kraft complimented as the two psions continued weaving through the air, attacking, defending, and/or evading in almost harmonic motion. *I must admit I am becoming quite enamored with you.*

I can't say the feeling is mutual, Lorelei rejoined, a rapid spray of violet energy surrounding and pelting the doctor, forcing Kraft to immerse himself in a forcefield sphere to defend, momentarily distracted.

She disappeared, then struck from above, reigniting her right-hand blade for a sweep at his waist, but Kraft managed to pull away in time. He fired a spray of his own, only for Lorelei to dive right through the air before they could arc down upon her, bringing both blades about to cleave Kraft's head. As such, she was taken off guard when Kraft – or more specifically the image of him – blurred away as her blades connected. Glowering, Lorelei ascended, narrowly twisting around to form a new barrier just as another array of psionic beam fire lashed out. All the while, Kraft flew to her right, firing in suppression.

Dancing around his shots, Lorelei generated multiple energy daggers that thrust and slashed upon Kraft. Diagonally, vertically, horizontally, the weapons threatened to sheer and cut into his legs, chest, and crossed arms.

But Kraft again evaded injury, deflecting the energy around the temple, reigning destruction throughout the space.

Kraft struck out again; a countering scattering shot, yellow bolts arced in from all directions. Lorelei was instantly bathed in a violet aura, absorbing the energy and redirecting it into a violet lightning blast aimed at her opponent. At the last moment, it was rerouted into the ceiling. The resultant shards fell as the two psions continued to battle, weaponized citrine and amethyst energy clashing repeatedly.

Once more, a true pity, Kraft continued regretfully. *I had hoped that, as one superior being to another, our first direct encounter would be more amicable than this.*

Another slash from Lorelei's psi blade forced Kraft to retreat again, Lorelei glowering after him. *"Superior?"* she questioned, though she already understood her opponent's intent.

Yes, Kraft answered, as though it were obvious. *Are we not holders of great power?* he posited as he dodged another burst attack. *Power that seldom graces the inhabitants of this galaxy?*

He quickly threw up another barrier to deflect her next blade attack, then ascended above and launched another energy spray.

And even among those select, privileged few… Are we not 'superior'?

Dodging, attacking, and forming barriers as she fought, Lorelei felt an emerging disgust toward that notion.

You truly are a vile one, she exclaimed as she countered, sending a ring of energy bolts swirling at Kraft.

And that is why it is a true pity, Kraft could only shrug in response evading and pressing the attack again.

———————————————————

It was a struggle to remain breathing at that point, let alone standing. Though he had only been hit once, that one psionic burst had struck him hard; much harder than a conventional beam shot. And that was before one accounted for the wounds he had taken earlier, as well as his sheer exhaustion from the initial fighting. Whatever happened now, Jon knew he was going to be out of it for a time, though thankfully not as long as he had been following Bonham IV.

Even so, he also knew that he couldn't afford to pass out, no matter how much his body strained. He, alongside the incapacitated Alex and Kaguya, were now within ground zero, a field of battle between two great powers that were as seemingly limitless as they were destructive. Great powers that were easily on par with Astaroth and Forneus, and much more unfathomable. Such that, as open and vulnerable as he was, Jon could not take his eye off the struggle above him, nor render aid to the fallen. Not that he would have been able to move to where Kraft had left them – at least not as fast as he would have liked to – much less help them in any conceivable way.

Thus, it was all he could do to stand and watch as virtual Armageddon thundered above, to observe the power of the White Siren firsthand.

Though Jon had witnessed Lorelei's powers several times before, from her "awakening" the Predecessor temples on Ephesus and Smyrna to the all too recent cataclysm on Nassau, this was the first time he had seen them directly, and in combat. To say he was taken back, and perhaps even in awe of her, would have been an understatement. He had always known her to be more powerful than she tended to let on; he was entirely unprepared for the full force in front of him now. A power that, as experienced as he was, he had never witnessed before, not even among others of her kind.

It was both magnificent and petrifying, the image of Lorelei flitting through the air, attacking and defending against Kraft. This opponent had outpaced he, Alex, and Kaguya at the same time in both movement and discourse. Yes, she had yet to inflict any serious damage upon the opposing psion, but at the same time, Kraft had yet to so much as graze her with his attacks. In fact, despite the sheer self-assurance he was projecting, it seemed as though Kraft was struggling to keep up with Lorelei, being more evasive than he had been earlier, as well as putting more force into his attacks. Yet again, nothing was connecting, and Kraft was required to retreat and maneuver more and more as Lorelei pursued him relentlessly.

At that moment, Jon felt himself recall much from before. The initial encounter on Aurora, Davis holding a gun to the psion's head just after the *U-7501*'s theft, her redirecting a sniper's rifle on Kurzis, Drake's trap on Bonham. All events in which she had been under threat, all events she either dealt with subtlety or let others handle for her. Only at Nassau had her power been on display for the first time, and that had been against her will.

What did it all mean? Why would a being of such tremendous power not wish to use her abilities? Even when her life and ambition were on the line?

Jon felt as though he somehow knew the answer, had always known the answer. Yet, in his exhaustion, it did not come to his mind. And even then, it would not change what was occurring now. Thus he remained a captive audience, one helplessly drawn toward an object of beauty and terror. Ironically, the very same object he had fated himself, and those around him, into following.

———————————————— ————————————————

Snaking through the oncoming energy swarms, Lorelei charged once more, blades ignited. Kraft fought back, forming a line of pulsating rings around his opponent and converging them. Another timely, dance-like maneuver on Lorelei's part prevented the rings from connecting. She pressed on, another slash at the doctor's waist and one to his back. This time the blade connected, and though it wasn't deep enough to cause a serious wound, it did, however, hinder the doctor for a brief moment, allowing Lorelei to bank away from Kraft's responding onslaught. Unrelenting, she twisted around, triggering another sequence of her energy rays, forcing Kraft on the evasive yet again. With more precision than one might have expected, the doctor maneuvered around the line of beam fire, allowing the rays to impact the temple wall behind him. Explosions of stone, glass, and metal added to the chaos of the battle.

Another hastily formed barrier prevented the amethyst blade from connecting again. Kraft developed an energy burst – smaller but no less intense – and struck at Lorelei's head. Lorelei immediately moved her head out of the flight path, then spun, bringing her opposite blade to bare. This one came closer, but Kraft still managed to form a new barrier in time, keeping the edge mere millimeters away from his skin. Knocking the blade away, he used his power to pull Lorelei closer, his grinning face beaming over her fierce glare. Lorelei noted the cut in his back had all but disappeared; even the tear in the doctor's clothing had seemingly been repaired.

Even so, Lorelei was far from finished. Dodging Kraft's follow up blitz, Lorelei slashed again with both blades. Kraft dematerialized before she could touch him. That was when Lorelei did something Kraft didn't expect or foresee. Anticipating his new location, she spun around as if to follow up with another slash, but instead, she executed an energy enthused kick. Caught off-guard, Lorelei's heel connected to the side of Kraft's head, knocking him away and seemingly disorienting him. That was enough for Lorelei to close in again, launching two more spin kicks against Kraft's head and waist, respectively, then firing a lightning burst that struck Kraft square in the chest.

Startled, Kraft flew back, with Lorelei charging after to finish him for good. Yet, despite the fierce offensive, Kraft was far from beaten down. Instead, gathering up his energy, he unleashed a full telekinetic shockwave before Lorelei could reach him. The result was instantaneous as the great psionic wave ravaged around the temple, obliterating various objects and edifices throughout. The structure was in serious jeopardy of collapse.

For their part, Lorelei and Jon were both forced to raise protective barriers, Lorelei extending her protection to the incapacitated Alex and Kaguya. Pressing his advantage, Kraft fired another concentrated psionic wave at the psion, shattering her barrier and driving her backward.

Reorienting herself in midair, just before she was to slam into a nearby pillar, Lorelei returned her glare to Kraft as the latter hovered in place. She brought her hand up to her mouth, wiping away a smear of cobalt blood. All the while, the doctor was, yet again, seemingly undamaged despite the ferocity of the on-going battle.

My compliments, Kraft projected as he hovered, yellow eyes fixed directly onto Lorelei's amethyst. *It has been quite some time since I was forced to use that level of power. Indeed, you truly are a superior being.*

Kraft then turned his gaze toward Jon, the pirate's hate intent in his glare. *Why you concern yourself with such meager creatures is beyond me, even if they are a cut above the average pirate.*

I have my reasons, Lorelei responded, quite far from finished. *Not that I would share them with the likes of you.*

Another disappointed contortion marred the "too perfect" face of the doctor. *No, I suppose not,* Kraft acknowledged. He raised his hand to attack the barely conscious Flint brother but was momentarily frozen in place. The surprise on his face was raw and fleeting.

If you have any desire for my understanding of your wishes, you will keep the battle between us! Lorelei threatened forcefully.

Warning acknowledged, Kraft moved back to the subject at hand. *As you now comprehend, I am also quite superior. I am not about to let you go, especially after all the trouble my associates and I have had seeking you out.*

Kraft's smile reemerged. *And more to the point, you possess the means toward reaching the Moon. That makes you all the more essential.*

To what? You and the Pisceans conquering the galaxy? Or do you, being a 'humble scientist and researcher,' simply hold academic purposes for the Moon?

With seeming regret, Kraft shook his head. *Neither I'm afraid. I have no interest, much less desire, toward this pitiful galaxy. And as intrigued as I am toward this subject matter, it is not science and understanding that drives me.*

He then granted a flat smile. Which, if nothing else, appeared strangely solemn. *Rather, it is for but a simple dream that I must reach the Black Moon.*

That was one explanation Lorelei didn't expect. Not that it mattered, as Kraft went on the attack again, firing another, far more powerful energy blast at his target. Lorelei raised an amethyst field around her form, holding it in place against the continuous assault.

For time innumerable, the new battle, one between sheer willpowers, took place. Kraft, despite whatever actual damage he received from the initial fight, maintained his attack while Lorelei held her defense, both psions locked in their respective positions. Gradually Kraft intensified the beam, adding more and more energy to it, only for Lorelei to do the same with her barrier. As such, neither appeared even close to overcoming the other.

Or so it seemed. In truth, Lorelei had no intention of prolonging the conflict and allowing Kraft to remain hale and hearty. She had learned what she needed to know. In addition, the 'good' doctor might choose to ignore her edict and attack the three defenseless warriors, or the surrounding structure could collapse at any time, trapping the Flint team members. Thus, while maintaining her barrier, she gathered more and more energy of her own, such that the amethyst aura around her began to crackle and pulse, bolts flying around the temple yet again. For all of his power and bravado, Kraft was still nothing to her. Nothing compared to…

And then, her eyes widened, realization, and remembrance dawned. Down below, she sensed Jonathan Flint, watching her, analyzing her. What exact emotions he held upon comprehending her powers she did not know, but all the same, she recognized that they were there. And those emotions would spawn another series of thoughts and feelings from seeing her as thus, not the "mere" scholar and songstress. That recognition instilled nothing less than pure dread and apprehension within the deepest parts of her soul.

Consequently, for all of her obvious reluctance, she knew she had no choice. She could not afford that repudiation… not from *him*.

And so, as she closed her eyes in finality, the barrier shattered, and the beam struck her dead on. Though it was a powerful blow, it had not been designed to kill; instead, the shock and resultant explosion rendered her unconscious instantly. Unmoving, she remained in the air as Kraft used his telekinesis to keep her afloat, a dominating smile now across his lips.

Acting without further thought, Jon rebrandished Astaroth and launched himself into the air, intending to strike at Kraft's left side before the worst could occur. Unfortunately, Kraft foresaw the assault as he had everything else. Reaching out with his opposite hand, he froze Jon in midair.

"She's mine now," the doctor spoke in full triumph before hurling Jon aside, slamming him into the furthest wall of the temple. The pirate's consciousness, as well as Astaroth's physical form, vanished immediately upon impact.

Kraft surveyed Lorelei's dormant figure again. This time, there was no responding glare as his grinning expression gazed over her, taking in every aspect.

Indeed, you are the one who will lead me, Kraft mused, eyes looking upon Lorelei's impassive face with contentment, and, though much less apparent, newfound hope. *Through the Dreamlands to my Sunset City.*

Flint Pirates umbra *Black Sun*
Timas IV

Though it was taking much more time and effort than he would have liked, Barbarossa could see that the damage was mounting on the enemy fleet. Many of their ships had been destroyed or brought out of commission by that point, and the Corsairs had made great headway with the enemy fighters. And while there was no indication of retreat, much less surrender, the warrior of the Third Terran Jihad knew that it was only a matter of time before victory would be gained.

"Enemy battleship now moving toward us!" the tactical operator called out in warning, just as the designated *Gnaiih*-class began to shift toward them, her guns reorienting themselves simultaneously. "She's firing!"

Once more, the *Black Sun* shook as enemy beam fire slammed against her shields, and once more, said enemy fire failed to pierce her defenses. Though the *Sun* had taken a very heavy beating, far more than the average umbra would have endured, she still retained her defenses, as well as her capability of inflicting harm.

Suppressing a snarl, Barbarossa glared at the enemy battleship, which had finished its turn and was proceeding against the *Sun* head-on. All the while, several other Piscean ships moved to support her.

They're going to concentrate their fire and attempt to overwhelm our shields, Barbarossa surmised, recognizing the tactic. That would certainly bring the *Sun's* shields down to the bleeding point, but that wouldn't matter. Not when the enemy flagship, and the rest of the heavier Piscean ships, were destroyed by the responding counterattack.

"Target the battleship with our torpedoes. Fire when…"

"Picking up new signals from the surface!" Gran announced, drawing all attention to her. "Enemy shuttlecraft now ascending!"

"What?" Barbarossa growled in surprise, lowering the command scope again. Indeed it was as Gran stated; the Piscean troop shuttles had just exited from Timas' sea and were ascending toward space.

And that wasn't all.

"Increased comm. chatter from the Pisceans!" Gran added. "The flagship is signaling fleetwide!" She looked up after a few more seconds of analysis. "They're withdrawing!"

Even before Gran's announcement, Barbarossa had recognized the signs. No sooner had the shuttles broken the atmosphere and entered space did the Piscean ships, while still maintaining their attacks upon the *Sun*, began turning away, moving further out of Timas' orbit. Simultaneously, the remaining fighters had abandoned their engagements and were returning to their motherships, who retrieved them at an accelerated rate. Only a few remained to escort the shuttles back to the lone battleship.

To Barbarossa's horror, that all culminated into one outcome.

"Pursuit course!" he roared, much to the crew's surprise. "Target the flagship's engines and set to disable! Raiders, prepare to board!"

Though the orders were carried out instantly, with the *Black Sun* firing several more crimson beam shots into the *Gnaiih*'s aft quarter, it remained for not, regardless. All too abruptly, the battleship engaged her arc drive and accelerated into arcspace. The rest of the Piscean fleet quickly followed, the last ship disappearing mere seconds later. Only the *Black Sun* maintained orbit over Timas IV.

Cold and discomforting confusion soon embraced the bridge, until Anna, at last, spoke up, voicing what all others present were wondering.

"What just happened?" she questioned. "What…what does this mean?"

Gravely, Barbarossa closed his eyes as he answered. "It means we lost, Miss Reed," he answered solemnly. "We lost."

Chapter XVI: Inveniam Viam

Abruptly Lorelei awoke and immediately frowned. Without looking around, she realized where she was, the starlit city, still set against an eternal night. It was only natural, she supposed; she had taken a very hard hit, just as she had at Nassau. And even more, now that she possessed the means to reach beyond the Sea, she imagined her "client," for lack of better description, had more to say to her.

"I see you have accomplished the task," that damned familiar voice spoke from behind.

Much like her surroundings, Lorelei didn't need to physically look back to see who – or *what* – was standing there. She could feel "her" presence, as well as she could with any other being. Perhaps even more so.

"Somehow," Lorelei replied as she turned around, once again facing a younger iteration of herself. Even now, gazing into her own amethyst eyes still disturbed her, though she did well to keep that feeling in the back of her mind. "And not quite as planned."

"So I understand," the other "her" answered, a frown crossing the child's face. "I cannot say I find this…pleasing."

Upon Lorelei arching an eyebrow, the child seemed to clarify. "The power and desire I sense from the one who apprehended you…" she continued. "They are…unsettling."

Enhanced unease welled up in Lorelei as she remembered her battle with Kraft and the maligned power she had felt throughout. If the one before her was unnerved, once again for lack of better description, by him…

"Yes," Lorelei agreed, in a tone that did not bode well for the subject at hand. "I find him distasteful as well."

Again she suppressed the feeling. "Unfortunately, I am presently under his care," she exclaimed, somewhat dispassionately. "And it seems he holds quite the interest in you."

Her younger self seemed to consider that thought – or so Lorelei surmised – but then dismissed it just as quickly.

"Regardless, you have succeeded," the other "her" affirmed. "And now your course lies before you."

"Right," Lorelei acknowledged, though with some reservation. She knew – and only to a certain extent – what truly lay before her. "Though I'm still unsure what exactly you want me to do when…"

"Do not worry," the other stated with assurance. "You will understand when the time comes."

The younger self nodded, seemingly for the last time. "For the moment, however…"

With that, the great light emerged once more, encompassing all and causing it to fade away.

Piscean *Gnaiih*-class battleship *Grah'n* Arcspace

Upon her awakening, it was the silence that hit first. Not that she had expected any music this time around, but it was enough to reinforce the fact that she was not aboard the *Black Sun*. Just as the man sitting off to the side, apparently monitoring her, wasn't the honorable Captain Flint.

At last, Kraft telepathically announced over the book he was reading. Lorelei blinked her eyes to focus. *I was beginning to think you would be out for some time yet.*

Resisting the urge to glare, Lorelei sat up, inspecting her surroundings. Even compared to the somewhat bland metallic interior of a Terran ship, she was not impressed with what she saw. A room in a dismal gray-green tone, with curving walls, an arched ceiling, and pale lighting placed at specific points, accompanied by a strange dampness and odor in the air. It was as if the vessel had just been raised from the darkest of seas. All permeated by a sickly cold that Lorelei could feel through her clothes, which she was thankful to be still attired in.

Kraft seemed to pick up on that last part. *You need not be worried about that,* he reassured her, without looking away from his book. *I am a gentleman first and foremost, and would never lower myself to that disgusting practice. As for my hosts, I'm afraid Pisceans have different standards toward attractiveness, which you simply do not fill.*

I'll take that as a compliment, Lorelei answered dryly before sliding to the side of the bed. Even now, she loathed the opposite psion's presence; it took every bit of her willpower not to reach out and psionically crush his heart. Assuming he possessed one, of course.

What do you want with me?

It was only then Kraft closed his book. *I believe that's long been established,* he replied as he stood and placed the book on a nearby counter. *I want you to guide me, and my associates, through the Sea.*

He wandered over to her, his pale yellow eyes scrutinizing her face. *Once we have reached the Black Moon, and have gained what we wish, you will be released and allowed to return to the Flints,* he stated, a smirk folding across his lips. *Assuming you still desire it, of course.*

Up close, Lorelei realized the psion's lips were an unnatural pale color. Undaunted, she stared back in defiance.

And if I refuse?

At that, Kraft felt a wave of energy wash over him. One that held enough power to cause the surrounding lighting to dim and various objects to shift in their places.

You are free to start where we last left off, Kraft responded with another grin as he moved to a nearby cabinet, which held, curiously, a Terran tea set. *But you and I both know that you won't.*

Lorelei watched carefully as her host took the steaming teapot and poured a light brown liquid into two cups.

I may not understand why, but you weren't fighting at your best earlier, he said, replacing the pot and picking up the two cups and saucers. *It should have taken much more effort on my part.*

Kraft approached the bed and graciously, with a slight bow, handed a cup to Lorelei. Despite her reservation, she took the proffered tea.

Or…. perhaps I wouldn't have won at all, he posited, taking a knowing tone. *Maybe you would have decimated me at the very beginning.*

Ignoring the bland glare from his "guest", Kraft took a sip of his tea, appearing to savor it.

Regardless, you had your chance to avoid all this. Now, you have no choice but to comply with our wishes.

Smiling, he placed his cup on the saucer with a distinct 'klink'. *You will not catch me off guard,* he exclaimed as he emanated a psionic wave. *I will always be anticipating and aware.*

Again Lorelei said nothing, though she used some of her power to dispel her "host's" energy. Even feeling it against her skin was repulsive.

Besides... Kraft continued. *What would you do afterward? Even if you did kill me, as well as every Piscean on this ship, you would be unable to return to the Flints, I assure you.*

Taking note of the underlying message in that statement, Lorelei scanned the *Grah'n*'s bridge and frowned.

Your associates have engaged this ship's auto-navigation system, she observed. *And encrypted it with a random code.*

An obvious precaution, Kraft nodded in confirmation. *Given your well-re-corded tenacity.*

He moved back to the counter and replaced his teacup, precisely where it had been before. *You cannot extract the code from the crew, as none of them know it. Nor can you force any of them to break into the system, as we will arrive at the Sea long before any progress could be made.*

Despite the obvious prodding, Lorelei did not respond but continued to sit on the bunk and hold her untouched tea. Kraft decided to conclude this first discourse.

As you have discerned, you are at our tender mercies, for the time being, he expounded. *I suggest you make yourself comfortable.*

Turning to leave, he stopped before opening the door. *Oh, I almost forgot,* he turned back with an apologetic expression. *For obvious reasons, I am afraid you must remain here.*

Again Lorelei said nothing.

For whatever reason, our hosts are quite apprehensive about allowing you access to their ship. Even so, I have convinced them not *to restrain you or place you in the brig, as long as you are not disruptive.*

Kraft let that sink in for a moment if only to ensure his "guest's" cooperation.

And now, he continued, giving off an overly dramatic bow, *I must leave you. I look forward to our next time together, Miss Lorelei.*

With a smile, Kraft turned and made his exit. Glaring after him as he left, Lorelei waited for a few more moments in the resulting silence. Then, once she was assured that he was gone, she disdainfully poured her tea onto the floor.

——————————— ———————————

Kraft was no more than a few meters away from his guest's quarters when his eyes picked up a familiar figure. In truth, he had long felt the Pisceans' presence, even as he was speaking with his fellow psion, but he had simply chosen not to contend with it…until now.

"Do you realize how rude it is to eavesdrop?"

Inanga naturally glared at Kraft. His glare was not nearly as intense as Lorelei's, Kraft mused.

"That woman will be more trouble than she's worth," the Piscean spat in clear disdain. "Make no mistake."

"I strongly disagree. Her connection to the Moon more than justifies our possessing her," Kraft retorted. "And though she may try at one point or another, she will be contained easily enough, I assure you."

Inanga snarled. "As if your assurances hold any kind of weight," he shot back in clear contempt.

Kraft smirked at his host's displeasure. "Without her, my dear Dagon, you will have no chance of reaching the Black Moon, much less asserting your sovereignty over your fellow Pisceans. It will do you well to appreciate her value."

"I do not care if she has been 'touched' by the Moon, the White Siren on my ship is an aggravation I can do without," Inanga countered. "Or have you not heard the stories surrounding her?"

"I've heard them, yes," Kraft nodded. "I particularly like the one where she made off with the Platinum Scales. How she got it away from the Librans…"

"The most notorious, and daring master thief in the galaxy. One who is well versed in the art of escape, as well as a psion powerful enough to challenge *you*," Inanga interrupted, accusingly. "And she is here, aboard my ship."

Though he was tempted, Kraft resisted the urge to shake his head dispassionately. "As I said, her connection to the Moon more than justifies her presence," he clarified, his patience sorely tried by Inanga's hassling. "You will see that when she leads us through the Sea to the waiting Moon."

Inanga remained doubtful regardless. "Somehow, I do not think she is entirely adamant about aiding us."

"Leave that to me," Kraft answered, again with a reassurance that put off Inanga rather than instilled confidence. "We have plenty of time before we reach the Sea. I'm sure I can sway her by then."

"Of course," Inanga spoke with obvious dubiety. "And the Flints?"

Kraft tilted his head questioningly. "What about them?"

Inanga nearly rolled his eyes. "Surely, they don't appreciate us taking their benefactor…"

"Ah, yes," Kraft exclaimed as if remembering a particular detail. "I suppose it would be inconvenient if they intercepted us."

"I would imagine," Inanga replied dryly. "Especially as the *Grah'n* is *alone* now."

Kraft didn't need his telepathy to pick up Inanga's ire over that last statement. Over half the Rohu fleet, which had been small to begin with, had been wiped out at Timas IV. Those that managed to survive the *Sun*'s onslaught had sustained extensive damage. As a result, Inanga had ordered the remnants of his once prized armada back to Piscean space, leaving only he and his flagship to proceed. Any other action would have been an unnecessary risk, but the Dagon remained hurt and humiliated regardless.

The Terran scientist was far from bothered by their status. "Well then," he retorted blandly. "I strongly suggest you get us to Sognare as…*piscinly* possible."

Inanga's gills flared, much to Kraft's minor delight.

"Once we're in the Sea, the Flints will have no choice but to break off pursuit."

The Doctor moved to step past the Dagon, but Inanga spoke up once more.

"And how do you know that?" he challenged. "They are not ordinary pirates, after all. What will stop them from pursuing regardless?"

This time, Kraft smiled scathingly. "I imagined it was obvious. Without the Siren to guide them through, they would be invariably trapped within the Sea. As well as left vulnerable to its terrors."

The Doctor then shoved by, walking down the corridor. "You will see my good Dagon. Kadath is within reach, and our dream-quest is well set."

Again the Terran's words came across as blades against Inanga's flesh, causing the Dagon to shake his head in disgust. *"Mgn'gha azbthnkor,"* he growled before moving away in the opposite direction.

Flint Pirates umbra *Black Sun*
Arcspace

"What…" Alex gaped, effectively voicing what everyone else in the room was thinking. Even Jon and Barbarossa weren't bothering to conceal their shock. "What in the Sixth Circle is this?"

The profile on the shared vidscreens read out as "LAURENTIUS KRAFT", and the accompanying data texts certainly held a detailed history on a person named Laurentius Kraft, who even held the title of Doctor within his life-time. Yet the face that came with the profile, whether it did, in fact, belong to the genuine article, was *not* the face of the man that Jon, Alex, and Kaguya had fought only an hour earlier. The face could have been that of an entirely different entity altogether, given the sheer contrast.

Rather than the overly, perhaps *artificially* handsome face from before, the best one could say about this one was "unassuming" and "ordinary". From the ovoid-shaped head to the oversized ears and nose, dreadfully combed over dark brown hair, somehow undersized dark brown eyes and uneven, unsmiling lips, the man in the picture looked more like a standardized depiction of Terrans than one who possessed unique traits. That face that could be found anywhere and everywhere in the galaxy, no matter the race or creed.

And yet, somehow and in some way, that face held its own uniquely terrible aura, which also contrasted what had been felt prior. For it was not the chaotic, destructive ambiance that the man in the temple had held, but rather a cold, somehow sinister countenance. As though the man in the picture was completely unabashed to the darker sides of the universe. As though the soul within had long been tainted by the greatest of horrors, to the point that no form of light – warm, wholesome light at least – could ever be found within.

As horrific as that face was, however, it was not the most disturbing part of the profile. Rather, it was a certain line just next to the image. A line that declared "DECEASED", with the accompanying date following at 700.03.15.

"An imposter then," Barbarossa offered as he folded his arms, fighting back the disturbance within. "Whatever this *creature* is, it must have assumed the good doctor's identity…"

"No," Kaguya countered quietly, as she continued to gaze at the image, straight into the projected eyes. "Those are the same eyes."

She looked over to the others to clarify. "The one we fought before held those very same eyes," she stated with utmost certainty. "Somehow."

Davis was quick to follow Barbarossa's example. "He could have had them transplanted," he exclaimed, trying to force back his anxiety. "Not to mention cosmetic surgery…"

"No, she's right," Jon put down the argument once and for all, staring hard at the image. "I don't know how, but the two are indeed the same. Just two hundred plus years removed."

"How is that even possible?" Anna let out. "Even if he had faked his recorded death, there's no way he can still be alive two centuries later!"

"That is a long lifespan for a Terran," Apache added, frowning. "Yet somehow I get the feeling he hasn't been hibernating up to this point…"

"No, cryo is out," Alex answered. "We would have seen the effects, and it doesn't account for his change in appearance."

"Okay, so we're apparently dealing with a zombie," Davis grumbled, forcing the meeting back to the main subject. "Where do we go from here?"

The other faces looked as though the answer were obvious.

"I would think the plan remains the same, Davis," Alex blandly rejoined. "Head for the Moon, get Lorelei, save the galaxy and then shoot back to Ryugu in time for dinner…"

"I get that, Alex," Davis responded, much as he didn't want to.

Unfortunately, even if they weren't obligated to rescue their wayward siren, the fact remained that there was just too much at stake, not least of which was the Pisceans enslaving or enraging an all-powerful godthing, to cut and run. Besides, Davis knew better than suggest it; after all, he had made his protests before, and they had gone to Timas regardless.

"What I mean is what's the plan to accomplish it all? Because last I checked, we lost our only means toward reaching the Moon." The helmsman glared over at Jon. "And with all due respect Captain," he pointedly stated. "Even you aren't badass enough to take us into the Sea as we are now…without a course or a guide."

That assertion hung in the air for several moments. Indeed, without Lorelei, they had no hope of making their way through Sognare. Not when so many had tried and failed, with the only survivor ending up maddened from the voyage. All the same, however, everyone, including Davis, knew that they couldn't leave it at that. No matter how much some, once more, namely Davis, would have been tempted to.

And then the helmsman spoke up again. "By the way…" he said, looking up and around the ceiling. "Has anyone else noticed?"

When the faces turned back to him, he continued. "Lorelei's not aboard," he pointed out, both verbally and with an upward angled finger. "Yet, the autodestruct hasn't activated."

The realization quickly spread across the table.

"Now that you mention it," Alex let out as he looked around. "It has been rather quiet around here, hasn't it?"

"You think Miss Lorelei did something just before she was captured?" Gran added.

"Perhaps…" Braun considered. "She may have entered in the cancellation code at some point prior."

That earned nods of agreement from the others, though Jon wasn't convinced. Somehow he had a feeling that it was more than that, but he didn't dare say it aloud at that time.

"That aside," Alex spoke up again. "I guess our only choice is to intercept them before they reach the Sea…"

"Can we do that?" Anna inquired.

"Not in arcspace. At least not without a high risk factor," Davis explained, professionally. "The best point would be after they drop out of arc upon final approach, but we don't know where that final point is going to be."

"And they may not even drop out period," Gran vocalized for Kaiser. "Depending on how *vespertilio stercore insanus* these Pisceans are, they may just actually dive right in." Kaiser then motioned for Gran to add, "Pardon the expression."

"So, where does that leave us?" Anna frowned. "There's no way we'll reach them once they cross."

Davis shrugged. "We could wait at the edge of the Sea for when they come out again…"

"Sure," Alex deadpanned. "With or without the all-powerful abomination backing them up?"

"Or worse," Apache added. "It could very well go after them for disturbing its nap, and then us next."

"That would be the worst case scenario, wouldn't it?" Barbarossa agreed. "As advanced as this ship is, I admit to having reservations toward fighting a godbeing. Even a false one."

"It'd make Ephesus look like a trip to a theme park on Bellerophon," Alex muttered in apprehension. "And just may be the prelude to Armageddon."

"So what?" Davis countered. "We take our chances with the Sea? Blind and open as we are?"

"Couldn't the Psi Disruptor counteract the Sea's effects?"

"Not likely," Braun shook his head sadly. "It would need to be enhanced a million times over just to hold against the basic effects. And we would still be without any form of navigation."

"But we can't just wait it out," Anna stated, before eyeing Davis. "Much less turn around and pray it leaves us alone."

Davis glared. "I never said...!"

"That's enough," Jon suddenly spoke up, his voice level but easily overriding the others. "Davis, how long until we reach the Sea?"

The air seemed to grow colder with that question, such that it took a moment for Davis to answer.

"Approximately seventy-two hours, present speed."

Jon nodded. "And there is no way we can intercept them before?"

Already knowing what the captain was thinking, Davis could only resign himself to the outcome. "Not without knowing exactly where they will drop out of arc."

The chill only emphasized the brief silence that followed. And then Jon, looking as though he had made the crucial decision, glanced at the others.

"Then we have but one heading," he stated with finality. "And we will follow it."

Another brief pause, as though the others were attempting a response to that ultimatum before Jon finally commanded. "Dismissed."

Knowing better than to speak further, the rest of the table, resigned to their destination, rose and made their way toward the door. Alex, however, cast his brother a final, questioning glance, to which Jon nodded inexpressively in reply. And though the younger Flint wished to press his brother further, he knew it wasn't the time, and so departed as well.

Now alone in the briefing room, Jon stood. However, instead of walking out the door, he turned to a blank, unadorned side of the room and closed his eye. Visible discomfort briefly appeared on his countenance, but the elder Flint forced it back. Anxiety would serve no purpose in what he was about to do.

"You have been with me since the beginning," he suddenly spoke, eye remaining closed. "And not once have I ever asked anything of you."

Slowly, he reached his right hand up to his face. "You have showed me much since that time," he continued. "To which I am grateful, though I can only question whether you did so for my sake, or for some other purpose."

His hand reached for his eyepatch. "Regardless," he stated, grasping the black cover. "I am in need of your...*wisdom* once more." Then, gently and reverently, he drew away the patch, though his right eye remained closed.

"And this time, I ask of it, not for myself, nor for those around me..." he specified, his voice gaining strength as he said. "...but for *her*."

He tilted his head down, as if in humility. "The one that has brought me unto this juncture," he said. "The one I will see unto that which awaits."

Though he couldn't be sure, he thought he felt *it* respond to his words, enough to cause his body to tremble.

"Thus I beseech of you," he said, solemnly yet imploringly. *"Show me the way."*

With that, Jon opened *both* of his eyes... and all became clear to him.

Black Sun
Call of the Moon

Chapter XVII: Toward Kadath

Piscean *Gnaiih*-class battleship *Grah'n*
Arcspace

A steady sigh escaped Lorelei's lips as she lay staring up at the ceiling, hands behind her head. It had been just over a day since her capture, though it felt more like over a year with the way it was proceeding. She couldn't remember the last time she had been so bored; even sleep felt less like rest and more like a chore. Not that the bedding she was lounging on would have helped much. One wondered if the Pisceans really did sleep upon shallow rock bottoms.

If there was one major downside to her present state, it was the sheer lack of stimulation. There was simply not much to do, short of the necessities for living and planning out her daring escape. Besides the fact she did not have direct access to the rest of the ship, not that she wanted to move further into it, her lodging was threadbare, containing little more than a bed, the Piscean equivalent of a washroom and one or two vidscreens that she could not access. Oh, and Kraft's book, which he had left on the stand earlier, but Lorelei was apprehensive about touching the tome. Like the good doctor himself – *it*self – the volume had a strange aura to it.

Unfortunately, that left her with very little else but her escape planning, and that had long hit a dead end. Sure, she had figured out the layout of the ship by this time, and could have easily gotten out of her "cell" and made it toward the hangar deck at least five different ways. Alongside, she could have readily taken Dagon Inanga's personal shuttle, which was outfitted with an arc booster, and either made her way back to the *Sun* directly or designated a rendezvous somewhere distant. And she could have done all of this by either eluding the Pisceans completely or taking Flints' example at Rochelle and seeing them all dead on her way out.

The reason why she didn't escape was the same reason she was there to begin with. Though he had been largely keeping to his own affairs since his initial visitation, Lorelei knew Kraft was out there, watching and waiting. She didn't need her special power to know that, nor to pick up his unsavory presence; the setup alone made it obvious enough. He would come after her the moment she made a move he didn't like, and she would end up in a worse space than she was in now. Perhaps even be in a worse state of mind and being; the thought alone discomforted her immensely.

So, like it or not, she was stuck for the time being. She would have her chance to escape, but not now. And much more, she still had her original task to accomplish; to "free" the Black Moon, or whatever it was, from its form of incarceration. For better or worse, this was something she could do before or alongside her escape; after all, whether aboard the *Black Sun* or the *Grah'n*, she would have been on the same heading. As such, she might as well take advantage of it, especially when she knew the *Sun* wouldn't be far away.

Still, that left her original dilemma. What could she do in the meantime? She already had been sleeping off and on. She had long been denied access to the ship's media and entertainment systems, lest she utilize those as a means toward her escape. Her wristcom had been confiscated during her initial capture, which also denied her access to the cortex. And her hosts saw no apparent reason to accommodate any desire, short of providing scheduled meals. Not that she preferred their company, any more than Kraft's.

That left her one option. Unfortunately, it remained there, upon that counter, waiting to be picked up and read once more.

She frowned at the thought. Obviously, that was Kraft's intention, the reason he had deliberately left the book behind. And though she didn't know exactly how it fit into his purpose, she knew it would somehow tie in toward his interest in the Black Moon. Perhaps even provide her some background to his motivations and character as well.

He's about as subtle as a battleship's cannon barrage, and just as cliché, she thought disdainfully.

Before the inevitable exchange may begin between them, Kraft first wished for her to learn something about himself. Something that he chose not to explain directly, thereby enticing his audience's curiosity.

Using a book for the allegory only adds to the mystery, as well as the accompanying drama. And you are all about the drama, aren't you, Doctor? Lorelei mused, staring at the offending volume.

Disgusted, she knew that ultimately there was no choice. Even if it hadn't been Kraft's intent, she would have wanted to ascertain as much as she could about him, and his weaknesses, for the next time they crossed. It was her nature to desire knowledge and to learn. It was one of the primary factors toward her seeking Arcadia, among other things, and it was the main reason why she was who and what she was. As the Terran saying went, knowledge was power, and Lorelei knew better than to refuse the opportunity...even when it was deliberately offered.

Thus, with a resigning shudder, she telekinetically lifted the book off the stand and drew it toward her waiting hands. She could tell it was an old book with the accompanying pungent scent that could only be generated by timeworn paper and dilapidated cloth. The cover was a washed-out green with the barely legible title displayed in faded golden Terran lettering. It was also relatively thin, much slimmer than the books she usually read, thus establishing it as a novella. Yet all of that took a backseat to the unpleasant surrealness it generated, as though, like its owner, it was not meant to be.

The Dream-Quest of Unknown Kadath... Lorelei read, her interest somewhat piqued. There was no author's name, which indicated that the story had been written in the First Age and had been reprinted upon its rediscovery within Alexandria. Or, as improbable as it sounded, it was a surviving ancient First Age edition that Kraft had somehow acquired. The wornness alone could have been evidence of this.

Regardless, she would not accomplish anything by studying the exterior. Thus, once more biting back her reluctance, she opened the book and began.

Three times Randolph Carter dreamed of the marvelous city...

Flint Pirates umbra *Black Sun*
Arcspace

It was a grim environment within the *Black Sun*. Not quite as grim as it had been prior to Ephesus, but the effect was more or less the same. It was composed of accumulated, though not overwhelmingly so, fear and apprehension from all those gathered and presently laboring. An environment that only existed upon the eve of battle.

The battle will only be the last part of this. The main fight will be getting to the Moon, Anna contemplated as she walked down the ever active deck, passing several working crewmen as she read a set of reports on her datapad, all the while fighting herself to keep from cringing. *We're sailing through one of the most unstable, chaotic areas of space ever to exist. A sea which no ship has ever crossed successfully, with the only survivor of one expedition unhinged by the experience. Unbelievable!*

Several of the crew were just as anxious, though they weren't as efficient in concealing it as Anna was her anxiety. It was only natural. Unlike Ephesus, nobody knew what to expect from the Sea, nor what they would find at its heart, but the pirates were gearing up for the expedition and coming battle regardless.

Weapons were being checked and rechecked, the arc engine was being retuned virtually by the hour, the shields were being recalibrated for the *known* parts of the Sea, and operational optimization of every team, system, and piece of equipment was being verified. Admittedly not much from Anna's perspective, but it was enough to give the inclination that the Flint Pirates may just may survive to fight again. Or at least make the return trip to Ryugu in one piece.

"Report," a familiar, growling voice sounded.

Anna resisted the urge to smirk. She had grown so used to that voice and its commanding presence that it no longer made her jump every time its bearer approached unnoticed. So, apparently, did the rest of the crew, who continued their work undisturbed.

"All departments on schedule," she answered. "Estimating less than six hours before overall completion."

"That quickly?" Barbarossa questioned as he moved next to Anna, projecting a curious expression.

Anna resisted the urge to comment on what that sort of emotion did to cats. Instead, she simply shrugged. "Considering all that we're about to do, I imagine the crew would rather spend the rest of the time at their leisure," she replied. "Besides, there's only so much that can be done to prepare."

Barbarossa nodded solemnly. "Unfortunately," he exclaimed, allowing a small portion of his discomfort to show. He had to admit this would be a first for him as well, and he didn't like it in the least. "Morale?"

Anna nodded toward a pair of crewmen moving down the deck, carrying some large piece of equipment. "As you can see, they're still working, but I wouldn't pretend the outlook to be positive."

"It never is," Barbarossa stated in turn. He surveyed the area to make sure no one else was in earshot. "I also take it the Captain remains indisposed?"

The operations officer looked up from her datapad. "Seemingly," she answered with a slight tone of uncertainty. "And even then, you would know before me."

"Heh," Barbarossa growled. Ever since Ianessa, the Captain, as well as the First Officer and Raider Commander, had been largely keeping to themselves. They still attended to their respective duties, but they were hardly seen or heard beyond that, even amongst the other officers.

It was understandable. As far as everyone knew, they were still recovering from their previous battle, as well as gearing up for the coming one. To Barbarossa, however, while he could believe that with Alex and Kaguya, a part of him wondered if it was the same with the Captain. After all, it was by his directive that they would brave the Sea; surely, he had a means or was developing one, to successfully cross it and reach the Moon.

"You're also wondering, aren't you?" Anna exclaimed. "What does the Captain have…"

"It would be best not to vocalize such thoughts," the Leo interrupted. They were, after all, in the open, and Barbarossa knew what kind of effect those words would have on any who overheard. As such, he simply nodded one final time. "Carry on, Miss Reed."

"Aye, sir," Anna answered as Barbarossa moved away. She watched his back for a little longer then promptly returned to her datapad.

———————————————————

"So you think we have a shot at this," Davis questioned as he stood by and watched Braun and the other engineers go about their work. The Professor was presently in front of the arc engine, continuously inputting adjustments while shifting between the readings on the display screen and the keyboard. "Actually crossing through the Sea."

"I would say a fair one," Braun replied as he entered another set of commands then checked the display screen. "Among other things, this ship was specifically designed to cross through even the most hazardous areas of space."

"Right, but an expanse of unstable psionic energy?" Davis questioned, seeing no reason to hide his skepticism. "Isn't that a little much, even for us?"

Braun considered. "I admit the Sognare is well out of the ordinary and perilous, as best indicated by the late Captain Jennis." The professor then shrugged. "Otherwise, I fail to see it any differently from a particularly volatile nebula, a radiation induced asteroid field or the Devil's Triangle," he continued, a smirk coming across his bloated lips. "Just another sea."

"An especially rough, stormy sea that can wreck minds as well as ships," Davis grumbled.

Braun nodded in acknowledgment. "But a sea nonetheless. Something that can, and will, be traversed, with proper preparation beforehand, of course."

"Right," the helmsman muttered, shaking his head in disbelief. In truth, he felt uncharacteristically envious, wishing he had that same confidence. Unfortunately, no matter how much he searched within, he just couldn't give credence to faith, much less hope.

Outside a superior ship, what exactly was going for them that hadn't existed for Jennis and those who attempted to cross before and after? Surely they had taken precautions to brave the Sea; surely, their ships and crews had held much in the way of capability and skill. And yet, like in some ancient mariner's tale, they had all been lost regardless, never to be heard from again.

Davis shivered, his thanatophobia, he had since looked up the proper term, briefly rearing its ugly head. It was short, thankfully, but still enough to emphasize his doubt and apprehension. As much as he was aware of his mortality, and therefore his inevitable demise, he did not want to die in this particular manner, forever lost in a nightmare made real. Yet, wasn't that what awaited him, and the rest of the ship, upon sailing off the edge of the map?

Braun seemed to notice the helmsman's discomfort, and a small chuckle escaped his lips. "This reminds me of the time before Ephesus. You were just as apprehensive back then."

It took a moment for Davis to remember, a frown crossed his expression. It had been well over a year since that fateful night in the Lounge, where he had confessed the full extent of his fear to the good Professor.

"And you're just as aloof about it," he shot back. "I don't suppose that somehow factored into your 'assurances.'"

The engineer smirked. Unlike Davis, death was not a large concern for the semi-immortal Braun, not when he had existed for centuries and had watched all he had cared for pass beyond him.

"Well, for what it's worth, I don't wish to die just yet," he stated simply. "I am doing everything in my power to prevent it, as are those around me."

Davis didn't need to look around to see the other engineers, at least the ones within earshot, also grinning.

"But no, that particular state of mind has nothing to do with my outlook," Braun gleamed. "I simply believe, despite the apparent factors to the contrary, that Sognare will not stop us. Especially when there is still so much left for us to do."

Hope flickered within the helmsman. Indeed, they had come a long way, and it would be anticlimactic if it were all to end in the Sea. Strangely, he found some assurance in that thought.

"Well, when you put it that way," Davis spoke with deference. "Far be it for me to claim otherwise, Professor."

Earning one last nod of acknowledgment from Braun, Davis decided that was the best time to take his leave. The task that sent him to engineering had long been fulfilled. As much as he enjoyed talking to Braun, eccentricities, and scientific jargon aside, he didn't want to keep the professor from his work. Besides, he had other duties to complete, especially if he wanted to get to the Lounge before the day's end.

Still, despite his burgeoning hope and Braun's assurances, a part of him retained uncertainty. Especially since he, and as far as he knew everyone else on the *Sun,* had yet to figure out *how…*

Piscean *Gnaiih*-class battleship *Grah'n*
Arcspace

Kraft could barely suppress his grin as he approached the door. It had taken a bit longer than he would have liked, but eventually, his guest had succumbed to her curiosity and done exactly what he had wished her to do. He couldn't help but feel elated; he had taken one step closer to the Moon.

When he came to the cell door, he paused, barely glancing at the flanking guards, whose shared glare and accompanying thoughts he ignored like a bad odor. Slowly, he allowed his smile to unfold before the door shifted open, providing him entry. His guest remained upon her bed, reading the book he had left behind.

I sense you're captivated.

Lorelei frowned but didn't look up from the book. *"Captivated" is a strong word,* she retorted, before deciding to give a more lenient answer. *Though, it is admittedly enticing, despite its prose.*

Kraft nodded in acknowledgment. *Yes, the original author was, ironically, not a gifted writer. I find the vision to matter more than the way it is described.*

Lorelei grimaced as she snapped the book closed. The faux casualness was enough to make her wretch, just like nearly everything else about her captor.

Let's not beat around the bush, she stated, telekinetically flinging the book at Kraft, who caught it with his power and placed it neatly back on the counter. *You didn't leave this here for my entertainment.*

Only then did she turn and glare at the apparent scientist; he merely shrugged as he took his seat.

You're right, of course, he said, looking toward the book fondly. *That is the last remaining article of my original life. The life I lived over two hundred years ago.*

Lorelei simply raised an eyebrow in response; her bored, disinterested glare remained unchanged. Kraft laughed out loud.

Come now, a woman so intuitive would have easily realized it, he explained, his grin taking a much creepier tone. *I am, in fact, dead.*

Again Lorelei did not reply, vocally or telepathically. She had surmised as much from their first encounter. It had been quite obvious Kraft's present form wasn't his original. It was too artificial, as well as too horrifically unstable, for that. Lorelei sensed that much of the good doctor's energy was focused on keeping it composed and functioning, much like a worn, broken down machine that only remained operational through extensive engineering efforts. One lapse moment would result in the body disintegrating; dust to dust as another Terran saying went.

Sheer improbability aside, there could be only one explanation for Kraft's present state. He had long exceeded his natural lifespan, and only through sheer psionic will had he remained physically active, or "amongst the living".

It wasn't easy at first, Kraft continued, ignoring Lorelei's disgust as much as he had the guards'. To emphasize, he raised his arm and withdrew his sleeve. The skin underneath rippled with psionic energy. *My first attempts to recompose myself were quite...limited, such that I came out looking anything but living.*

A tone of solemnness overtook Kraft as he recalled his initial attempt after "passing on". Had he been his original self, he would have undoubtedly shivered at the *abomination* he had become, but now he felt...nothing. A status that was becoming commonplace as time went on, but he didn't dwell on that, much.

After a couple of decades, however, I managed to get the process right, though it requires me to change form now and then, he continued, withdrawing his arm. *The longer I hold onto a single form, the harder it becomes to maintain. Eventually, I have to develop a new appearance and body structure for myself.*

How inconvenient, Lorelei answered with appropriate blandness.

Kraft shrugged. *Inconvenient but worthwhile,* he replied, flexing his hand to emphasize. *Until I reach my Sunset City, I cannot afford to pass onto the afterlife, or whatever awaits on the other side.*

The doctor cast a determined gaze at Lorelei's bland one. *And I will reach my city!* he declared. *I will gain what I have sought from the beginning, just as Carter had.*

With that comment, Lorelei felt his power wash over her again, but with a softer effect, akin to his caressing her cheek. She barely suppressed her disgusted shiver.

And you will help me do this, my dear siren, Kraft affirmed, his dominant smile returning.

Glare firmly in place, Lorelei telekinetically repulsed his 'touch'. Another moment of silence elapsed before Lorelei, at last, spoke.

And what is this "Sunset City" that you seek? Lorelei inquired, knowing full well she was playing into his hands, but not caring. The more she knew…

Kraft's smile intensified. He had waited for just that query.

Indeed, that is the question, isn't it? What have I sought for so long that I have even transcended death as Carter had transcended the Dreamlands? He then shrugged. *As embarrassing as it is to admit… I don't remember.*

An expression of regretfulness then came over him. *Time may have a way of healing the living, but it is the direct opposite for the dead,* he explained. *As the years pass by in abundance, all that I am, and was, slowly passes with it. I remember very little of my original life, including what it is I searched for.*

Again he nodded toward the book. *And just as this is the final remnant of my life, it is also the only indication of what I seek. For just as Carter pursued the Sunset City, to the point of risking his very existence to gain an audience with the gods of Kadath, I seek my own.*

Dubiousness entered Lorelei's eyes. *And you believe the Black Moon will grant it to you?*

Kraft nodded. *The Black Moon is said to be the dwelling place of Gods or Devils,* he smiled knowingly. *Just as Kadath had been the dwelling place of the Great Ones.*

Lorelei crossed her arms. *Seriously?*

Her sarcasm earned another laugh from Kraft. *No, I do not believe the Black Moon to be such either. But I do recognize its awesome power. Surely, the power that created Sognare, the power that has influenced so many minds, including yours, would be enough to grant what I seek,* he stated, regret infusing his words. *And more to the point, it is my final gamble.*

Rather than explain, Kraft closed his eyes and relaxed his control. Lorelei watched as his body seemingly and rapidly deteriorated. His form thinned as the visible skin dried out and tore, while his eyes sunk and collapsed into the back of his skull, and his hair and lips receded to mere wisps of their previous appearance. Bone was quickly exposed, drying, and minimizing by the second, as his clothes shrank and became ripped and tattered. All while his psionic energy diminished in luminosity, much like a dying star.

Lorelei remained undaunted by the grotesque image. After all, she had gathered as much during her earlier assessment.

I do not know how much longer I can continue, Kraft stated through his corpsified form. *Every day, every hour, it takes more and more energy to remain, as well as to function. Energy that is far from infinite.*

And then just as abruptly, Kraft reverted to his "passable" form, running his fingers across his suit jacket, as though brushing away any remaining dust. *It's safe to say I will not last far beyond this year, as you can see.*

The mania returned to Kraft's eyes. *Thus, I will reach the Moon. Regardless of the sacrifice or consequence, and you will be my guide.*

Another brief silence, during which the blandness returned to Lorelei's expression. *Forgive me,* she replied dryly, *if I feel unmoved toward…this.*

And, just as Kraft had done before, she used her power to project her disdain. *Any of this!*

With a snicker, Kraft waved away her telepathy. *I thought you would react that way,* he replied, with a hint of disappointment. *And I find it as regretful as I did back on Timas IV.*

Lorelei started to speak, but Kraft spoke first. *Surely you understand my plight more than anyone else? The desire, the drive, to seek what others have dismissed, to put everything that you are, and were, toward its acquisition.*

Again Lorelei felt his power surge over her, though this time, its effect was different. This time, it struck a feeling of familiarity.

Surely you would do the same, Kraft pressed on, *to reach Arcadia...*

Immediately, Lorelei sent out a telekinetic wave, throwing Kraft back from his seat and across the room. He landed hard against the bulkhead, sliding down to the floor.

Hate emanated from every pore of her body. It took all of Lorelei's power to restrain herself from inflicting any further damage on her captor. That and the knowledge it would require far more than she wanted to expend, especially given her isolated position.

Knowing she had realized as much, Kraft physically rose from the floor, again dusting off his clothes.

Once more, regretful.

Before any more could be said, or done, the intercom came online. "Doctor Kraft, your presence is requested on the bridge," a Piscean voice called out. "Doctor Kraft to the bridge."

Sighing, Kraft shook his head in mock frustration. *Well, I suppose that's all the time we have, at least for the moment.*

With one final smile, he moved toward the door. *I'll let you hold onto that,* he said, again nodding toward the book. *If only so you may consider...*

Not bothering to wait for an answer, the undead scientist exited, leaving his guest alone once again, all while ignoring the murderous intent that radiated from her being.

Flint Pirates umbra *Black Sun*
Arcspace

Alex was in a somber mood, emphasized by the music playing over his quarters' sound system. Though he was not as obsessed with the classics, or the other artful parts of Ancient Terra, like his brother, there were times he felt such works were appropriate. In this case, *Who's Crying Now.* The song contained a sweet, sad melody, while the even rhythm was enough to keep him awake and working. And he certainly had reason for the latter.

Stifling a yawn, the younger Flint gazed somewhat exhaustively over the data on his monitor. An arrangement of datawindows was displayed across the screen, from Kraft's bio to recorded statistics on the Sognare Sea and various mythologies centered on the Black Moon. All of it informative in some way or another, Alex had spent the better part of the hour verifying as such, but not to the extent that he wished. If anything he, and the rest of the Flint Pirates with him, were still going into this fight blind.

The data, or lack thereof, on Kraft, was especially frustrating. What Alex found had been enlightening, but not enough for him to derive some sort of advantage. Outside the doctor's early life, career, and accomplishments as one of Terra's leading psionologists, there simply wasn't much else to glean. Especially over the last two hundred years following his "demise". As far as the "official" sources were concerned, Kraft was long dead and buried somewhere on Terra. Alex doubted any of his sources would have much else; even Ciel had not mentioned him during the discussion concerning the Pisceans. Subsequently, only rumors and speculation remained, none of which could be validated in the present.

Of course, there was still the matter of reaching the Doctor and the Pisceans, and the Black Moon. For the life of him, Alex didn't know how they were going to accomplish this one. The *Black Sun* had no defenses against the Sea's effects. Even the Psi Disruptor wouldn't be effective against a psionic force that size. Yet, he knew Jon had a plan, as he always did. He wouldn't be taking them into the Sea otherwise. Just as he also knew his brother, in his usual manner, wouldn't reveal said plan until the "right time", which would likely be upon entry.

All in all, there were just too many unknowns for Alex's liking. And nothing instilled apprehension, and at other times captivation, in the younger Flint than the unknown.

The door chime interrupted his musings.

"Enter."

The door shifted open, allowing Kaguya entry. "Anything?" she inquired, having known what Alex had been doing for the last few hours.

The younger Flint shook his head. "Nothing beyond the basic information. And things we already knew."

Kaguya nodded, her expression just as solemn. "To be expected," she replied as she came over to stand beside Alex, her own eyes upon the monitor screen. "Though still dismaying."

"Tell me about it," Alex exclaimed, frustration apparent. "How are Cheney and the others doing?"

Kaguya pursed her lips before answering. "Still recovering," she said simply. "Their participation is…doubtful."

Alex inhaled, having expected as much. Besides their physical wounds, the raiders had also suffered massive psionic backlash from Kraft's entry to Ianessa. Their recovery time could be lengthy.

"I get the feeling there won't be much ground fighting in this one…"

"We would still have to board the enemy battleship," Kaguya posited, though she reneged on mentioning the exact reason why.

Alex shrugged. "True enough," he replied. *Though with any luck, Lorelei will have taken care of things by then,* he thought, pausing before his next question. "And Jon?"

Kaguya shook her head. "Still sequestered in his quarters."

"Yeah," Alex rejoined, turning and steepling his fingers as he thought about his brother. "I figured that would be the case."

Kaguya resisted the urge to sigh, uncertainty in her expression. In response, Alex adopted a flat, but reassuring, smile.

"Don't worry; he's just refining his plan."

The kunoichi nodded. "I've surmised as much," she agreed, somewhat hopeful with Alex's reassurance.

Inwardly smiling at his handiwork, Alex decided to move things along further.

"We'll survive this one, Kaguya," he said, smile expanding as he reached up to grasp her hand. "We may get hurt from it, perhaps badly, but we'll survive it. After all, only fools dare enrage dragons," he stated determinedly. "In this case, fools that taste yummy wrapped in rice and seaweed."

That earned a small smile from Kaguya, alongside an equally small, almost uncharacteristic laugh, all while her doubts slowly drained away.

"Yes," she agreed, her hand folding into his. "We will survive," she stated with the same determination, her smile fully blossoming as she added. "And we will be victorious."

She gazed at the projected image of the Sea. Somehow it appeared smaller.

"For only dragons may rule the heavens," she declared. "And only the Blue and the Gold may rule all."

Alex grinned, *Black and Gold, actually*, he thought with his hand clasping hers tightly. Yes, the Flint Pirates would survive Sognare. Though he had yet to understand how they would proceed, or even what horrors awaited them therein, they would survive.

And much more, they would *win*… despite the unknown.

<u>Chapter XVIII: Sea of Madness</u>

Piscean *Gnaiih*-class battleship *Grah'n*
Sognare Sea

"We have arrived at the Sognare Sea," the helmsman proclaimed to the rest of the bridge. "Auto-navigation has disengaged."

No other words were spoken as all eyes fixed upon the main monitor. Though Inanga and his followers had seen their fair share of anomalies, in space and elsewhere, what lay before them now was entirely incomprehensible. And with that understanding, abject terror began to spread across the bridge crew, infecting all up to and including the Dagon.

Before them and their mighty battleship lay the infinite Sea, as boundless in scope and dimension as its name alluded. From their present perspective, it appeared as nothing less than a solid wall of shifting energy, turbulent, and fluctuating like the most ferocious storm. Powerful discharges – not unlike terrestrial lightning – swept about at varying angles and vectors, while fiery cyclones danced majestically across the scape. Colors of every spectrum, and beyond, shifted to and from, appearing for the briefest of times before changing once again, while substance crystallized, liquefied, and/or vaporized in tandem motions. A curious intertwining of horror and beauty that transfixed and appalled those who dared gaze upon it.

Chaos, Inanga thought. Pure chaos was the best, perhaps only, way to describe the Sognare. A realm that truly contained the domain of gods and devils, for no mortal could ever hope to thrive here. Not for the first time, the Dagon reconsidered what he was about to do; what oblivion he was about to take his ship and his followers into. An oblivion that had consumed so many before them.

Indeed, as his flagship now loitered above the precipice, Inanga recognized this to be a fool's errand. How could the *Grah'n* ever hope to sail through such a discorded Sea? How could he ever hope to reach beyond it, to what lay at its center? Surely he had been brazen to presume any of it attainable, let alone possible. To bring his ship into a nightmare given form and dare believe with any semblance of hope that he could best it. As though those who had failed before had done so out of consequence and nothing more.

Yes, he admitted to himself, he had been arrogant to presume. He could see that now, gazing upon the pandemonium before him. All the same, however, he knew he could not turn back. To do so was to abandon any hope of reaching what was perhaps the greatest power in the universe, a power that, if convinced of his behest, would allow his Dag to subjugate and *properly* unify the rest of his civilization. And afterward, the rest of the galaxy with it, thereby bringing equally *proper* order and administration to what had been fragmented and turmoiled. Only a fool would let such a power, and the affirmation it represented, slip away from him.

But then it is said only fools dare brave this maddened Sea, Inanga thought with no small measure of irony. At the very least, it would be an eventful voyage. That much was assured.

Thus, he tapped the control panel on his chair arm. "Doctor Kraft," he began. "Please report to the bridge, and bring our 'guest' along."

Flint Pirates umbra *Black Sun*
Sognare Sea

"God in Heaven…" Davis breathed as he viewed the Sea, watching as it surged and shifted before him and the rest of the *Black Sun*'s bridge crew. It was not the first time he had felt his entire body go numb from fear, but as he gazed out into such an abyss, a fitting description, in spite of its rainbow colors, it was the first time he felt that fear cut so deep. As if it reached into the depths of his soul.

The rest of the bridge looked on much the same; even Barbarossa could not keep the disturbance off of his face, nor did Alex or Kaguya. Only Jon held a passive expression as he gazed upon the ever-changing color and matter, though he would have been lying if he claimed to have not felt unsettled. Now that it was in front of him, he could see the Sognare lived up to both its name and its reputation. A sea of dreams – or nightmares – which one could very easily get lost within, never to return.

Even so, he wasn't about to turn away now. Not when so much, up to and including the return of their beloved patron, was riding on their entering and making it through. Thus, Jon rose from his chair.

"Mr. Davis," he commanded. "Please relinquish the helm."

The air seemingly cooled as further uncertainty encompassed the bridge. And not just because it would be the first time the captain would helm the ship.

"Mr. Davis," Jon repeated, this time with a tone of impatience.

Swallowing, Davis did as he was commanded. "Aye, sir," he replied, rising and stepping away from his station.

Piscean *Gnaiih*-class battleship *Grah'n*
Sognare Sea

The turbolift doors shifted open, admitting Lorelei and her undead escort onto the bridge. Greatcoat swaying as she stepped forward, she ignored the mixed gazes from the bridge crew as she, more to Kraft's indirect prying than of her own will, stepped up to Dagon Inanga. As she did, the Dagon turned his single functioning eye to her, looking her over.

"So you're the much-debated Siren," Inanga began as he observed Lorelei, who remained impassive. "Forgive me if I'm not bowled over with awe."

"No forgiveness necessary, Dagon. I have neither use nor desire for your reverence," Lorelei answered, her tone forwardly respectful yet underscoring her disdain.

It was quite clear, especially to her increasingly agitated audience, that she looked upon the Piscean leader as though he existed under the sole of her boot.

"Though your subservience would be appreciated…"

Several of the crewmen began to rise from their posts at this insult, but Inanga signaled them to remain. The last thing he needed now was for any of them to play into the Siren's schemes.

"I'm afraid I cannot provide that either," the Dagon retorted, almost genially. "As a Dagon and a member of the Chtenff, only the Dagoth may accept my submission."

Lorelei didn't need her telepathy to discern the Dagon's obvious disdain on that subject.

"I'm sure you understand," Inanga stated contemptuously.

The psion simply shrugged. "The universe is full of disappointments," she rejoined, nonplussed. "As I'm sure you discovered firsthand at Timas."

A flood of ire surged through the bridge, more than a few crew members straining to attack. Lorelei smiled banefully, her eyes never leaving Inanga's.

"But do not worry," she exclaimed all too pleasantly, underlying her virulence. "That humiliation will not hurt so much after all is said and done."

Her eyes sparkled as she gazed into Inanga's one eye.

At least… she telepathically proclaimed, her power extending over the whole of the bridge, overriding all within. *It won't hurt as much as what I have in store for you...*

Enough, Kraft responded, exerting his power to dispel Lorelei's force. The effect was almost immediate, as though Inanga and his fellows were just coming out of a daze. *None of our purposes will be served with this sideshow.*

Scowling, Lorelei nonetheless acquiesced to Kraft's indirect demand. Shedding her greatcoat and passing it dismissively to some random crew-men, she then moved past the still recovering, now glaring, Inanga, and came over to the helm. With her approach, the helmsman rose from his station and, with great hesitance, allowed Lorelei to take his place.

Flint Pirates umbra *Black Sun*
Sognare Sea

Silence persisted as the bridge crew, while remaining at their posts, watched as the captain dissipated his greatcoat, and proceeded to man his new post. For their collective part, no one knew what to think of this development, as none could recall when the elder Flint actually piloted a starship, as opposed to a fighter or shuttle.

Even Alex was unsure of what was happening, a feeling that was as unnerving as it was disconcerting. He was the only being in the universe that held his brother's trust, the only one that truly understood his processes and workings. If anyone was to understand what Jon was intend-ing, it should have been him. The crew certainly believed that, as more than one of them cast Alex a questioning glance while his brother worked, to which the younger Flint simply nodded that it was all according to plan and said and did nothing beyond.

Yet, despite his outward reassurance, Alex was just as bewildered as they were. Jon had not spoken to him once on their course and action toward the Sea. And all attempts to inquire on Alex's part were met with utter silence.

That mere line of thinking made Alex increasingly sick to his stomach. Why hadn't Jon answered him? Why had he felt it necessary to hide this from his brother and loyal first officer?

Alex was no fool; he had known Jon had somehow found a safe passage through the Sea. He had known it the moment they had been ordered to proceed to Sognare, regardless of their losses at Timas IV. Even with so much on the line, Jon would never have given that command without first finding a means. Nor, for that matter, would he have willingly sailed them into oblivion, no matter how desperate the situation was.

So once more, why? Why had he left Alex in the dark with the rest of the crew? And, as much as Alex hesitated to think, if Jon was so reluctant to fill him in on something like this, then…then what else could he be hiding?

———————————————   ———————————————

Ignoring the surrounding gazes, Jon took his seat at the helm. As several had gathered, it would be his first time piloting something bigger than a shuttle. All the same, however, the station was familiar enough to him, being not far removed from the control interface of a fighter or a shuttle. And even if that had not been the case, he would have been able to operate it anyway. Through the same means he had used to learn anything and everything about his ship, right after her liberation from Rochelle.

After looking over the controls, he turned his back to the Sea. Even with the means to move forward, it would still be a difficult voyage through the abyss. The swirling, spectral chaos had claimed so many ships, and it showed no signs of calming at any point. Had Jon believed it to hold sentient will, he would have thought the Sea *hungered* toward the *Sun*'s approach. One more ship to devour, one more line of souls to damn. Shaking his head at the thought, Jon withdrew and tapped his wristcom.

"All hands, this is the Captain," he began. "We are now about to enter the Sognare Sea."

He allowed a moment for that to sink in.

"You have all heard the stories. An infinite sea of nightmares, which no vessel may sail through. A realm of pure madness, in which no safe passage exists," he continued. "I tell you now that last one is untrue."

Incredulousness was the best way to describe the general response. All across the ship, heads turned to glance dubiously at one another, while different crewmen wondered what in the Eighth Circle was their captain thinking. More than a few, however, dared gain hope toward his words.

"Much like the eye of a cyclone or the center of a maelstrom, there exist areas of calm within the Sea," Jon explained. "Select spaces in which the chaos and turmoil do not reach."

He did not need to turn to see the questioning gazes from those behind him.

"These spaces are continually shifting, and are otherwise impossible to detect with either sensors or the naked eye," he went on. "Only a select few may be able to glean their existence, and much more their state of being. But once they are found and isolated, they can be utilized for passage."

The pirate captain gazed down slightly.

"The late Captain Jennis intended to use one of these passages to reach the Black Moon, but ended up losing his course to the Sea's ever-changing nature," he said, remembering what he had seen in Ianessa. "We will not make that mistake."

Jon gazed back at the Sea. This time determined.

"We will sail through and reach the Black Moon. And we will also regain our missing crew member," he stated firmly. "For this is the *Black Sun*, and we are the Flint Pirates."

Again, he did not turn to see the expressions behind him. He could already feel their resolution.

"Nothing may lie beyond our reach," Jon declared with his firm resolve. "Nothing may prevail against our might."

Allowing another moment to pass for those words to resonate, Jon then finished.

"Nonetheless, the path before us remains a treacherous one. Even within the passages, it will still be possible for the Sea to reach us," he said. "Damage control teams will go on standby immediately, and all crew will keep watch for any abnormalities toward the ship or their fellows."

He clarified that last one.

"Remember that the Sea is considered a realm of madness. As such, its influence is over the mental as well as the physical. I cannot explain what effects may be suffered, but if the late Captain Jennis is any indication, it may manipulate the mind at any given time. Thus I reiterate, you are all to keep watch of both the ship and your fellow crew and to take appropriate action where necessary."

That caused more discomforted glancing about, but not nearly as much as before. Jon knew that they were as ready as they would ever be.

"May the wind remain on our backs," he concluded. "Flint out."

Signing off, he waited a little longer for the bridge crew to settle back into their stations. Though several of them, especially Alex, still had questions, Jon knew they would at least wait until it was over before asking. Until then, they would keep to their duties, and continue to trust their fates to their captain.

Taking some solace in that trust, Jon pushed the throttle forward, causing the ship's arc engine to flare. With that momentum, the *Black Sun* entered the Sea.

Piscean *Gnaiih*-class battleship *Grah'n* Sognare Sea

Gently yet skillfully, Lorelei guided the *Grah'n* into the Sognare, the mighty battleship entering into the passageway as gracefully as she would have into water. It was a surprisingly easy entry, with little physical resistance met as the hull exited open space and ventured into the spiraling mayhem. There hadn't even been a shudder, let alone sheer madness overtaking the ship or worse. Those behind her took it as a positive sign, though Lorelei doubted that would last. Anything could still happen after all.

Chaos reigned around the *Grah'n* as she passed, her bridge crew gazing into it via the main monitor and sensors. It was even worse than what they had seen from the outside, with the constant force of energy moving and shifting in unfathomable patterns and spectrums. Violet lightning bursts surged off the port side, arcing around the ship like ribbons for several moments, before flashing and disappearing just as instantly. A stream of pure green ran just off the starboard side, a virtual river in space, which then crystallized and shattered into countless shards, each as brilliant as the most precious of emeralds. Multicolored "stars" flickered in and out of existence, flaring around the ship in dazzling vividness only to die out in the next moment. All while the earlier depicted cyclones, now appearing as large as planets and as destructive as the greatest of storms, continued their dance throughout.

Yet, for all of their ferocity, none of these things reached the *Grah'n* as she sailed onward. Though several of these phenomena came close enough to touch her hull, the Piscean battleship remained unblemished by the maelstrom. As if an invisible wall now existed and encompassed her, keeping the disruptions at bay.

Several of the Pisceans were starting to gain hope as a result, while Kraft looked on with intrigue. What generated these passageways, as Lorelei had explained to them just before entering? Were they natural phenomena, or were they created by the will of the Black Moon?

There was, however, one element of the Sea that managed to permeate the apparent barriers and onto the *Grah'n*, traversing the shields and hull. Each of her crew heard a strange melody chiming throughout the Sea. A mysterious song, made up of what sounded like an infinite chorus, which called out from somewhere ...beyond. A slow, sorrowful refrain that carried through one's auditory systems with graceful harmony. Perfectly accompanying the surrounding chaos, as though performing a ballad.

Lorelei wasn't sure what was generating that music. It was obviously psionic in nature as opposed to acoustic, which meant that it was another one of the Sea's productions. Perhaps it was a result of the sheer psionic resonance, as well as the environmental conditions within the Sea. Or perhaps, as some of the present crew suspected, it was the souls of those who had attempted sailing the Sea before, forever trapped within and forced to sing of their collective despair in unison. Or, it was simply another one of the Moon's more direct manifestations, much like her 'younger self' had been prior.

Regardless, it did nothing to hinder the *Grah'n*, so Lorelei simply abided by it as she maneuvered the ship through the passageways. Like everything else about the Sognare, the passageways were ever-changing in shape and route, such that it took much of Lorelei's concentration to remain within its boundaries.

Yet she persevered, having no interest in turning out like Jennis and those that had gone before. And it wasn't like the others, not even Kraft, were able to comprehend the passageways as she could, as they remained invisible even to direct senses.

If she had been able to think amidst her concentration, Lorelei would have wondered *how* she was able to "see" them. Or, more precisely, "feel" them, as they were beyond her eyes and telepathy. It was more akin to one moving through the dark, using a mixture of instinct and perception to guide one's self when physical sense proved inadequate. Obviously, this was how Jennis guided his fleet so deeply into the Sea, only to lose his way amongst the chaos, likely through a single moment of doubt or question.

Once more, Lorelei did not wish to share his fate, and therefore, did not fixate on the "how". She simply focused on reaching the end, which remained between the turmoil and alteration.

All while that haunting chorus continued to sing from beyond...

Flint Pirates umbra *Black Sun*
Sognare Sea

Lightning flickered about as the *Sun* sailed onward, moving through the passageways with relative ease. It wasn't quite the smoothest of voyages, as she continued to pitch and shift with the energy currents, but at least she avoided the absolute worst of it by remaining in the calm. The crew, who kept watch over their surroundings as their captain stipulated, appreciated that much. Though several of them were already wondering how long it, as well as their apparent fortune and safety, would last.

That same intensity resonated on the bridge, even as the crew members remained at their posts. An eerie silence, the kind in which no one dared speak lest they invite ill fortune, dwelled there, contrasting the ghostly melody that sang out from the Sea. Gran, in particular, had been affected by the latter, almost entering a trance from the song's "beautiful yet terrifying" spell. Only through her comrades' efforts was she able to force it back and maintain her post, though it was quite apparent that exertion consumed vast portions of her energy.

Seemingly as much as Jon was expending on the helm, strenuously keeping the ship within the continuously shifting passageways, while advancing gradually. Nobody envied the captain in his labor, no matter how he was accomplishing the task.

We've really gotten into it, Davis thought as he looked out over the viewscreen, where the Sea went on about its turmoil and discord. Since his usual post was taken, he had settled for Lorelei's science station at the rear of the bridge, on the port side. It was his only choice, as its owner was not present, and Jon would never have allowed him in the captain's chair. And he would rather not be standing with the way the ship was pitching.

On the whole, the Sognare wasn't as bad as he thought it would be. Yes, it wasn't the smoothest ride he had ever been on, and that damned singing could get annoying after a while, but as long as the ship remained within the calm, it wasn't so terrible. Just like flying through a nebula, really. A particularly stormy nebula, in which some unseen, unnerving chorus line sang in the background, but otherwise…

Davis quickly shook his head at the thought. Who was he trying to fool? Just because nothing horrific had happened to him or the ship, yet, didn't mean that he wasn't terrified out of his skull. Even looking away from the viewscreen and focusing on the science display didn't help, It was as though he could feel the chaos outside against his skin, just waiting for the *Black Sun* to slip out of the safe zone, where it could reach out and…

"…engage beam cannons…!"

Davis suddenly looked up as the apparent command was given. Yet, after a moment, he realized it hadn't been Jon's voice that had spoken it. In fact, it sounded rather distant to him.

"…set target to six-four-one, mark two-one-nine…!"

Quickly the helmsman looked about the bridge, attempting to find the source behind those commands. Yet, strangely, he could not identify the origin.

"…Fire on my command…!"

"…Sir…!"

"…Captain, these people are innocent! There's no need to…!"

"…I would appreciate it if you didn't refer to those things as 'people', Commander…"

"…Sir…!"

"…a lesson must be given, and so it shall! Now fire!"

"Mr. Davis?" Davis suddenly heard to his right. Turning, he found Gran looking over to him from her post, her face projecting concern.

Blinking and momentarily wondering what had just happened, Davis shook his head.

"It's nothing," he spoke to the comm. officer reassuringly. "Damn music is just getting to me."

Though the concern did not retract from Gran's face, she nonetheless turned back to her station. Leaving Davis, upon gripping the arms of his chair as the ship pitched yet again, to wonder even further. And to fear.

Piscean *Gnaiih*-class battleship *Grah'n* Sognare Sea

Had he still been "alive", Kraft would have likely yawned in lethargy. As he was very much incapable of doing this, the doctor instead settled for folding his arms as impatience started to emerge from within. He had anticipated it would be a lengthy, as well as "bumpy" trip, but he had hoped it would not go any longer than a few hours. Unfortunately, the Sea's expanse was seemingly as infinite as its depth, such that the *Grah'n* could take days before she reached her objective. Kraft cursed for not considering that beforehand.

If he had known the voyage would be this tedious, he would have brought his book to the bridge alongside Lorelei. A part of him was tempted to retrieve it now, but he ignored the desire. He could not risk turning his attention away from his captive, not even for the briefest of moments. Though she forwardly kept toward the helm, guiding the *Grah'n* through the chaos, he could tell that she was still keeping watch over the ship, looking for another opening to exploit. It would have been beneath her not to, especially in her present environment. Thus, Kraft kept his gaze, both physical and psionic, on her, ensuring her compliance. All while remaining alert for when she did, in fact, make her move.

He wasn't so focused on her, however, that he didn't feel something else waver within the bridge crew. Enough that he cast a corner glance, as though a small gust of wind had swept over his shoulder. Though they were well away from the chaos outside the passage, that didn't mean the Sea couldn't entirely reach them. There was always a possibility, even with he and Lorelei present, that…

A cry of anguish sounded across the bridge, causing Inanga and the others to look up. Clasping his hands against his face, the executive officer let out additional cries, falling from his chair and convulsing as though he were on fire. The *Grah'n*'s captain and several others immediately rushed to his side, muttering to him in Piscean while trying to get him under control. Unfortunately, their efforts were for not, as the officer became more and more violent despite their attempts.

Kraft closed his eyes and sighed in dismay, namely toward the unaffected Pisceans and their futile attempts to calm their fellow crewman. The situation was already volatile enough, and this didn't help their chances any more than Lorelei's earlier stunt. As such, his eyes snapped open once more.

With a very audible crunch, the executive officer's head twisted violently to the right, snapping his neck. That more or less took care of the distraction, as well as the noise, but it also directed all attention back to Kraft. Attention that was less than pleasant.

"Shuggoth mgathg!" Inanga cursed in vehement anger. "Was that...!?"

"Completely necessary," Kraft answered simply. "Even if he could have been saved, this is neither the time nor place for it."

He glared challengingly at Inanga. "Any deviation, no matter how slight, will only doom the entirety of this ship. Not just the one," he stated to the Dagon. "And that includes questioning me or my methods."

Inanga was about to reply, but Kraft suddenly looked up as the operations officer spoke.

"I'm getting reports of additional episodes throughout the ship," the Piscean announced with evident dread. "They're demanding orders."

The captain started to answer, but Kraft spoke up once more.

"Tell them this," he ordered, ignoring the dubious glances around him. "Any crewmen that show signs of affliction are to be struck down immediately."

Shock and rage instantly flooded the bridge; it was readily apparent the officers were poised to attack Kraft.

314

"You do not command us…!" Inanga bellowed in protest.

Impatient with the insolence, Kraft responded by telekinetically grasping Inanga by his throat. The Dagon struggled for breath as he was lifted off the deck, hands clawing at his esophagus.

"Do it," Kraft repeated his command with force, in case the flaying Inanga wasn't enough. "Before the worst occurs."

Harnessing his fury, the operations officer nonetheless complied. Only upon his doing so did Kraft drop the coughing Inanga back onto the deck. Murderous rage remained on the Dagon's face; he contemplated ending their partnership, and Kraft with it, immediately. However, the doctor was indifferent toward this thought, and it showed in his expression. All would be justified once they reached the Moon.

Thus, he faced the front of the bridge, where the still, forwardly at least, compliant siren guided the ship.

Flint Pirates umbra *Black Sun*
Sognare Sea

"Get her out of here!" Braun commanded to the three crewers, who were struggling to contain their latest afflicted comrade. One grasped the crew-woman's legs while the other held the arms and torso. Trying to be careful not to grab anything 'private', they carried her out of the engine room. The cries of anguish continued, only silencing when the turbolift doors closed.

The engineering crew went back to work, but tensions remained high. That had been the third team member that had fallen to the Sea's devilry, and there was little doubt that even more were dropping in torment throughout the ship. Not that anyone spoke of it, of course, purposely focusing on their duties up until the inevitable occurred. Both to keep their minds engaged, not contemplating the rampantly emerging agony, as though their inattentiveness would prevent it from happening, and to keep the equipment functioning in order to reach their destination. Preferably in one piece.

Braun followed the rest of his subordinates, turning back to his monitor.

At least the Sea didn't seem to affect the arc engine. It was performing as well as it did in open space, a few minor adjustments notwithstanding. This strangely assured Braun, as it meant their ship would continue toward the Moon even if her crew didn't. But even then, she had to remain in the passages throughout. He didn't want to think about what would happen if the *Sun* slipped into the open Sea.

He shook his head at the whole thing. How much longer would it last? How many more would fall to the affliction before they finally reached what they sought? And even then, would it all end upon their arrival? Or was there something just as terrible, if not worse, waiting for them at the terminus?

Regardless, he reminded himself, they were here now. They could not afford to leave Lorelei in captivity, nor could they allow the Pisceans to gain the Black Moon's power. And as for the Moon, Braun did not know enough about it to make a firm decision, but something told him that they could not let it be. That, perhaps even more than the crew around him, it was suffering, and they were the only ones that could alleviate that suffering, or at least help Lorelei perform the deed.

Braun focused on his monitor, entering a few more adjustments to the arc reactor, all the while waiting for the next sign of affliction to appear in the other engineers. And himself.

———————————— ————————————

When Anna opened her eyes again, she was not aboard the Black Sun. *Rather, she stood dressed in a white gown, in an all too familiar chapel, in front of two filled rows of seats and next to another man thrice her age. One whose handsome face belied the most unsavory of characters. A priest was speaking at the altar.*

"You may now kiss the bride," the priest finished.

Suddenly, Anna was pulled into her groom, his lips forcing themselves onto hers, while his hand wandered down her backside...

"No!" she cried, shoving the man back. She tried to hit him, but she had no strength. "This isn't right!"

"But it is."

Anna turned to face a formally dressed, white-haired man. A man she had grown to fear as well as hate throughout her life.

"Did you think you could get away from me, Camille?"

Fury radiated through Anna. "Don't call me that you bastard! My name is Anna! Anna Reed!"

"No, it's not. You are Camille; my daughter…and my slave."

"Well, our slave." An elderly woman stepped up beside the man. She shook her head in dismay. "Seriously, Anna, running away? As if we didn't see it coming."

The woman gestured toward the ground in front of the altar, where Jon and Alex's bodies lay, riddled with beam shot wounds. Their blood splattered across the hem of Anna's gown.

"So sloppy and distressing," the woman stated. "Our child wanting to play pirate. Shameful!"

Anna's eyes teared as she shook with rage. "You're shameful! I kept you, the damned family, and your thrice-damned Company from failing for years!"

"So you did the heavy labor," a woman marginally older than Anna sneered. "But really little sister, isn't that your God-given function in this universe?"

Anna tensed as she felt restraint against her arms. Looking down, she saw that she was now chained to the floor by the wrists.

A smile passed over the opposite woman's meaty lips.

"Surely you didn't think I would work?" she said, just as new chains clamped on Anna's ankles. "I am the chosen heir and face of the Company, not the workforce."

One more voice joined the derisive chorus. A woman, smaller in frame, her face highly marred, her appearance unhealthy.

"I can't be expected to work!" she whined, just as Anna felt more chains

wrap around her, pulling her downward. "That's your responsibility."

All talking at once, her family continued to spew both ridicule and demands.

"Shut up!" Anna cried, struggling to pull free as more and more chains snaked across her body. "This is not real; I left you all behind! I escaped!"

Contemptuous laughter filled the chapel as the chains pinned Anna to the floor. Her screams were drowned out by the noise.

——————————— ———————————

Anna's eyes snapped open; a hand grasped her arm. Looking up, she realized she was aboard the *Black Sun*, dressed in her Flint Pirate clothes and at her operations station. And much more, her right arm was now grasped at the wrist by Jon's left hand.

Glancing over, she saw that the captain remained at the helm, focused on guiding the ship, but somehow had taken notice of her plight. He seemed to be the only one, as the rest of the crew remained attentive to their stations, while those looking forward only watched the viewscreen. None of them voiced any form of concern but concentrated on their duties with utmost caution.

Sensing she had returned to reality, Jon withdrew his hand without a word. Whatever had happened to her, whatever the Sea had done to her, Anna realized the captain had acted fast enough to prevent any degradation of her work and to keep anyone else from noticing. Not even Barbarossa, who was sitting at the tactical console on the opposite side of the helm, sensed her distress.

Resuming her duties, she quietly mouthed "thank you". Jon subtly nodded in acceptance.

All while, further back in the bridge, Alex shook violently at the command station, his fingers clawing, fire flickering from their tips…

Chapter XIX: Beyond the Wall of Sleep

Piscean *Gnaiih*-class battleship *Grah'n*
Sognare Sea

Lifting the newly rendered corpse, the two crewmen proceeded toward the nearby turbolift, taking their "cargo" off the bridge. It was a grim task, especially as this was the third to be inflicted and struck down, but the couriers dared not voice their objections. Not to a being, Terran, or otherwise, that could kill with a mere thought at any moment. Thus they brought their former comrade into the lift and disappeared behind the closing doors, speaking not a word.

Watching as they parted with growing ire, which he barely kept concealed from his subordinates, Inanga would have loved nothing more to repay the "favor" by snapping Kraft's neck. Only the knowledge that he would inevitably fail kept him from doing so. Even with the doctor turned away, his attention fixed on the viewscreen and the Sea beyond, Inanga knew the impudent bastard was reading his every thought and intent, waiting precisely for the Dagon to make his move. Then the wretched psion could easily dispatch him, claiming he had succumbed to the Sea and thereby assert complete, finalized control over the *Grah'n* and her crew. Oh, how convenient that would be for the doctor, Inanga mused.

Stifling a growl, the Dagon could only return to his bridge chair, where he would at least appear to retain authority. Not that any of his subordinates would notice by this point. Between the Sea's torment and Kraft's standing order to execute any who displayed even the smallest signs of "corruption", it was all they could do to concentrate on their duties. To think or dwell upon anything else would invoke terror.

How did it come to this? Inanga thought, uncaring if Kraft or that white witch overheard it. It was a rhetorical question, as he knew the answer all too well. It had been him. His ambition had brought him, and the rest of his dag, to this precipice. And, at this point, they were well beyond turning back.

He should have seen it coming, the Dagon supposed. There was many a story, among Pisceans and the other races of the galaxy, in which one's desire for power became his or her folly in the end. A fair number of those tales descended from actual history, such that Inanga recalled several once-prominent leaders who, through one means or another, yearned for too much and went on to lose everything. He had originally thought he had learned from their examples, that he would not repeat their mistakes, but here and now, it was clear that he had learned nothing. That, through a simple arrangement with a force he could not control, he, and those around him, would follow in their footsteps to the very end.

Certainly, they hadn't reached the Moon yet, nor had he made his appeal. But if he couldn't even keep one renegade Terran with abnormal power under control, what chance did he have with the Gods and Devils who dwelled there? If their powers, their very existences, were beyond his comprehension, then why would they deign to parlay with him? Surely he would be little more than a microbe in their sight, a sub-being whose abilities and aspirations were beneath their notice. At best, they would be amused by his attempts to bargain, and at worst…

Inanga shivered at the thought, once again uncaring if the two telepaths picked up on his discomfort. He was well beyond caring about anything now. Anything that didn't pertain to their survival, and perhaps saving what little remained.

Still, he hadn't forgotten why he was there, why he had sought the Moon to begin with. Yes, he yearned for power and authority, but there was more than that. Too long had Rohu been little more than an afterthought amongst the dags, too long had his brethren been considered a minority within their society. Alongside, too long had their so-called brethren squabbled with each other over nonsensical things, such as status and prestige amongst themselves. There was an entire galaxy beyond Pisces, made up of different races and civilizations that were unified in will and purpose. Twelve, in particular, were equal to Pisces' supposed standing, each as hostile to Inanga's culture as they were to each other.

Why did the Pisceans have to be divided? Why couldn't they unify under a central creed, one beyond sharing common enemies? How much further could they go before they gave into their fractures? Or better yet, how much further could they go before one of the other Twelve took notice of their division? It sickened Inanga that he was, seemingly, the only one among the Dagons who realized the truth behind those four questions. Not even the current Dagoth, the one who was supposed to lead *all*, saw the proverbial wall writing, much less retained the intellect and charisma to do something about it.

The Black Moon was to be the answer to all these things. If Inanga could not unite his kinsman by his abilities, then surely he could do so with the Moon's power. And from then on, lead his civilization to the greatness that none had so much as dreamed of. All while their enemies, including the aforementioned Twelve, lay under them destroyed or enslaved.

It was through that rationale that Inanga was once more resolved. For better or worse, he was in the Sea now, and the fate of his entire civilization rested on his shoulders. Even his survival paled in comparison to that of Pisces itself, and Inanga knew all too well what would happen if he turned away now. He dared not consider the ramifications of abandoning this one chance, his one attempt to save his nation from itself. His people, whether within or without his dag, from themselves.

Thus he took a drawn breath and then focused his eye forward. The Sea remained as infinite to him as it had when the *Grah'n* first reached it. Even so, he knew, in some way or another, that they were drawing closer. Closer to their decisive reckoning…

―――――――――――――――――   ―――――――――――――――――

It was the smell that reached him first. The smell of fire mingled with metal and flesh. It was a scent he had picked up many times before, in just as many different settings, yet this one was more familiar. For it was a particular scent, one he had drawn in long ago. One that he would never forget, no matter how badly he wished.

Sight and sound were quick to follow, and Alex despaired at what those two senses detected. The image of a burning starship corridor. A segment that had been beautifully ornate once upon a time was now reduced to a fiery ruin. Alarm klaxons sounded in the background, and lighting flickered, signaling the alert status of the vessel. Fire was in abundance, crackling with an almost insidious quality, while damaged circuitry sparked with the erratic deck lights. In the distant background, the sounds of weapons fire and death cries could be heard, faintly yet discernable enough to instill terror, even in him.

"The Morgan,*" Alex breathed as he surveyed the ruin, despair threatening to consume him. There was no mistaking his late mother's flagship, any more than the reason behind its condition. Only one event, one terrible battle, had caused so much destruction, casting a dark shadow over his life and those of his brother, and many others. "Ephesus."*

"Indeed," an unfriendly voice responded, causing Alex to jerk in alarm. He heard the being's approach, its footsteps echoing throughout the corridor, drowning out the background fighting. The younger Flint could barely depict a silhouette, moving through the deck like a specter, closing in gradually. Through the shadows, Alex glimpsed its cold, bemused smile, as well as felt the sheer malevolence that emanated from its form.

At first, Alex was unable to identify the approaching entity, save only for a foreboding sense of familiarity. Whatever was moving toward him, it was as though even the light was repulsed by its apparition.

Slowly, recognition came. Not unlike ice flowing through his veins, Alex felt his body tremble in abject terror.

"No..." he whispered as he stepped back, Forneus materializing in his hand. "No...!"

Yet the specter continued forward regardless.

"You're dead!" he exclaimed in horror. "She killed you!"

"Did she?" the specter replied.

Alex saw its smile increase with maliciousness. Rage overcoming terror, the younger Flint unleashed a fire wave down the corridor, engulfing the specter, leaving no apparent remnant behind. Yet it was not to be.

"Volatile as ever," the wraith, having reappeared, chimed with sinister amusement. "So much has changed, and yet so little. It's no wonder you're a mere second to your brother."

Alex's ears burned at the casualness of his adversary's tone. "Why are you here!?" he snarled. "Of all the people I could have met in this place, why you!?"

"Simple, I am not through with the Flints," the specter sneered. "How could I remain in Hell while the Golden Queen's bastards live?"

Its chilling laugh filled the air.

"Did you think my vengeance would end with my 'death'? Surely you of all people understand one can live past the grave!"

"But, you didn't!" Alex growled as he launched another fire wave, once more engulfing the specter. "Mom killed you!"

"And I killed her," the apparition laughed once more before disappearing. "Cursing her children to walk this universe in anguish and despair!"

"Bastard! Things are different now!"

"So you would believe," its voice echoed. "Yet we both know the truth, don't we, Alex? You will die in glorious pain and agony. You and all those with you."

"Shut up!" Alex commanded to no avail.

"It hurts," the voice taunted. "To know no matter how far you run, you will never escape your fate."

"I said, shut up!" Alex yelled again, searching for the being.

"Nothing will save you. Not the Black Sun, *not your crew, not the dream of resurrecting the Gold Dragon. Not even the hand of Lord Fuma's daughter."*

Though Alex couldn't see it, he knew another smile flashed.

"Nothing you do, nothing you gain, nothing you hope for will save you from the pain I inflicted upon you here."

Alex turned and found himself facing the specter.

"The Flints," it stated. "Will fall.*"*

Enraged, Alex brought a now enflamed Forneus downward, moving to cleave the apparition in fiery halves…

Flint Pirates umbra *Black Sun*
Sognare Sea

"Alex!" a voice, seemingly distant but growing apparent, called out to him. *"Alex!"*

Alex blinked his eyes, abruptly returning to the present. Once more, he was on the bridge of the *Black Sun*, which remained sailing through the Sognare. Only now, he was standing in the center of it, staring straight into his brother's eye as the latter crossed Astaroth with Forneus. The rest of the bridge personnel were also on their feet, their respective weapons drawn, yet held back by a combination of hesitance and Jon signaling them to stand down. All while the ship continued to sway as it moved further through the Sea.

Blinking again, it took another few moments for Alex to process what had just happened. Upon doing so, however, he stepped back, Forneus dematerializing from his grasp.

"I'm sorry," he stammered, finding himself out of breath and unable to look Jon in the eye. "I…"

"I know," Jon answered as Astaroth disappeared from his hand. He then stepped forward and rested his hand on his brother's shoulder. "It's not your fault."

Hesitantly, Alex looked at his brother, finding no condemnation in his gaze. Instead, Jon simply gave off a calm assurance that no damage had been done. Scanning the rest of the bridge, the younger Flint found the rest of the crew holding similar expressions as they lowered their weapons, retaining visible relief that they had reached him before anything bad could happen.

Overcome by his emotions, Alex reached up and grasped Jon's hand. "I saw him, Jon," he murmured, still feeling breathless. "I saw…"

"I know," Jon repeated with an understanding expression.

Momentarily Alex felt the urge to question his brother but decided not to. Somehow, Jon knew exactly, as he always seemed to.

"He…" he again stammered. "He was so real…"

"But he wasn't. He died long ago," Jon stated with a tinge of disdain. "Our mother saw to that."

This time, Alex didn't need to look up to see the sympathetic glances around them, even from Davis. Though they lacked the elder Flint's understanding, they could easily guess what Alex had just gone through.

"At any rate, we're nearing the end," Jon moved on, withdrawing his hand and nodding to his brother. "Can you hold your post?"

Alex nodded back. "Yes," he confirmed, before looking on curiously. "Wait, if you're talking to me...?"

Smiling, Jon stepped aside to give Alex a clear view of the helm. Much to Alex's surprise, his brother was still there, guiding the ship along. Thus, the one before him was an Astaroth generated clone.

"A good captain must be able to think on his feet," Jon exclaimed as he glanced back at his real self. "As well as multitask."

Alex laughed, shaking his head. "I'm good now. Don't let me hold you up, brother."

Nodding again, "Jon" closed his eye and allowed his form to dissipate back into darkness, allowing the bridge to return to its original state. For better or worse anyway, given the continuing voyage.

Retaking his chair, Alex spared one last glance to his brother. With no further distractions, Jon had concentrated his focus on the Sea, guiding the ship along the currents. Alex wasn't sure if the elder Flint noticed his younger sibling's gaze, though somehow he was sure he felt it.

"Thank you," he whispered, before turning back to his station. As previously stated, they weren't far from the finish now. Alex focused on his tasks, ready and willing to meet the Black Moon head-on when the time came.

Piscean *Gnaiih*-class battleship *Grah'n* Sognare Sea

Lightning sparked and flashed across the main monitor as the *Grah'n* continued onward. By now, she appeared to be traveling through a large, multicolored passage lined with illuminated orbs, energy, and flickering matter. Despite those outbursts, the immediate space was eerily calm, as though the Sea's earlier turbulence was all but forgotten here. Only the song remained in performance. Its choir seemed to have grown even louder and more melodious over the last few minutes, projecting a beautifully ethereal harmony. One that indicated, at least to a certain occupant, that they were drawing close.

Gazing further into the Sea, Lorelei used both her eyes and telepathy to see beyond the ship. Now that they had left the more violent areas of the Sea, she was able to "safely" scan her immediate surroundings, all the while guiding the *Grah'n* further. It seemed that the closer they came to the source, the more stable the Sea became. It also seemed to become "denser", for lack of better description, the energy more composed and less erratic, not unlike actual solid matter in comparison to liquid or vapor. It made the *Grah'n* more difficult to steer, but Lorelei kept her steady well enough. If anything, she appreciated this more than the earlier shifting tides, as well as the fact now she didn't have to worry about ever-changing calm zones.

However, it was what she sensed with her telepathy that gave her the most hope. Through the abundance of physical energy, she could feel *it* out there. A sentient consciousness, vast in scale and depth, such that it felt like a sea within itself. Presently dormant, but far from inactive. Even now, she could feel its slight motions, shifting and fluctuating from within the heart of the Sognare. Motions that grew more and more as the *Grah'n* approached, not unlike the throes of a sleeping giant. A vast and formidable giant.

Kraft appeared to sense it as well, as the opposite psion drew closer to the helm, his own eyes remaining fixed forward. For once, Lorelei barely noticed him. Such was the power that they were both drawn to, that even the doctor's vile presence was but a blemish in comparison. Lorelei also noted that the doctor lacked his usual arrogance, his awe toward what they were advancing upon quite apparent. Awe, and perhaps a semblance of fear?

Soon enough, the passage ended, bringing the *Grah'n* ever deeper into the Sea. Though it remained illuminated, there was a distinct feeling of darkness here, as though the surrounding color and substance had taken more subdued tones. Even more disconcerting, the energy seemed more... *transient* as it shifted, being far more measured and refined in movement when compared to the Sognare's outer boundaries. There were no further lightning bursts either, no disturbance of any kind. Only a realm of serenity, entirely contrasting to the rest of the Sea.

That was where they found it.

At first, it was barely noticeable. Little more than a small span of black that appeared behind parting clouds. As the *Grah'n* drew closer, however, the clouds gradually shifted away, revealing more and more of its mass. Until at last parting entirely, revealing the full form to the bridge crew. And instilling them with utter trepidation.

There, within the very heart of the Sea, was the Black Moon. A strangely apt title, given that it was the size of a traditional moon. Yet, at the same time, an understatement, for the Black Moon was unlike any celestial body that those aboard the *Grah'n* had ever seen before. A perfect black sphere, one that held no flaw or disfigurement of any kind, yet retaining a dark intensity that was as deep as space, seemingly infinite in scope. As though its "surface" was not an actual substance, but of the void itself.

Even Lorelei had been wholly unprepared for what she now gazed upon. Before, she had only seen a minute portion of the Moon, and in a disarming, cordial form no less. Now, she stared out at the whole, both in the physical realm and in that only she and Kraft could comprehend. A power that was unlike anything she could ever have perceived.

And though she could not quite verify it, she was all too sure that as she, and those around her, gazed upon the darkness before them, something within gazed back.

Flint Pirates umbra *Black Sun*
Sognare Sea

"God, help us…" Davis breathed, effectively summarizing the thoughts of the rest of the bridge.

Neither Jon nor Alex could blame his outburst, for they were just as awestruck and as fearful of what they saw. The Black Moon was even more immense than they had imagined. And not merely in size; in its entirety, the Moon was beyond anything they had ever experienced.

The domain of gods and devils, Jon mused to himself. So far, there didn't seem to be anything of that nature along the Moon's surface – if it could be called a "surface" – but the elder Flint wouldn't have been surprised. The Black Moon certainly projected that kind of power, even in its passive state.

"Sensors?"

Barbarossa shook his head. "Nothing, Captain," he answered, sounding as intimidated as the others. "Sensor waves are not even reaching the Moon."

Alex looked up. "Are they being absorbed or repulsed?"

Again Barbarossa shook his head. "Neither. It's as though they aren't even making contact."

"Hm," Jon wondered. Was the Moon actively blocking their sensor scans? Or were the *Black Sun*'s sensors, no matter how advanced, simply not attuned enough to decipher their target? Jon had a feeling it was more the latter, as the Moon didn't appear to be reacting to their presence in any way. That only made him question what they were dealing with that much more.

Suddenly, the sensors beeped in warning.

"Piscean battleship directly ahead," Barbarossa announced.

At that, the viewscreen shifted to display the designated warship, which was some distance away from the Moon.

Alex frowned. He had almost forgotten that they would be there. "Should we cloak?"

Now it was Jon's turn to shake his head. "I don't want to lose our shields," he exclaimed, before adopting a frown of his own. "Besides, they've already seen us."

Piscean *Gnaiih*-class battleship *Grah'n*
Sognare Sea

"That's impossible!" Inanga gaped as the *Black Sun*'s profile was magnified on the viewscreen.

Indeed, even Lorelei and Kraft were taken back by the umbra's presence. How had she gotten there? How had the Flints managed to navigate through the Sea? There was no way they could have without Lorelei to guide them. Not when so many ships and crews had fallen to the Sea's wrath before her.

And yet there she was, before the Moon. Now turning to face the *Grah'n* head-on.

It was then, just as Inanga called for battlestations, causing alarm klaxons to sound and the crew to scramble, that realization dawned on Lorelei. Her chance had come.

Flint Pirates umbra *Black Sun*
Sognare Sea

"Battlestations!" Jon commanded as he retook his proper chair, allowing Davis to resume helm control.

"Weapons online," Barbarossa reported from tactical. "Cannons and phalanx powering up, missile and torpedo tubes loading."

"Vector change on enemy battleship!" Anna announced. "They're turning toward us!"

Jon nodded, having expected as much. "All ahead full, combat speed," he ordered, lowering his command scope. "Bring us into torpedo range."

Piscean *Gnaiih*-class battleship *Grah'n*
Sognare Sea

"They're advancing!" the tactical officer alerted. "Range ten thousand and closing!"

The *Grah'n*'s captain nodded toward the helmsman. "Retake your station," he commanded, then looking toward tactical. "Arm weapons and…!"

He never got to finish. Just as the helmsman moved toward his station, he was suddenly flung across the bridge via telekinetic force, slamming into the bulkhead. From the helm, Lorelei rose, launching a surge of violet lightning into the captain, followed by energy bolts into two more officers, killing them instantly. She then propelled herself at Inanga.

Reacting just as quickly, Kraft interjected himself between the Dagon and the opposing psion, deflecting her intended blade strike. Sneering at the doctor's intervention, Lorelei pressed the attack, slashing at the doctor's head. Kraft narrowly evaded. Amethyst and citrine energy clashed once more.

Flint Pirates umbra *Black Sun*
Sognare Sea

"Firing range now," Barbarossa reported, bracing himself for what was to come.

Through his scope, Jon watched as the Piscean battleship drew closer. "Target their weapon systems," he commanded. "Fire on my…"

The light overtook him, and the rest of the *Black Sun*, before he was able to finish that order.

Piscean *Gnaiih*-class battleship *Grah'n*
Sognare Sea

Moving fast, Inanga managed to wrestle himself away from the raging psions and turn toward the tactical station. As luck would have it, Lorelei had managed to kill the tactical officer before she had made her attempt on him, but the station itself remained active. As such, Inanga pulled the tactical officer's corpse away, flinging it onto the ground before taking his seat.

Amidst the flurry that had overtaken the bridge, the Dagon keyed in the weapon systems, setting up a targeting solution on the approaching umbra. She had more than likely entered her own weapon's range already, but Inanga was not about to give up without a fight. Once she got close enough, he would…

The light encompassed the *Grah'n* as well.

Sognare Sea

So focused were the two warships on each other that their respective crews had effectively turned their attention away from the Moon. As such, they failed to notice that its "surface" began to ripple and fluctuate, not unlike the Sea itself. At first slow and gradual, but picking up speed quickly, until the whole of the Moon seethed with intensity.

Regardless, the effect was instantaneous. Before any of the respective crews realized it, a great force emerged from within the heart of the Moon and rapidly expanded. Engulfing both ships and the Sea within a matter of moments.

Chapter XX: Within the Moonlight

"Welcome," her younger self – no, the Black Moon in projected form – greeted. "I had hoped you would arrive quickly."

Once again, Lorelei found herself within the ethereal city, standing directly in front of her host. It took her a few moments to refocus from the apparent transition, but eventually, she adopted a frown.

"I don't suppose you will tell me what you just did."

The Moon nodded in understanding. "You need not worry about your comrades," it answered. "I simply intervened before any dissension could initiate. Rest assured, they are alive and well, as are your other hosts."

Lorelei's frown remained regardless. "Why?" she questioned, causing the Moon to blink those amethyst eyes. "I thought you were unsettled by the good Doctor Kraft."

The Moon tilted its head, seemingly piqued. "This remains so," it confirmed.

"So why did you intervene?" Lorelei persisted, almost vehemently. "If you hadn't…"

"Because," the Moon interrupted. "As strange as it may sound to you, I despise conflict."

The projection then turned and walked to the side, as if pondering. "I cannot recall exactly, and yet I still know," it continued with increasing hesitance. "That I have seen much chaos and destruction in my time."

Much to her disbelief, Lorelei though she felt vestiges of horror enter the projection.

"Something truly terrible," the Moon trembled. "Something that I *feel*, even as I am now."

Lorelei said nothing, though she felt a similar disturbance. What sort of cataclysm could have been so terrible? Especially to have instilled such apprehension into the one before her?

"For this, and perhaps additional reasons," the Moon went on after taking a moment to recompose itself. "I would rather this advent, and any other that may follow, be resolved without further violence."

Crossing her arms, Lorelei mused toward what she had just heard. A part of her remained hesitant, after all, she had no way of knowing if the Moon would keep this proclamation once it was freed, or even if the chaos and destruction it had witnessed *hadn't* been caused by itself. Yet, something inside her gave her reassurance that what she had heard was real, that this was the Black Moon's true form and being.

Incredulity and disbelief fell upon her as she gazed over the projection. "*This* is the ultimate power?" Lorelei proclaimed after another moment or so. "'The dwelling place of Gods and Devils? The power that may subjugate the galaxy for any who gains its favor?"

Deciphering the irony, the Moon gave a small, bemused smile. "So it would seem," it replied, after another moment of consideration.

Despite her present circumstances, Lorelei burst into laughter. It was almost too much for her to take, and she could only imagine how others would upon learning this. So many interests, political, personal, or otherwise, were riding upon this singular power and what it could inflict upon the galaxy. All of them would be rendered null and void once the truth was made clear. However, that was the least of her concerns now.

"Well then," Lorelei spoke again once she calmed down, remembering why she was there. "Shall we begin?"

The Moon gleamed. "Yes," it answered all too happily. It then gestured down the avenue. "If you would please…"

Nodding, Lorelei followed as the Black Moon led.

———————————

"Okay…" Alex commented as he looked over their newfound surroundings. "I would say we're not on the *Sun* anymore."

Jon easily concurred. Wherever they were now, it was clearly not the bridge of the *Black Sun*. In fact, he wasn't even sure if they were still in their original universe.

What is this…?

Laid out around them in pristine order, the interior of McHale's Island appeared as inviting as it did enigmatic. Outside the lack of patrons, it was arranged precisely how the brothers had seen it not too long ago, before their abrupt departure. Even the liquor shelf behind the bar held the same bottles as that eventful night, as well as the same number of them.

Seeing this, Jon walked behind the bar and picked up one of those bottles, alongside an accompanying glass. As Alex watched him work, the elder Flint then poured a small shot of liquid into the glass, before putting the bottle down and picking the glass up. Then, after a short moment of hesitance, Jon drank the liquid in a single motion, before taking another moment to evaluate his finding.

"It tastes real," he exclaimed before putting the glass down with a dull thud. "Even has the same burn to it."

"But none of this can be real," Alex admonished, taking off his glove and wiping his finger across the countertop, feeling the smoothened polish of the wood. "This has to be a psionic construct of some kind."

"You are correct in your assessment," another voice spoke up, causing the brothers to turn around, Devilblades in hand. This did not disturb the speaker in the least, who casually stepped into sight. "This is indeed but a replication, designed from what I have observed from your memories."

The speaker then gestured over its apparent stature. "Alongside this form," the projection of Ernie stated in an uncharacteristic matter of fact tone.

Even without that explanation, both Flints could tell that the entity in front of them was not their friend on Nassau.

"Are you the Black Moon?" Jon questioned.

The projection seemed to consider. "That seems to be what you know me best as, yes. Though I rather doubt that to be my true name."

The Moon gestured with its hands. "You may lower your weapons," it spoke with calm reassurance. "I am no threat to you."

Though retaining their caution, the brothers dissipated their Devilblades. They were unlikely to do actual harm to the entity before them anyway.

"Interesting form you chose," Alex commented, observing the image of Ernst McHale. "Was there any particular reason behind it?"

The projection shrugged, much like its form's basis would have. "It was my intention for you to feel at ease," it explained. "For this, I required a form that you were both familiar with and held no hostility toward."

It then tilted its head. "I did find another potential basis in your memories, but after some careful consideration, I felt it best to go with something less provoking toward you. Or perhaps you would have preferred it?"

"No, this one is suitable," Jon answered. Both he and Alex knew exactly what 'form' the Moon was referring to. "And we appreciate you considering our feelings."

The projection nodded as it took a nearby seat. "As I said, I am no threat to you," it continued. "Once she has accomplished the task I need of her, she will be returned to your care, and you may resume your voyage thereafter."

Jon and Alex took seats, just across from the projection.

"By her, you mean Lorelei?" Alex asked.

"Yes," the Moon confirmed. "In the present time, I felt we could have a 'chat', as you Terrans refer to such exchanges."

Its eyes narrowed upon the brothers. "Your galaxy has progressed much since my internment, and though I have kept watch of its development since my reawakening, this will be the first time I have interacted with any of its present inhabitants."

Alex let out a small laugh. "This is a first for us as well," he answered, now deeply interested. "It's the first time my brother and I have ever had a 'chat' with an actual, true to the stars god."

"Or the all-powerful domain of Gods and Devils," Jon added.

The Black Moon smiled sadly. "I'm afraid you are both mistaken. For I am neither."

"Really?" Davis exclaimed with apparent disbelief. "With all the power you possess, not to mention all that you've done to this point, you could have easily fooled me."

"Is that so?" the Moon's projection inquired with an arched eyebrow. "I appear so powerful to you that you would believe me omnipotent?"

Davis practically choked back the irony. If all the chaos and destruction the Moon had caused hadn't been evidence of its power, then the present scene he was in certainly did. A replication of Old Billy Riley's back on Nassau, before its untimely destruction, with Davis sitting at the exact table he had previously occupied. The projection of the redhead, whose name he could not recall at the moment, was placed directly across from him, with two filled tankards between them. If the other patrons had been there, it would have been a complete replication, but it was instead deserted of all except Davis and his "date".

Either way, Davis could think of no other being capable of such imagery.

"Perhaps not omnipotent," Davis answered evenly. "But more than powerful enough, especially to us mere mortals."

The projection chuckled, much in the way its base would have. Davis couldn't tell if that was the Moon's actual response, or if it was simply mimicking the original. Nor did he know if it was laughing at his sarcasm, or what he had exclaimed.

"Powerful I am, seemingly," the Moon admitted. "But neither divine nor eternal."

It shook its form's head. "Your depiction of God is many things, a parent, an artisan, a lawgiver, a guide. He used His power to create all of existence, and then he spent even more power in guiding that existence, causing all within to grow and develop toward the fulfillment of his unseen plan."

Now it was Davis' turn to arch an eyebrow, but he otherwise said nothing.

"Though I have yet to remember all that I was, I know I am none of those things," the Moon went on. "As powerful as you believe me to be, I am not capable of creating such a vast universe. And even if I were, I do not possess the capability to guide it so intricately, nor am I so proactive and forward-thinking as to have plans for it that span eternity."

The projection shook its head once more. "No, I am no god," it proclaimed, apparently once and for all. "And I'm certainly not a domain for such powerful beings."

Davis dared take a sip from his flask. "Many would claim differently," he said, appreciative that the projected grog tasted the same as the genuine article. "Starting with the Pisceans that sought you out in the first place."

"Yes," the image of Yusuf exclaimed sadly. "It is a strange pity, to expend so much energy and resources in seeking me out, only to find them all utterly wasted."

"I don't know about that," Barbarossa retorted. "Inanga and his miscreants desire power, not divinity. And god or not, you retain great power."

"Perhaps," the Moon acknowledged, considering. "And what they wish of that power is simple enough."

Barbarossa took an uneasy drink from his tankard. "Does that mean you're going to give them what they want?"

"Of course not," the Moon replied as if it were obvious. "As I said before, I despise conflict. And they would use my power to cause conflict across the galaxy."

Barbarossa didn't know how he stayed composed over that statement. He didn't want to imagine what would happen if the Moon had answered differently.

"So, what will you do?"

The image of Yusuf shrugged. "I cannot answer that until your Siren completes her task."

"Ah, yes. Forgive me," Barbarossa exclaimed, having nearly forgotten. "In the meantime, I am rather curious."

"Yes?" the Moon asked, seemingly interested.

Barbarossa thought about his words for a moment. "You claim yourself to be neither divine nor eternal," he started. "Nor are you, by your own words, a parent, an artisan, a lawgiver, or a guide."

The image of Yusuf gazed back curiously as Barbarossa went on.

"And yet, on the other side of the spectrum, you are not evil or maligned," he posited. "Past events notwithstanding, you look down upon violence and destruction. And you don't seem any more interested in temptation or corruption."

"Indeed," the Moon confirmed, seeing where Barbarossa was going. "I am neither god nor devil."

"Which brings me to the object of my curiosity," Barbarossa said, looking the projection square in its apparent eyes. "What do you see yourself as?"

——————————— ———————————

The image of the Pavon merchant blinked, apparently having been taken off guard. "That is a peculiar question."

I'm sure the answer will be too. Anna thought, almost pursing her lips in anticipation. Despite herself, she was actually intrigued.

After another moment, the Moon flashed a sad smile. "I'm sorry," it said. "I haven't *been* for so long; it's rather difficult to fathom…"

"Take your time," Anna spoke softly. "We seem to have plenty of that, after all."

"Yes," the Moon concurred, then took another few moments to come up with a proper answer. "At the risk of sounding needlessly arrogant, I see myself as something beyond such conventional labels."

The image leaned forward a little. "Not to say I am above what they represent," it clarified. "But rather that I am something that cannot be classified within your realm of understanding. Something *different* from all that you know."

"Interesting," Anna exclaimed, tilting her head in thought. "Do you think you came from somewhere else?" she posited. "Somewhere beyond this galaxy?"

"That is a possibility," the Moon concurred. "I do appear to be very different from its present inhabitants. Yet, all the same, I cannot be sure of where I could have come from."

"That's alright," Anna replied sympathetically. "I'm sure it will come back to you when Lorelei is finished with whatever you're having her do."

"I hope so," the projected image answered, shaking its head in apparent frustration. "It is truly disconcerting. To exist, but not to know nor understand your own identity."

"I wouldn't be sure of that," Anna replied, momentarily recalling what she had beheld in the Sea. "Sometimes, it's tempting to forget."

The avatar looked on curiously. "Why?"

─────────────────────── ───────────────────────

"Because the memories can be painful," Braun replied to his audience. "To the point, you wish they were never there, to begin with."

Once more, the scientist was in Old Billy Riley's, standing in front of the vidscreen where he gave his "lecture". Only this time, he had only one 'pupil' in his 'class'.

"You speak from experience," the projected image – that of a beautiful young woman in a floral top and mechanic overalls – observed.

Braun nodded. "Yes," he answered in apparent solemnity. "Ultimately, however, I know I would be doing myself a disservice by forgetting."

In an apparent example, he raised his right arm. "No matter how hard the memories are, the truth of the matter is one's background is, by definition, where one came from," he explained, flexing his metal fingers. "It is one of the key components to what we are, for better or worse."

"Indeed," the Moon concurred.

Point made, Braun attempted to lower his arm, but even in the present setting, it refused to cooperate. Thus he was forced to beat it back into place, as he normally did.

"In that regard, I confess I am rather captivated," the scientist proclaimed as he forced down his rebellious limb. "Where could such a fascinating creature like you have come from? And how could you have ended up in such a mundane setting?"

"I wouldn't say your galaxy is mundane," the Moon replied. "Quite the contrary, I find its present inhabitants to be utterly fascinating."

"Oh?" Braun responded.

The Moon took that as an exclamation of interest. "Terran, Piscean, Leo, Geminian, Taurean… No matter your biology or origin, you each have progressed through countless eons to reach this point, where the stars are within your reach."

The avatar turned its gaze to Braun directly. "Throughout that span, you have triumphed and errored, risen and fallen. Yet through each, you learned and grew, developing gradually yet continuously. It has never been easy for any of you, and several of your brethren have perished along the way. Yet through your pain and struggle, you have each emerged into something extraordinary to behold."

The Moon smiled as the meaning of its words sunk in. "Each, according to your gifts, has entered the realm of possibility," it said. "In which only your respective gods may limit you."

For the first time since he could remember, Braun was taken back. He had known the Black Moon was an ancient entity that it had existed in this universe for as long as anyone could remember. Yet it was only through those words that Braun truly fathomed how primordial, how venerable, it truly was. As though it had observed the galaxy, and the universe around it, since its very beginning.

Could that mean...? Braun began to think before the Moon interrupted him again.

"But now," the Moon spoke up. "It is time that I look away from that which is around me, and simply concentrate on *me*."

It then gave off a flat a smile. "No matter how tempting it may be to forget once more."

———————————————

After several minutes of walking seemingly without aim, the Moon at last presented Lorelei with their destination. There, in the short distance, was a peculiar looking tower that extended well into the darkened sky. At first, it looked little different from the other buildings that made up the starlit city, but for some reason, as Lorelei gazed toward it, she felt something was out of place. A kind of ominousness, as though the building contained something of extraordinary power and presence. As though it were reacting to her approach.

The Moon's projected image took clear notice. "So, you sense it," it exclaimed, gazing up at the tower as well. "That which rests within."

For a time, Lorelei attempted to concentrate her power through the building, but each time she did, she felt as though she were rebuffed. Not through any conscious effort, but rather for the simple fact that whatever lay within was incomprehensible, even to one such as her.

"Do you know what's in there?"

The Moon shook its avatar's head. "Only something that has been dormant for countless ages," it replied. "Not unlike what you found on Ephesus and Smyrna."

Indeed, Lorelei found the comparison to be quite apt. And yet, not so much. To her perception, the Babels had "simply" been machines that had not been utilized in time uncounted. This presence, whatever it was, was a living breathing entity by comparison. Which, in turn, caused Lorelei to remember an Ancient Terran quote, regarding the waking of a sleeping giant.

Again the Moon seemed to notice. "Does this trouble you?" it inquired.

The psion considered for a moment. It was still not too late for her to refuse. And much more, despite their earlier exchange, she still had no idea what kind of force she would be awakening. Yes, it was passive, but at the same time capable of much destruction as both Nassau and Timas IV indicated. Awakening what slept within that edifice may, in fact, not be the best course of action for her or the rest of the galaxy.

In the end, however, she forced those temptations away. Despite all that had occurred to this point, she had come all this way. And much more, she had assured her host that she would follow through.

Thus, taking a moment to resolve herself to whatever would occur, Lorelei answered. "No."

The Moon once again tilted its head, this time in acknowledgment. "Very well, then."

No further words were exchanged as both entered the skyscraper.

Chapter XXI: Ex Oblivion

Eyes flickering open, Kraft found himself staring upward, toward an unfamiliar ceiling. He was no longer aboard the *Grah'n*, as the ceiling, the *wooden* ceiling indicated. His vision clearing and focusing, the doctor could barely fathom where he was, while it took him several moments to remember the previous events. It was as though, having slept for some time, he had only now awakened.

That was when a chord of familiarity struck within Kraft, in turn leading toward dawning, if imprecise, recognition. Rising, he saw he had indeed been resting upon a bed. This, alongside the archaic architecture and furnishings of his apparent bedroom, was of little importance to him. Rather, it was the light that shone through the nearby window panes that drew his attention. A golden light that was strangely entrancing.

Upon opening the window, he saw it. The Sunset City, in its sprawling, magnificent glory. The veined marble walls, temples, colonnades and bridges, the silver-basined fountains and perfumed gardens, the wide streets set between delicate trees, the blossom-laden urns, and gleaming ivory statues. It was exactly as it had been described in his book, yet far more beautiful than he had ever imagined. And just like Randolph Carter before him, Kraft could only stand in awed breathlessness, wholly captivated.

For some time, Kraft was satisfied to simply remain there and gaze over the great metropolis, once more as Carter had done in both the beginning and the end. For a similar amount of time, he wondered if he was, in fact, Carter, having just traveled to the end of all that was, only to find that his prize had always been before him, set right outside his housing in the Ancient Terran city of Boston, awaiting his return.

Ultimately, however, he remembered who he was, and more importantly, why he was there. He was not Randolph Carter, nor had he ever sought an *actual* Sunset City. Rather, he was Doctor Laurentius Kraft, and the object of his quest was nothing so simple or apparent. And the god he wished to bargain with was far more indecipherable, as well as difficult to reach, than the whimsical inhabitants of Kadath.

"Welcome," a voice, a distantly familiar one, spoke out. "I trust this is a preferable setting?"

Abruptly Kraft turned to his side, just as the origin of the voice moved out from the shadows. And for the first time in quite a while, the doctor felt astonishment as he looked upon the one before him.

"Are you...?"

"Indeed," the Black Moon, appearing in the original, living form of Kraft, confirmed as it moved into the glistening light, dark brown eyes meeting the other's yellow. "I am that you have sought."

Kraft could barely hold himself in. At last, he had come face to face with the great and powerful Moon. Despite the doctor's best efforts, his expression betrayed his emotions to his host.

"I am quite intrigued," the Moon continued as it came to stand in front of Kraft, effectively contrasting original to present form. "For one such as yourself to have endured for so long and at such cost..."

"I have," Kraft exclaimed, feeling almost breathless. "It was a difficult journey, and much had been sacrificed throughout. But that no longer matters."

Tears began to stream, the first that Kraft had felt against his face in a long, long time.

"I have finally reached you."

His original form nodded. "Yes," it concurred impassively, once again, in contrast with the actual Kraft's emotional display. "You have."

———————————————

Bemusement welled within Lorelei as she and the Moon's projected form crossed the skyscraper's threshold. It was an all too familiar scene to her. The widened amphitheater-like space, walls, and steps in faded gray with stained glass-like iconography lining the former, all leading toward a great maw at the center. Indeed, it was exactly like what she had found on Ephesus and Smyrna.

"I thought you would appreciate the familiarity," the Moon commented as it stepped down toward the maw. "I trust this to be a correct assumption?"

Lorelei nodded. "Yes," she concurred. "This will make it so much easier."

Now understanding, Lorelei reached her hand out, causing the designated tile to lift off the steps, levitating before her. Upon inspecting the tile, she found it missing the slots meant for Aurea and Argentum, as well as the Predecessors inscriptions. Only the control orb remained.

"There is no need for activation keys here," the Moon clarified. "Nor any form of inscription."

"So I see," Lorelei replied. "Will the process be the same?"

"I cannot say," the Moon answered, shaking the head of its projection. "I know not what will happen beyond this point. Any more than what lies within that abyss."

Lorelei frowned as she gazed into the maw. Indeed she found it quite doubtful that it contained a Babel. She suspected that whatever slept within that darkness was something beyond even her comprehension…for better or worse.

Still, she understood. Even for a supremely powerful being, her host could only do and know so much, especially while remaining in its captive dormancy.

"Well then," Lorelei sighed as she stepped before the console. "Let us see."

Nodding, the Moon moved back and watched as Lorelei placed her hand upon the orb. Energy began to surge and pulsate around them, flowing directly into the open maw.

——————————— ———————————

"I'm sorry," Kraft continued, wiping the tears from his face, trying to look a bit more dignified. "It's just... to finally come before one such as you... to finally gain that which I seek..."

"I understand," the Moon replied softly. "It is a natural reaction. For you have wandered and struggled much throughout this existence. All so you could reach this place."

"Yes," Kraft nodded, finally regaining himself. "For centuries, I have wandered and struggled against the universe and my mortality. All for the sake of obtaining my Sunset City..."

He then laughed at his choice of words. "My apologies," he said, glancing out the window. "Though it is a brilliant and spectacular projection, I did not mean *this* city..."

"I am aware of this," the Moon answered sagely, looking out over the "city" itself. "This is merely an appropriate addition to our present environment. A reflection of your idealized setting, as described in the book you prize so much."

"Yes, right," Kraft responded, glad that the deity understood.

"What you seek is something not so simple," the Moon observed. "Nor so apparent as this twilit realm."

Kraft gleamed that much more. "You know what I desire?"

"I do, yes," the Moon confirmed. "It is but one facet, though a critical facet, of the existence that was Laurentius Kraft."

For a brief moment, Kraft thought he sensed something dark within the projection's tone of voice. Something that was an anathema, it caused him to blink in uncertainty. He pushed the thought aside, however, simply deciding that he was misinterpreting the deity's words.

"Critical indeed," Kraft concurred. "Enough that I have transcended Death to obtain it."

The Moon tilted its head. "Have you?"

Again Kraft felt something amiss, and again he forced it back. "I have, though it was not easy. Nor can I *remain* so for much longer…"

"So it is estimated," the Moon observed, gazing over Kraft's body. Seeing passed its apparent form and to the degradation within.

"I must…" Kraft stammered, once more unable to hold back his emotions. "I must gain what I have sought for so long. Before I relinquish myself."

Thus, taking a breath, Kraft turned to the projection. "You can grant this, right? With such power, it should be easy for you, yes? Just as it was to reach out to the Siren? Or to create this great city before us?"

The Moon said nothing, instead only watching as Kraft looked upon it pleadingly.

"Please," the doctor begged. "I promise you anything in my power for this, anything that you would ask of me."

Tears again began to stream. "Please grant me that which I seek! My *true* Sunset City!"

For a time, silence reigned throughout the setting, as though all had become frozen. His plea given, Kraft could only gaze longingly and earnestly at his original self, waiting and willing for an answer to be provided.

And then, the answer came. Though it was not at all what Kraft had expected, nor wished.

"I cannot do this," the Moon replied.

Kraft suddenly felt as though all warmth in the universe had just drained away. "What?"

"It is as I said," the Moon spoke, closing its eyes in apparent resignation. "I cannot grant you that which you seek."

The doctor could not believe what he had just heard. No matter how much he wished, he could not interpret it otherwise.

"But..." he stammered again, this time with incredulousness. "You are the Black Moon... The domain of Gods and Devils..."

"That is what I am called, yes," the Moon confirmed. "Yet it is a mistaken assumption, for I am no god. Nor am I haven for such beings."

The Moon dared to draw closer to Kraft. "And even if I were, I would be unable to fulfill your wish. Not only because it is beyond my capability, but also because it has long since passed."

"But..." Kraft faltered, feeling his body weaken from a newfound strain. "For so long, I..."

"Yes," the Moon continued sympathetically. "For so long, you have wandered this plane, searching for that which Laurentius Kraft could not in life."

Kraft looked up again, this time in abject uncertainty. "What...?"

"It is as I said," the Moon went on. "Laurentius Kraft died two hundred years ago, his being long since transcending this reality."

The entity looked upon the specter, once more impassively. "You are but a fragment, a remnant that did not follow with the whole. The culmination of yearnings and desires left unfulfilled, cursed to wander, to seek out what he could not before passing on."

"No..." Kraft breathed, at last collapsing onto his knees in sobs. "It's not true...!"

"I'm afraid it is," the Moon answered as it knelt in front of him, reaching out its projected hand onto Kraft's shoulder. "You are but a shell of the true Laurentius Kraft. A 'nothing' left to walk in a realm that is of neither light nor darkness."

Kraft continued to sob as the Moon squeezed its hand comfortingly.

"Even the emotions you believe yourself to feel are but falsehoods," it said solemnly. "For you simply remember what Laurentius Kraft would 'feel', and act accordingly."

"Even…" Kraft stammered once more, this time in disbelief. "Even these tears…"

"A physical byproduct, created and affected by your memories of feeling," the Moon explained with finality. "Nothing more."

Hearing that, Kraft stopped his crying, instead choosing to remain motionless. The Moon took this as a form of acceptance.

"There is but one wish I can grant you," it countered, now speaking cautiously. "I can have you pass on from this existence."

No response was given, so the Moon continued. "To move beyond all that you have suffered," it offered. "So that you may rejoin your whole."

Again no response. The projection blinked, unsure of what to make of its ward.

"What say you?" it inquired. "To this promise of reunion?"

Only then did Kraft respond. "I say…" the specter suddenly hissed.

Before the Moon could react, Kraft reached out and grabbed the projection's neck with both hands.

"You are a liar!" Kraft thundered, strangling the projection. "It's not that you *can't* grant me my city, it's that you *won't*!"

The Moon struggled but could not break the hold, for Kraft concentrated the entirety of his power into his grip.

"So be it!" Kraft roared with apparent fury, his body rippling with psionic energy, causing both the room and the city outside to dim and crack with thunder. "If you won't grant me what I seek, then I will *force* it out of you!"

Again the Moon attempted to repulse the aggressor, but Kraft forced it back. With much of its power restrained, the Moon couldn't even hinder the opposing psion, resulting in both its projection and everything around to break.

Abruptly the sunset faded into darkness, while the room and the formerly magnificent buildings and edifices shattered and fragmented. Energy crackled and swept across the domain, increasing the destruction, while project debris churned within an invisible whirlwind. All while Kraft continued his strangulation within the epicenter.

"GIVE ME WHAT I DESIRE!" Kraft bellowed, generating further chaos across the scape as the Moon, still in the form of the true Laurentius Kraft, struggled in the psion's hold.

———————————— ————————————

Lorelei's hand flew back from the console, as though it had been repulsed with an unseen force. Before she could question it, she felt the ground shake and saw cracks appear in the walls and stairs.

"What's going on?" she turned to question her projected younger self, which, much to Lorelei's horror, was grasping its head in apparent pain. "What's happening!?"

Only one answer came. An enormous powerful scream, which seemingly echoed through the cosmos…

Chapter XXII: Ira Furor Brevis Est

Flint Pirates umbra *Black Sun*
Sognare Sea

"What in the fifth circle just happened?" Davis exclaimed as he suddenly found himself back on the *Black Sun*'s bridge, with a potentially major headache starting to set in.

The rest of the bridge crew, having returned to their stations, felt much the same. It took several moments for them to focus, and that much more to realize they were, in fact, back on the ship. Not that they were sure they had actually left it in the first place.

Jon and Alex, however, were more concerned with what occurred *before* they had seemingly reverted. Without any warning whatsoever, the projection of Ernie had doubled over in pain, grasping at "his" head as though it were about to explode. Right before eliciting that very unnatural, very intense scream.

Knowing what his brother was about to ask, Alex already began scanning the Moon. Nearly cringing as he looked over the readout.

"Picking up massive fluctuations from the Moon," he reported. "Like nothing I've ever seen before."

Instead of questioning his brother further, Jon lowered the command scope. Indeed, it was exactly as Alex had said. Not unlike a star or planet in its death throes, the Moon rippled and surged, energy crackling across its apparent surface. Though retaining its spherical shape and dark color, its form was in constant oscillation, shifting in shape and structure with violent compulsion. All while the Sea around it churned, seemingly in reverberation.

"My god…!" Anna gaped as she, along with the rest of the bridge, watched the action on the viewscreen.

A resultant lightning burst struck against the ship's shields, causing the *Sun* to pitch. Davis just barely managed to keep her steady.

"Forgive my bluntness, Captain," the helmsman hollered through the shuddering. "But, I recommend turning tail immediately!"

"For once, Jon, I agree with Davis," Alex followed up, still looking over his readout. "The Moon's getting more unstable by the second, and the Sea with it!"

Jon cursed. He didn't want to leave, not until they had Lorelei back. After all, that was why they were there. But at the same time, his first obligation was to the health and safety of his crew. Both of which would be rendered mute if the *Black Sun* remained in the Sea for much longer.

Besides, it wasn't as though Lorelei were within reach anyway. Though Jon had no way to verify it, something told him that she was no longer aboard the Piscean battleship. Thus, with more reluctance than he should have felt, or so he believed, Jon began to give the order.

"Helm, come abo…"

Alex's sensors beeped again. "Now picking up energy readings from the Piscean ship! It's…" he began to say.

Just as Hell unfolded before them.

Piscean *Gnaiih*-class battleship *Grah'n*
Sognare Sea

Inanga groaned as he rose from the tactical station, nearly stumbling as he moved back to his actual chair. His head was throbbing, and his body felt further strained. He could only wonder what that sudden scream had done to him, let alone its source.

We should never have come here, Inanga thought disparagingly through the excruciating throbbing. Indeed, it had all been for naught. For all of his plights and desperation, the Black Moon had openly refused all of his requests, claiming it could not help Inanga with what he wished. Even worse, it had gone as far as to insult him, belittling him as a power-hungry madman that did not care for anything. That even his devotion to his people and wish to unify his race were superficial at best, mere excuses that concealed his desire to stand above all others. Or so it had claimed.

Overall, Inanga had finally had enough. As much as that impudence bothered him, the fact remained the Moon would not aid him in his endeavors. Nor could he force it to, its power quite evident.

"Helmsman, take us about," he commanded just as the rest of the bridge crew focused back on their stations. "I want out of this *epshuggog* at the earliest…"

I'm afraid I cannot allow that, a certain, ever detestable Terran voice called out in Inanga's head.

Suddenly realizing that the good Doctor Kraft and that other psion witch were not physically present, the Dagon glowered that much more.

"Kraft," he hissed. "I don't know where you are now, nor do I care."

Through the outside chaos, the Piscean leader glared at the violently fluctuating Moon, briefly wondering what was causing it such turmoil. Ultimately, however, he failed to care about this either.

"You can keep that wretched thing for yourself," he continued. "Neither I nor my dag will have any further part…"

Oh, but you will, Kraft stated, something in his "voice" causing a great chill to run down Inanga's spine. *I'm not about to let her friends remain. Not after all the trouble they have caused me.*

The image of a dark smile then entered Inanga's mind. *And just to make things a little more* interesting…

A sudden wave of nausea hit Inanga before he could say another word, causing his breathing to heighten and his body to convulse. The same was true with the rest of the *Grah'n*'s crew throughout the ship, the Pisceans all feeling as though something was occurring within them. Something dark and horrific.

Doubling over as though he were about to retch, Inanga attempted to force his body back under control, only to find himself completely powerless. Whatever was happening, whatever was being done to him, it was beyond his ability to cope. To the point that, much like the Moon before him, the Piscean leader and his subordinates began to throb and fluctuate in form. Each eliciting choked, gurgling screams as they writhed and thrashed, now in immense, overwhelming anguish.

And then, all at once, it culminated. Letting out a final, desperate cry, Inanga's body exploded into a bloated organic mass, almost immediately followed by the rest of the crew, all shifting and expanded with terrible alteration, while the ship around them warped and distorted, ferociously changing from metal to organism itself. All merging as one apparent flesh.

Flint Pirates umbra *Black Sun*
Sognare Sea

"By the hand of Dajjal…!" Barbarossa breathed as he witnessed the horror erupt before them, unable to keep the fearful astonishment off of his face. An expression that was matched by all others that watched, up to and including his captain behind him.

Before all of them, the enemy battleship expanded and bulged, writhing, and festering as only organic matter could. Under violent distortion, the entire craft morphed from a Piscean warship into something else, something that could only be described as *other*. A spherical, bloated aggregation covered in orb-shaped blisters, continuously swelling until it took on the size of a smaller moon. Multicolored eyes and contorted mouths rippled across its surface, yawing open with tortured ferocity, while a multitude of tendrils sprouted and variously lengthened, thrashing and flailing against the surrounding space.

A true nightmare given form.

Eyes focusing upon the *Sun*, the mouths let out a great collective shriek that surged through space. Powerful enough to move through the umbra's hull, all but one of her crew reached and covered their auditory organs or otherwise braced. An unnatural shrill that one felt within as well as without.

Remaining firm against the outcry, Jon watched as the abomination began advancing upon them, tendrils thrashing even more violently as it approached. Already he could tell there was no running from this one. The horror had been designed to hunt them specifically, and that singular purpose would drive it until it was fulfilled. No matter where or how the Flints chose to hide.

"Hard to port!"

Davis didn't know how he heard the command through the shrieking, but he fulfilled it all the same. Moments later, a collection of yellow energy materialized around the monstrosity and launched as beam fire, blasting through space where the *Black Sun* had been moments ago. At least one of them came quite close to striking, causing the umbra to shutter from the near-miss.

Jon glowered at this, and what it indicated. Though the creature was driven by a singular purpose, it lacked actual intelligence or conscious will. Which meant it would be nigh impossible to predict in action.

"Alex!?"

"It's a biological construct, generated by the Moon's psionic emissions,"

Alex reported as he examined his readout. "Skin, muscles, organs, nervous system… I'm picking up all sorts of data, but no obvious weak points!"

Jon stifled back a curse. He should have known it wouldn't be that easy. "We'll go with the old fashioned approach then. Helm, combat speed! Main cannons and missiles, fire!"

Also aware that there was no retreating now, Davis brought the *Sun* about, allowing Barbarossa to fire all four cannons and the starboard side missile launchers in a great broadside. Somewhat surprisingly, the beams and projectiles hit the monster, striking with enough force to burn its apparent skin and draw gobs of yellowish blood from underneath. For a time, it appeared damage had been done to the horror.

The feelings of triumph terminated abruptly as the creature let out another bellow. The burns on its skin diminished while the cuts and tears sealed themselves. All at an accelerated rate, such that the creature was healed within seconds.

"Of course," Alex deadpanned. It figured the thing had regeneration powers that matched the *Sun*'s Moebius System. As if killing it would have been easy.

Reacting in apparent anger, the monster launched another barrage of energy. This time one of the beams struck the *Black Sun*'s forward shield, causing the ship to quake violently upon impact. Responding just as fast, Barbarossa returned fire with the bow cannons. Again the eldritch was struck, and again its wounds healed, even as the cannons pounded against it in rapid succession.

Until we find a weakness, our only choice is to wear it down, Jon thought as he surveyed his "adversary", which withed and convulsed against the *Sun*'s cannon fire. It then counterattacked with additional beams, nearly throwing the attacking ship off its vector. *Strain its regeneration to the breaking point…*

"Di…iii…iieiiiieeiii…!" the abomination garbled in a ghastly, abhorrent cry, the mere tone of its "voice" causing the pirates to shiver.

"Diiiiiiieeeee...!"

Another beam struck the *Sun,* throwing her about. Through the shuddering, Jon and Alex glared at the mutation, as did Barbarossa. Horrific it may have been, but it still bled. That was more than enough indication that it could be killed.

"All weapons fire at will!" Jon commanded just as Davis maneuvered the *Black Sun* around, bringing its torpedo tubes to bear. All six of the projectiles launched and were promptly followed by the bow cannons, blasting into the horror with even greater force.

———————————

Greatcoat swaying as she stepped forward, Lorelei surveyed the new setting around her. Compared to the splendor of her previous environment, this one was far more desolate. Ruined buildings and fragments littered the dreamscape, both across the ground and floating aimlessly in the sky above. The air, if it was that, felt stale and degraded, not unlike that of a tomb or a mausoleum. While a wavering, ethereal green light permeated the area, emphasizing the apparent lifelessness of the ruin.

Standing with his back turned to her, Kraft patiently waited as she approached. With his arms folded behind him, the Doctor appeared as though he were looking toward something else in the distance, beyond the decrepitness. However, as the opposing psion came up to him, Kraft looked down, his anticipating smile reforming across his lips.

I was hoping you would come here, he telepathically exclaimed to his 'guest'. *You, who the Moon has deemed worthy.*

Lorelei didn't fail to note the derision in that exclamation. *I'm only going to say it once,* she warned. *Let her go now.*

Kraft sniffed at the ultimatum. *And if I refuse?* he posited as he, at last, turned to face his opponent. *If I decline to cease my efforts to merge with the Moon and take its power for my own?*

The White Siren glared. *I believe you already know what will take place.*

The scientist looked on wearily. *It is quite a shame, you know. In spite of your disdain, I thought you of all people would understand why...*

I do, Lorelei interrupted. *I know precisely what drives you. That force of will that presses you onward, even at great cost and burden.* A frown crossed her expression. *As loathe as I am to admit it, you and I are indeed the same. For it is the same will and desire to seek that drives us both, as you claimed before.*

Despite all that was occurring, Kraft's smile turned appreciative of that admittance. Lorelei wasn't through, however.

However, that understanding means little to me. In the end, you are just a remnant that should have left this existence long ago.

The smile faded as ire entered Kraft's visage. *So you proclaim as well.*

Lorelei nodded. *She showed me everything before I came here,* she explained, derision becoming more apparent...*before all of this.*

Her hands clenched, a surge of violet energy materialize. *Consequently, that is where our similarities end. As much as I desire Arcadia, I would never lower myself to what I see in you. An empty shell living for but one purpose, holding no other attributes or desires beyond, no concern for the effects or collateral damage of its actions.*

Kraft folded his arms over his chest, preparing for the fight. *Do you truly believe yourself so different? Even though you are living for a singular purpose, a singular* obsession, *as well?*

Again Kraft was interrupted, this time with a harsh laugh and a serene smile. *As if Arcadia were my* only *obsession.*

That took Kraft off guard, such that he attempted clarification. However, Lorelei was faster in her reply.

But we're straying off the subject. I made her a promise that I would set her free. A promise I intend to fulfill. She rose slowly off the ground, readying herself. *No matter who or* what *stands before me.*

Lifting off the ground as well, Kraft glared at his enemy in an open challenge. *You may try.*

In response, Lorelei launched forward, violet blades forming in her hands while Kraft materialized numerous energy bursts and fired in turn.

Flint Pirates umbra *Black Sun*
Sognare Sea

The *Black Sun*'s cannons thundered, sending four scarlet beams into the horrific mass. As had several times before, it cried out in apparent pain, and then responded in kind by launching several more yellow-tinted beams into the lone umbra. The *Sun's* shields held, yet the power behind the beams was more than enough to cause the ship to quake and pitch, nearly triggering a roll toward its portside. Only Davis' stringent hold kept it from doing so, thereby allowing Barbarossa to follow up the cannon blasts with another starboard missile barrage.

Jon's frown intensified as he watched the projectiles streak into the abomination, peppering its outer hide with harrowing explosions. Large quantities of yellow blood flowed into space. Unfortunately, while the entity shrieked and thrashed in pain, the newly inflicted wounds were just as quick to heal.

Subsequent barrages from the beam cannons and phalanx weren't able to inflict any permanent damage, while the monster closed in and returned fire even more viciously. Fortunately, Davis was able to evade the responding beam fire, as well as the successive swipes from the tendrils, but that only gave them a little more time.

"Alex!"

"Still working on it!" the younger Flint responded as he continued scanning, still looking for a point of weakness. He knew there was one, as did Jon, but there was just too much organic material. Even the *Sun*'s highly advanced sensors were struggling to analyze the monstrosity. They were generating data, but not as fast as Alex or Jon would have liked.

The beast roared again before firing new energy bursts. This time, however, the bursts were smaller and more numerous, effectively swarming over the *Sun* as Davis strained to maneuver. Those that struck were deflected by the shields, but the damage still mounted, as the damage alerts indicated. In turn, Barbarossa fired back with the stern cannons as Davis brought the ship about, attempting to gain some distance.

Jon sneered as he watched the apparent juggernaut surge after them, forcing itself through the crimson beam fire while lashing out with its tendrils. Again Davis maneuvered the ship around the swiping appendages, while Barbarossa fired a pair of torpedoes directly into one of the creature's gaping mouths. Yet even with the resultant explosions, which ended up blowing out said jaws and a good segment of the creature's form, it still reformed.

"Maintain fire!"

"Acknowledged!" Barbarossa responded as the ship turned to port, presenting its broadside.

Additional beams and missiles rained across the beast, this time obliterating several of its mouths, eyes, and tendrils alongside much of its skin. Another great shriek of rage and agony sounded as it started to regenerate, with one of the newly sprung tendrils thrashing out toward the *Sun*. This time Davis was unable to evade, with the appendage slamming directly against the umbra's upper shield.

Struck with even greater force than the prior attacks, the *Sun* pitched downward, nearly throwing her bridge crew about from the impact. They managed to remain in their respective posts, but just barely.

"Report!" Jon demanded.

"Shields down to fifty-seven percent!" Barbarossa responded while firing more cannon shots at the beast. Knocking one of the other tendrils away before it could impact. "That hit drained away twenty percent alone!"

"Diiiiiieeeee!" the monstrosity howled as it formed and fired additional beams. A combination of larger and smaller ones this time.

Biting back a curse, Davis threw the ship into a starboard turn, narrowly evading the fire. In doing so, the *Sun* presented her portside to the horror, allowing Barbarossa to respond with another missile spray.

Watching as the missiles impacted across the hide, Jon spotted the creature's first weakness. Aside from its regeneration power and bulked organic mass, it had no real defense. It could only absorb attacks, not deflect or guard against them.

Granted, that didn't make much of a difference at the moment, with the creature's regeneration capabilities more than compensating for that flaw. Even so, Jon kept that detail in mind, knowing it just may make a difference later on.

Assuming we last that long, he thought grimly as he lowered his command scope, hurriedly analyzing the tactical readout therein.

All while the beast let out another haunting, wrathful bellow. One complimented by further beam and tendril attacks.

Yellow lightning rained around her, forcing Lorelei to alternate between dodging the oncoming bursts and deflecting them. As soon as an opening presented itself, she responded in kind, firing off several energy bolts at Kraft's retreating form. The doctor generated a barrier to deflect.

Lorelei utilized this opening by flanking the opposing psion and charging forward, slashing at Kraft's left side. Kraft naturally withdrew, but Lorelei was able to execute three more slashes before another yellow burst spray forced her to defend. She retaliated, firing a surge of violet lightning. At the last moment, Kraft managed to impose one of the free-floating buildings between him and the attack, right before launching it at her.

Reextending her psi blades, Lorelei slashed the edifice across the middle, both halves flying away as she charged after her opponent. Kraft responded with a swarm of yellow energy spheres, which Lorelei was forced to weave around. Two came dangerously close to hitting her, but she managed to disperse them with a well-placed slash right before coming upon Kraft again.

Kraft reformed his barrier and repelled her initial attack, forcing Lorelei to try different angles, maneuvering to find an opening. Unfortunately, the undead psion's defense held against her onslaught, allowing Kraft to counter with two converging enhanced energy bursts. Lorelei deflected the motion as she ascended, away from the doctor.

Sneering in derision, Kraft hurled several more cluster bursts after her. Rather than move around the new attack, Lorelei quickly spun, generated a barrier shield, and propelled through the oncoming bursts, effectively striking at her opponent from overhead. The doctor was caught off guard, his only available action to drawback just as the White Siren slashed at his head. He saved himself from massive head injuries but incurred a prominent cut across his cheek.

Blood running down his cheek and neck, Kraft glowered with hate as he fired off more sprays of energy. Lorelei danced around them with ease before executing additional slash attacks, keeping her opponent from regaining any footing. It was presently her choice of an offense; Kraft was too powerful and skilled for her to do anything elaborate yet. She had to fight fast as well as up close in order to overwhelm him.

Just as Lorelei was about to reconnect, Kraft demonstrated he was both cunning and resourceful. Another ruined building shard flew in from the side, slamming into Lorelei's left hip. The collision threw her sideways. After flying a large distance away, the White Siren landed on another, larger piece of ruin, specifically what appeared to be an avenue of some kind.

Just as she reoriented herself, Kraft landed on the structure fragment, running across the surface, firing more bursts as he rushed her. Again Lorelei formed a barrier, then dove over the side, generating and firing crackling violet bolts as she fell. Kraft was forced to deflect, distracting him from the Siren coming over the other side of the fragment to move in and slash, this time at her opponent's right. Kraft repelled this as well, but Lorelei, once more in the fashion of a dancer, twirled behind him and caught him against his left side, inflicting a deep cut that would have incapacitated any other.

Letting out a responding bellow, Kraft focused his power onto the remnant, crushing and fragmenting it. Then bounding upward, he forced the shards to encompass and rapidly converge upon his adversary, attempting to pummel her from all angles. Knowing better than to try and flee, Lorelei spun again, sweeping her blades around, disintegrating any fragments that came close, executing several flourishing arcs in the process. Then, upon reaching the apparent end of her pirouette, she reoriented and outstretched her arms, sending out a telekinetic shockwave that obliterated the remaining projectiles.

Besides the primary effect, the shockwave was also powerful enough to knock Kraft off-balance, flinging him across the space. By the time he halted his flight, Lorelei was upon him once more. A hastily formed barricade blocked her attack, but this time Lorelei held her blades in place, attempting to overwhelm the shield.

For a moment, the psions glared into each others' eyes, projecting the full intensity of their respective hate and disdain, their will and resolve to see this fight to the end. And then Kraft amplified the strength of his barrier, forcing Lorelei back again. He pressed the attack by firing more bursts, to which the Siren reformed her defenses.

Hissing yellow energy bolts clashed with violet forcefields; skillfully, Lorelei evaded the onslaught as she drew closer for the intended kill.

Black Sun
Call of the Moon

Chapter XXIII: The Blind Idiot God

Flint Pirates umbra *Black Sun*
Sognare Sea

The eldritch bellowed once more, sending a psionically empowered wave rippling across space and over the *Sun*. Though her shields held, she still shuttered from the cry, nearly listing to port. Struggling, Davis managed to keep her level, allowing Barbarossa to "reply" with a follow on broadside. Four crimson beams blasted into the horror, obliterating much of its flesh and causing it to writhe violently, its mouths eliciting various shrieks from the apparent pain. Yet again, this triumph did not last as the creature's regenerative powers revitalized the damaged areas in a matter of seconds.

Immediately, the tendrils swiped at the *Sun*, forcing Davis to put the ship into a steep dive to dodge. Additional beam bursts complimented the latter, furthering the evasive maneuver. In turn, Barbarossa counter-attacked by directing several of the umbra's phalanx against the creature's previously wounded areas, the rapid-fire shots peppering its outer surface, ripping and tearing any form of matter in its way. Dual missile sprays and repeated cannon fire soon followed, intensifying the harm and eliciting further cries of anguish.

Even targeting the regenerated areas, the result remained the same. No matter how much damage the *Sun* wrought upon her opponent, its injuries would heal, and its anguish would recede. Only its rage would increase, furthering its drive to destroy its apparent foe. Its attacks were becoming more and more erratic and savage, as well as more problematic for Davis to evade, as another tendril lash, one that would have struck at the bridge tower, emphasized.

Jon stifled a wince as Davis was just able to dive under the tendril. Though the bridge tower remained protected by shielding, Barbarossa had already verified the kind of damage only one strike could do. Thus he didn't want to think of it somehow managing to break through the *Sun*'s primary means of defense.

Either way, Jon thought as he glared at the eldritch, which writhed and twisted under the renewed beam cannon fire, *we can't keep this up forever.*

"Hard to port! Concentrate your fire on the eyes!"

It wouldn't do much he knew, but it just may cause more destruction than hitting the rest of the body over and over. Barbarossa seemed to agree as he wasted little time in redirecting the cannons against the nearest receptors. Additional crimson beams fired from the *Sun*, the ocular organs rupturing with each hit, spraying offal and ichor throughout space.

Yet another anguished cry erupted, this one more pronounced than those previous, while the flailing tendrils and responding beam fire became even more randomized. Whether it was due to the resultant blindness or pain was anyone's guess.

Though it ended up healing itself again, Jon couldn't help but feel reassured over what he observed. First, the rejuvenated eyes appeared slightly mutated as if the regenerating process was being stressed. Second, the monstrosity seemed to be in a constant state of pain now, obviously brought on with the spontaneity of its "birth." That pain became more and more emphasized with each passing second, as though its body was further strained through its continued existence, which was why its responses to the *Black Sun*'s attacks also became more and more tormented and uncoordinated. Granted, that made it more dangerous, especially as the battle progressed, but for the moment, Jon took some affirmation in his ship's immediate effect.

At least we're causing it an additional amount of agony, Jon thought, just as the thing let loose another star shattering bellow, which washed over the *Sun* like a nova, again throwing the ship about through its overwhelming force.

"Shields down to fifty-three percent!" Barbarossa warned as another psionic barrage followed, several of the bursts striking against the *Sun*'s shields. "Now, forty-six!"

"Damn it," Jon exclaimed through clenched teeth. However they were going to destroy it they had to do it soon before they lost their shields and were left exposed to the Sea, which had grown even more chaotic since the start of the battle. Not even the Psi Disruptor would protect them from the Sognare.

"Continue bombardment!"

The cannons thundered, obliterating much of the eldritch's form and eliciting further cries of agony from the monstrosity. Missile fire followed, adding to the damage, burning, and blasting apart entire segments of the entity's flesh amid other less than positive effects. All culminating in it regenerating, and promptly executing counterattacks, forcing the *Sun* to maneuver even faster.

All while the Moon churned and fluctuated.

Kraft glared as Lorelei charged, just managing to raise a shield before her blades could strike him. The twin amethyst blades were deflected, but Lorelei quickly spun, making a backhanded attack, one that would slice her opponent's head down the middle. However, while she moved too fast for Kraft to form another barrier, he still managed to dodge the carving motion. The tip of the blade swept precisely where his head would have been.

Lorelei completed her maneuver and twisted around to fire another barrage of energy bolts, but Kraft teleported into the distance just as the first shots launched. The doctor intertwined another piece of the broken city, a five-story edifice, in between himself and the next few shots, before telekinetically throwing the structure at his opponent.

Rather than attempt to dodge, Lorelei chose to fly through the remnant, slicing it into fragments with her blades as she moved upon Kraft again. Though the undead psion predicted the action somewhat, Lorelei was still faster than expected in her approach. Snarling, Kraft responded by generating a large swarm of energy flares that blitzed the White Siren at subsonic speed.

Again alternating between evasion and deflection, Lorelei maintained her advance, eventually coming upon her opponent and slashing at his abdomen. Surprised at her ability to thwart his attack, Kraft was slow to evade; Lorelei moved too fast for him to form barriers. In defense, he fired twin bursts of energy at point-blank range. Immediately reversing her advance, the Siren moved behind another immense structure levitating in the distance. Just as the energy hit the fragment, Lorelei descended to the ground and unleashed pulsed psionic waves designed to disorient followed by a massive field of jettisoned rubble from the surface, forcing Kraft back on the defensive.

An eerie yellow glow surrounded the undead psion as the first psionic wave hit. The field of wreckage ricocheted in all directions. The floating structures surrounding the doctor began to explode due to the vortices created by the deflected waves and debris.

Unrelenting, Lorelei pressed her attack. Kraft redirected a pair of intact remnants to fly at her, attempting to crush her between them in a pincer attack. Frowning, Lorelei rapidly vaulted over the careening ruins, which disintegrated upon their thunderous impact. Stopping her ascent, she took control of the mass of shards and launched them at Kraft, who again was forced to erect a barrier, a more powerful one, to defend. Lorelei, however, anticipating that response, at the last possible second, redirected the fragments to encompass Kraft in a maelstrom rather than fly straight into him.

Only upon the closing of her fist did the swirling wreckage converge, effectively blotting out the enemy psion.

Or so Lorelei would have preferred. Unfortunately, right before impact and impalement, Kraft focused his power and generated a psionic flare, one comparable to a newly born sun. The shards were completely vaporized before they could so much as graze him. Lorelei, taken off guard, was forced to look away and cover her eyes, leaving her open to the follow on shockwave. It flung her across the space and slammed her into another, larger remnant.

Smashing through the outer "wall", Lorelei ended up landing on her back against the apparent floor. The remnant, as it turned out, was a still relatively intact building of some kind. Not that she was able to think about it too much, as another barrage of yellow energy soon followed, penetrating the remnant from different angles. Rather than evade by flying, Lorelei decided to take a cue from Kaguya, employing a line of acrobatic moves to avoid the bursts, even going so far as to deflect the last attack with a well-executed knife hand, sending it flying into the wall.

That was when she noticed cracks suddenly appearing in the floor, walls, and ceiling around her. She frowned, realizing the implications immediately. Kraft had chosen to plagiarize her earlier attack.

The remnant imploded, but a few moments later, violet energy infused the destruction generating a large dust cloud. Lorelei launched out, ascending back into the open space. It had been close, closer than she wanted to admit, but ultimately not enough to finish her.

That outcome seemed to incense her opponent even more. He surged after her, firing energy bursts as well as weaponizing the surrounding remnants, further maintaining the offensive. Instead of forming a barrier, Lorelei followed up on her previous evasiveness, reforming her blades and dancing across the immediate space, dodging and slashing down all that flew at her. She moved fluidly and majestically, the grace of an accomplished artist again apparent, ensuring that none of the projectiles would reach her.

Flint Pirates umbra *Black Sun*
Sognare Sea

"Jon, I think I found something!" Alex announced right as the *Sun* was struck by another energy burst. Tapping a few more keys, the younger Flint sent the readout to the main monitor for all the crew to see. "If I didn't know any better, I'd say this thing has an arc reactor!"

Jon easily saw what his brother was alluding to. Buried deep within the twisted, construed organic mass was a particular looking organ, for lack of a better word, that seemed to function much like the powerplant of a starship. At least, that's what Jon, who was nowhere near as scientifically inclined as his sibling, gathered from the recorded data. Even without the latter, the functionality and energy distribution still looked similar.

"Probably the Piscean ship's original plant," Jon observed as his mind ran over the information. This discovery presented much for the Flints, as it was the very weakness that they had been seeking. Unfortunately, it was also very well protected, placed deep within the horror, and shrouded by its thick mass. And that wasn't discounting its regenerative power.

"Will it detonate?"

Another energy burst struck against the *Sun*'s shields, the resultant quaking underscoring the direness of their present state.

"I don't know," Alex shook his head after going over the additional data. "I've never seen a 'reactor' like this before. The organic composition alone…"

"Alex," Jon softly interrupted, just as the umbra's cannons returned fire. The resulting destruction and anguished cry again underscored the present, as well as the Flints' desperation within.

Taking another moment to consider, Alex nodded in confirmation. "Yes. Yes, it will," he spoke with clear assuredness. "After all, if it weighs like a duck and is made of wood…"

"It's a witch," Jon finished, matching his brother's smirk even as their vessel shook once more.

It may not have been a conventional reactor, but if it worked like one, then it would have all the same flaws. Namely distinct susceptibility to a well-placed beam, missile or torpedo shot.

Of course, the projectile in question would have to reach it first, which fell back on their immediate problems. Their target was buried within layers upon layers of organic material, which would heal almost instantly when damaged. And if the latter healing process worked anything like the *Black Sun*'s Moebius System, then Jon knew it would take a whole fleet, one of equivalent size to Drake's forces at Ephesus, to overwhelm it.

He and the rest of the Flints had their work cut out for them. As if the next energy burst didn't emphasize that fact.

"All weapons, fire for effect!" Jon commanded, just as the *Black Sun* turned to face the eldritch yet again. The elder Flint sneered. "Full barrage!"

―――――――――――――

Despite her best efforts, a speck managed to evade Lorelei's defenses. It struck her across the cheek, eliciting a fair-sized cut. Ignoring the sting of the wound, she retaliated, slashing an amethyst blade against Kraft's neckline, forcing her opponent to form another shield to deflect it, as well as the two following attacks. However, that was simply her initial assault. She drew back and swept to her left, forming a line of bolts as she moved. Upon her command, the bolts then launched out as one, converging upon Kraft with singular ferocity. And this time, Kraft wasn't able to deflect them all, with at least one striking him and taking out his right shoulder.

Nearly screaming out against the sudden pain, Kraft barely reformed the obliterated shoulder as Lorelei again surged at him, sweeping her blades at his torso and head. Unable to defend against her rapid attacks, he instead concentrated on evasion, moving his body out of the blades' reach as much as he could. Relentlessly, Lorelei pressed the offensive. In turn, Kraft managed to withdraw into the distance twice, firing a barrage of yellow energy each time, to which Lorelei simply pressed on, simultaneously dodging the bursts while moving in closer.

Charging once more, Lorelei crossed her blades as she slammed into Kraft, who barely managed to reform a shield before she could strike. Again that mattered little as she focused her power on her momentum, sending both of them streaking across the void, eventually crashing through another ruined, free-floating building. Breaking through several walls until reaching one of the larger rooms within, Kraft landed across the "floor" in a sprawl, skidding across the surface before managing to stop. In contrast, Lorelei touched down gracefully and casually wiped a speck of dust from her shoulder.

Spitting out a goblet of blood, which almost immediately turned to dust upon hitting the floor, Kraft glowered with exasperation up toward his enemy.

Why can't you be a good girl and die… the undead doctor snarled.

I've never *been a good girl. And I have an aversion toward dying,* Lorelei dryly retorted, taking no shortage of bemusement in Kraft's aggravation. *Not that you need to worry about either of those things, at least not for much longer.*

Gritting his teeth to hold back his scream, Kraft faced the opposing psion with all the disdain he could muster. *You are the most infuriating woman, even more infuriating than your reputation claims.*

Lorelei only smiled. *I try,* she replied as though accepting a compliment. *After all, I am the White Siren. One who brings disaster upon those who hear my song.*

She flexed her right hand; amethyst energy crackled and surged around it. *Now, would it be possible for us to resume? Or should I just finish you here and be done with it.*

Kraft actually elicited a laugh as he rose to his feet. *So proud, and so assured,* he exclaimed, yellow eyes glaring into purple. *You really do see me as a villain to be slain, don't you?*

Aren't you? Lorelei shot back, smile fading to a snarl. *After all the things you did to get here? All the innocents that perished? What you are doing in the Sea now?*

I did what I had to do to gain what I seek, Kraft glowered even more deeply. *And I will continue to do what is required, even if I have to burn down the galaxy around me!*

Now it was Lorelei's turn to glare. *How villainous indeed.*

As opposed to yourself? Kraft retorted. *As you said, you are the White Siren. A thief and a murderess who went as far as to conspire with the vermin of the galaxy to gain her desire.*

A malicious smile soon folded over Kraft's lips. *Oh yes, I'm well aware of your activities, my dear, before and after you obtained the* Sun. *All the things that you did to get here now.*

His smile then grew even more. *If anyone would be willing to see the galaxy, and all within, burn to reach that final destination, it's you.*

Much to Kraft's surprise, however, Lorelei simply frowned. *Perhaps...*

Kraft suddenly felt his throat painfully constrict. As well as his body involuntarily lift several meters into the air.

Once more, however, Lorelei viciously exclaimed as her adversary struggled in her invisible grasp. *That is not something for you to worry about.*

She then flung her opponent through another set of walls, until he burst into the open space again. Moments later, she surged after him, blades reextended, just as Kraft twisted around to meet her, roaring as he fired off another barrage.

Flint Pirates umbra *Black Sun*
Sognare Sea

Another blast thundered against the *Sun*'s shields, causing the ship to quake all over again. She responded once more with her cannons, but the results remained the same. In fact, Jon was almost certain that the creature's healing factor had accelerated in the last few minutes, such that its regeneration had taken even fewer seconds to complete.

"Alex!?" Jon demanded, just as Davis maneuvered the ship around another flailing tendril.

"Still working!" Alex responded as he continued to run through the data. He knew there was something there; he just had yet to find it. He could only hope that the ship still existed by the time he discovered it.

A hope that Jon also held as he lowered the command scope, gazing through the eyepiece. Taking a bit of the action for himself, he fired off another missile barrage into the creature's eyes. Unhindered by the creature's lack of point defense, the projectiles slammed into each of its ocular organs, the resulting explosions obliterating them and eliciting another pained cry. From this, Barbarossa took his cue and fired several more cannon and phalanx shots into the holes, causing even further damage.

For a time, the creature trembled, twisting about in utter grotesqueness as it apparently fought to force back the pain. The display was enough to make more than one of the bridge crew nauseous, as were the unnatural cries that accompanied it, which was precisely when something even more horrendous occurred.

"What in the Seventh Circle...God help us?" Davis exclaimed as he and the rest of the bridge watched the horrifying display. Once more for a time, it seemed as though they had severely damaged the creature to the point of fragmentation. Breaking off much like dead leaves from an autumn tree, these fragments, each of varying size and shape, floated away from their host, hurling aimlessly across the immediate Sea. Initially seen as little more than deadened pieces from the whole.

Unfortunately, this was far from the truth, as these fragments were not mere pieces...they were spawn.

Flailing tentacles, fanged jaws, twitching eyes, and various other forms of mutation erupting, each of the fragments came to life, sending out lesser psionic cries as they "birthed". Each appeared to hold the same virulence as their "parent," and all turned and started flying toward the *Sun* with predatory intent.

"My god…!" Anna let out, feeling especially sick now. It would have been loathsome enough had the "children", for lack of a better word, not been inclined to attack. But their intent was soon verified as several smaller energy bursts struck against the *Sun*'s defenses. Far less powerful than the "parent" but much more numerous.

Alex quickly shouted out the appropriate commands in his brother's place. "Scramble the Corsairs! Setup for anti-fighter combat!"

"I'm going out as well," Jon added as he raised the scope, stepping out of the command chair. "You have the conn!"

"Got it!" Alex replied as he took the command chair while his elder brother moved to the turbolift. No sooner had the lift doors closed did Alex lower the command scope again, scanning the spawn. They were already quite numerous, and it was all too likely the main body could produce more if necessary. Even so, that wasn't about to stop him, or the rest of the Flint Pirates.

"All phalanx, target incoming small craft!" the younger Flint ordered, all while bringing the data he had been going over into the scope's monitor, effectively resuming his work. "Fire at will!"

———————————————

Energy bursts zoomed about in abundance now, either flying aimlessly through the void or striking random fragments. Undeterred, Lorelei continued to maneuver, evading most of the assaults while erecting shields to deflect the remainder, all the while counterattacking when she was able. Unfortunately, she wasn't able to perform the latter all that much, as Kraft had long since forgone any kind of defense and instead concentrated on keeping Lorelei from attacking at close-range. Thus it was all she could do to fire off an opposing energy shot or two whenever the opportunity presented itself.

Regardless, she evaded the saturation attacks, spinning, twisting and turning around each with an efficiency that Kraft, now thoroughly consumed with rage, could not countermand. Then, without warning, she emulated one of her opponent's favored tactics and telekinetically threw a large building fragment at him, forcing him to concentrate and fire off a larger energy burst to obliterate it. Supprising her opponent, Lorelei, her approach hidden by the building fragment, drove through the resultant shards and attacked, slashing at Kraft's chest and inflicting a deep cut, one that would have killed a "living" being immediately.

Howling in both fury and pain at the wound, Kraft instantly retaliated, telekinetically flinging Lorelei away. This mattered little as Lorelei easily flipped around and fired off a concentrated barrage as she flew, blasting Kraft all over. Angry bellows filled the air before he recomposed his otherwise heavily destroyed body. Another swarm of yellow energy flares soon followed, but this time Lorelei had even less difficulty in evasion, effortlessly dancing around the spinning flames despite the increased volume.

She spun and closed in again, this time unleashing a full-on combo attack that slashed Kraft in several areas. Both arms were removed, while several more cuts appeared in his neck and torso. All culminating in a slash at the waistline, dividing Kraft's upper body from his lower, and then a solid, psionically empowered kick into his top half. One that sent him careening into yet another fragment. And finally, upon his attempt to recompose his body, Lorelei dove over him, impaling both amethyst blades through his chest.

Her offensive complete, Lorelei released the two blades from her hands, leaving them embedded in Kraft, before drawing back. Taking a moment to observe as her opponent struggled futilely.

This... Kraft hissed while attempting to recompose his arms and rip the blades out of his chest. It was for not, however, as Lorelei had specifically ensured those blades would disrupt his regeneration power. *This... is impossible...!*

Lorelei sniffed derisively. *You said it yourself,* she replied, whipping her right arm about to extend another blade. *I could have beaten you in Ianessa had I not held back so much.*

She then raised the blade into Kraft's line of sight. *Obviously,* she coldly finished, *you were correct.*

With that, she stepped forward, intent on finishing Kraft for good. As long as he could not recompose, it would be easy to destroy his body, his final anchor in the world of the living. And though he had earlier proclaimed his own intention to merge with the Moon and take its power, Lorelei knew he had been unable to do so while fighting her. Otherwise, he would have been far more powerful.

Thus, this was it. The final remnant of Doctor Laurentius Kraft would be removed from this realm once and for all.

A fact that did not fail to register on Kraft, who struggled fervently as his executioner approach. No, he couldn't let it end like this! He was so close! So close to gaining what he had sought for so long! So agonizingly long! He had to fight on! He had to win! Even if he had to sunder the galaxy itself as he had declared before!

He had to reach his Sunset City! His *true* Sunset City!

Determination merging with mania, Kraft concentrated all his power that remained and focused on the blades holding him down. At first, he could not overpower them, but eventually, as he let out another pained, anguished roar, he broke through. And in the process, generated another psionic blast that threw Lorelei back. Frustrated, she flipped around and landed on the opposite end of the remnant.

No! Kraft bellowed as he again recomposed his body. Pure psionic energy, intermingling between black and yellow, emanated from him as his body trembled, rippled, and convulsed. *No, it's not over! Not yet!*

Letting out another roar, this once much more anguished than those prior, Kraft again concentrated his power onto himself. Generating a form that Lorelei, for all of her experience, had never seen before, yet instantly came to dread as she watched it emerge.

Initially appearing as a psionically generated shadow, the black form extended behind Kraft, then took discernable shape. A black, hulking giant that rose well above its master, appearing humanoid in form but with little resemblance to any sentient creature. Gold lines and emblems appeared across its muscle mass, while glowing yellow eyes, ones that Kraft soon matched, permeated its "face". A lipless grin folded across its "mouth", while a curious black and gold striped headdress appeared on its head and fused with the rest of its form as a helmet-like carapiece. Finally, a golden "beard" extension materialized on its "chin," and a single crest, one shaped like a Terran cobra, appearing over its forehead.

Even Lorelei could not keep the astonishment off her face as the apparent shadow took full form. Recalling her Ancient Terran history, the thing held a distinct resemblance to the monarchal rulers of the tribal nation of Egypt. At the same time, the power it emanated was many times more than what Kraft had originally utilized against her.

She didn't have time to analyze further, however, as Kraft, seemingly having forgone what little sanity he had left, let loose another inhuman roar, apparently directing the giant. The shadow reared up and launched twin energy bursts from its fists, far more powerful than those prior ...

Chapter XXIV: Crawling Chaos

Flying out as one, the twenty-five Corsairs took off from the *Black Sun*'s launch bay and throttled after the oncoming hellions. The latter were very quick to detect their approach, with a fair number of the spawn turning away from their original target, firing yellow energy bursts as they drew toward the fighters. Fortunately, their attacks were quite erratic and ill aimed, exploding almost harmlessly as the Corsairs charged, firing their vulcans and missiles in turn. Shortly, the two sides converged, with the pirate craft mingling with the beastlings in a spectacular melee, while their "parent" continued to trade blows with the *Sun*.

At least they aren't regenerating, Boss thought as she fired her vulcans into one of the spawnlings. Sure enough, the monstrosity ripped apart in bloody fashion, the fragments *not* merging back together or into anything else. Some of the remaining chunks ended up bouncing off of her shields as she flew through, but there were no other effects. The ace took that as a plus and banked right, searching for additional uglies to kill.

She didn't have to wait long, of course, as her warning sensors indicated. Three of the things had turned after her Corsair and were now firing on her. And though they remained as inaccurate as from the start, one of the bursts still managed to get through and take a fair-sized chunk out of her back shield. The impact was enough to elicit a very descriptive curse. She banked and dove, maneuvering away from the other energy beams, right before twisting her fighter about and firing a vulcan burst. She managed to catch at least one of the beasties, riddling its form apart as she had its "sibling", but the other two returned fire more quickly than she anticipated, forcing her to break away again.

They're fast little fraggers, Boss admitted as she maneuvered around the erratic fire. *Not all that intelligent, obviously, but fast.*

Combined with their animal instincts and psionic abilities, the hellions were vastly more capable than the Flints' usual opposition. But then considering the beast that had spawned them, that wasn't any real surprise. And again, they died easily enough.

Such was the case when Boss stylishly barrel rolled to her right, and then maneuvered around once more, this time firing her beam cannons. It may have appeared to be overkill, but her target was larger than the last two spawnlings she destroyed, and Boss couldn't be sure if it would absorb more fire as a result. Regardless, it obliterated all the same, and her Corsair was again barraged with organic fragments, while the remaining spawn let out a harsh bellow and an accompanying bombardment. Again she barrel rolled away, firing her vulcans as she flew. This gave her the fourth kill, and she was thankful her shields were active to block the remnants.

Upon the last of the chunks flying past, Boss took a moment to survey how the rest of the fight was going. Much to her appreciation, the other Corsairs were having similar successes against their targets, with more and more of the spawnlings being blown back to Hell. Yet, the accomplishment was limited, given the sheer number of the monstrosities. Even worse, due to their spontaneous generation, the beasties came in various shapes, sizes, and accompanying strengths and weaknesses, resulting in some of the Corsairs and Buccaneers having more difficulty in making kills than others.

Such was the case when Boss witnessed one of the spawnlings spray some kind of fluid at Buccaneer Five. Apparently acidic in composition, it rapidly ate through his shields and struck the fighter underneath. The Corsair began to dissolve, spinning wildly in the process, until finally detonating. Whether that had been an effect of the attack or Buccaneer Five willfully self-destructing, Boss would never know.

"Damn these things to Hell," Boss hissed as the glare of the detonation died away. For what seemed like the hundredth time, she repeated the question. *Just what in the Seventh Circle are we fighting?*

Her sensors then beeped in warning again, just as a larger ugly flew after her, one of its several jaws opened wide. Gunning her sub-arc engines, Boss sped away as the entity clamped down. Bellowing in response, the thing launched several enlarged energy bursts, while its tendrils extended and attempted to ensnare the fighter. Expertly maneuvering around each, Boss flipped her Corsair around and fired her cannons, scoring several hits across the giant and even managing to blow off one of the tendrils. It psionically bellowed in apparent pain, but the thing didn't slow down, forcing Boss to reorient her Corsair and dart away.

Continuing to bank and maneuver, Boss was successful in evading the tendril swipes and energy bursts, though the rapid attacks of her pursing beastie kept her from countering. She weaved about, trying to throw it off, but she just wasn't able to shake it, much less find an opening for an attack. All while the thing bellowed and thrashed, apparently frustrated over its inability to kill her.

Sorry, but I'm not that easy, Boss snidely thought as she performed an Immelmann, again gunning her engines in the process. She looped up and twisted around, bringing her fighter back toward the monstrosity, which elicited another psionic enthused bellow from its several jaws. Maneuvering around its further attacks, Boss banked right just as the thing was about to crash into her, or vice versa. Then, while maintaining her flight vector, she spun the Corsair around and fired several cannon salvos, blasting the monster apart before it could correct its vector and retaliate. The explosion was as grisly as the rest, but somehow even more spectacular. And this time, Boss didn't have to fly through its remains.

Five down, Boss thought somewhat cynically, just as her sensors picked up more bogeys moving after her. *Many, many more of you disgusting bastards to go.*

She again went to full throttle as the next round of monsters gave chase.

A newer, much larger burst oncoming, Lorelei immediately threw up a barrier to deflect. Unfortunately, the attack was far more powerful than she had anticipated, and so her barrier shattered all too easily. The resultant shock flung her threw the space, until she crashed into one of the nearby remnants, her back slamming into a broken fountain, her head striking against what was once a decorative accent. Unrelenting, Kraft charged in, the avatar moving to slam its fist into the opposing psion. Lorelei just managed to recover her senses and ascend as the entity struck, the impact shattering the fragment and flinging smaller shards outward. These, however, Lorelei had little issue evading or defending against.

She attempted to attack, but the construct was faster, firing an additional line of black energy orbs. Forcing back a curse, Lorelei returned to evading, moving around the oncoming bursts. Not only were they more powerful now, but they were also being generated and launched at a much greater rate. Consequently, she found it very difficult to avoid them, and she knew it would take much more on her part to form a strong enough barrier against them. Once the opportunity at last presented itself, she counterfired, launching violet lightning at Kraft. However, the opposing psion was just as fast in repelling all of Lorelei's attacks.

Seeing this, Lorelei withdrew as Kraft and his familiar pursued. Though it was more or less a simple psionic manifestation, Kraft had invested the bulk of his power within the grotesque monstrosity. The result was a conduit through which he could project that power, all without the strain and limitations on his main form. A focusing point, in other words, that bypassed Kraft's inherent weaknesses and allowed him to fight much more effectively, as well as much more erratically.

So it was when Kraft launched after her, the specter generating an energy field around itself as it rocketed through the air. Knowing better than to try and deflect *that*, Lorelei vaulted out of the way, and then retaliated with three energy bolts to her opponent's exposed back. The avatar twisted around and swept its arm, knocking away the shots as if they were but thrown rocks. It returned fire, sending out an even larger black and gold fireball.

Lorelei withdrew away again, moving so fast she almost appeared to vanish. However, the fireball immediately pursued her, Kraft having anticipated her response. Unwilling to waste energy playing tag with the hellfire, Lorelei spun rapidly, creating an outward, rotating tornado that forced the flames away, dissipating their strength. Although successful, she still felt its sheering energy as it passed, nearly knocking her away with its force.

Again, Kraft closed in, the avatar extending a set of claws from its right hand and slashing. This time, Lorelei only barely dodged the worst of it, with the claws raking against her left midsection, drawing cobalt blue blood in the process.

Eliciting a sharp hiss to stem off the responding scream, Lorelei slashed at Kraft with her blade, only for her opponent to telekinetically throw her into a nearby ruin. The avatar immediately fired another twin set of energy bursts, pulverizing the structure and directing it to collapse, burying the psion. Violet light glowed through the rubble as Lorelei exploded out of the mass and performed a running slash against the specter. She struck, drawing a black mist from the entity's left side, causing it and its host to recoil violently. The latter even let out a pained cry, right before the avatar turned and fired several more yellow bursts after her.

Once more, Lorelei evaded, moving around the energy fire as best as she could. It was becoming more and more difficult for her now, between her adversary's increasing relentlessness and the ever-growing power behind its attacks. She continued her retaliation, succeeding in another slash to the shadow's side. The avatar let out another inhuman cry, but other than a black mist emission, it and its host both remained in the fight.

Suddenly, Lorelei's pain intensified, nearly causing her to lose her coordination. Gazing at her side, she saw that the earlier wound she had received was also eliciting black wisps, with the effected tissue beginning to deteriorate. Cursing, she had to take a moment to dispel the injury completely, which allowed Kraft to move upon her again. Lorelei was just barely able to evade the full impact of the avatar's fist, but it still managed to brush against her left cheek. More black wisps and accompanying pain followed thereafter.

Forcing back an anguished cry, Lorelei focused her power and generated a psionic "flash" at point-blank, encompassing the area in bright violet energy. Her opponent temporarily blinded, she withdrew to another distant splinter, what was once part of a grand boulevard. Momentarily hidden in the rubble, she reached up to heal her new wound. Apparently, the energy that made that familiar had acidic properties, such that even a graze could be lethal if unattended. She did well to keep that in mind.

Unable to locate his opponent, Kraft directed the giant to begin obliterating the levitating fragments, eliminating any hiding places. Explosions sounded throughout the space, debris and dust clouds filled the air as black, and yellow energy shots flew in all directions. The entity generated a yellow orb, not unlike a small sun, and threw it at Lorelei's location. Her respite at an end, the White Siren re-entered the melee.

She had a mere second before Kraft launched after her, the avatar's fist flying forward. Lorelei crossed her blades to block the strike; she knew better than to try and form a barrier against the fist. That precaution was for naught, as she barely lasted several seconds before she was overpowered. Blades shattering, the fist struck Lorelei dead center, sending her flying out yet again. Trailing more wisps from her now burning greatcoat, she smashed through several more fragments as she flew.

Damn it, Jon cursed as another Corsair was struck down, impaled by a line of launched needle-esque spines from one of the creatures. That made three fighters down already, and they were barely repelling the monsters away from the *Sun,* let alone exterminating them completely.

Twisting his Corsair around, he made toward that particular eldritch, firing his vulcans as he charged. Unfortunately, it was not only covered in quills but chitin-esque armor, which managed to repel his fire. Gritting his teeth in response, the pirate captain banked away, right as the thing launched another salvo of spines in his direction. As with its "siblings", the creature's fire was wildly inaccurate, but simultaneously high in volume, forcing Jon to evade. Fortunately, it wasn't long before he drew a bead on it again, firing his cannons into its side. This time the armor did not hold, resulting in the monster being blown into fiery bits, a final psionic empowered screech signaling its demise.

He didn't have time to feel satisfied; however, as one of the larger entities was soon upon him, emitting a psionic bellow of its own. Maw opening wide, three slender, fleshy red tendrils lashed out like missiles, their barbed ends nearly striking the Corsair. Jon barrel rolled out of the way, but one of the tendrils managed to graze his shield, and much to Jon's amazement, it almost pierced it. The tendrils were shielded with energy, much like torpedoes. Worse, the creature had more of them in reserve, which it launched in salvos. Jon put his engines into full burn to evade.

Responding cannon shots took a fair chunk out of the creature, but what remained was now was quite enraged. More tendril attacks soon followed, the barbs zigzagging after the Corsair, forcing Jon to put more and more effort into dodging the appendages. At the precise moment, he turned and fired a vulcan spray, managing to blast the tips apart on some, but there remained too many for him to destroy at once. They continued to flail after him, retracting momentarily just to be shot back out again.

Glowering toward the oversized spawnling, Jon obliterated another chunk of it with his cannons, causing the creature's many mouths to yaw open and elicit pained cries. Acting quickly, the pirate captain forced his fighter through the psionic emission and fired off two missiles, both of which streaked down into the gullet. Only then did the monstrosity at last die, exploding like an overripe fruit, the resultant offal hurling throughout the immediate space. Jon banked around it, using his vulcans to clear away one or two of the larger pieces.

We're not getting anywhere, Jon reflected gravely as he gazed over the battle at large. Despite the losses, the Corsairs and Buccaneers were holding out, and the *Sun* was still very much in the fight. However, outside eliminating much of the hellspawn, he could see that little progress was being made in destroying the main abomination. He watched as the *Sun*'s bow cannons fired again, only for the entity's resultant wounds to heal just as quickly as before.

"Come on, Alex," Jon whispered as he watched the *Sun* turn away from another retaliatory barrage, maintaining her fire against her much larger target as she did. It was at that point that his sensors beeped in warning again, just as two more of the spawnlings launched after him. One had no apparent tendrils, but held a single, oversized eye at its center, while the other had multiple organic and insectoid limbs, all of which were equipped with some kind of claw or barb.

Exhaling in disdain, Jon banked his fighter away just as the one with the eye generated a single, concentrated beam, which swept after the Corsair. Simultaneously, the clawed entity extended two of its arms, the crustacean-like pincer on one snapping together as both lunged after the fighter. Jon maneuvered around each attack, right before twisting around again, firing his vulcans and cannons in tandem.

Flint Pirates umbra *Black Sun*
Sognare Sea

"You just won't die, will you?" Alex sneered as the horror healed itself from yet further beam cannon fire. "You've got to be getting tired, at least!"

It seemed to answer him with another bellow, as well as several accompanying energy bursts, to which Davis put the ship back into evasive maneuvers. Despite his best efforts, however, two of the shots managed to strike against the *Sun*'s starboard shields, jolting her quite violently while causing several screens and monitors to flicker. Barbarossa retaliated with additional beam cannon blasts, but the effect remained the same as before.

"Diii...diiii....iiii....iiiiiieeee!!" came another psionic cry from the eldritch, which washed over the *Sun* in an even deeper tenor, sounding more wretched and haunting than previously.

Forcibly ignoring the sounds, Barbarossa continued to pound the thing with both cannon and missile fire, creating several more transient wounds. *Too* transient, however, as they healed within seconds, allowing the beast to counterattack just as quickly. Between the energy bursts and the flailing tendrils, Davis all but strained himself in keeping the ship out of the impact zone, with Barbarossa having to redirect the cannons to blast away one of the encroaching limbs. It too obliterated...only to heal within moments.

The younger Flint stifled a curse as he watched the newly reformed tendril lash at the *Sun* again, with Davis putting the ship into a narrow climb to evade. Alex couldn't remember the last time he had fought such a frustrating opponent, whether with a ship or Forneus in hand. The thing would not remain incapacitated, no matter what they threw at it, while the contrasting agony of its birth made it increasingly frenzied as the battle progressed. It was taking more and more out of Davis just to keep the *Sun* out of its reach. He wasn't having very much success as another burst slammed into the umbra's shields.

"Shields down to thirty-five percent!" Barbarossa shouted from tactical, causing Alex to scowl that much more. The battle was taking far longer than it should have, yet they weren't making any progress.

If we could just reach that damned organ, this would all be over, Alex thought as he lowered the command scope again, studying the projected image of the beast's singular weak point. Destroying the 'reactor' would easily destroy its host, but it was deep within the creature's anatomy. Too deep for the *Sun*'s weapons to penetrate even with a concentrated barrage, and unless they knocked it out in one go, it would just heal itself all over again just as it did now, following another torpedo shot.

And then, as Alex watched the gaping wound seal itself, something occurred to him. He didn't know what exactly had caused the thought to emerge, but when it did, the younger Flint realized its significance. Perhaps the creature had one more weakness after all. One that, if exploited correctly and precisely, may just win them the day.

With that newfound starting point, Alex input numerous commands into the scope, adjusting the *Sun*'s sensors. Several new readings appeared within the scope's monitor, allowing Alex to begin his analysis. It would take some time, unfortunately, which they had very little of now, but it remained the Flints' only real chance at victory. He had to trust that Davis and Barbarossa could keep the thing beaten back until he found what he sought.

As well as hope the ship remained in one piece.

⸻

Flipping onto another shard, Lorelei immediately shed her inflamed greatcoat; it disintegrated the moment she flung it into the air. Through the vanishing flames, Kraft surged after her, his avatar's fist again extended to strike. She leaped up and away as the ground under her shattered. Another slash at the avatar's extended arm resulted in another gust of black mist, but other than that, Lorelei did very little damage. On the other hand, it did seem to increase Kraft's madness, as the avatar slashed at her with its opposite arm, but she managed to evade this as well.

Violet lightning slammed into Kraft's chest, inciting his wrath. Both he and his avatar with him thrashed and recoiled, but little damage resulted from the salvo. The avatar retaliated quickly, a virtual hailstorm of energy bursts inundated Lorelie's position. Initially forming a screen, she was forced to abandon it as she quickly became overwhelmed. She moved to elude the remaining floe, but the sheer volume ensured strikes against her shoulder and midsection, knocking the air out of her as well as throwing her back.

Both avatar and master grinned viciously. Kraft pressed the offense, firing additional blasts at his target until she was encompassed with eruptions. As she emerged from the explosions, the doctor surged again, his avatar's fist moving to strike Lorelei in the face. Lorelei dodged and spun, attacking the construct's back. The familiar whipped its right arm about, generating a shockwave that smashed into her at near point-blank range. It would have easily overpowered her, but she managed to absorb the force at the last second, which also allowed her to evade the avatar's successive bursts.

That was when Kraft performed a new attack. Focusing energy around the avatar's fists, it generated a multitude of energy beams, which swept across the immediate space. Cursing, the psion watched several of the nearby fragments get cut apart by the sweeping beams. Evading, alternating between straight out dodging or moving around other remnants, Lorelei ensured that she remained obscured from the rays. There was no point in erecting a barrier against these, as they would easily cut it apart as they were everything else.

And then Kraft decided to get even more creative, sweeping one of the beams across another large fragment, as it came above Lorelei's current location. Repeating his earlier tactic, he generated a virtual meteor shower, launching the shards as one. And this time, as strained as she was, Lorelei was unable to dodge them all. Several pieces slammed into her form; multiple eruptions of cobalt blue blood, as well as an accompanying cry of pain, followed.

Without hesitation, Lorelei responded with a surge of violet lightning straight into Kraft's face, catching him off guard. For the briefest of moments, the scientist's head was reduced to a charred, fractured skull. He quickly regenerated the bone and tissue that had been "lost". However, he could not withhold a scream as he fought against the accompanying torment.

Additional pain soon followed as Lorelei, having taken the opportunity to close the distance, smashed her heel into the doctor's newly reformed left cheek. Her opponent's head proverbially spinning, she executed several punches into his torso. Standard fisticuffs that were not psionically enhanced, she was attacking too fast to concentrate her power, yet were still enough to knock the wind out of Kraft, as well as cause him further disconcertion. She completed the combo with a solid kick into his gut, sending both him and his avatar flying back several meters.

She would have attacked further, but Kraft recovered even faster than before, allowing his avatar to fire twin bursts that struck Lorelei simultaneously. Letting out a cry, this one of surprise as well as pain, her body was flung through space, yet again. Kraft, taking a dark and highly distinct pleasure in watching her fall, pursued with relish.

Flint Pirates umbra *Black Sun*
Sognare Sea

"Shields down to twenty-five percent!" Barbarossa warned as another blast struck against the *Sun*'s starboard side, rocking the ship furiously.

"Concentrate all available power to shields!" Alex commanded without taking his eyes away from the scope lest he miss any vital piece of data that would throw his calculations off. "Redistribute from weapons if you have to!"

Discomfort within the bridge crew, along with some disbelief, was evident, but Alex ignored it all. At this point, their firing on the horror was ineffective. They were keeping it from overpowering the ship, but not inflicting damage, and the thing was only becoming more belligerent.

As the younger Flint scanned over the projected data, however, he was assured more and more that his idea could work. No, it *had* to work. Like it or not, it was their only real card to play now, before they were eventually overwhelmed. Whether by the horror, or the increasingly unstable Sognare, which had become progressively violent since the battle began.

Still, this is going to be close, Alex thought as the ship took another hit from an energy burst. He withdrew the scope and tapped a switch on the chair arm.

"Bridge to Engineering!"

Chapter XXV: Collapsing Cosmoses

With no shortage of severe impacts, Lorelei slammed through building after building before finally coming to a halt. She had been able to psionically cushion most of the blows, enough to keep from incurring any critical harm, but otherwise, little difference was made. The impacts were jaunting, more than enough to disorient her, generating blurred vision, alongside the dull, throbbing pain brought on by physical shock. Even the taste of her blood did not stop her, as she was more than able to anticipate her opponent's next attack.

Sure enough, Kraft charged through the debris after her, the fists of his avatar raised to strike and finish the fight. She dodged right, firing a barrage as she gained some distance. Kraft pursued faster, shielding himself from the energy bolts as his doppelganger fired off another selection of energy discs, forcing Lorelei to maintain her evasion. She countered by telekinetically launching several of the nearby fragments, but Kraft shielded himself from these also, right before rushing after her once more. This time Lorelei was unable to dodge in time and raised a shield to deflect the giant's fist, simultaneously maneuvering toward Kraft's left flank, her right arm blade extending to slash.

She never made contact. The avatar swept its massive arm at a tremendous speed, effectively backhanding Lorelei across the field and slamming her into another large piece of ruin. The crazed remnant of a psion then proceeded to bellow, firing a continuous line of energy bursts at her location, obliterating it wholesale. Shaken, Lorelei utilized the force of the energy impacts to fling herself upward, returning fire as she ascended. Her shots struck their target. Unable to defend himself in time, Kraft's form was thoroughly riddled and decimated as a result. Lorelei attacked, amethyst blades cutting into the doctor while the avatar's haphazard attempts to protect were ineffective.

Yet even that did not finish Kraft. Through the slashes and point-blank fire, his power and wrath, already a considerable force unto itself, intensified. Further pain and vexation merged with anger and despair, seething, simmering, convulsing, until at last overwhelming and erupting.

With a sudden surge of power that stunned the White Siren, the undead doctor let out a terrifying, formidable roar as he forcibly regenerated. The uncontrolled, bestial rage he projected flooded throughout the space. An ire that was no longer centered on Lorelei, nor even the Flints or the Black Moon, but toward all things that he would see destroyed. The will and desire to realize the universe around him rendered unto oblivion for daring to obstruct him from what he sought.

Such was the force of his wrath. It struck Lorelei harder than the resultant shockwave, requiring her to raise a shield against it. Indeed, she had wondered when it would finally happen, when the last semblance of Laurentius Kraft would give way to the ever consuming nothingness within his remnant shell. When all that well and truly remained was the yearning toward the Sunset City that was forever beyond him, and the resultant fury against any for keeping it out of his reach. An existence, or lack thereof, now fully consumed by its obsession, the anguish at being unable to see it fulfilled, and the maddened rage at those it believed to be responsible. Whose final, lingering resolve was to destroy and nothing more.

Her shield did not last, eventually cracking and shattering before the sheer force struck her head-on, pitching her back as Kraft, or what little truly remained of him, surged against her.

Flint Pirates umbra *Black Sun*
Sognare Sea

Braun concluded, assuming his optic sensors were transcribing the data to his brain correctly, this was going to be a close one. Even though it had just been transmitted from the bridge, he already saw that he had a formidable task ahead of him, if the readings were accurate. And yet, as he felt the ship jolt again from another energy burst, he knew that there was little choice and little time to act.

"Confirm Professor," Alex spoke over the comm., sounding understandably anxious. The ship shook again, further emphasizing the direness.

"Confirmed," Braun responded as soon as the tremoring died down. Inwardly preparing himself for the new task at hand, and the precise delicateness it would require. "Standby."

Taking that as good an acknowledgment as any, Alex dropped the comline, allowing Braun to turn back to his station. As luck would have it, two of his more competent subordinates were within earshot.

"You, and you," he called, pointing to the engineers. "With me, now!"

Knowing better than to question, especially as the ship shook violently, the pair followed Braun into the nearest turbolift. The rest of the engineering staff continued with their duties amidst the chaos.

———————————

Jon banked just as the blue plasma launched, nearly striking his fighter's left wing. He counterfired with his vulcans as he flew past, spraying the spawnling across its outer surface, causing some amount of wounding. It wasn't enough to kill it, however, as the entity became further erratic in its actions, eliciting a pained psionic cry as it fired additional plasma. Sniffing in disgust, Jon barrel-rolled then twisted around again and fired his beam cannons, striking off a fair chunk of the creature and finishing it with cannon blasts into the wound.

Moving through the resultant remains, Jon had selected his next target when something struck his fighter...hard.

Alarmed, he abandoned his attack vector. Looking about, he realized the source of the blast as he watched another discharge from the Sea erupt just past his fighter, generating additional tremors.

It's all coming apart, Jon fumed as his Corsair pitched about in the turbulence.

One of the hellions detected his plight and came after him, its enlarged maw opening to bite down. Jon banked away, firing both his vulcans and cannons into the creature's side. Though the damage was considerable, it was the sudden lightning burst from the Sognare that finished the thing for good, randomly striking and obliterating it at once. Another such discharge nearly hit Jon's Corsair, but now alert to what was transpiring, the pirate captain managed to avoid it at the last moment.

"Are you seeing this, Corsair Zero?" Boss chimed as she banked away from another hellion; a pair of missiles later, one more entity was destroyed, with yet many more still out there.

But that was not the Flints' main problem now.

"I am Corsair One," Jon acknowledged as he looked over his sensors, his gut clenching from the readings. By now, the Sea fully embodied its name, evoking a tempestuous madness. The turbulence was sweeping erratically throughout the space, while additional, vibrantly colorful lightning bursts flashed. Far more violently and frequently than when the *Sun* had first traversed its span.

We're running out of time, Jon thought as he maneuvered around a suddenly manifested cyclone, which would have easily swept in and torn his fighter apart had he not gotten away.

The Sea had been winding down since the battle had started, but now it was firmly within its final throes. The Moon appeared even worse off; it's fluctuating now more violent as well as continual, energy rippling and pulsating throughout its sphere. All combined into a destructive force that neither Jon nor anyone else present had ever perceived before.

Not far from his position, a powerful gale struck Boss' fighter, forcing her to gun her thrusters through the turbulence. Through her canopy, she watched as three of the monstrosities were blown away to parts unknown.

"Recommend we…!"

"Maintain combat," Jon answered sharply, even as he struggled with his control stick. As much as he wished he could give that order, he, more than anyone else, knew they were well beyond the point of breaking away. Not even having the *Sun* go to arc from within the Sea would save them. Their survival lay solely on Lorelei's efforts, as well as their holding out.

Swallowing, Boss turned her fighter toward the nearest piece of refuse, sweeping her vulcans across its scaled hide before moving away as it counterattacked. It was becoming more and more difficult to control her fighter, but unfortunately, she knew why Jon had given that order. Either they finished what they started here, or they would be swept away with the Sea. There was no middle ground…nor escape to be had.

Thus she continued her attack, spraying another vulcan barrage across the spawnling, which retaliated, firing scales as projectiles. All while the Sea and the Moon both churned with increasingly anguished fury.

Flint Pirates umbra *Black Sun*
Sognare Sea

So not good, Alex thought as he analyzed the sensor readings. The deterioration of the Sea was accelerating and becoming much more violent and erratic. The psionic equivalent of a terrestrial hurricane or a much, much larger expansion of the storm Lorelei espoused on Nassau. Alex and everyone else were all too aware of what happened to ships that were trapped in such storms.

And of course, that wasn't discounting their primary concern, which was now hurling another barrage of yellow energy after them. As though to compliment the much more recurrent, as well as intense, lightning emissions.

"Hard to port, forty-five degrees!"

With considerable effort, Davis forced the helm into compliance, bringing the ship about to present her starboard side to the beast. More than a few energy bursts slammed into the shields, but they held, allowing Barbarossa to retaliate with another broadside of cannon and missile fire.

As Alex had ordered, the former's power had been diminished considerably to keep the shields active. The latest round of damage reflected this, as the entity healed in barely a fraction of its original time. Even so, it still hurt and wailed in considerable torment, its tendrils whipping erratically. One nearly swept over the *Sun*'s bridge tower, though Davis maneuvered under it at the right moment.

"Helm is becoming harder to maneuver!" Davis called out as he virtually wrestled to keep the ship under control. The *Sun* began to list to port as if to emphasize his point, though the helmsman managed to put it back on course. "I don't think I'll be able to hold her down much longer!"

"Just keep us out of Cuttles' reach!" Alex answered back, understanding Davis' plight for once. The ship was badly tremoring, even without the endless maneuvering.

Concentrating his efforts, Barbarossa triggered the main cannons once more, striking the juggernaut head-on. Again the beams did far less damage than before, "merely" burning and scarring the outer hide, not actually penetrating it. Not that it mattered any more than the previous attacks had. The eldritch regenerated yet again, its shallow wounds fading from sight as the once marred flesh was reborn.

Once revitalized, the juggernaut pressed its attack, coming after the *Sun* faster and much more violently. The excruciation of its desultory was now almost overwhelming. Its movements were also become increasingly fren-zied, seemingly without any form, control, or conscious act. Completely uncoordinated, its flails and barrages were disheveled and poorly comprised, but at the same time unpredictable as well as varying in the application of force. Therefore, far more dangerous than in the beginning, while its anguish only grew with its writhing existence.

"DIIIIIIIIIIEEEEEE!" came the next wail, as well as the resultant psionic shockwave. Bolstered by their shields, both the *Sun* and her fight-ers managed to plow through, but damage was still done. Through his strained, hand covered ears, Alex barely heard the alarm klaxons sound, signaling that another large chunk had been taken out of the shields.

"Shields now less than fifteen percent!" Barbarossa alerted urgently. "We'll lose them completely if we take another hit like that!"

"Damn it," Alex hissed under his breath.

Losing their shielding had been a bad enough worry during the initial trip when the Sea had been relatively stable. Now, in its erratic, mercurial state, Alex could only imagine what it would do to the exposed *Sun*.

"Divert remaining weapons power to shields! Do not let them break!" He almost ducked as another tentacle waved over the screen. "Helm, go for distance! Hard burn!"

Davis abruptly maneuvered around another swaying set of tendrils, simul-taneously riding through another flurry as he gunned the main engine. A massive cyclone took form by the ship, forcing Davis to bank quickly, while lightning flashed throughout. One such burst clipped the *Sun* across her starboard. Though it was not enough to finish her shields, it still emphasized the urgency.

Indeed, Alex knew, this was the endgame. This was where they either slew the beast or all they all died. As it stood now, the latter was much more likely than the former, as the worst of Alex's fears had come to light. The beast was outlasting them, its regenerative power not diminished in the least. Yet the *Sun*, for all her power and abilities, was down to her final defense, heavily strained and near the breaking point. All while the Sea deteriorated with each passing second, as though it also intended to kill them.

Thus, all he could do was retreat, having the *Sun* present her stern as she raced for distance, the Corsairs falling in around her in the process. The original beastie had generated more spawn in the interim, and Jon and the rest were no closer to eradicating them than Alex was with their parent.

Unfortunately, this also enticed the monsters into pursuit, racing after their battered, beaten prey while firing all manner of projectile against them. Two more Corsairs fell while the *Sun*'s rear shields were hammered continuously. Even with their augmented state, there was little doubt they would soon fail.

This isn't it for us, Alex thought as he again glared at the juggernaut and its spawn, who were now fixed toward the *Sun*'s stern. *This* can't *be it for us.*

Indeed there remained hope. By now, Braun and any he brought with him had reached one of the weapon bays and were feverishly working on their ace. Their one chance to finish the beasties *and* live on at the same time.

Yet, as the beasts gave chase, that hope seemed increasingly forlorn. More and more, as the stern shields dwindled, the killing strike, whether from the monsters or the Sognare, drew ever closer…

———————————— ————————————

The yellow bursts were almost continuous as well as widespread, triggering explosions across the near entirety of the field. It now required the majority of Lorelei's energy simply to dodge or deflect the bursts, all the while exploiting any opening she could to counterattack.

She banked right, generating and firing another line of violet shots, they launched out in sequence and struck their target head-on. Despite the damage inflicted, however, Kraft drove through the attack, his avatar responding even faster, firing off another responding barrage, forcing Lorelei to generate a shield to deflect.

There was very little semblance of Kraft now, as Lorelei both saw and felt. His body was cracked and broken as the finest porcelain, while his avatar fluctuated violently in shape and form, bleeding off energy as one would blood. Regeneration was no longer a concern obviously; the fiend simply powered through every attack, uncaring about the damage it took. Indeed, as Lorelei felt from its seething rage, all that mattered now was that she be destroyed. Her and everything else that the specter could reach before it ended.

Espousing another forceful bellow, the avatar fired a massive burst at Lorelei's shield. It shattered, but not before Lorelei abandoned it, then reextended her blades and charged. Several more energy bursts launched as she approached, but she dodged them all. The firepower was intense, yet uncoordinated as a side effect of her opponent's unrestrained fury.

The avatar slashed its clawed arm at Lorelei's head, but she dodged this as well, right before spinning and executing a deep cut across the main form's torso. Once more, it broke and shattered, fragments of its ruined being exploding out into space. More energy bursts launched, but she focused on her attack, dodging right and slashing at Kraft's shoulder, shattering it entirely. Both it and the upper arm it was attached to fragmented away, yet the lower arm remained folded with Kraft's right, seemingly unaffected. Another black claw slash forced her to withdraw, but not before firing a follow-up line of energy shots directly into Kraft's torso, blowing out much of his lower body.

And yet the specter did not slow, instead it drove after her as its guardian reached to ensnare her again. She evaded once more, then counterslashed the extended arm, drawing away more black "blood". The resultant wisp lashed out at her – whether a conscious act of Kraft's or not – striking her face like a spray of acid. She reflexively let out a soft cry, closing her now blinded eyes.

Unfortunately, that was enough for Kraft to regain the initiative. Reaching out with its opposite arm, the guardian grabbed Lorelei and viciously swung her about, releasing her into another nearby fragment. She collided with a meteoric slam, the ruin exploding into splinters from the impact. Yet Kraft did not stop, *could* not stop. Bellowing once more as it manifested a virtual sphere of yellow energy, it threw it at Lorelei, engulfing her in a great, unrelenting salvo…

Chapter XXVI: Slaying the Monsters

Flint Pirates umbra *Black Sun*
Sognare Sea

"Modulator," Braun ordered, his right hand reaching out to take the requested piece of equipment as soon as it was offered. The ship quaked again as another attack struck her wavering shields, but the chief engineer paid it as little mind as possible, lest it distract him. He focused mainly upon his urgent task, taking the tube-shaped instrument and applying it to the bundle of circuits and machinery in front of him, gradually working toward the desired effect. Once he was through, at least with that phase, he handed the tool back and requested another piece, continuing the adjustments. All the while, it seemed the *Sun* would break apart around him and his colleagues.

No, Braun knew better than that. The *Sun* would hold as she had many times before, just as he had built her to. And she would do so long enough for him to finish his present work, though that was a different subject matter in itself.

It wasn't anything overly complicated, especially for one such as him, but that didn't make his present task any less difficult. After all, he wasn't just reconfiguring mechanics or implementing additional parts. He was trying to accomplish a *specific* effect, which required precision and a delicate touch, as well as a reasonable level of mechanical coordination. Not ideal factors given the present environment; the quaking especially threatened to disorient Braun in his task. Fortunately, it was far from the first time, much less the *only* time, he had been forced to work in such an environment, and so continued about his task without hindrance, at least as much as he could.

With the *Sun's* tremoring increasing, Braun was barely able to keep the modulator in its precise position. Once more, he was going for an *exact* effect, something that even a millimeter difference could nullify. Or much worse, cause his work to blow up on him, and the rest of the ship, quite literally.

"Plasma inducer."

Eager hands passed him the requested instrument, which he started to incorporate into the device in question. It was a tight fit, but he managed to insert it and connect it to the controls. The task complete, his right hand shifted into its welder configuration, allowing him to unify the parts of the device that the inducer didn't quite fit. Throughout, Braun noted the sweat faced nervousness of his assistants, which he easily ignored to focus on his task. Not that he could blame them; however, this was indeed one feat of engineering that none of them wanted to see fail, lest it be the last thing any of them saw…

Suddenly the ship veered to port, nearly causing Braun and the device to topple over to the side. He managed to keep both himself and his work grounded; however, his assistants were somewhat less fortunate. Shaking away the minor disorientation, the professor continued his work as his subordinates picked themselves up off the floor, muttering about their impending demise.

No, Braun resolved to himself yet again, *we aren't going to die here*!

He would complete this assignment, no matter what he had to endure to see it through. Too many lives, many of which were fighting to the last to buy him time, depended on his success. Depended on him to ensure that they survived and returned to their original mission.

Depended on him so that they may reach Arcadia.

Thus as his right hand reached out to grasp another offered tool, Braun concentrated entirely on completion and completion alone even as the *Sun* was again struck by eldritch force, once more threatening to break and shatter around him.

Another oncoming burst slammed into his rear shields, forcing Jon to bank away as one of the beasties closed in. Barbed tendrils extended outward as a fang center opened wide; a shrill cry elicited from the latter as it surged after the Corsair. Sneering at its approach, Jon flipped around and fired his cannons straight into the maw, obliterating the eldritch.

Unfortunately, two more of its siblings immediately took its place. One fired a blast of plasma that nearly struck the Corsair's left side. The second was spewing acidic spores. Only a timely roll followed by an equally timely dive prevented the attack's success.

Weaving his way through the dual fire and the rest of the surrounding battle, the pirate captain kept ahead of the two spawnlings, purposely drawing them in. Sure enough, the hellions overcompensated, allowing Jon to bank away and fire his cannons into the exposed flank of the plasma shooter. The spawn all but disintegrated, its remnants instantly swept away, while Jon turned and fired his vulcans into the spore carrier. The concentrated fire tore it apart as well, its destruction producing a large pale green cloud. The captain quickly banked to avoid flying into it. Even with shielding, Jon couldn't risk another surprise. Not when the end was already nigh.

Through his mounting exhaustion, the pirate captain managed to steal a glance at the oncoming swarm. They were still distant, the larger spawn and their genitor not quite able to keep up with the *Sun* and her fighters, but they remained in pursuit. Those that possessed long-range firepower continued their barrage while the smaller, faster spawn attacked directly, hounding their "prey". Just then, the "parent" produced another harrowing bellow, creating additional turmoil in the Sea, nearly knocking Jon's fighter and the rest of the Corsairs off their flight path.

Reorienting his fighter through the resultant swells, Jon managed to evade a launched projectile, some sort of warped barbed "maggot". The attacking spawnling, little more than a flying wyrm with deformed wings, released a high pitched screech as it swooped at the pirate in avian fashion. It fired another of its "ammunition" at the Corsair. Jon veered and rolled, then inverted and shot a quick burst of vulcan fire, piercing the beastie's skin but not finishing the little monster. Angered, it blasted another "maggot", hitting Jon's Corsair on the right side. His shielding withheld the onslaught, but just barely.

Feeling as though a comet had struck his fighter, Jon executed a high yo-yo, just as the wyrm fired twice more. His tactic worked as the wyrm overshot. A successful hit would certainly have pierced his shields. Jon didn't want to discover what would happen if he were left vulnerable to the Sea, whose violence had escalated exponentially in the last few minutes.

The dogfight, or "maggotfight", continued as Jon had to contend with multiple projectiles along with their home beastie. At last, an opening developed, another vulcan spray into the wyrm, and this time it was successfully destroyed, the oozing remnants spiraling away, disappearing into the ever-churning Sea.

A little more, Jon thought, taking a breath. It was a risky move in the middle of a dogfight, but he needed to do it. He needed to reaffirm once again. *Just a little more...*

The Sea was collapsing around them, their monstrous adversaries were forcing the initiative, and all means of escape were firmly cut off. Even so, Jon knew all too well that they were far from finished. Knew that Alex had found a chink in the original eldritch's fleshy armor that could be exploited, and was now having Braun modify one of their torpedoes for that exact effect. Knew that Lorelei remained undefeated in her battle, and would yet triumph against Kraft. Knew that they would all live beyond this, just as they had Ephesus.

All if they could just hold out a little more.

Resigned, Jon banked his Corsair toward his next target, vulcans firing as he attacked.

Flint Pirates umbra *Black Sun*
Sognare Sea

Alex grimaced as the monster, and some of its larger spawn launched another collective barrage. Their combined fire seemed to fill the main monitor. On cue, Davis executed evasive tactics, but it was obvious that he wouldn't be able to dodge them all. Several of the bursts and projectiles blasted into the *Sun*'s stern, against her reinforced but ever faltering shields. The ship pitched violently, lights, and consoles flickered erratically as the klaxons seemed to grow louder.

"Report!"

"Shields down to ten percent!" Barbarossa responded, just as the *Sun* was struck once more. "Make that seven percent! We're a stone's throw away!"

"Keep those shields up no matter what!" Alex bellowed, swallowing his anxiety.

It was hit or miss now, and they were cutting it way too close for his liking. It helped even less that weapons and select other systems were fully offline, their remaining power already funneled into the shielding.

More shots were fired, but this time Davis was able to maneuver around them. The beasties still had power, but not the intelligence to use it properly, just as in the beginning. Unfortunately, this was contrasted by the Sea, whose rate of chaotic deterioration had increased again. Enough that Alex could tell the helmsman was straining at his post, ensuring that they remained beyond the monsters as well as on their heading. How much longer it would stay that way was anyone's guess.

Come on, Professor, the younger Flint thought, tension flaring as he continued to watch the action on the main monitor. His gaze was primarily focused on the originator. Alex had a hunch; if the parent were destroyed, the spawnlings would follow. And if not, then they at least removed the genitor, which would allow the Flints to mop up the remnants without further replenishment. Yet none of that would matter until Braun had finished with the instrument in question, and they were fast running out of time.

Yet another of the projectiles struck. By some miracle, the shields remained active, but the force was more than enough to reverberate through the bridge.

"Shields at four percent!" Barbarossa hollered, the anxiety now fully embedded within his tone.

Beside him, Davis and Anna both visibly shivered as they worked, the beastlings again seemingly enticed by their weakening.

"Three percent!"

Closing his eyes, Alex, at last, gave in to the inevitability. It looked like it was going to be it for them, after all. He could not think of anything else that could be done, not even to buy more time.

"Reverse course!" Alex ordered, bracing himself for what was to come. "Reroute all available power to weapons and fire everything we still have at the big one!"

As if in anticipation of the *Sun's* attack, the "big one" generated another daunting bellow, the psionic shockwave jarring the *Sun* brutally as Davis reluctantly brought her into a hard turn. Alex was undeterred; his glare focused on the monstrosity. If nothing else, they could at least wound it one final time, not that it would live much longer. Between the worsening Sea and its deteriorating state, its end was also inescapable …and soon.

Here's looking at you, Mister Smiles, Alex thought derisively as the bow cannons and torpedo launchers came back online.

———————— ————————

Rage wholly manifest, the final fragment of Doctor Laurentius Kraft continued its onslaught, launching thousands upon thousands of yellow bolts into that single point. It roared, repeatedly and with undying fervor, as the fire converged from all possible vectors, bringing ultimate destruction upon the object of its ire, its unrestrained hatred. The very same object that had denied its fulfillment, though the fragment was no longer capable of comprehending that far, much less remembering exactly why it hated so much. By its remaining nature, it could only hate and seek destruction and no more, being little more than the lingering wrath of its original whole.

Thus the barrage continued for a time seemingly innumerable, its originator, once more bound by its deteriorating nature, unable to cease it. The rain was as relentless as it was destructive. Surely it had long obliterated that which it hated at the onset. Surely nothing remained at that point, nothing but a perpetual fire that blazed against the surrounding green. Surely it was all finished now. Surely *she* was finished.

And then, amidst the barrage and the resultant flames, a small glint of violet began to flicker from the epicenter. So concentrated on its endless attack, the aggressor barely comprehended it from the sheer annihilation. It was only when that small glint ignited with full force that it at last registered, as did the great shockwave that struck Kraft and his guardian, hurling them backward, further than those before.

That is when an entirely new advent began.

Once more from the center of that yellow inferno, the violet seemed to launch out over the vastness, shifting all that it touched. The green of the makeshift sky darkened, while the remaining fragments of the destroyed city began to churn. Rather than further obliteration, they wholly altered, turning from physical pieces into rays of light, before launching outward. Flying into the apparent distance to create a vast galaxy, whose "stars" shone against the dark in the brightest magenta. All complemented by the wisps and clouds of an amaranth nebula.

And yet, as beautiful and spectacular as that scape was, it paled in comparison to what lay at its center. A great light that shone like a white sun, seemingly burning against the vastness. As bright as to cause even the lingering fragment and the avatar to shield their eyes, all wrath momentarily displaced.

Then, as that light receded, she reemerged once more. Floating in the middle of the "space", Lorelei gazed at Kraft's remnant. Her eyes alight with the same violet as the surrounding stars, only *far* more intense, while her body was now cloaked in a great aura. Energy danced and crackled about her form, with one burst lashing out at Kraft as lightning drawn to a rod. The avatar reached out to deflect it, only to recede upon contact, as though its outstretched hand was burned.

For the briefest of moments, the fragment lingered, its glowing eyes fixed upon the opposite psion. It seemed to hesitate, against everything that it was, it seemed to *fear*.

And then the moment passed, as Kraft let out a vengeful roar. The guardian drew its right fist back and charged once again, intent on finishing that which it hated once and for all. Smiling slightly, with but a flick of her hands, Lorelei reignited her psi blades…

Flint Pirates umbra *Black Sun*
Sognare Sea

And…there! Braun thought as he incorporated the last piece into the correct position. No sooner than it had snapped into place did the mechanism light up, its various mechanics functioning as intended. The time was nigh.

"That's it! Load it up!"

As the two assisting engineers moved the instrument toward its designated place, Braun quickly engaged his wristcom.

"Braun to Bridge! It's all set!"

He then watched as his subordinates loaded the projectile into the tube, and sealed it shut.

"You may fire when ready!"

Finally, Alex breathed with no shortage of relief. They would survive just yet.

"All ahead full! Drive us straight on!"

Davis hit the gas, bringing the *Sun* to her full sub-arc speed. More attacks were flying at her now, both from the original beast and its spawnings, a fair number of which turned away from the Corsairs to pursue. However, with their poor accuracy combined with the *Sun*'s attack vector, none of the fire so much as grazed her. All the while, the umbra charged on as an obsidian dagger, moving to plunge deep into the original monstrosity.

Lowering the scope once more, Alex went over his readings one final time, both to wait until the ship was at the ideal firing point as well as to ensure that his attack would have an immediate and catastrophic effect. Had he not been so pressed, he would have wished for more time to verify his calculations, as any man of science would have wanted. Unfortunately, there were now mere seconds between life and death; it was going to be close. Alex hoped and prayed that his plan was sound as he watched the original monstrosity grow more apparent in the scope's monitor.

The thing must have realized the attack that was to come, as both it and its "armada" unleashed a firestorm at the fast-approaching *Sun*. Using what little maneuverability he still had, Davis weaved around and through the onslaught, some shots coming close but never striking. Any hit they took now would be fatal; if they weren't destroyed at the onset, the last of their shields would give way and leave them open to the Sea. At the same time, however, the helmsman also knew that they only had one shot to end this and that they had to make it count in absolution. Thus ignoring his anxiety, he drove the ship through the inferno and toward their objective, those around him watching and also praying.

"From this little spark," Alex found himself reciting in the manner of his brother. *"May the great flame follow."*

And then, it was time.

"FIRE!" Alex roared.

Upon that command, the torpedo launched out of its tube and accelerated toward its target.

———————————————— ————————————————

"That's it!?" one of the remaining Corsair pilots managed to blurt out through the melee. "What in the seventh circle is...!?"

"Wait for it," Jon ordered. He had an inclination about the nature of the attack, an approving smile folded over his lips.

Her instrument launched, the *Sun* veered away, allowing the torpedo to charge headlong through the fire. With its already considerable acceleration augmented by its mothership's original charge, the beastlings had no hope of intercepting it, no matter how many attacks were launched. Alongside, Alex had timed the shot well, as it passed through the bulk of the fire in a matter of seconds, proceeding directly into the originator. The monster, as though instinctively sensing the danger, lashed its tendrils out in succession, yet was unable to so much as gleam over such a miniscule projectile. Contact was made less than five seconds after launch.

Focusing its shielding forward, the torpedo followed its original programming and pierced into its target, forcing itself as deep inside as it could "burrow". Eventually, it could move no further, and so came to a complete stop within the eldritch. However, it did not detonate as it was originally designed to do. Instead, following its recent modifications, the torpedo began to vibrate. Slowly at first, at least by the standards of the function but building up rapidly, generating copious amounts of heat through it all.

Eventually, the heat began to melt the entire frame, deforming it into slag in a matter of seconds. This was but a secondary, non-essential effect, for it was the oscillation of the torpedo's frame from within its target that the defenders had been counting on. An oscillation rate that was set to a precise resonance frequency, which despite the target's gargantuan size, ran throughout the organic mass as music through a tuning fork. The result was just as immediate.

Eliciting a colossal agonizing bray, the monstrosity tore apart from the inside out, its bloated form all but exploding as a fleshed star. Multitudes of organic substances burst out into the Sognare, while the core vainly fought to keep itself whole. Fragments in all physical states launched out aimlessly into the churning Sea, obliterating those spawnlings within the wake. Those that were not struck directly were also torn apart in the resultant upheaval, being psionically linked to their parent.

While the lesser spawnlings were destroyed completely, and quite gruesomely, the parent's regeneration powers remained in effect. Organic matter reforming as quickly as it was ripped away, the monster maintained a continuously horrific state of flux, unable to do any more than wrestle itself to retain some shape. Even so, it managed to keep itself largely intact, all while the torpedo core temperature continued to rise as the oscillation increased in intensity. Watching the torpedo's effects, more than one crewmember aboard the *Sun* began to sweat.

Suddenly, a new wound opened up. One that revealed the specific "arc organ" that was originally buried deep within the miscreation. Now exposed and vulnerable to the surrounding space, and more importantly, the *Black Sun*'s reenergized weaponry.

Flint Pirates umbra *Black Sun*
Sognare Sea

"FINISH IT!" Alex commanded.

Barbarossa immediately complied. Cannons, missiles, and torpedoes firing as one, the *Sun* let loose the full force of its remaining offensive power. Concentrated on that singular point, the beams and projectiles slammed into the organ in overwhelming repetition, piercing and rupturing it entirely. To the last, the monstrosity tried to regenerate and remake itself, but against the *Sun*'s sheer firepower, it could only hold out for but a few moments. Eventually, it gave way, right as the original torpedo reached full resonance.

With a final cry, which may have been of defiance as well as terminal anguish, the eldritch exploded, its destruction generating a wave of light that erupted across the Sea, eclipsing all within the surrounding space…

———————————   ———————————

With a thundering vengeful cry, Kraft's avatar fired a salvo of yellow bolts against its charging adversary. They were ineffective, as were the previous attacks; their energy unable to break through Lorelei's aura. Unhindered, the White Siren advanced with her reignited blades, completing two slashes against the avatar and one upon Kraft, causing additional broken shards and gouts of black to erupt. The remainder now visibly struggled against the damage, a very noticeable change from but minutes ago.

Again the guardian slashed at her, and again Lorelei did not bother dodging, the attack easily deflected. She countered just as quickly, cutting the arm off with a flying slash. It did not regrow, forcing the guardian to use its opposite arm to fire an enlarged bolt against her back. Lorelei responded by waving her left hand, effectively knocking the energy blast aside. A burst of violet soon followed, the beams lancing through Kraft and its construct as a battleship's guns through weakened armor, resulting in additional destruction, with more of Kraft and his guardian's form breaking away like glass.

Even so, Kraft's undying nature, the very last of it, remained functioning, driving the remnant to continue the fight. As diminished as it was, it still attacked, firing another barrage of yellow blasts after Lorelei. It fell against her, all but wholly engulfing her as it had mere moments ago. Yet now, it could not harm her, was completely incapable of harming her. For no matter how much Kraft fired, it could not pierce her aura.

At this, the fragment again seemed to hesitate, but once more for the briefest of moments. Fortifying as much energy into its avatar as it could, the entity raised its remaining arm, generating no less than a miniature sun within its palm. The avatar flung this rapidly enlarging artificial star at its master's adversary, turning it into a virtual comet. One that exploded with the force of a supernova.

Only then did Lorelei move again, launching through the glare at an accelerated velocity. She executed another charging slice against Kraft, causing most of his left side to break and heave away. The avatar attempted a counterattack, but with flashing blades, she struck, cutting off its remaining arm. Moving at a speed that rendered her little more than a violet streak, she continued her assault, hacking and breaking Kraft down more and more with each pass. Whittling him down to his barest form, bereft of much of his remaining body as his guardian disintegrated into a black haze, fading into nothingness.

And then, Lorelei turned and launched for the final time. Charging straight through the fragment's center and opening a massive hole. Furious and overcome with a strange confusion, Kraft, utterly astonished at what had just occurred, lingered for a few moments more as Lorelei came to an abrupt stop just behind him, whipping her blades with distinct and stylish finality.

As last feeling itself give way, the final remainder of Doctor Laurentius Kraft uttered one last agonizing cry as it disintegrated and dispersed. Light erupting in its place…

Chapter XXVII: What the Moon Brings

Flint Pirates umbra *Black Sun*
Deep Space

It was beautiful. A brilliant, strangely rainbow-esque glow that shown like a beacon against the darkness of space, completely unlike any light that the *Black Sun*'s crew had ever seen before. A hue that seemed to eclipse the surrounding black, belying the great power that had been dormant but minutes ago, now at last awakened. Now, at last, returned to its proper state, or so those who brought their eyes upon it hoped.

As the turbolift doors opened, Jon's gaze fell upon the light; it filled him with the same awe felt by the rest of the bridge crew. For what lay before him and his ship could only have been the Black Moon's true form. The very thing that he and the rest of the Flint Pirates had placed their lives upon the line for, finally brought to fruition.

"Incredible," Alex murmured as his elder brother moved to stand next to the command chair, neither sibling's eyes drawing away from the light. Truly a wondrous thing, they both felt, certainly beyond either of their expectations. Not at all the domain of gods and devils, yet strangely neither a god nor devil in itself. It was just as had been claimed before, seemingly to be beyond any such titles or any other point of reference that the Flints could consider. Indeed beyond anything within the scope of their galaxy.

That being said, neither Jon nor Alex was so captivated that they weren't aware of everything else pertaining. First and foremost was, as a clear result of the Moon's full awakening, the Sognare Sea no longer existed. With the source now free from its dormancy, the excessive psionic emissions had ceased, causing local space to return to normal. Through the Moon's sheer radiance, one could depict the distant stars that also shone in the void.

The second, and perhaps most important, point was that the Moon, or whatever it identified itself as, was not attacking them. Nor was it speeding off to obliterate or devour the closest star system. In fact, it didn't seem to be doing anything in the present, much to the relief of the majority of the bridge crew. After all they had been through, not a single one of their number wished to engage in another fight, much less with another eldritch entity. Not that the Moon, in all of its luminous beauty, could be considered so horrifically, of course.

And finally, there was the third point: Lorelei. Nobody knew what to make of that one. Had she survived her battle or was she beyond them now? More than a few couldn't help but wonder.

All except for Jon, who chose to remain silent on the matter. Though he couldn't quite tell where the *Black Sun*'s patron was precisely, he had yet another inclination. And much more, that she would be returned to them in but a few moments.

--------------------------- ---------------------------

"So this is your true form," Lorelei observed.

Though the Moon was still projecting her younger image before her, she easily felt its "light", for lack of better description, and the sheer energy it now emitted as compared to its inert form. Indeed as opposed to a

Black Moon, it was now equivalent to a sun. A sun whose luminosity, and selected color, was beyond compare.

"Yes," the younger her confirmed, holding a radiant smile toward that exclamation. Once more, in contrast to the passivity she held before, the projection now beamed with elation. A state of emotion that was reflected by their surroundings, which took the form of a simple, yet warm light.

Lorelei couldn't help but smile. "Do you remember everything now?"

"I do," the Moon responded with great delight. "In my own right, I was an explorer. A wanderer that moved from cosmos to cosmos, galaxy to galaxy."

The Moon looked up in remembrance, entirely pleased with what it recalled. "Through my travels, I had come to this galaxy long, long ago, 'when the stars were but children and the planets but seeds.'"

Astonishment immediately weighed upon Lorelei. "You were here during the time of the Predecessors?"

"Yes," the Moon again confirmed, once more with visible recollection. "I walked amongst them, proverbially speaking, and quite often spoke with them."

The projection then smiled almost sardonically. "And no, I'm afraid they never told me what Arcadia was," it stated. "I'm afraid you'll still have to find that out on your own."

"I actually prefer that," Lorelei replied. In truth, she had thought that would be the case, and wasn't even going to bring it up. "It's more fulfilling to learn for one's self."

The Moon beamed in acknowledgment. "Since that time, I have witnessed much throughout the ages," she continued. "Events that have since been rendered unto myth and legend, or otherwise long forgotten."

The child's eyes seemed to take on a gleam of reflection. "Some of greatness and wonder," it went on. "And others…"

This time, Lorelei was tempted to inquire about these events. However, upon remembering the Moon's intervention to the prior fighting, as well as the horror it had shown therein, she held herself back.

Once again, the Moon sensed Lorelei's thoughts and nodded in gratitude. "At some point, however, I ended up depleting myself," it explained. "I entered into a profound sleep that I could not awaken from, no matter how hard I tried. A slumber that, as the eons past, I fell deeper and deeper into, eventually losing all knowledge and comprehension of myself."

"Until I came along," Lorelei summarized.

The Moon smiled again. "Until I heard your song," it concurred, before taking on a more chiding tone. "The perfect wake-up alarm, as it were."

Lorelei could not help but feel rather taken back to have her singing compared to a 'wake-up alarm.' However, upon closer inspection, she realized that the Moon was simply exaggerating. That, once more in direct contrast to its dormant self, it had rediscovered humor.

"I've never heard it described quite like *that* before."

The Moon quickly realized it had misstepped. "I'm sorry, I didn't mean to…"

"It's perfectly fine," Lorelei answered back facetiously. "I wouldn't be an accomplished songstress if I couldn't stand some criticism."

That earned a surprising laugh from her host. It was rather heartening for Lorelei to watch.

"Whatever your melodic qualities, it was your song that broke me from my slumber," the Moon went on. "Not enough to fully awaken, of course, but just enough for me to become aware again. Everything else fell into place thereafter."

The projection then took on a more remorseful expression. "At great cost, admittedly."

"Yes," Lorelei agreed, sharing that same expression.

From Timas IV and Nassau to those Flints who lost their lives in the recent battle, much had been expended to awaken the Black Moon from its timeless slumber. Far more than Lorelei would ever have wished.

Even so, it was what it was. For whatever had been lost to reach this point, it had all come to pass at this very moment, which brought to mind a new inquiry on Lorelei's part.

"What are you going to do, now that you are no longer bound to your sopor."

The Moon nodded. "For time innumerable, I have voyaged from one universe to the next, witnessing and experiencing much throughout."

It then looked down, in seeming recollection. "Now, however, I feel that I have reached the end of this journey," it said with renewed melancholy. "It is time to return from whence I originally came."

"I see," was all Lorelei could say, now strangely unsure.

The Moon regarded her for a moment. "I would ask you to join me, but you still have your journey to fulfill and your own experiences to gain," it spoke with apparent regret. "A true pity, I feel."

"As do I," Lorelei agreed, looking down with similar regret. She could only imagine what spectacular realm the one before her had originated from, and all the marvels and oddities it would hold.

But no, such a realm was not for her. Not especially when she still had Arcadia to reach, as well as…

"With that understanding, I'm afraid this is where we part ways," the Moon declared at long last, the projection already starting to fade into the light. "In spite of our short time together, I will indeed miss you, dear friend."

"And I will miss you as well," Lorelei answered as she watched her younger self gradually vanish, little by little. "I fear this galaxy will not see another like you."

The Moon smiled once more. "Give it time," it said. "Just as the universe is infinite, so are its wonders. And not all of them as far beyond as you may believe."

That was when the Moon seemed to recall something else. "There is one thing I want you to have, however."

Before Lorelei could ask, that very thing materialized in her hands. She was quite surprised when she saw it.

"Are you sure?" she queried, very uncertain.

"Yes," the Moon replied reassuringly. "Such a thing should not be wasted."

Though still somewhat dubious, Lorelei ultimately chose not to refuse. Thus tucking it under her arm, she gave the departing Moon a final sendoff.

"Farewell, Domain of Gods and Devils."

The Moon chuckled one final time toward that description, the light embracing it – no, *her* – entirely. It seemed strangely appropriate to her, despite everything.

"Farewell, Siren of the Rhine."

Flint Pirates umbra *Black Sun*
Deep Space

"What…?" Barbarossa muttered, effectively voicing what the rest of the bridge crew was observing.

For a very short moment, the light of the Moon fluctuated, producing a vivid spectrum of color and vibrancy before the onlookers. They reacted defensively, all too recent events still lingering, with Davis about to maneuver the *Sun* away as Barbarossa moved to reengage her tactical systems. However, before any of them could perform any such action, each one of the *Black Sun*'s crew heard something. A distinctly soft voice, one that could only have been held by a child, called out.

"Thank you."

And then, it was gone. With the abruptness of a thunder peal, the light vanished instantly from the void. Leaving but the dark openness of space, and the familiar glint of nearby stars.

For but a moment, the Flints could only wonder what exactly they had just witnessed.

"She is free now," a familiar voice spoke from the rear of the bridge.

At that, all eyes turned to find Lorelei, casually sitting at her station, looking upon those surprised gazes with utter bemusement.

"She has returned from whence she came," she stated. "And all remains well in the universe."

Out of those present, only Jon couldn't help but depict a tinge of sadness within the psion's voice. However, rather than inquire toward that in particular, he instead turned his eye toward the object in Lorelei's hand.

"What's that?"

Solemnly Lorelei brought the book out so that she could gaze over the faded cover. "*The Dream-Quest of Unknown Kadath*," she explained, running a gloved finger over the title lettering. "A parting gift, as it were."

Drawing a small smirk in response, Jon faced forward again. "Helm set a new course for Ryugu," he ordered as Alex rose from the command chair, allowing his elder brother and captain to retake it.

Letting out a long and deliberate breath, Davis entered the commands. "Aye, sir," he replied dutifully. "Arc Drive standing by."

Jon smiled. At long last, it was time for them to return as well, to Ryugu, to their original quest, and their pillage and plunder.

"Arc Three," he commanded, settling back into his chair, somehow anticipating the trip. "Make it smooth."

At that, the *Black Sun* turned about. Then, with a final crimson flash from her main engine, she accelerated into arcspace, disappearing into the void.

Epilogue: Till A'the Seas

Flint Pirates umbra *Black Sun*
Arcspace

"There and back again," Anna exclaimed after taking a swig. "Like it all never happened."

"Could have fooled me," Davis retorted. He was too exhausted to think of a more sarcastic response. "Feels like eons since we first hit Nassau."

"Please don't bring that up. I still have aches and pains from that night," Apache added as well, taking a sip of his usual foul-smelling beverage.

Such was the general mood throughout the Lounge, as those crewmen who were not on duty drank and laid their recent ills to rest. Only the relatively upbeat melody of the present song, appropriately called *Bad Moon Rising,* broke up the somberness somewhat.

"And it's not like I heal overnight like some species…"

"You should eat more vitamins," Gran translated for Kaiser, who then shook his tankard. "Prunes would also help, given that you were hatched two years before Tiberius."

Apache looked far from pleased. "At least I was hatched, rather than chisel…"

"Alright, alright, stop it right there, Woody, and you too, Thinker," Cheney interrupted from his end of the table. He was still recovering from Ianessa but was well enough to be present. "It's been a bad enough experience for all of us, and I'd rather it end on a low note. At least as much as this crowd would allow."

Despite the outburst, Anna smiled at the raider's presence. "It's really nice to see you back with us, Master Chief," she stated as she looked over his present shirt.

The Dread Pirate's shirt proclaimed "THIS IS MY RIFLE, THIS IS MY GUN, THIS IS FOR FIGHTING, THIS IS FOR FUN" in bold lettering.

"You had us going there for a while."

"I had me going there for a while, ma'am. I hate to admit it, but that piece of dead shit came damn close to killing me," Cheney admitted, downing a fair portion of his coffee. Unlike most of his kind, he wasn't fond of alcohol. "And the worst part is I never got to repay him the favor."

He glowered with disdain as he remembered Kraft's entrance into Ianessa. "Are we sure he's well and truly gone?" he inquired, actually sounding hopeful. "He did unlive for two whole centuries."

"Don't know, but we're all betting on it," Davis answered, visibly shivering at the idea. "Between all that happened and how vicious his opponent can be, I don't think we'll be seeing him again."

"Damn," Cheney sniffed in apparent disappointment. "Guess there's always dancing on his grave," he muttered, taking on a rather vicious smile. "As well as taking a latrine break…"

"Anyway," Davis purposely interrupted, turning toward Kaguya. "How are things back home? Your father still waiting for us?"

"*Hai,*" Kaguya responded with a shrug. "Though he expressed much displeasure toward our tardiness, and that 'honor must be restored' upon our arrival."

A sudden coldness swept across the table as Kaguya casually drank from her *ochoko* cup. That same coldness also haunted the other tables in proximity, while at the bar area, Lloyd almost dropped the tankard he had been cleaning.

"Just kidding," she said without changing her expression or tone, causing more than one set of shoulders to sag. "In truth, he understands all that has happened and will once more provide us haven as we replenish our numbers and equipment."

Blinking somewhat toward the rather uncharacteristic display of humor, Anna could only shake her head. She had the distinct feeling Alex was rubbing off more and more on the Dragon Princess.

"Did he say anything about the aftermath of the Sognare's disappearance?"

"Nothing specific," Kaguya reported. "The Pisceans and the Aquarians are standing down, as are the other Powers. There is some lingering tension toward the space that the Sea once occupied, but until something of real interest is discovered, it's little more than a curiosity."

"That is a rather intriguing thought, however," Braun thought out loud as his artificial hand stroked his bloated chin. "Could there have been planets and star systems within the Sea, which only now may be reached? Perhaps even other wonders that have yet to…?"

"With respect Professor, I wouldn't give a Leps' ass," Davis interrupted. "The saucerheads can have those strange new worlds, new life, and whatever."

A small chuckle circled around the table. Saucerhead was an ancient derogatory term for an explorer, based on the stereotype that their ships were all saucer-shaped at the bow. Nobody knew where that presumption came from, especially when exploration ships were as various in shape and design as any other vessel type. Even so, the phrase stuck, as did the narrow-minded do-gooder, couldn't-handle-themselves-in-the-real-universe image.

"Myself, I go where the gold is," Davis declared with a raise of his glass, earning no small amount of cheers from around the Lounge. "That and the women," he added, causing even more cheers to erupt.

Stifling a deliberate exhale, Anna yet still agreed. They were what they were first and foremost. The heavens may fall, and the universe may burn. Days of fortune may lie ahead, as well as days of struggle. They may not always get what they sought, and there would still be "side ventures" like this one.

In the end, however, the Flint Pirates remained what they were. Rascals, scoundrels, villains, and knaves. And all else entailed.

Thus she raised her glass for the inevitable toast. "Gold and glory then," she called out to the Lounge. "Till A'the Seas dry out!"

With that, the entire Lounge let out a resounding cheer as the occupants all took their drinks.

"Overall, the whole experience was downright agonizing," Alex exclaimed as he and Jon walked down the corridor. "As if tracking down the Babels wasn't a big enough pain in the ass."

"At least it's over," Jon answered, exhaustion in his voice. He couldn't remember the last time he felt this tired, not since Ephesus anyway. "Though we'll be staying a little longer on Ryugu because of it."

"Yeah," Alex replied solemnly, remembering the crew they had lost through the voyage. Though none of the dead had been especially close to him or his brother, they had still been Flint Pirates. That meant they had been brethren in arms and fortune to the end.

Jon couldn't help but grin at his brother's melancholy. "Don't take it personally," he reassured. "It was thanks to you that we were triumphant at all, albeit by the skin of our teeth."

Alex cast his brother a bland look. "You don't have to embellish it, Jon."

"I'm dead serious, Alex. This was your best command performance to date. And to top it off, it was your tactic that killed the thing when the rest of us were struggling to survive, let alone inflict damage."

He placed his hand on Alex's shoulder to underscore his statement.

"So hold your head up high, little brother," Jon emphasized. "As agonizing as it might have been, the final victory remains yours."

Alex seemed to take some measure in that declaration. "I suppose it is," he answered, feeling vestiges of pride begin to emerge.

If nothing else, it was a far cry from his performance at Ephesus, where only late in the battle had he managed to get into the rhythm of command. Like so many other things, that too seemed like a long time ago.

"Still, it would have been better if we had everyone come home with us."

"It would have, but that is seldom the outcome," Jon said. "Take solace in that you got as many to survive as possible and move on from there."

Alex couldn't help but grin at his elder. "Is that an order, Captain?"

Jon matched that grin. "Consider it sage advice from your wise older brother," he shot back. "But since I am also your captain, I suppose I could make it an order…"

That earned Jon a small punch to the arm. "As usual, you're full of shit, bro," Alex laughed. "When we get to Ryugu, drinks are definitely on you."

"I can go with that," Jon said, just as he and Alex approached a specific part of the ship. The elder Flint frowned at a particular doorway, and what he was about to do therein. "Just don't expect it to always be like this."

"'Seldom the outcome' as said," Alex rejoined. "But at the same time, I do believe it will happen that much more in the future."

Jon sniffed in mock exasperation. "I said hold your head up high, not to let it swell," he retorted, then moving before the doorway and letting out a small sigh. "We'll be with you soon enough. Make sure that part of the ship remains intact until then."

"Can do," Alex dutifully replied as he turned toward the Lounge's direction. Though he wasn't sure how much of it was still intact, he had a feeling that there was still plenty of grog to go around.

However, before he made more than two steps, Alex found himself looking toward his brother one more time.

"Jon?"

Jon stopped and turned to face Alex again. "Yes?" he answered, seemingly ignorant of what his younger brother was about to ask him.

For a long moment, Alex was indeed tempted to ask that question. Just how did they get through the Sognare? Without their guide, it should have been impossible for them; they should have ended up among those multitudes lost in prior voyages. Yet Jon had somehow navigated through it, and for the life of him, Alex still could not understand. Which ultimately led to another question, one that Alex hoped he would never have to ask his brother. Finally, Alex decided not to pursue the answer.

"Nothing," he stated, shaking his head as he turned away. "It's nothing."

Ignoring his brother's confused gaze, Alex resumed his trek to the Lounge. That wasn't the end of it, he knew. Sognare might have been the most blatant point, but now that Alex considered it, there were many times when his elder had said or done something that he should not have been able to. Whether providing vital pieces of information or, as with the Sognare, getting them through the obstacles and straight to the prize, Jon seemed always to be several steps ahead when he shouldn't have been. And though Alex would have liked to just leave it at his brother having honed intuition, he knew, deep down and against all that he wanted to believe, that there was more to it than that. Possibly more than even he could fathom.

However, that was for another time and place. For now, he would drink and celebrate with the others, having ensured that they would survive for another day. As Jon had said, it was his victory most of all, and he would be damned before not living it up. And if it could be at Davis' expense, then so much the better.

430

Watching his brother disappear into the nearest turbolift, Jon kept his expression neutral as he turned back to his intended destination.

———————————————

It was strange, Lorelei reflected, to read this particular book a second time through. The first time it had otherwise been forced upon her by a captor, and as a result, she had been rather biased toward the story. Now, however, while it was not the best work, Terran, or otherwise, she had ever read, it captivated her, yes, by that actual definition on some level. Namely, the conclusion, whose meaning, again due to the conditions under which she had been reading, she had missed the first time through.

So to the organ chords of morning's myriad whistles, and dawn's blaze thrown dazzling through purple panes by the great gold dome of the State House on the hill, Randolph Carter leaped shoutingly awake within his Boston room. Birds sang in hidden gardens, and the perfume of trellised vines came wistful from arbors his grandfather had reared. Beauty and light glowed from the classic mantel and carven cornice and walls grotesquely figured, while a sleek black cat rose yawning from hearthside sleep that his master's start and shriek had disturbed...

An ironic and rather fitting conclusion by her standards made even more so by all that she had just endured. In the end, the Sunset City was none other than Randolph Carter's home of Boston, as reflected and idealized by the memories of his youth. The very thing he had sought, to the point of treading the forbidden Dreamlands, was outside of his window the entire time. Whose means of access was but not to dream, but to *remember* out of love and wonder.

What made it even more ironic was that, somehow, she had the feeling Kraft, or at least his remnant, had missed it as well. She had no way of knowing, but she would like to think that whatever Sunset City that Kraft had sought had been much the same: so close as to be right in front of him, and well within his reach. The remnant had clearly not understood such a simple concept, which was why he had gone as far as he had. Expended so much, as well as what little existence he had remaining, to obtain something that may or may not have been before him all along.

Or perhaps that was why the remnant had existed in the first place. Perhaps, somewhere through his original life, Laurentius Kraft had realized the truth and had, at last, gained what he sought, which was why he had passed on, leaving behind the part of himself that was incapable of accepting that obvious truth. Leaving it to wander aimlessly as the original whole moved, fully immersing itself into whatever lay beyond. Such would be a poetic conclusion to this particular story, at least in her opinion.

Regardless, it was all over now. Kraft was fully dead, the Pisceans vanquished, and the Black Moon freed at last. Only Ryugu remained before them, after which they would inevitably return to their original pillage and plundering. And Arcadia.

For one final time, Lorelei hoped that, wherever he had ultimately ended up, Kraft had indeed found what he had sought in the end. She laid the book on the table next to her chair, precisely as the doorway to her quarters opened, allowing the one she had been expecting to enter. She closed her eyes as she sensed his approach from behind.

"I had wondered how long it would be before we had this inevitable 'talk.'"

"I wondered as well," Jon stated in turn, not trying to hide his anger. "How long you would keep up this charade."

"So you knew, or at least suspected, long before?" she observed as she rose from her chair, resolving herself for what was about to occur. "How long?"

"Since Aurora," Jon responded, folding his arms, wrath radiating from his being. "My only question…why?"

Lorelei sighed as she cautiously stretched her arms, feeling the exhaustion weighing on her yet needing to maintain her calm.

"And you only ask now?" But there was no explanation from the obviously very irate pirate captain. "You wouldn't begin to understand."

"Try me," Jon growled, refusing to back down. "You're much more powerful than you've been letting on. So powerful, in fact, you could have prevented all of this from occurring. Prevented deaths, injuries, as well as given us great aid in the fighting."

He dared to move closer, only then causing Lorelei to turn and face him. "So, I will ask just once more, why?"

The psion closed her eyes, seemingly processing her answer. By the time she spoke again, it felt as though hours had passed.

"I do not want this," she began, rather hesitantly. "I have never wanted this…"

When she opened her eyes again, anguish shone from deep within. "I cannot explain to you how I have suffered because of it. How, despite all that you would think, it made me *less* than I could have been."

The captain glared back, unyielding.

Refusing to face away from her accuser, Lorelei continued. "This power, this potential, whatever you choose to call it, is not something that I desire to use so forwardly. Even at the risk of my own life."

"But what of the lives of others? What of the lives aboard this ship, including mine?" Jon shot back. "Your blatant disregard for the safety of this crew, *your* crew, unnecessarily placed us in mortal danger multiple times. You selfishly allowed members of this crew to die to attain your goals when it could have been prevented. "

Flinching inwardly at the harsh words, Lorelei again refused to let Jon see the impact of his accusations.

"And what of you, Captain?" she responded. "What is this office, this ship, worth to you?"

The psion probed more deeply. "These newly honed leadership skills that only come from repeated experience and responsibilities? As you learned after Bonham, this crew relies on your knowledge and governance, but will not tolerate any weakness or incompetence. If I had prevented any difficulties, eliminated any dangers, provided minute directions, you would not be the captain you are now."

"So, this was all for my education, my development?" Jon hissed. "That's rich…and a damned poor excuse!"

"But accurate," Lorelei countered, her agitation increasing. "I, and this crew, require a strong, experienced, steadfast leader in that center chair, not a puppet."

Her gaze took on an additional challenge. "You just put your brother through a similar 'trial by fire.' You didn't eliminate the danger, or do the work for him, but allowed him to discover his capabilities. Forgive me if I implemented the same tactics. "

"And the lives lost?"

Undeterred, Lorelei pressed her point, though she did turn away again. "Before you were Captain Flint, how many previous jobs under your direction resulted in lives lost, considered unavoidable to gain your prize? When I could intervene to prevent death without jeopardizing the long term goals, I did."

"*Daedalus* …" Jon recalled in admittance. "That Imp sniper."

"Yes, and others. Only when we are activating a Babel, I cannot help as it requires all my power and concentration."

"And Ianessa?" Jon admonished. "You could have finished Kraft and stopped the Pisceans then and there before they took so many lives."

His glared deepened with accusation. "You pick and choose your involvement as if lives are pieces on a board."

"And you demonstrate your ignorance with your analysis," the psion bitterly retorted.

Jon's eye flared as Lorelei turned again to face him but now with resentment.

"Kraft would have used you, your brother, and all others as chattel," she slowly enunciated. "He sensed my attachments and immediately targeted you and them to inflict maximum pain. To wage war with him in that enclosed space was to forfeit all your lives."

"I'm not buying that answer. With your powers, you could have done a lot more to stop him and mitigate the ensuing battles," Jon rejoined. He sensed her words were true, but the real reason for her surrender at Ianessa was still not revealed. "Stop obfuscating the root motive!"

Several long minutes past as the captain's final words lingered between them. Through that time, Lorelei withheld her response, somehow managing to keep her lip from quivering. Finally, looking down, she began to speak in a soft voice.

"For as long I can remember, I have been feared," she at last admitted. "Feared even by those who would call me one of their own."

She turned away yet again, biting back the resultant tears somewhat. "And as a result, I grew cynical. No other lives besides my own mattered to me. No other opinions or assessments were of importance. With impunity, I used my powers for whatever I needed to gain."

The psion woman drew in a long breath and paused. "Until I met you," she at last stated. "Until I came aboard this ship."

She turned back to face the one person that mattered.

"At Ianessa, I was afraid."

"Afraid?" Jon arched an eyebrow.

"That if you, or anyone else," she nearly stumbled over her words. "Had seen…realized my capabilities… you would have chosen to walk away."

This time it was Jon's turn to take a breath. As incomprehensible as it was to think of her as afraid, somehow he should have known that would be the explanation. Between those words and the tears shimmering down her face, tears that he, somehow, knew to be true, he felt something inside him begin to stir. Something inside of him that had been dormant for a long, long time.

"I might be furious with you," Jon began again. "I might not understand or agree with your reasoning, but I'm not going to renege on our accord. You should know that."

"I do," Lorelei answered. "But for the longest time, I was afraid to take the risk."

Jon glowered. "There was no risk," he countered. "If this were going to be a problem, especially between the two of us, I would never have signed on with you, regardless of the incentive."

He came over and rested his hands on her shoulders. "The way I see it, we all have our strengths and weaknesses, and admittedly some of the latter are more trying than others. But that doesn't change that we are part of the same whole."

If only you knew... Lorelei thought, but for whatever reason didn't say aloud.

"For better or worse, you are here. You are a part of this crew," Jon continued. "And unless you demonstrate a valid reason, you will remain so, regardless of what others may think of you and your 'gifts'.

"Having said that, however, I very much do not appreciate you holding back," he stated forthrightly. "Not when there were battles we could have won, if only at a lesser cost."

Lorelei sighed, looking away once more. "I truly wanted to aid you and the others in those battles," she admitted once more. "If only more directly."

Again she closed her eyes. "However, I truly was afraid," she confessed as certain memories began to weigh upon her. "Afraid that, if you saw even the barest glimpse of my true power, you would turn away from me as so many others had done."

With considerable effort, she forced back those memories, one after the other.

"I couldn't take that chance," she continued, even more hesitant now, her voice almost a whisper. "Not with...you."

His remaining anger dispelled by her honesty, Jon, feeling as though his body were somehow moving on its own, took her hands into his. Surprised, she opened her amethyst eyes to look directly into his one sapphire blue.

"As I said, there was no chance to take," Jon reiterated, this time more softly. "And there never will be."

Then, in what came across as an eternity, both drew forward, their eyes drifting away as their lips at last found each other. Time all but faded as they remained there, entirely to themselves and far beyond the dark and frightful galaxy around them. Alone but with the feelings, the sheer *yearning*, that had nurtured upon them since Aurora. Drawing them further and further on, before either could begin to grasp what was happening.

Breaking apart for a brief moment, they both acknowledged their reality. Yet, as either found themselves held in the other's gaze, they could do nothing to stop it, would do nothing to stop it. The very force that had been in motion between them since that fateful encounter in Neverland, since those very same sapphire and amethyst eyes first fell upon each other, against all possibilities and likelihoods. Since that fateful pistol shot, and all that came after.

Thus bringing his hand up to her cheek, Jon once more drew Lorelei to him, to which she rejoined with all that she was, all that she held for only him. From that point on, not even the universe itself held any further sway over them…